IMPACT

Rosalind Minett

ISBN: 978-09927167-2-1

Uptake publications,
The Cottage, Kingswood Manor,
Tadworth, KA20 7AJ

IMPACT

Post-war – the fall-out

IMPACT is the third volume in the trilogy, A Relative Invasion.

1937-1940. In Book One, INTRUSION, five-year-old Billy Wilson is introduced to his frail, artistic and manipulative cousin, Kenneth. Against the background of impending war, Kenneth begins his invasion into Billy's life and the rivalry begins.

1940-1945. Book Two, INFILTRATION, finds the two boys evacuated to the country. Billy finds nurture in his foster home that has been missing with his own parents, but a family tragedy enables Kenneth to invade Billy's life wherever he is.

1945-1951. Book Three, IMPACT, begins in July, with VE Day celebrations fading into memory as Billy leaves his billet and returns to his home in Wandsworth. Kenneth is about to move in with him.

ACKNOWLEDGEMENTS

My thanks to the following people:

Ron Large for interesting and useful information about post-war Wandsworth; all the Records Offices I visited, but especially Wandsworth Archives at Lavender Hill, and Surrey Archives at Woking.

Louise Lawrence for her interest and support.

My especial thanks to the talented cover designer, Pradeep Premalal.

"We are responsible for what we are, and whatever we wish ourselves to be, we have the power to make ourselves. If what we are now has been the result of our own past actions, it certainly follows that whatever we wish to be in future can be produced by our present actions; so we have to know how to act."

Swami Vivekananda

Chapter One

July 1945
Inside the car, the seat felt rough and hot. A tuft of
stuffing was poking out of the covering beside him. Billy
fingered it. It felt like the fur of Noah and Japhet, Mr and
Mrs Pawseys' farm dogs, when they greeted him every
morning. In Wandsworth there would be no dogs. No
pigs, no chickens either. He stroked the stuffing over and
over to calm himself as the car moved forward and away
from his sanctuary.

Uncle Ted drove, not very well. Billy had so longed to
see him, but not strange like this. He searched the lean
face in the driving mirror and met its staring eyes. Uncle
spat out three questions. 'Billy – been living there all this
time? Twelve now, are you? And your sister, seven?'

Billy nodded. Even Uncle's voice sounded odd.

Mother took over. 'I told you that already, Ted. We've
all been evacuated since the Blitz. The vicarage could
only take me and Jill, so Billy was billeted here. We have
sent you our news regularly.' She turned to look at him.
'But perhaps you've been in no state to take it in.'

'No state,' Ted laughed, if that croak could be a laugh.
'Bet you're glad to go home,' he directed at Billy.

'We certainly are,' Mother said. 'I'll say!'

Billy didn't answer and slumped back into his seat.
He'd dreaded leaving the Pawseys even more than Hitler
invading. Ever since VE Day he'd felt sick at the thought,
but hadn't been able to picture it actually happening. It
was truly terrible to leave the people who'd loved him
and given him a safe home; but it was wonderful to see
Uncle Ted at the door, back safe from war. That

excitement had muddled his dreadfully sad feelings, and then how different he looked! The Uncle Ted he remembered from before the war had made jokes, played magic tricks, done handstands.

Billy had stood at the door with his suitcase, confused, and made the shortest of goodbyes to Mr and Mrs Pawsey when there were so many words in his heart. His misery about leaving, excitement and bewilderment just couldn't sit together inside of him. It was a wonder he wasn't sick all over the place before even getting into the car.

A car! Billy hadn't been in one since the vicar had delivered him back here four years ago. He wriggled uncomfortably. He'd expected to make his goodbyes to the Pawseys privately, when he was on his own, with Jed the carter collecting him. The arrangement had been for him to meet Mother and Jill at the railway station, where he'd go in the horse and cart. But an officer at the hospital had lent Uncle this car to take the family home, so they'd all come to the Pawseys' to collect him.

It turned a corner rather sharply just then, so that Jill slid across Billy's lap. 'Whoops,' she giggled.

'Mind the eggs.' He clasped the basket Mrs Pawsey had given him close to his middle.

The car jerked into the lane that led to the main road. 'I bet Uncle hasn't driven before,' Jill whispered.

He frowned at her.

'Thank goodness,' said Mother. 'Evacuation's finally over. It's been so long since VE Day, waiting to get away. Such an imposition, expecting me to work another six weeks at that wretched garage. Home! I can't wait to get my shoes onto proper pavements. Just look at those muddy ruts.'

Jill nudged Billy and rolled her eyes. She didn't seem at all in awe of Mother. Then she whispered, 'Who's that little girl crying and waving at you?'

He pushed his face to the window. Sally! Her little figure pushed away from the girls around her as she ran forward, waving wildly and calling. He couldn't say anything; his throat was choked. His hand didn't feel it belonged to him as it lifted and waved. The car passed and left her behind, crying alone.

'Billy?' Jill nudged again. 'Who is it?'

He swallowed hard. 'Sally Youldon, from where I used to live, the first time I was evacuated.'

'Oh, I know. That little girl you saved from drowning? The peasant family?'

'They weren't peasants!'

'Mummy said they were. She didn't like you minding them. Anyway, Sally's all sad you're coming away.'

He swallowed harder. 'Yes.'

Mother called over her shoulder, 'Open the window wider, Billy, please. It's still so hot. I never have liked high summer.'

He wound the handle a few more times. The wind blasted his face as it whistled past the window. It felt as if his heart was sucked out too. He imagined it whisking away to Mr and Mrs Pawsey, then flying past bushes to Mrs Youldon, Sally and Tim. How would they manage without him? He pressed the hard bit of his chest where it hurt. Something vital had surely gone and left his stomach churning up and down with every rut in the road.

'Awfully bumpy, Ted,' Mother complained.

Uncle grunted. 'Better than queuing for a coach for hours, or squashed up on the train, standing all the way.'

'That's true. I had that awful experience in 1940, coming down here with Doreen and the children. Never again!'

The car juddered to a stop. 'Oh, for heaven's sake!' Mother sounded cross already. The farm's herd of cows had begun to cross the top lane, back from milking.

Uncle Ted put on the brake and groaned. 'Just my luck.' The engine spluttered.

'Better not let it stop, Ted. You don't want to crank the handle again.'

As the cows lumbered past, one of them lowered its head, peering straight into the car. Mother and Jill squealed. Its huge eyes penetrated to the back seat to look at Billy's misery. Did cows feel sorry for people, like dogs could?

It mooed, its breath smearing the windscreen. Mother screwed back into her seat. 'Oh make it go away, Ted, do. Great, horrible thing.'

It lurched off as if it had heard. The car engine spluttered again as the line of cows ambled past and into the field. Uncle Ted drummed his fingers on the wheel. Mother sighed.

The wicker basket on his lap scratched Bill's legs below the edges of his trousers. The basket held eggs laid by the chickens he'd fed every day. Tucked underneath to save them from cracking was a green checked napkin from the set Mrs Pawsey used every meal-time. Now she'd have one missing. The paper bags beside the eggs were filled with cakes made with the last of their rations. They'd gone without to send Billy off with all the best of what they had. He'd known he was special to them, just as they had become to him. When Mother unpacked the basket in Wandsworth he'd save the napkin, secretly. Then he'd always have something of the Pawseys'.

'Come on, cows. We want to go home to London!' Jill chirped, making the words into a little song. 'Lon-don, Lon-don, we're off to London town.'

The last cow flicked its tail before stepping leisurely into the mud lake by the open gate, and Uncle Ted bent to the controls again with shaky hands. He didn't look very sure about which knob did what.

4

Jill's dark curls brushed Billy's neck as she leant close to whisper, 'Uncle Ted's a bit loopy, isn't he?'

'Of course not!' he muttered back. 'He's just out of hospital, recovering, that's all.'

'Kenneth said—'

He pressed a hand across her mouth to shut her up.

There was a new noise from the engine and the car lurched forward. The farmer lifted a hand in a wave and the gate shut behind the black and white backsides of the cows.

'We're off!' Jill bounced a few more times, Billy protecting the precious eggs by holding the basket in the air.

Mother gave a triumphant sigh. 'And now back to a civilized normality, I trust. Foot down please, Ted. Let's get away from this' – she waved a hand towards the field – 'smell of cows and pigs. Billy's billet.'

Billy scowled at his lap. There weren't ever cows at the Pawseys' and this farm was two lanes away from their smallholding. He kept his eyes on the eggs. Mother should see how unfair she was.

The car turned left at the main road. Billy turned, trying to see out of the back window, but it was set too high on Austin Eights. Outside, all sight of the village would soon be gone, even the church spire.

'Now you can put it right behind you –' Uncle Ted's fingers were twitching through his white forelock. '– your evacuation. They told me to do that about my service, now that war's over.' He leant forward over the wheel as if his ribs needed propping up. 'Easily said when you're a doc in a white coat, safely away from sh—'

'Ted!' Mother put a hand on his arm. 'It *is* all over.'

A growl came from his throat, 'Over? Rotten war, rotting—'

Mother put a hand over his mouth. 'Shh.'

'Will we get home before dinner time?'

Mother turned to Jill, still bouncing happily up and down on the back seat. 'No. And pull your bow up. It's slipped right down to your ear.'

Jill took the side lock of hair and shoved the ribbon a little higher. 'Will we have to eat in a restaurant? I've nev-er e-ver ea-ten in a re-stau-rant.' She bounced in time to her words.

'For heaven's sake, child. Can't you sit still?'

Uncle Ted had the car under control now. It began to speed up once on the main road. There were fields outside the car window, and then arches of trees blocking sight of anything else. The trees became skimpier and further apart revealing a set of huts in a clearing. A wooden signpost near the road read 'NAAFI' and someone had scribbled 'Not known here'.

Billy's legs were sticking to the cracked leather seat. It would take hours and hours to get back to Wandsworth, his insides were screwed into a ball, everything was awful. The car sides and roof were a shell around him, like being in an Anderson shelter, but sheltered from where he wanted to be, instead of from bombs. He hadn't felt worse, not even in the cellar with the noise of bombing, Kenneth shaking beside him, and that scary whining squeal of the air raid warning.

Gradually he became aware of Mother's one-way conversation in the front, and Jill's excited chatter beside him in the back. He stopped pulling at the stuffing. It wasn't their car and he was making the slit worse. He put his hands in his pockets and gazed at the back of Uncle Ted's head where the hair was still black. Nanny and Grandad would be so happy to have him and all of them back again. Mrs Pawsey had urged Billy to think of all these good cheery things. He shook himself sensible and let himself hear the end of Jill's chatterings, realising they were intended for him.

'...And I said to him, "it will be such a squash and you and Billy will quarrel and I don't want to sit in the middle of you two," and he said, "Anyway, Mummy's taking me to visit some of our relatives. They haven't seen me since I was four".'

Billy jerked to attention. 'Who?'

'Kenneth of course!'

'I thought they were going to London by train.'

'They are, but that's what I've just said. *Not yet.* They're going to Northampton first. That's where they live, Kenneth's grandad and grandma. It'll be two whole weeks before he and Aunty come to settle in.'

Billy sat back, imagining two grandparents fussing and adoring Kenneth, just as Aunty did. Two weeks. That was something. At least he could get used to 'home' before Kenneth invaded the place.

Jill nudged him. 'Won't it seem funny, all of us there? I'm used to having Mummy to myself, and funny people coming in and out to see the vicar. But I shan't miss them.' She giggled. 'Or the tellings-off and sermons at dinner. I saw Kenneth and Aunty every day because their billet was down the road, but I can't imagine all of us in the one house every day!'

'No.' He felt for a hanky and wiped the back of his sweating neck. It was flipping hot in the back, even with the wind blowing in. Jill's chatter wasn't helping. It was so rotten to leave this place, and doubly rotten to think of Kenneth living with them.

'I can't even remember our house, can you?'

'Yes,' he said, thinking about it. 'I can. But it will seem strange now.'

Mother came to the end of her conversation and overheard. 'We shall all find everything strange, children. You'll both have to buckle to.' She turned back to the front.

Jill leant towards Billy. 'And, I will have my very own bedroom, instead of sharing with Mummy.' Her voice dropped to a whisper. 'I'm going to have secret things in it. There'll be treasure. And if I make a friend at my new school, I'll bring her home to play in it. It will be ever so private. You won't be able to join in.'

He managed a smile. 'Don't worry. I won't.'

Jill nudged him in the side. 'But *you* won't have your own bedroom now.' She chuckled. 'We're opposites. I'm getting my own room at last; you've had your own bedroom all this time, and now you'll be sharing.'

'Yes.' The last time he'd shared a room with Kenneth had been the dreadful night after Uncle Frank had died, while the grown-ups were at the funeral. That was definitely the worst night of his life.

He kept quiet while Mother and Jill went on chatting. Uncle Ted was silent too. Outside the window, fields of blue spread like ball gowns across to the gentle hills beyond. Flax. Mr Pawsey had told him flax was important during the war. The blue might change to some other colour now, just like men's trousers would change from army khaki to business black. Billy couldn't imagine Dad's legs in khaki, but he wouldn't see them until Dad was demobbed.

Billy started as Uncle suddenly spoke. 'You'll be *Bill*, I suppose, now that you're big.'

Immediately, he decided he must change. 'Yes,' he said out loud, and turned to Jill. 'You must call me Bill from now on.'

'Jill, Bill. It rhymes,' she squealed.

'I know,' he said grimly. 'I told Mother that when I was your age. Can't be helped.'

Uncle went on as if no-one had spoken, '—and you can call me Ted.' After that he said nothing. He didn't answer Mother, just nodded to her chat.

It had been a long while of her talk and his silence before she turned round to them, 'Uncle Ted has to concentrate on driving, so don't talk to him.'

'*She* has been,' Jill whispered, thumbing towards Mother below the seat level.

Bill frowned at her. She was getting quite cheeky.

The next sound was Jill again. 'Are we halfway yet, Mummy? This is a proper town.'

The fields had given way to streets of houses. Mother peered out of her window, looking ahead. The houses became closer together and there was a church. 'Is this halfway, Ted? Shall we stop for something to eat? We'd better, I suppose.'

'Goody,' said Jill. 'I'm ever so, ever so hungry.'

Ted pulled into the kerbside beside some public toilets. The engine spluttered twice and then stopped. He opened his door and the full heat of the day swept in.

Jill was pushing Bill forward. 'Go on.'

'Wait for Uncle to open the door on the pavement side. It's dangerous to get out onto the road.' He looked out at the row of houses and the shops ahead. Everything looked big and brick and not like places you could just run past, whooping and calling out as he'd been used to for the last four years.

Ted opened the door for Mother. She swung her legs as one towards the pavement, just like the lady film stars in the newsreels. 'Oh what a relief to stretch my legs. Proper pavements! Wonderful. I'll ask a local if there's a restaurant. Surely there'll be something.' She tip-tapped away down the road.

Uncle wrestled with the front seat until it swung forward and they could clamber out. He went into the Gents.

Jill spotted a chalked hopscotch game on the paving outside. 'I used to play this at the village hall, in the yard at the back where they kept the fire engine. My friend Iris and me got ever so good at hopscotch. Can you do it, Billy-Bill?' She lifted one foot and started hopping.

'I can, but Mother wouldn't approve of hopping in the street.' He remembered his shock when Mrs Youldon first told him to 'play out' and Mother's horror when she found out that he played in the street.

Jill carried on hopping and jumping, as if he hadn't spoken. 'And Iris lives in Wandsworth, too.'

Mother reappeared as Ted came out of the Gents. 'I asked at the post office. Two streets away up there, the WVS run a British restaurant at the Workers' Institute. It's the only place.' Her face spoke about how she felt about that.

Ted said, 'I'll eat there, whatever it's like.'

'We'll go and wash our hands first. You, too, Bill.' Mother grasped Jill's shoulder, stopping her mid-hop, and ushered her to the toilets.

Afterwards, Ted led off down the street, forgetting to take Mother's arm as he should have done. Jill nudged Bill. 'Look. He does look loopy, whatever you say.'

Ted was flicking his head as if he had a long lock of hair over his eyes, but he hadn't. His hair was army short. His walk did look odd, fast and jerky. Mother wasn't hurrying to walk beside him. They followed Ted past the few shops and across the road at the Belisha beacon. On Mother's far side, Jill leapt from each metal stud to the next all the way across the road. 'Oh, for heaven's sake!' but Mother didn't stop her.

A short way on, a dirty brick and stone building with a pointed roof had its doors open and a WVS lady standing at the entrance. Jill spotted her. 'Look, a lady like Aunty, green uniform, see?'

'That'll be it,' said Mother.

They joined the string of people paying and collecting their tokens, one for each course.

'Can I keep them afterwards, Mummy, they're so nice?' Jill held up the bright blue counter and then the yellow one. 'I could use them as Ludo counters.'

But the tokens were taken as they paid. At a counter, more WVS ladies handed out their plates of mince, mash and peas and dishes of spotted dick and runny custard. 'Is there rice pudding?' Mother asked, but the WVS helper said it was *off*.

Mother only tutted, but Uncle Ted turned his mouth down. 'Rice pud's off. Doesn't matter where you go, this is off, that's off. All set out to make you feel miserable.'

'Yeah, so much worse than eating rats in the trenches, isn't it, mate?' A large man wearing part of a check shirt, a flat sleeve where his lower arm should have been, leaned over Ted's shoulder. 'Demobbed early, like me, eh? But without a good reason. Like this.' He jerked his head at his flat arm sleeve and then at his foot, which was in some kind of box with a metal strip under it. 'Where did you serve, then?'

'Belgium,' Ted muttered trying to squeeze past Mother to take his tray to one of the four long trestle tables.

'Oh, yeah. Until it was occupied by Kraut thugs, 1940. It's been a long time since then.'

'Better help my family get to a table.' Ted followed Mother and slid quickly along the bench beside Jill. Bill closed the gap behind Ted, who looked very uncomfortable. How could he help Ted out?

Lumbering awkwardly, the man followed Ted. The metal bar clanged on the floor like a bell tolling. 'What regiment, mate?'

'East Surreys.'

'Royal Hampshire, me.'

Mother sat down opposite Jill so Bill hurried forward to flank Ted's other side.

The man put his tray beside Mother's as best he could, one-handed, and sidled along the bench. 'Good-day, Missus. All right if I take this space beside you?'

Mother nodded briefly, then turned her face away.

Ted now had to face the man over the plates of dinner. He picked up his knife and fork and began to eat hurriedly.

The man shoved his plate along the table, gravy slopping onto the table. 'Yeah. We had all the worst. France, Belgium, Algiers, Salerno, Egypt, back to Italy and that's when I copped it. Lucky to be alive.'

Ted's face looked hard as a brick.

Bill turned his face sideways so that Ted could seem totally involved in a separate conversation. 'It's quite nice this mince, Ted, isn't it?'

The man hadn't shaved very well. His stubbly face and way of speaking wasn't what Mother was used to. She was ignoring the man, looking across to Jill, as if checking what she ate.

He didn't care. 'Good to have hubby back home so soon, Missus?'

'This is not my husband. He is still serving.'

'Oops. Sorry. Didn't mean to embarrass you. Enough said!'

Mother drew herself up until her back was as straight as a soldier on drill, and raised her eyebrows alarmingly. She didn't look at the man. 'I am eating with my brother and my children, thank you.'

'Yeah. Course you are.' He pushed his chin forward towards Ted and gave a huge wink to Bill since Ted was looking down at his plate. He took his fork in his one good hand and lifted a large dollop of mash and gravy to his mouth. Several drops of gravy dripped onto the table. Mother flinched slightly. He leant towards her. 'I was just asking your *brother* where he served after Belgium. Escaped to Dunkirk and rescued, I expect.'

Ted nodded.

'Then?'

Bill needed to rescue Ted again. What could he say? He knew Jill would be staring but with Ted between them he couldn't nudge her. She hadn't met many younger men before, especially not one with only one hand. He bent forward to his plate and tried to catch her eye. Sure enough, she was watching the man, fascinated. The man noticed.

'Do you have lots of uncles, Missy?'

She smiled back at him. She was too little to know that 'uncle' could mean something else. 'No. We did have one other one but he got killed by a bomb.'

'Jill.' Mother threw a stern warning glance across at her.

The man sat up. 'In Belgium?'

'No. In Balham.'

'What, on leave there?'

'No. He wasn't a soldier because he was a tax inspector, wasn't he, Mummy?'

She frowned at Jill. 'Just eat up.'

The man snorted. 'Love them! Exempt, weren't they!'

Mother bridled. 'That's quite enough about our personal business, if you please.'

The man turned his attention back to Ted.

'You serve in first battalion?'

'Various.' Ted was busy with his plateful. He'd found hard lumps of potato in the mash and was pushing them to one side.

'Were you in the BEF?'

'No.'

'I knew a bloke in the East Surreys. Harry Thorpe. Know him?'

Ted shook his head.

'Not much to say for yourself, have you?'

13

Mother still didn't look at the man but put her knife and fork neatly crossed on her plate. She would have touched her mouth with a napkin if the place had such a thing. 'It's best not to worry my brother with too many questions. He is only just out of hospital.'

'Ah. Right. Where's the injuries?'

'Internal,' said Mother crossly and picked up her knife and fork again.

Ted was eating bit by bit as if swallowing poison. Actually, the food wasn't too bad although the mince was very runny. Bill had nearly finished his plateful and so had the man, even though he only had one hand.

'Anyway, Harry Thorpe was off to Africa when I last saw him, so I guess that's one place where you were.'

Bill jerked his head up. *Africa?*

Jill squealed, 'Were you in Africa, Uncle?' Several nearby diners looked up as her voice echoed around the hall.

Ted stood up and flung his knife and fork on the plate. 'Enough flaming questions.' He swung one leg over the back of the bench, and then the other. He moved back away from the tables. 'See you back at the car in fifteen. I'm going for a walk.'

'Go for a walk. Lucky you,' the man called after him. 'Wouldn't I like to! Only I never can again.' The man moved onto his spotted dick and custard. 'My word, this is tasty.' He raised his voice. 'You've left yours, mate. Waste not, want not.'

Ted was already at the door ignoring the WVS lady who was saying, 'We all clear our own dirty plates, dear.'

Bill looked at Mother for guidance. Her face was tight and red. 'I did say that was enough, Jill. Now see what's happened. Eat up. The custard is good for you. Then we must go.'

Bill finished his own pudding and then started on Ted's.

The man leant over to him. 'Better appetite than Uncle, eh? You looking forward to soldiering then, now you see how smashing it is?'

'Please leave my son alone. He isn't even thirteen yet.'

'Flipping heck. He's the size of a sixteen-year-old.'

Mother ignored him. 'If you've finished, children, let's clear the plates and get going.' She stood up and waited for the man to stand so that she could side step to the end of the bench. When he raised himself, taking his time, she moved her skirt aside as if she didn't want it to touch him. Bill held the packed-up plates and signalled a *Hurry up* to Jill with his eyes. She rolled hers back, but followed behind him.

Outside, Mother walked them very briskly along the road, as if worried that the man would follow them. A little way ahead she said, 'You must be careful of talking to strange men, Jill.'

'But he had no arm! When we had the collection for wounded soldiers, you gave me sixpence to put in the tin.'

'Even so. Men you don't know. Just – don't talk to them, and certainly don't discuss our private business.' She strode on.

Jill lagged behind, sulking.

Mother turned her attention to Bill. 'I know that was very awkward and the man was obnoxious, but he's bitter because he's been badly wounded. He'll have difficulty getting any sort of work again, and that means his useful life is over. It was surely dreadful enough being in trenches under fire.'

That would have been awful for Ted too. Bill's heart didn't have room for the man's problems. 'I knew Uncle Ted was in France first. No-one said where he was afterwards.'

Jill caught up. 'Was Uncle Ted really in Africa, Mummy?'

'Yes, and other countries. He really doesn't want to talk about the war, so please, both of you, no questions.'

'Oh,' Jill whined. 'But Africa is where black people are and piccaninnies, and great big fruits grow on the trees and it's baking hot all the time. I want to hear all about it.'

'You'll have to learn about it in school, then. Not from Uncle Ted. Mind, I shall be very cross if you disobey, Jill.'

Jill tossed her head and skipped ahead. Did that mean she would or wouldn't obey? He'd have a quiet word with her. Ted had been in Africa. The GIs had been sent there in '43. Supposing they'd met!

Ted was leaning against the car, waiting for them. He wasn't wearing army trousers like the man in the restaurant. Where was his uniform and what had happened that Ted didn't want to talk about? Bill remembered how he'd been in a dreadful state after Dunkirk, but he did talk about that. This time he was like a shop with the 'Closed' sign.

Ted stood up as he saw them. 'Ready, then? Let's get going.'

Jill sprang forward. 'Can I just press the horn?' It was attached to the front of the car, its rubber ball just asking to be squeezed.

Ted shrugged and Jill sprang to squeeze it before Mother could say *No*. It gave out a satisfying honk. Bill wanted a go himself but Mother was waiting at the passenger door with the seat tipped forward for them.

Bill squeezed in, changing seats so that Jill could be on the pavement side for seeing London. Ted leant down to crank the engine and it started obediently. He got into his seat and placed his hands on the wheel firmly enough.

As the car moved forward Jill's voice rang out. 'London, Lon-don, off to London town.'

Ted looked moody and Mother didn't chat either. Jill filled the silence with chirpy singing until Mother said, 'Enough, dear. We've heard enough songs.'

'Will it be long before we get to London? I want to see all the famous buildings.'

'What's left of them,' muttered Ted.

Bill sat back and closed his eyes. Best to pretend he was sleepy to avoid saying the wrong thing.

Jill nudged him, but when he didn't move, she pulled a comic from her little bag and turned the pages slowly. She couldn't read much yet. He'd read to her, now they were going back to live together, like a proper brother and sister again.

Chapter Two

It surely wasn't long since he'd closed his eyes but he must have slept, for now they were passing the ruins of buildings. Piles of rubble and wooden work huts sat alongside blackened brick walls. Factories, pubs, banks or homes had once stood there. It was difficult to believe it.

Jill shrieked. 'Look at that house! Its insides are all showing. I can see a bath upstairs.' She giggled. 'Look, Bill, you can see the stairs and everything.'

The dingy houses and blocks of flats were so close together and had no gardens. There were holes in the pavement where railings had been, dirt on the walls, cigarette stubs all over the pavements. The streets of houses had cleared spaces surrounded by brick rubble. London was different from what he remembered, lighter, yet blacker. The buildings looked filthy, an edging of black fluff on every surface. Even with blue skies and strong sunlight, it wasn't a cheerful outlook. Bill stared hard another ruin of a home. Supposing they'd stayed home in Primley Road instead of escaping to the country!

'Oh my goodness,' said Mother. 'What a mess! We've lost the London we knew.'

'Look! Red buses, buses with upstairses!' Jill squealed as one thundered past.

'Double-deckers,' Bill muttered. They looked huge after the village bus. He peered at the next one passing. He'd almost forgotten what they were like. 'Upstairs, Jill, at the very front, you can see all around, and you're right close to the buildings.'

Mother turned around. 'We're coming into the centre of London, now.' She turned back to Ted. 'Do a little tour, Ted, can you? Goodness, how long since I've been here!'

Another squeak from Jill. 'Look at those ladies in high heels.' The people in the streets did look different from the country folk.

Ted drove grimly on. Mother had gone quiet.

Bill saw that, to Jill, this was all new and exciting. She'd grown up with no knowledge of London.

'Ooh, look at that great big church thing.'

'St Paul's Cathedral. It's famous.'

'All over the world? Did Hitler know about it?'

'Yes,' Ted suddenly joined in. 'He'd have bombed it if he could. Look how it's bombed all around.'

Last time Bill was here, tall buildings had blocked the sight of St Paul's apart from its dome. Now they could now see the whole of it, flanked by the blackened bases of ruined buildings and a great cleared patch in front. But it still looked magnificent, a king amongst paupers.

'St Paul's Cathedral,' Jill murmured. 'And what's that, Bill?'

It was rather nice having a little sister wanting him to point out everything. Jill had been Kenneth's shadow for the past four years. Bill pointed out the Houses of Parliament, not that she'd understand what 'government' meant. He stared himself, everything so close together, so big. So damaged. It was a strange thrill to be back after so long, but shocking too.

Ted drove over Westminster Bridge.

'Let me see the river. Is it big, is it blue?' Jill was as near to standing as she could manage, her face pressed to the window. Bill eyed the muddy banks full of debris, slightly green on top of its satiny surface.

'Oh it's nearly black and all the bank is mud. Ugh.' But the boats pleased her and she stayed excited as they drove past the dinginess of Stockwell, Oval, Elephant and Castle.

When he saw the crush around Clapham Junction and heard Mother breathe, 'Arding and Hobbs,' Bill knew they would soon be home.

They passed the common. Even the stretches of green were soiled. It was blighted by corrugated iron huts, piles of iron, bricks, unkempt grass and overgrown bushes. They drove down roads with gaps where a house had been the unlucky hit. All this had been happening while lucky people were safe away in evacuation.

Jill laughed at another sliced open house, a stray bath lying in the garden and the upstairs rooms displaying the sad broken furniture. 'How funny! It looks as if someone's just gone out.'

'Just gone,' Ted said bitterly.

Bill felt queasy. Would Primley Road look this bad?

Mother looked out of the window, holding her handkerchief in front of her mouth. Bill had known, of course he'd known, that loads of buildings had been hit, but while he was living with the Pawseys he'd been so safe that the news was like a wireless play; scary but not real.

Mother said, 'We're not far from Wandsworth now.'

The buildings did look more familiar, and he looked keenly in case he recognised something. 'Isn't this the road we used to walk to Mr Durban's, Mother?'

'Yes, that's right.'

'Who's Mr Durban?' Jill piped up.

'He's Dad's friend, he works with him.' A bright orange feeling joined all Bill's black ones. He couldn't wait to see Mr Durban and the precious sabre. Once his secret photo of it had been stolen, he hadn't had its magic protection. Now he'd be seeing it for real.

The car turned a corner into a road where nothing was bombed. Primley Road looked the same as the day he'd left, carrying his suitcase and a bag of food, with his parents pushing Jill's pushchair ahead of him. He screwed up his eyes and tried to remember the scene through the smeared glass of the car window.

Mother got out of the car while Ted collected the luggage from the boot. He set it all in a line, military style.

Jill had already pushed the front seat forward to scramble out. Bill waited. If he placed his feet on this pavement it was like accepting that he belonged here. He looked up at the front of the house. It was strange, recognizing it so well yet feeling so apart from it. He stayed sitting until Mother waved him to get out.

'Help, then, Bill!'

'Is this our house or that one?' said Jill, pulling a case onto the pavement with one hand and waving a finger with the other.

Bill pointed to their black gate. He wasn't sure the house had a friendly look. A flickery feeling swirled inside his tummy.

Ted stretched. 'Long drive. I won't come in, Sis.' He put their suitcases at the front door. 'I've got to take the car to the station for Lieutenant Trent's brother to collect. But I'll do that in the morning. First, it's time to settle back home with the parents.'

Mother held him at his elbow and her voice was kind. 'You must be so relieved to be back with them at last.'

He shrugged, his face stiff. 'It'll all be changed there. You'll see.' He drove away with a brief wave of a white hand.

Bill looked around, trying to remember this road. When he was six and seven, he used to run down to school that way. Turning left led to Reg's house, and a few streets on, to Andrew's. Would he see any of them? Not when it was time to go back to school. They were all too old for junior school now. He turned back. Jill was standing still, large-eyed, until Mother put a bag in her hands and ushered her through the front gate. Then she gave Bill the keys. He opened the front door, quite slowly.

A damp and musty smell met him. He and Mother dumped the suitcases in the hall. He picked up a large pile of post and put it on the hall stand.

She sniffed. 'You can tell how long it is since your father was here. I can positively smell abandonment.'

The cream gloss wallpaper under the dado rail was far dingier than Bill remembered, and the patterned tiles on the floor needed a good clean. He glanced out at the road again before shutting the door. How close together the houses were, pressed in, like people on a crowded train. He shook his head. No fields between houses here. There wouldn't be any smell of country. Perhaps he'd never smell it again. *But when I'm grown up, getting there will be down to me.* Only, it was such a long time until he was twenty-one.

'Phew,' said Mother. 'Home at last. I can't believe it! My own home again after all this time.' She opened the front room door and started pulling dust sheets off the chairs.

Jill was silent, standing with the bag Mother had passed to her, like a party guest who was waiting to be welcomed.

He said, 'Shall I go round and open some windows?'

'Yes, do that, Billy.'

'*Bill*, now.'

'All right, all right. And collect the dust sheets. Tea. I need some tea. Surely there'll still be a packet of tea in the caddy. There won't be any milk. We'll have to open a tin of condensed, but at least we'll have a fresh pot of tea for a nice change. Pray your father didn't use it all before he left.'

He heard her footsteps down the passage and then a cry of glee. 'My old kitchen. All to myself! I shall have to remind myself where everything is.'

22

'I don't know where anything is,' Jill piped up. 'Can you show me, Bill?'

He pointed to the front room and she put her head round the door.

'Front room, we don't use it much. You mustn't touch the ornaments in it. Anyway, it's to be Aunty's room now. The next door's the cloakroom. I'll show you the rest of the house later. I'm going to help Mother, so why don't you go upstairs and find your old bedroom.'

'Where is it? I'm going to put all my secret things there.'

He smiled. 'Your room's the furthest one. Go on. You might find your old toys in the cupboard.'

He felt better for the sound of Jill's voice counting the stairs while she hopped up them. He went back slowly into each room, pulling the sheets off the chairs, turning the pictures to face the right way, removing the blackout and opening each window. It felt slightly shocking to do these things without asking permission first.

Each room brought a memory: galloping horsey out of the front room, helping Mrs Donnington polish the spoons in the dining room, watching Dad smoke his pipe in the parlour where the wireless voice doomed misery, the pack of unopened colouring pencils on the garden room bookcase and Dad's disappointed voice, 'He has no interest in drawing, whatsoever', Uncle Frank measuring Kenneth and himself back-to-back against the hall wall; the wrestling, the exercises, Uncle Frank's death. He shuddered. It was uncomfortable, those past times flitting into his mind, one fragment after another.

It must be ages since Dad was here, and even more years since Mrs Donnington had been in to clean. Would she come back now war had ended? Everywhere was terribly dusty, cobwebs were hanging from all the corners of the ceilings. He took the dust sheets into the hall. The dust would have to be washed out now.

Mother called out, 'Bring down some sheets from the airing cupboard, Bill. We'll peg them on the line to freshen while there's still sun. They haven't seen the light of day for years, so I hope there's no moth.

He bounded upstairs. His room hadn't been touched since 1940. Before Dad was called up in '43, he probably only came for the post and a night's rest, and to keep the house from being requisitioned. He was mostly wherever Court was sitting.

Horsey was propped in one corner. Bill remembered putting him there after returning from the first evacuation, because a seven-year-old was too old to play with hobby-horses.

He closed his door and leant back against it. He'd enjoyed his own space here, way back before he'd known there was a man called Hitler, before he heard bombs or saw dogfights. He stretched his arms out trying to occupy the whole space. Horribly soon he'd be sharing it.

Along the passage he could hear Jill squeaking in her bedroom, then her footsteps as she peeped into Mother's room, the bathroom, the spare room, and finally his. 'It's big this house, like the vicarage, but there's only one upstairs.'

'There's the loft, but you need a ladder to get up there.'

'Golly, I can't remember anything,' she said. 'I'm like someone who's never been here.'

'But you were. I remember the day you were born and a nurse was with Mother in her bedroom. When you were a toddler, I read you stories up here, sometimes. Once I found you a little bear. It fitted just snugly into your hand.'

She looked at her empty hand as if he was making it up. 'Can't remember. Do you like being back in your old bedroom?'

'Yes, quite.'

24

'Where's Kenneth going to sleep?'

He took a big breath pressing what felt like a metal band round his chest. 'There'll be bunk beds. This one will have to go.' He looked around, imagining the changed room.

'You've never shared before.'

'Actually I have. My first evacuation. Alan and I shared: and not just a room – it was more like a cupboard – but the bed, a little camp bed.'

'Goodness! That must have been a squash.'

'It was, but we got used to it.' If only it was Alan he had to share with, not Kenneth.

Jill used her grown-up's voice. 'You can get used to anything if it goes on long enough. The vicar said that once when I wanted jam on my bread and there wasn't any. Come on. You said you'd show me the downstairs rooms and I want my tea.'

He collected the sheets from the airing cupboard and led Jill downstairs. He found Mother laying tea in the kitchen instead of the dining room. The mound of dust sheets now filled the scullery doorway.

'Take a cloth from the scullery,' she said to Bill, 'before you hang the clean sheets outside. You'll need to clean the washing line first.'

He went outside and ran the cloth along the line of rope that stretched from the scullery to the shed, the ugly part of the garden. Mother was right, when he got to the end of the rope the cloth was filthy. He looked up and remembered the searchlights, the flak and planes overhead. The cloth was thick with dirt from the war in the skies as much as the smoke from London chimneys. The top of a factory chimney in the distance had a steady plume to join the rest. How it spoiled the blue sky! He spread out the sheets for their first night home.

He washed the cloth and his hands in the scullery sink. Through the doorway, he saw Mother putting the teapot on the kitchen table.

'Come on, Bill. We'll eat here for now. I've got everything to do now we're back, and I've only the one pair of hands.'

'You'd look funny with more.' Jill giggled.

'Don't be smart.' Mother looked at them both as if they might suddenly multiply into several children. 'I expect you're both hungry. I'm not sure what I can find you to eat.'

Bill picked up the basket from Mrs Pawsey. He slid it forwards. Inside were eggs, fruit cake, butter, crusty bread and tomatoes.

'Bless her!' She unpacked it. She cut the bread, then three very thin slices from the fruit cake.

While she was busy, Bill managed to put the napkin in his pocket.

Mother rescued a raisin that had fallen onto the table and put it with the fruit cake. 'We're certainly glad of this today. We're used to rationing, but it will be much worse here in London, so you children will have to get used to it.'

Bill spread a scrape of butter carefully onto his bread. Mother had found some Bovril in the larder. The thick, sticky paste at the bottom of the jar was still worth scraping up. He looked at the padlock hanging from its metal loop on the larder door. Mother and Mrs Donnington had piled the stock there when war was expected. 'Do you remember Mrs Donnington, Jill?'

'Who?'

'Our Home Help,' Mother said. 'We shan't be seeing her again. No-one can get any help now. Everyone's told me that.'

Jill wasn't listening. She finished her tea quickly and got up without asking, but Mother didn't say anything until Jill started opening cupboards. 'Enough!' Mother shooed them both out of the kitchen. 'I want to clear up and find what tins are left. Then I must write the shopping list and a note for the milkman so he knows to start delivering again.'

'Show me round, Bill. You said!' Jill ran in and out of the downstairs rooms. 'Isn't it funny that I was here, sitting in my highchair.'

'And hiding,' Bill said. 'Come here.' He opened the cellar door and peered under the stairs. There was no light and Dad hadn't left the torch hanging on its hook. He pushed Jill's head down in the right direction so that she could make out the outline of the camp bed where they'd sat those scary nights. 'Do you remember being down here in the middle of the night sheltering from the bombs?'

Jill shook her head.

'Not the noise?' He pointed. 'That's where we had to sit. Next to the coal hole.'

'Ugh. Bet there are spiders down there.'

'Probably. They have to live somewhere. Can you see the round iron flap up at the end of the cellar? That's where the coal comes shooting down when the coalman comes. Mother let me stand here sometimes and watch. I thought that was very exciting.' He smiled. 'You can stand there, next time he's due.'

'Not likely! Why would I want to put my head in a horrid, dark stairway and see coal coming through!' She wriggled back out of the doorway, brushing cobwebs off her hands. 'Ugh.'

He wasn't used to having girls around. It was odd, the things they liked and didn't like. He took her back to the kitchen where Mother was opening the post. 'There's one for you, Bill, somewhere.' She rifled through the pile. Could Dad have written one just for him? It couldn't be from Mr and Mrs Pawsey already. Mother pulled out a postcard. 'Here.'

His excitement dashed down to the floor. It was from Kenneth.

> *Billy,*
>
> *I am having a lovely time with my granny and grandpa. They have given me loads of things. They took me to the pictures and I saw Anchors Aweigh with Gene Kelly and Fred Astaire. It was funny and excellent.*
>
> *Yesterday, Mummy heard that I have been awarded a place at Dulwich College. It's the best school in the whole of South London. Have you been told which school you are going to yet?*
>
> *Are you getting your bedroom ready for me? We will be coming soon.*
>
> *Kenneth*

Bill swallowed twice, then held out the postcard to Mother to read. Her head was bent over one letter after the other. 'Yes, dear, I've read it. Kenneth seems to be cock-a-hoop.'

'Come on, Jill, I'll show you the garden.' He took her outside. He wouldn't have her attention for many days more. Kenneth would take it over.

Mother had so much to do that it was late when they went to bed. The thin slice of fruit cake and two slices of bread felt like a long time ago and there was nothing more. He was hungry. Mrs Pawsey had always given him a good supper in the evening.

He sat on his bed with a thump. It was only this morning he'd been at home with the Pawseys, with the Youldons' cottage just a short run away. He was almost a son to the Pawseys, he'd been with them so long, and because they'd lost their only son, Graham. As for Mrs Youldon, whose little cottage he'd been billeted in on the first evacuation, she was the first person to make him feel special. She said he was her big boy. She depended on him for looking after her little ones. Now he'd gone from all of them forever. His eyes smarted. Mother wouldn't ever take him for a visit, that was for sure. He screwed up his eyes, trying to see them from memory. Were they all missing him? He pulled the green and white napkin from his pocket, hugging it to his chest. It was his little bit of the Pawsey home that he was going to keep always.

By his bed there was a certain crack in the wall which before evacuation, he'd always peered at as he dropped off to sleep, making it into a spider, a thin man, a steeple with bricks hanging below it. He could still do it. He pulled the blanket further towards his chin. The smell of his blanket, the iron base of his bed and the rail above it took his thoughts way back beyond the wail of the air raid siren to a time of soft toys, pyjamas with stars on them, hot milk in a blue chunky cup, and a faraway da-dit-dit-da of cross voices below the floorboards.

Chapter Three

Bill's eyelids felt too heavy to open but unfamiliar sounds around him stopped him from curling up into oblivion again. He thrust out his hand to feel for the damp nose of Macbeth or the thick ruff of Othello. Air blew through his searching fingers. They remained empty. He turned over and faced the crack in the wall. He heard gates opening, an exchange of *Good Mornings*. Primley Road people were off to work. He was not at the Pawseys' any more.

He pulled the sheet above his head, lying still to recapture the morning sense of restless dogs, the huff and puff of Mr Pawsey on the stairs, the whiff of honeysuckle and parsley, the snorting and clucking of piglets and chickens awaiting their feed. He wanted to remember all of it forever. One day, when he had his own money and was allowed to go away on his own, he would buy a train ticket and go back for real. His throat hurt. It hurt badly. He put his fingers on it in case there was a great lump Mother or Jill would see. No, only he would know it was there.

After another few moments of shutting his eyes to the new day, he sat up. The napkin fell off his front. He held it to his nose. He could smell the Pawseys' dining room, the home-baked bread. He wanted the napkin with him all the time. It was too big to keep on him without someone noticing, but he had scissors in his soap-bag. He got out of bed and found them. He cut the best piece, the middle, into a neat size. He could put that inside a full handkerchief every day, and no-one would ever know. He hid the rest of the napkin under his handkerchiefs and socks in his top drawer, and held the cut piece close. Mrs Pawsey had told him to think about cheerful things, like the people he'd be seeing again. She'd want him to do that.

Think of seeing the sabre again; Mr Durban, and Angela, a person who told him what was going on when no-one else did. She'd be pleased he was back. Nanny and Grandad's faces would glow when they set eyes on him. It was nearly five years since they'd seen him and Jill, who was still in a pram back then. They'd hold out their arms and their hugs would go on and on. They'd be amazed at how grown up he was. Uncle Ted would be absolutely fine now that he was safe at home. Everything would be back to how it used to be when he was small. Nanny would make a lovely dinner —— well, the best meal she could on rations. Visiting them had always been the best day of the week.

He slid out of bed and was the first washed and dressed. He put the piece of napkin inside a clean handkerchief and then in his trouser pocket.

After laying the table for breakfast in the kitchen, he went into the garden in case there were some flowers he could pick for Nanny. She'd like that. The garden was quite a mess, everything overgrown. He went to the shed but couldn't open the door. Swollen wood at its bottom pressed into the mud. The lowest two overlapping planks needed replacing where they had rotted. Perhaps there was a saw in the cellar. He had better see to this.

Apart from a patch of rotting rhubarb, there didn't seem to be any vegetables, and the flowers had been sabotaged by weeds. He kicked at a patch of soil. It was light brown, thin and stony, not like the rich ginger of the Pawseys' garden.

Mother always used to want something pretty to look at from her chair in the garden room. She'd never liked to garden, and hadn't wanted a vegetable plot, but with rationing, how would they manage without? Until Dad was demobbed, he'd better take the garden over. He'd learned so much from Mr Pawsey, so he could do it. He picked the largest stones from the patch where he would grow the carrots and things and threw them as far down the garden as he could.

When he went back indoors, Mother was in the kitchen holding the packet of cornflakes. 'This is only half full and it's probably stale.' She put round three dishes. 'You'll have to be the main food shopper, Bill, because people go early to queue. Even without this horrendous pile of washing, by the time I've seen to Jill and breakfast, everything will have been snapped up.' Her voice rose higher. 'And I don't know how I'm going to get this house clean and straight and feed everyone. Without Mrs Donnington, I have everything to do.'

He wasn't sure how best to help. He picked the ration books up from the table to see which shops they were registered at. Mother commented from the larder, 'Not even any oats. Goodness me, your father must have eaten loads of porridge. And all these shelves are so dirty! Pass me the Vim, will you?'

He found the cylinder of Vim under the sink, its cardboard soggy where the tap had leaked into the cupboard. He spoke towards the larder. 'We could keep chickens, so we'd get eggs. There's plenty of room in the garden.'

Mother squeaked. 'Ooh, I couldn't cope with feathery things. Suppose they got indoors? I wouldn't have a clue how to deal with them.'

'I would. I could look after them.'

Mother emerged from the larder holding the dishcloth and Vim. 'You did that at the Pawseys' of course. How out of touch I am with what you can do.' She put her dishcloth under the tap and wrung it out.

Jill came down in her dressing gown. Aunty had knitted it, but there hadn't been enough wool to make it all one colour. The top part was mustard yellow, the middle, grey and the bottom quarter was army green. 'Can I have my cornflakes before getting dressed, Mummy? I couldn't find any clothes.'

Mother pushed her hands through her hair. 'None? Not in the brown suitcase?'

'They were dirty when they were packed, remember?'

'Oh my goodness. All this washing on my very first morning home.' She fluttered her hands towards the largest suitcase, not yet unpacked. 'Who'd be me? There must be something you can wear, Jill.'

'Only these, if you mean in the chest of drawers.' She opened her dressing gown to show a tiny frilly skirt hanging off one hip and a blouse that must have fitted her when she was in her pram. Bill gave a shout of laughter and she burst into peals of giggles and rolled on the floor.

Mother wasn't amused. 'Get up, get up. You were far less trouble when you were that size, I'll have you know. Sit up for your breakfast, please.'

Jill didn't rush to get up or to finish giggling. Mother sighed and turned her back. She poured some milk into each cornflake dish.

When he was seven like Jill, the kitchen had been a place where he feared trouble. Jill, twisting round to make Bill laugh and in full view of Mother, obviously didn't have such a problem. She looked totally confident. Had Mother changed? He sneaked a glance as she placed a dish neatly into Jill's place, and another more randomly into his. No, she just preferred girls. He pulled his dish towards him and began eating the flakes, stale as old cardboard. No napkins for kitchen meals! How things had changed, post-war.

Jill munched away happily. 'My friend Iris lives right near here. She's the one I played hopscotch with and I want to go and see her.'

Mother didn't appear to be listening. She was eking out the last of the condensed milk into her pale beige tea, the pot 'hotted up' from last evening.

It would probably help Mother to have Jill out of the way. He said, 'What street does Iris live in?'

'Look. Her mummy wrote it down.' She passed over an old birthday card with an address written on the inside.

'That's near St Ann's Hill. I know it. Perhaps I can walk you there when I go for the shopping – if Mother says.'

Mother looked up, her mind probably on other things, and nodded. 'When you're dressed.' Then as an afterthought she added, 'If people are right about the length of queues, it will probably be dinner-time by the time Bill finishes, so he can collect you as well.'

'All right,' he said. If she wasn't in a hurry for him to get back, he could scout around a bit after delivering Jill. He might come across Reg or Andrew, or take a look at his old junior school.

'There are quite a lot of chores to finish before you can go,' Mother interrupted his thoughts.

He swept the larder and kitchen, pulling the bag of dirty washing from the large suitcase and piling it beside the dust sheets against the scullery sink. He checked the mangle. He remembered that if you left it unused for too long, the rubber rollers stuck together and left tiny flecks on the wet washing. Their last holiday, he calculated quickly, six years ago, they'd had a smashing two weeks at Cooden Beach. When they'd got back it was a baking hot day. Mrs Donnington had been sweating over the washing while she minded him. The mangle roller was soggy. He'd been sitting on a bucket in the scullery picking the rubber bits out of his knitted swimming costume when Dad came in to tell her the fearful news that war was almost certainly coming.

He wound the mangle handle a couple of times and grubby grey streaks showed on the roller. There was a stockinette dishcloth on the draining board. He was going to clean the rollers with it, but it had dried into such hard folds that it stayed stuck on the draining board, and when he yanked on it a splinter of wood went into the side of his hand. He didn't like wooden draining boards. Mrs Pawsey had an enamel sink and drainer. It was chipped and badly stained, but you didn't get splinters.

'Why are you sucking your hand?' Jill was now dressed in the things she'd worn yesterday.

'Here, can you pull this splinter out? I can't do it with my left hand.'

Her fingers were small enough, half the width of his. She leant over him and pulled it out. 'You see, I am a useful girl.'

'Thanks. Are you ready to go?'

Mother was sorting the remainder of the suitcase into piles on the kitchen chairs. She nodded at the table. 'There are the ration books and the form to show we're back. I've written you a list. Standard loaf, cheese, marmalade, two tins of beans, cornflakes, half a pound of biscuits – broken will do, they taste just the same – the meat ration, three pounds of potatoes, onions, carrots and a cabbage. Take two baskets to even the weight.' She passed them over. 'Here's three florins. That should be plenty. You can buy a comic each with the change.'

'Thank you!' That was a whopping surprise. He hadn't had a comic for ages.

Jill started saying, 'Don't get me *Sunny Stories*. I want a comic with more pictures.'

He nudged her to the front door. She was chancing their luck by sounding ungrateful. 'Tell me outside, silly,' he muttered. They left the house to its dank, neglected smell. Sunshine beamed onto the front path.

35

'It's hot!' Jill hopped towards the gate swinging what had once been a very smart lady's bag. Its gold coloured clasp hung open, revealing a number of small dolls and a Knitting Nancy.

'Where did you get that bag, Jill?'

'Aunty gave it to me because the clasp's broken. Look—.' She let it fall open wider and stroked the inside. 'This is satin.'

'If you take that, you won't be able to help me carry the shopping home.'

'No. I can carry the comics, though, under my arm.' She skipped ahead, her dark curls bouncing on her shoulders as cheekily as her words.

'I hope it'll be all right with Iris's mother, you coming without any notice. If not, you'll have to come with me.'

Iris's place had a low brick wall topped by a hedge. The double-fronted house with its bay windows looked inviting, and when Iris's mother opened the door to them, she smiled widely. 'Hello, Jill! Iris has been saying you'd be back home by now. It is a nice surprise to see you so soon. Come along in.' She pointed to the handbag. 'I can see you've brought things to play with. And you are Billy, the brother?'

'Bill, Mrs Nokes. I'm just dropping Jill, if that's all right. I've got to go and queue for the food. We only got back yesterday evening.'

'Your mother must be up to her ears. Tell me where you live and I'll drop Jill back after dinner. She can stay and eat with us.'

'Hooray!' Jill stood peering down the hall for her friend without a backward glance at Bill. 'We live in Primley Road and I know the way!'

'Thank you very much, Mrs Nokes.' Bill shut the gate behind him. Even better. Now he had time to scoot around for a recce.

The nearby roads still had their trees but many of the front gardens looked neglected, no fathers, no husbands to work in them on Sundays.

Around the common, the iron railings had been ripped out for the war effort. The regular gaps along the grass looked like a mouth with pulled teeth. The white S for Shelter was still clear over the entrance, but Mr Durban's ARP hut had been removed. That's where Bill had rushed for information and comfort when Ted returned from Dunkirk in boots that had gone green, a greatcoat and nothing else. Kenneth had scoffed that he'd been defeated but Mr Durban said Dunkirk was a miraculous success and asked for Bill's help in eating a bar of chocolate. Bill smiled. He realised, now he was older, that Mr Durban was just being kind. And it was probably his last bar. When sweets came off the ration, he'd buy Mr Durban loads of chocolate.

He walked to the top of St John's Hill overlooking the mess of London. Fulham was where Mr Durban's Cossack sabre lived in a cupboard, the scarlet top of its pommel just showing above its scabbard. How thrilling it had been, that first Christmas Eve of the war when Mr Durban told him its terrible tale and its special name - *shashka*. And now he had his own sabre story to tell Mr Durban, the one Alan had found in the Manor library last year.

Mother should hurry up and telephone Mrs Durban to say they were back. They must visit soon, before Kenneth got back. He mustn't hear about the sabre; it was Bill's secret that he had seen it, dreamed up its power, and Mr Durban's secret that he had told Bill its story.

He ran down towards the station. That's where there were a lot of bombed houses. One had bits of chairs, an exposed staircase, and a tree continuing to grow right through the rubble. Next door, a pram stood outside an undamaged house and a woman was scrubbing the step, as if nothing had ever gone wrong. Nearby, a house was sliced open from front to back. A small gang of rough children scrambled up to the first floor. Others were rummaging through rubble for war treasure: shrapnel, pennies, ornaments and crockery under heaps of brick dust. A group of girls played house in a back room that still had three of its walls and a mantle-piece. Two were 'cooking' in a battered saucepan with a long spoon, and a bigger girl was sweeping dust from under a horse chestnut tree. Another sat on a backless chair, pretending to be The Mistress. Several boys were playing tight-rope along one of the remaining joists on the first floor. It did look fun, but he didn't know any of them.

He stepped back onto the pavement. Joining in would be much better when he'd found one of his old friends. They'd do a whole tour of bomb sites. That would be spiffing. He turned away. He was supposed to be shopping. It would be awful if everything had been sold because he had been off exploring instead of queuing. He ran back towards Garrett Lane.

The line of women stared at him when he joined the baker's queue. He was a newcomer, just the same as when he was first evacuated. He wanted to shout out, 'I live here. I'm from Wandsworth.' After about ten minutes he got to the front. He handed over the ration books and took hold of the greyish National loaf. It had no smell. Mrs Pawsey had always baked her own, swapping her eggs for flour. He put the hard oblong into the basket. When would he enjoy a baking bread smell again?

It took longer to get served at the grocer's and after that, the greengrocer's had the longest queue of all. There was a whisper about a new delivery and when he reached the front he saw a carton of small oranges with a large notice, 'Children Only'. He passed the ration books over but the greengrocer only let him have one. 'You're too big to count as a child.'

Bill pointed to his ration book, but the greengrocer shrugged. 'Sorry.'

Bill hesitated. Should he argue?

The lady behind Bill said, 'Hurry up, ducky. We all want to get served, you know.'

He asked for the potatoes. When the greengrocer threw them on the scales, they were so thick with dirt that he didn't get much for the money. He wouldn't look forward to coming to this shop again, but you had to go where you were registered.

He got Jill's comic from the newsagents and although it had *The Wizard*, he bought stamps with his share of the change so he could write to the Pawseys and Youldons.

The baskets were too heavy to walk over to his old school. That would have to wait for another day.

Arms aching, he walked on until Primley Road stretched in front of him, unharmed and only slightly shabby, as if it had been unaware of the war. The gate was swinging loose as he came back up the path. He could mend that sort of thing now. He went to find Mother. She had emptied the large suitcase which was now propped against the door, while beside her on the floor, a tin bucket held the dreaded washing.

'Here's the shopping, Mother. I'm going to mend the gate later; the hinge is off. I know where the tools are.'

'Good. If you can, Bill. I've made a huge list of things that need doing.' She looked up as he started to unpack the baskets, holding out each item like a trophy.

'Loaf.'

'If that's today's bread, I'm a film star.'

'Cabbage. Potatoes.'

'They look as if they've brought half the garden with them.' Then she saw the orange. 'Ooh, an orange. What luck! Where is Jill?'

'Mrs Nokes is bringing her back after her dinner.' He hung the empty baskets on their hooks in the larder. 'Are we going to Nanny and Grandad's afterwards?'

Mother looked at the tin bath full of washing and sighed. 'Tomorrow. I have to wash a second load now and get it hung out.'

'Can't we go after that?'

'I shall be all in. Anyway, it's probably best to let Ted settle in properly before we go round there. They have to adapt to having him home. Find me some more pegs, will you? Then we'll have our dinner and afterwards, I can start dusting everywhere. It will take an age to get the living room clean, but we must have somewhere to sit besides the kitchen. We can't live as though we're paupers.'

The doorbell rang, and Mother went to thank Mrs Nokes for having Jill. Jill's voice trilled down the hallway in a sing-song. 'Thank-you-ver-y-much; can-I-come-again?' She skipped on towards the kitchen.

Mother followed. 'Jill, you are in luck. Bill got an orange from the greengrocers.' She passed it over. 'Give him a couple of pieces, will you?'

Jill took up the orange, sniffing it and closing her eyes. 'Aaahhh! We had one of these at the vicarage Christmas party.' The skin was very tough and the white stuff wouldn't come away from the fruit for ages. 'Here you are.' She handed Bill two segments.

'Thanks, Jill. Smashing.'

She sucked at one herself. 'It's not very juicy. How do I eat it? It's hiding under a white blanket.'

Bill couldn't help laughing, but Mother tutted and took a knife to the orange. 'Be grateful, child. Fruit's a rare enough treat. It's only you who got one.'

'You can have this boat, Mummy,' said Jill.

Mother slipped the segment into her mouth and chewed it slowly. 'Not very good, I agree.' She sighed. 'I remember real oranges. Before you were born, Jill.'

It was at the Manor party, with Alan and all the other vaccies, that he'd last had an orange. This one was a very poor substitute, but he kept the last mouthful of orange in his mouth for as long as he could as a way of bringing back the memory. He had a long drink of water to savour the taste.

Jill looked impressed. 'What a big drink, Bill! I saw your throat wobbling up and down. Isn't it lucky that water's not on ration?'

'Perish the thought, child,' said Mother. 'That's all we need!'

Bill hid his smile. Jill's funny comments were the only cheer in Wandsworth. 'Is it all right if I go back out for a bit, Mother? I'll fix the gate when I get back.'

'Yes, you go, Bill. I'll teach this young lady how to dust and tidy her bedroom, now that she has one.'

Chapter Four

Bill shut the front door behind him and started up the street. The air smelled full of bus fumes and coal dust. A grey mist spoiled the blue sky behind it. He turned away. He belonged in the country, not here.

A shout came from across the road. A rough lad on a bicycle with an overloaded basket on the front shouted, 'Hey! It's you, isn't it? Billy? Billy Wilson, eh?'

He saw a bony face, red from the sun, under unruly greasy hair. The lad wore a man's jacket that hung very loose. Something registered, but not the deep rasping voice. The lad swung his leg over the bike, making the pile of vegetables in the basket wobble dangerously. Bill lifted a hand halfway, not to seem unfriendly.

'You back then, Billy? Look at you, you're not half tall! Ages since we sat together in Mr Hendrick's class, i'nt it?'

It was Jim, the chunky boy he'd once played football with! He was so changed; skinny and rather grubby-looking. 'Goodness. Hallo, Jim. I'm just back – yesterday. Call me Bill now, will you?'

'Okay. What's it like, the country? You gone and went the first, di'n' you? I remember you lot all filing out for the station that day. It went flipping quiet in school after. I thought Ma would send me away, but she never. Bet you had all the fun.'

'Mm, it was good. I liked it. Did you stay here all through everything?'

Jim nodded. 'Yep. Dog fights. Bombing. V1s, V2s, seen it all.'

He was like an old soldier. All the stuff on the newsreels Bill had seen, Jim had been in it.

'What happened to the rest of our lot? Andrew, Reg and everyone? They didn't end up with us. Did they stay behind too?'

Jim's face lengthened. 'Andrew did. He bought it, him and his mum.'

'What – not...?'

'Yeah, on the way to the shelter. Both together, in '41.'

'*No.*' That was something Bill had been scared to think of, his own friends caught by bombs. It was shocking enough to lose an uncle, even a nasty one; far worse to lose a friend. He leant back against a low wall. He'd been looking forward to exploring bomb sites with Andrew, and now his house was one of them. No Andrew. He could almost see his back view, a rumpled shirt and pullover, the only boy with brown plimsolls, running after the tennis ball, the only thing they had to play football with at that time. It was Andrew who told him to stand up to Kenneth after a bad spat in the playground. Now he wouldn't say anything anymore. Bill wouldn't bump into Andrew around the shops or see him climbing on anything. He was gone. Just gone. He looked back at Jim. Who else might be lost? He managed, 'You've been okay, your mother and everyone?'

'Suppose.' Jim shrugged. 'Except she's been working nights; sleeping when I get up, getting ready for work when I get home. My dad's going to be demobbed, though. September, he says, 'cos he was one of the first went. Lucky he didn't cop it, over in the thick of it all.'

'Rath-er. I'm glad he's okay. Mine is, too. I'm waiting for him to be demobbed.' He hesitated. 'Sonia was in my village. She's staying on for a while, and the awful twins. Do you know about the others, Reg? Fred? Mavis? Danny? June?'

'I've seen June around, and been on the bombsites with Fred. Reg is okay but doesn't hang around with me any more now he's at the posh grammar. Danny got sent to Wales and he isn't back yet, doesn't want to come back but probably he will. He sent me a postcard with all these hills on it. He has to go up one to school every day, right beside the sheep and all. Which school will you go to, then? I'm at the Sec. Mod. Failed my eleven-plus. Mr Hendrick said I would.'

'Don't know. No-one's said yet. Anyway, another three weeks of holiday, isn't it? I only got back yesterday. I was going to take a look at the old school. I was hoping to spot one of you.' His voice faltered at the thought of the one missing.

'We can go up the bomb sites; there's loads. It's smashing fun. I'll call for you. I've got to go now or I'll get it in the neck. Have to deliver this lot to the prefabs up Spencer Park.'

'I'd like to see prefabs. I saw about them in a newsreel.'

'Yeah,' Jim was already back on his bike, 'they have refrigerators!'

'No. What like Americans?'

'Yeah, and I know how to squeeze into that secret park up Spencer. I can show you. Cheery bye.'

Bill watched the lean legs cycling off, the backs of Jim's heels showing above his sock tops. The socks must be three sizes too small. A bony Jim working with no mother at home; Reg up hills in Wales; Andrew dead, not even time to hide in a shelter. Meanwhile, the worst he'd had to suffer was leaving the Pawseys and the Youldons. He felt miserable enough about that, but now he felt guilty too, which was worse.

He pulled his socks up and went back home. Jill was sitting at the table with her comic in front of her. 'You got me *Chicks' Own*, Bill. That's for babies.' She was flicking the pages over, nevertheless.

'Sorry. You didn't want *Sunny Stories* and there wasn't anything else for girls.'

'Where's your comic, Bill?' Mother put another pile of socks to soak in the bucket.

'I used the money to buy stamps.'

'Goodness, I can give you stamps. But what for?'

He hadn't wanted to tell her. 'Writing to people back at the village,' he muttered.

'Oh, a thank you letter to your billet. That's polite, dear. You can take a sheet of the small notepad from my writing desk in the garden room.'

'Thank you.' Too awkward to explain that he needed large sheets, and several of them, to write all he had to say to the Pawseys and Mrs Youldon, as well as a drawing for Sally and Tim because they couldn't read much. Tonight he'd write to Mr and Mrs Pawsey in his bedroom privately, taking as long as he needed, without Mother looking over his shoulder.

He should tell Mother about Andrew, but Jill would hear. He would tell Alan, when he was allowed to telephone.

Chapter Five

Bill folded all the sheets ready for ironing after rolling them one way and then the other so that the damp was evened out. He smoothed the vests, blouses and shirts over the clothes horse, one by one, to air around the boiler.

'Good boy, that's helpful.'

While Mother was pleased with him it might be a good moment to ask if he could phone Alan. He waited until she had the iron running smoothly to and fro and then asked.

'Yes, you can phone him this evening after we get back from Nanny and Grandad's.' She clanged the iron onto the boiler to heat up again and turned to Jill. 'Going there will be exciting, won't it?'

Jill didn't answer. She fiddled inside her lady's handbag, arranging her small dolls.

Mother sprinkled water on the last sheet and the iron hissed as she pressed it along the top edge. She looked at the pile of folded linen. 'I'm going to put this first load away and then get ready. Come along, Jill, let's tidy you up as well.'

Bill locked the back door and tightened the handle on the boiler door. He was ready enough; he was longing to see Nanny and Grandad again.

Mother came downstairs red-lipped, Jill lagging behind. 'Here, take this, Bill.' She picked up a basket from the chair and passed it to him. 'It's important to take some food wherever you go these days.'

There wasn't much in the basket. Bill went to the larder. 'Can we take some of those eggs? They won't have any as good as these.'

'All right, take three, one for each of them.' Better not say that would only leave one egg for themselves.

Mother checked her appearance in the hall-stand mirror. 'Come along both of you. You won't need that cardigan, Jill.'

'Do we have to go?' Jill muttered to Bill.

'Yes!' He took her hand because he knew she didn't want to go.

'Mummy, can I stay here? I really want to play with my dolls and put things into my bedroom cupboards.'

'Not now. Nanny and Grandad will be longing to see all of us, probably especially you. You were a baby last time we saw them. They don't know you as a girl.'

'And I don't know them. I won't know what to say.'

'Then keep quiet for once. That will be a nice change.' Mother skewered her hat on. 'Let's go, and if Nanny's not up to making tea, we can be back for a supper here with whatever we can scrape together.'

Bill took pity on Jill's pouty face. As they walked together behind Mother, he said quietly, 'You don't have to say much, just answer their questions. And you can play in their garden. It's quite big and it has an Anderson shed with a bed and books inside, and there's vegetable patches.' He saw in his mind's eye the row of carrot tops he'd been pulling when Ted shuffled home from Dunkirk, filthy, his boots green from standing in the sea for three days.

Mother turned. 'And do try to be civilized for once, Jill.'

'Yes, Mummy.' She skipped along in front of them, a bow on her wavy bob that always matched whatever she was wearing. Passers-by smiled at her. Bill was glad. Jill would make Nanny and Grandad happy.

The walk there had always seemed very long while he struggled to keep up with Dad and Mother. Now he had to slow down for Mother and it seemed hardly any time before they were walking up the leafy street. A flutter in his chest matched the movement of the trees. He took Jill's hand. 'That's Nanny and Grandad's house. See the green gate? When you get up the path, there are two garden gnomes.'

He waited for the door to be flung open and dear Grandad and Nanny to be standing there with open arms, the smell of roast meat circling him as warmly as their hugs. But the door stayed closed until they had rung the bell twice and waited for achingly long seconds afterwards.

'Give Nanny time to answer,' Mother said as Bill paced from foot to foot.

Slowly a shadow grew into a shape on the coloured glass section in the middle of the door. Then there was the clink of a chain and a key turning. At last the door opened and an old lady with a chiffon scarf over her almost hairless head stood breathlessly saying, 'Oh, here you are, dears. Wonderful.'

Jill took two steps backwards. Then she gave Bill a small shove in the back so that he was jerked forward in front of her.

Mother suddenly seeming tall, bent over the old lady as she kissed her. 'At last we're home. Hasn't it been simply ages! It's all been so hard for you but we're back now.'

Nanny finished hugging Mother and looked up at Bill, blinking. 'Billy. My goodness me. Billy!' It was he who had to outstretch his arms to hug her, though gently, for he felt bones more than the flesh of her body. He scanned the folds of skin hanging from her cheeks, searching for the Nanny he'd known. She wasn't as he remembered and he stepped back, feeling uncomfortable.

She turned to Jill and hugged her stiff figure. 'Just a little mite, you were, dear, not even speaking when we last saw you. Now a big girl of six isn't it?'

'Seven.'

'Yes, a proper schoolgirl, dearie me.'

Mother put a hand on Jill's head and looked over it to Nanny. 'How are you both, really?'

'We're managing, Marcia.' Nanny turned away, motioning them down the hall.

'Are you managing Ted, or is he managing you?'

'He's settling down,' Nanny muttered, then she smiled at Jill. 'Come along in. Poor Grandad's stuck there in his chair. He can't wait to see you all.' She walked on carefully, her lace-up shoes bagging around her feet swaying outwards from her swollen ankles. Her shoe heels were worn down at the outer edges. Bill kept his eyes on them. If he could get Phillips soles he could build those up so that she could walk better.

They all followed her into the back room where a fire glowed, despite the warmth of the day. Grandad was in his old smoking chair, two sticks beside him. He was pressing hard on them, trying to stand.

'Sit down, Daddy, do,' said Mother moving forwards to him and kissing the top of his head. 'Here we all are at last. Here's Jill,' and she motioned Jill forward. Grandad held out a hand, smiling gently at her and nodded lots of times. 'What a lovely little lassie.'

She looked embarrassed, twisting one foot round the other. Grandad let his eyes travel upwards to Bill.

He stood awkwardly beside Mother. Was this the Grandad he'd sorted tools with in the shed? Should he bend forward to Grandad or stay upright?

'Our Billy! What do you know,' he said in a croaky voice, looking over at Nanny. He met Bill's eyes. 'I'm stuck here most of the time nowadays. No more gardening, not like we used to, you and me. Useless old'un I am now. And you're a man, nearly. Fancy that. All those dreadful years, keeping us apart.' He put a hand out towards Bill's, and nodded to himself.

Bill swallowed. The beastly war had changed them. There was no smell of roast. What smell there was seemed damp, almost unpleasant. The walls were dingy and the skirting boards needed cleaning.

'Where's Ted, then?' Mother asked them.

'In the garden, tidying up for us. I'm hoping he'll find some beetroot or something to dig up. I wanted to give you all something nice to eat but…' Nanny's voice tailed off, and Bill saw her eyes watering.

'Don't you worry, we haven't come for a meal,' Mother said quickly.

Bill held the basket up. 'We've brought you food. There's an egg each from the chickens where I was living.' He tilted the basket forward, showing them off.

'My oh my. That's a treat. Look at the size of them!' said Grandad turning to Nanny.

'Wonderful. We'll have those boiled tomorrow. What a kind boy you are, to think of us.'

Bill smiled. He'd cheered them up already. 'Nanny, I can help in the garden so you get enough vegetables.'

'Thank you, Billy. Grandad will be pleased.'

Grandad banged his stick on the floor in time with his words, 'Just too old for it all, Billy, that's the thing.'

'Never mind, Grandad. I'll go out to the garden now,' said Bill, hurriedly. He'd leave it to Mother to tell them not to call him Billy any more. 'I'll see whether Ted needs a hand.' He went out to where the vegetable patch had been. It was terribly overgrown. Ted was standing with one hand limply on the spade handle, gazing into space.

'Hallo Ted. We've all come over.'

Ted looked over at the house vaguely and did that tossing of his head again before pushing the edge of the spade into the soil.

'Shall I do that?' Bill reached forward to take the spade.

Ted reacted slowly as if his time was running at a different pace from Bill's. By the time he wrenched his gaze from space to consider Bill, the spade was turning the soil. Ignoring Ted's silence, Bill worked away to make a fair start at preparing a vegetable bed, but no beetroot or anything else showed itself.

'Found any vegetables here, then, Ted?'

'The old man hasn't been able to get out for months.'

'Time to get something sown, then. Are there seeds in the shed?'

Ted wandered a few steps towards it, and then came back. He watched the spade turning the earth.

'Ted, are you glad to be home? Is everything all right now?' Bill asked with a hopeful heart as he dug and dumped, dug and dumped.

'Everything all right.' It wasn't a question, more like the beginning of a thought. 'It can't ever be, though I thought of home long enough.' Ted took a couple of uncertain steps and then retraced them. His eyes moved vaguely in Bill's direction. 'The old man hasn't been out in the garden for months. His legs were damaged when that V2 nearly got them.'

'What V2?'

Just minutes after they'd left Woolworths at New Cross, a V2 hit it. They'd only gone there because it had saucepans for sale - not been able to get any for years. The explosion knocked them both off their feet. All the passengers on a passing bus were killed in their seats. That's why the old man still can't walk more than a step or two. But it's what they saw on the bus, all those bodies, they can't get over.'

Bill stood very still. His insides felt the same as when Mr Durban told him about the Great War in Russia; the fields and fields of dead bodies, stained with their blood.

'When it's your turn, Bill, the next time there's a war, don't get talked into it. Just say No.'

51

'Be a conchie?' Wandsworth prison with its grey brick and tiny barred windows was where Dad had said conchies were put as punishment. How scary! Dad was a pacifist, but he'd said he'd do his duty whatever his views.

'But you did your duty, Ted. Soldiers are heroes. Shouldn't I do my duty? If there's another war…'

'Another war. There will be. There's always wars. People wanting more than they've got, hating people who've got more, wanting other countries as well as their own. You stay out of it. It's evil. War makes you do things you know are wrong. It lets other people do awful things to you.' His voice trailed off.

Had the enemy done awful things to Ted? What had happened, in Africa or any of the other faraway places the army had taken him? In the newsreels soldiers filed onto trucks with big smiles on their faces, giving the thumbs up and V-sign. Why wasn't Ted like that? What could he say, to help Ted be happy again? It was as difficult as finding the right words for Kenneth had been, when Uncle Frank was blown up. He tried his best at a comforting voice, 'It's all over now.'

'All over for lots of people. Most of my mates, for starters,' and Ted wandered off along one row of the bare vegetable patch and down the next. He must have forgotten what he was there for.

It was all over for Uncle Frank and for Andrew and hundreds of servicemen, perhaps thousands. Best not to think about it. Bill shoved the spade hard into the earth and carried on digging until at last he saw leaves. He pulled out some limp beetroot and seven potatoes. 'A fork-over will soon bring this lot to rights, Ted,' he said encouragingly, just like Mr Pawsey would have done. 'Just needs a bit of attention. But we need seeds, or potato and carrot tops to start the rows off.'

'Yes.' Ted walked closer to Bill. 'You're right. I'll be able to have a go at that. Plenty of time now.' His vacant tone suddenly changed and he said, 'I've got to learn to cook. They can't really manage.'

Bill's heart thumped. This was awful. 'Isn't it just Grandad's legs?'

'No. He's got diabetes, lungs bunged up, hip joints gone. Mother's got a dicky heart.' He spoke in short sharp bursts, as if he was giving a report to his commanding officer.

Bill didn't want to believe it. Nanny had a lovely heart. Ted's head wasn't quite right, he knew that. 'I can come over to help nearly every day while I'm on school holiday.' He put his vegetable findings into a woven basket. It had many sections missing. 'I'd better take these into Nanny.' He moved towards the back door.

Ted moved slowly forward. 'I suppose Sis is here? I'll come in.'

Indoors, Bill put the few poor beetroot and potatoes into the kitchen sink, washed them clean and then his hands. He followed Ted in to find Mother and Jill sitting with Grandad, Jill at the furthest point of the room. Mother nudged Ted towards a chair. She had made a large pot of tea and Nanny had found a packet of rich tea biscuits.

There were little red threads in Nanny's cheeks. Her hands shook when she took her cup so that it rattled in its saucer. 'You must have such news to tell us, Billy, dear. This is so lovely, having you all back home. And safe. We must count our blessings.' She ran out of breath and her cup rattled again.

'We do count our blessings,' said Grandad. 'Ted home in one piece, all of you back from evacuation, your father unharmed and this dreadful war over. So now, fire on, young man. Fill us in with your last five years.'

Everyone's eyes turned to Bill. He felt a heavy weight of responsibility. Jill was sitting awkwardly with her milky tea, toes not quite reaching the floor, not looking at anyone. Grandad was stuck in his chair, not able to go into the garden he loved. Nanny was shaky and couldn't really cook. They desperately needed cheering up.

He put on a smile although his face hurt around it. Talking of the last five years meant thinking about the people and places he missed so much. The pain around the bottom of his ribs was there all the time. He couldn't tell that to anyone here. He must think of the war effort and talk about that.

Grandad leaned forward. Nanny said, 'Well, dear? We're longing to hear all about it.'

His mouth opened and he began to talk.

Chapter Six

There was still a tin of corned beef from before the war. The last one. It was rusty but the little key worked, the lid rolled off and the smell of meat hit them deliciously. Mother boiled some potatoes and Bill got the knife and chopping board and gave the cabbage a salty rinse.

The large saucepan had pock marks and thin patches. It made him think of Nanny and Grandad buying their new saucepan and only just escaping being blown up. The hateful smell of cabbage boiling made the image worse.

'Ted told me what happened to Nanny and Grandad. Why didn't you say? Why didn't you warn me that they're different?'

'You needn't take that tone with me. I do what's best for everyone, I'm sure. I thought you were too young to hear about it.'

'It's not as bad as what happened to Uncle Frank and you told me that.' Then he stopped. She hadn't told him. 'Sorry, Mother. It was Kenneth told me he was blown up on the Balham bus when the bomb dropped on the station.'

'Ah. I wondered if you knew as you never asked any questions at the time.' Mother's tight face hardened further when she mixed the egg powder into milk for custard. 'We'd better save half this milk for breakfast, so please don't complain if the custard is watery.'

Even the cruet was the Bakelite one, the proper one was still in the dining room, probably with the same pepper as it held in 1940. They ought to be settled in at home by now, but they were still eating in the kitchen as if proper meals wouldn't happen until Dad got home.

They'd just finished eating when the doorbell rang. Mother came back with Jim behind her, and Bill could see that she didn't approve. Jim's creased shoes were bent out of shape like old dinghies and had a crust of mud around each heel.

'Perhaps you'd leave your shoes on the mat if you're going upstairs, Jim,' Mother said, her tone making it clear that this wasn't just a suggestion.

'All right, Ma'am, Mrs Wilson.' As a delivery boy, Jim was used to dealing with customers. His voice sounded like the shop-keepers'. 'Fact is, I've got things to show Bill, here, he being away all wartime. We'll probably play in the park.' He winked at Bill behind Mother's back.

'We'll go now, Mother?' Bill hurried Jim out.

Outside, Jim grinned at him. 'Bit posh, your place. I remember it from that party you had when we were nippers; games, clown, presents, big cake!' He punched the air. 'Now I'll show you what's what. C'm on.'

He gave Jim a wary glance. 'Where to, then?' He shouldn't get up to mischief, with everyone relying on him.

'There's this really smashing bomb site. It was a church, empty inside now where the bomb fell, but there's a hole you can climb down to the secret part below. Fred 'n me found where the priest kept his robes and that. There was a kettle and cups all broken in bits. There's bits of statues, and I found a little pile of sixpences. Afterwards, we bought a football second-hand with it, and two liquorice sticks. Do you want to see? There's long slabs of stone and we reckon there's bodies buried under. Super fun.'

The thought of Andrew stopped him wanting to go there, and surely they'd get caught? He said, 'No. Let's go up to Spencer, those prefabs and the secret garden.'

'Right'o. Follow me.'

The prefabs looked quite ugly outside, low and made with some white stuff, no bricks. Some people had started gardens outside their doors and not just vegetables.

'Old Ma Fenchurch'll let us look round hers. Her old man's in the hospital and she's got a soppy boy who's in an institution mostly.' Jim took Bill round to the back door. A cat with tousled fur slid out as he opened it. 'Mrs Fen-church! It's Ji-im.' There was a pile of coins on a saucer on the windowsill. Jim took two and put them in his pocket.

Bill gasped. 'Don't!'

'It's all right. She often gives me stuff. She won't mind.'

A croaky voice called out. 'Jim? Come in here, then.'

Jim pushed open an inner door with a double bed and an old lady standing beside it. 'You can give me a hand. I want to put this blanket on the high shelf.' She saw Bill. 'Oho, who's this?'

'My friend come to see your prefab. He's never seen one.' Jim went to the bedside and took the folded blanket from Mrs Fenchurch. He nipped up onto the chair and put it on a shelf behind double doors. 'Look, Bill, see? The wardrobe's already fitted in.'

Mrs Fenchurch smiled at Bill. 'Yes, isn't it lovely? The prefab came with cupboards and shelves all ready to put our things in. Not that we've got much, thanks to the bombing. You wait till you see the kitchen. All cupboards there, and the refrigerator. Keeps the food fresh for ages.'

Bill followed them into the kitchen where there was a line of cupboards under a shiny surface.

Mrs Fenchurch pulled a cloth along it. 'See! Cleans just like that, no scrubbing.' She turned and pointed to a white metal cupboard. 'My refrigerator.' She pulled its silver handle to open the door and a shock of cold air blew over them. There was a bottle of milk on its door rack, a shelf for the meat and another with lard, a bowl of dripping and a plate of jelly on it.

'Goodness,' he said. Mother would think it was smashing.

They saw into a bright bathroom and then the sitting room with its fitted gas fire. 'Everything's very neat and convenient,' Mrs Fenchurch said proudly. 'We hardly know ourselves. Much better than what we lost.' She went to a sideboard where there was a large screw-topped jar. 'I expect you're both after sweeties.' She pulled out a few wrapped boiled sweets and passed them over.

'Thank you very much.' They weren't Bill's favourites, but it was very kind of her.

'Thanks, Missus,' Jim said. 'Can I take anything for helping you with the blanket?'

'There's tuppence in my purse. I might find you more when you bring my shopping. The list's in my bag, too.' She pointed to her bag on the easy chair.

Jim opened it and took out a piece of paper and the purse. Bill watched in case, and sure enough Jim took a sixpence as well as the tuppence and the shopping list. 'Thanks, Missus. We're off to the park, now, but I'll see you tomorrow. I've got your list. I'll sneak you an orange, if I get a chance.'

'Thank you, dear. You're a good boy.'

Jim grinned.

Bill nudged him, hoping he'd put the sixpence back, but he didn't.

'We have to go now.' And Jim yanked Bill's arm so hard that they were both at the door.

'Thank you for showing me around, Mrs Fenchurch,' Bill got out as Jim pushed him through the door. 'It's a lovely home.' Outside he said, 'That's awful, Jim. You took an extra sixpence as well as money from the saucer. That's wrong. And all you did was put a blanket on a shelf.'

'People like her, old, rely on me to help; there's bits and pieces I get back. That's fair.'

'I don't think it is.'

'Yah.'

Bill knew it wasn't fair but he wasn't going to get Jim to understand that.

Jim handed him another sweet. 'Come on. We're going across to the garden now. Quick, while no-one's about.'

The secret garden was exciting. It meant squeezing through a section of wire fence on one side of Spencer Park, and running like fugitives until they reached the part that had little walks, hedges and a stream. It was private, only for the rich people who lived in the nearby big houses, but now it was overgrown and neglected. It didn't seem so very wicked to play in it because it was being wasted. Most people didn't even know it existed.

As they were scrambling out again they heard footsteps, and Bill was on the wrong side! 'Get down,' Jim whispered, and Bill crouched beneath a bush while Jim pretended to do up his shoelace. The footsteps passed and Jim's arm came through the gap to pull Bill out. Half of him was out when the footsteps stopped, and a voice called, 'What are you up to, boy?'

'Nothing, Missus. My friend's just getting his...'

The voice came from a lady bus conductor with untidy black hair and Bill knew her straight away as Mrs Donnington. It was very embarrassing. Luckily, she was turning away with a shake of the head and hadn't seen Bill.

'Cor, that was close!' Jim grinned at him.

'Yes, not half. We could've been for it.' There was no way he wanted to go on a bomb site now. 'I'm going back now.'

'D'you have to? We haven't done the bomb sites.'

'Later. See you another time.' It wasn't comfortable playing with Jim. He wasn't going to again.

Running fast, it was easy enough to catch up with Mrs Donnington. He walked a little way behind her until she turned down a narrow road and into a doorway. She was getting out a key. It must be where she lived. He stopped, then as she opened the door, ran forward. 'Mrs Donnington?'

'Yes?'

'I'm Bill Wilson, remember? You used to help in our house.'

'Billy! Well, I never. The size of you! Look at you, away all of the war and now you're back, eh?'

He nodded, smiling with hot cheeks.

'It's a long time since you were helping me polish the fire brass, isn't it?'

He nodded. 'I just thought...' How could he ask about coming back as their home help?

'Come on in, Billy. Have a cup of tea with me.' She led him into a small hall past a row of hooks smothered with coats, cardigans and jackets. Boots and shoes were paired neatly in the corner left by the stairs. Another front door was at one side on the second stair. How funny. There must be a separate flat upstairs.

Mrs Donnington led the way into a room where the settee was jammed under the window and the easy chairs almost touched the cooker and sink. 'It's a real treat to see you after all this time. How's that baby of yours, although I suppose she must be a little schoolgirl by now?' She took the clippie's uniform jacket off and hung it on the back of a hard chair, then filled a kettle. Her piled up hair on the back of her head wobbled just as it always used to.

'Move those blankets off the settee and sit yourself down.'

By the time he'd answered her questions she had a cup of tea in front of him and popped in a lump of sugar.

'There. I was saving that for Colin, but he's gone over to Croydon to try for a job with his uncle. I don't expect he'll get it. No experience, see.'

'Colin?' He only just remembered Mrs Donnington's son. 'Is he demobbed?'

'Class A, conscripted first, demobbed first, only fair. It's lovely he's home safe, only we're a bit crowded,' she gestured to the settee. 'He has to bunk down on that. I'm so proud of him, our hero.' She pointed to his photograph on the sideboard, smart in his uniform. 'Such a tough war, they had, North Africa, Sicily, Italy. They weren't allowed to say at the time, but he's told me bits now.'

'Africa? My uncle served there.'

'East Surreys, Colin was in.'

His heart leapt. 'Yes, Ted was too.'

'Was he? Then I'll tell Col when he gets back. They'll want to go for a drink together.'

Bill sipped at his tea. Perhaps it would be better not to mention hospital. Ted wouldn't like that and Mrs Donnington might ask what his injuries were. He said, 'Ted's back with Nanny and Grandad. He won't talk about the war.'

'No. They want to forget all about it and protect us from knowing what they suffered. Best let them concentrate on knowing we won the war, ducky.' She drank from her chipped cup. 'Your mother must be glad to be home after all this time.'

'Yes, but she finds it ever so difficult to manage the house all by herself and she has to get it ready for my aunty and cousin to move in.' He explained about Uncle Frank's death.

'Poor souls. It was a terrible disaster, that Balham bomb. I knew the driver, poor chap, though he survived. Mind, we had bombs all the time then. Day, night, we just had to put up with it.'

'Are you going to do Home Helping again?'

61

'No, ducky, no-one's doing home help these days. We've all been doing war work and mine's the best paid for a woman. We get the same wage as the men! Our worry is the men taking back their jobs when they come home.'

'I suppose Mother will have to make do with me helping.' He drank the last of his tea.

'Your aunty will help in the house, don't you think? And you'll have another boy for company. Just what you need.'

He smothered his sigh and looked back at Colin's photograph. 'Mrs Donnington, I could pop in to run your messages if you like.'

She smiled. 'Maybe. I have got Colin to help, but you drop round when you're passing. You're a fine lad, tell your mother, and give her my best.'

He made for home, without the good news for Mother he'd hoped for, but if he saw Colin next time, they might talk about Africa.

Chapter Seven

He'd gone to help Nanny and Grandad but when he got back home, it was difficult to answer Mother's 'How were they?'

Ted had burned the food dreadfully and Nanny had told him it was best if he just did the clearing up, not the cooking.

Bill said, 'Ted's doing his best to help,' and then changed the subject. 'Grandad got stuck on a difficult crossword clue.'

Mother nodded. 'Poor Grandad. He'd love to be doing more than a crossword.' She pushed a knife into a lump of swede simmering on the stove. 'Let's see whether this economy recipe is something Madam Jill will eat.'

Jill was perched on a stool, pinching her nose. 'Your dinners are much worse than the vicarage ones, Mummy. That smells horrible.'

It did, but Jill said the same whether it was porridge, mince or boiled fish.

Mother snapped, 'You can be horrible yourself, Jill. Just wait until you're a mother!' She pulled out the newspaper Aunty had bought that morning and jabbed a finger at the first page. *There is a world shortage of food. In this country there is enough bread for everyone. Don't waste a crumb!* The Ministry of Food is talking to people like you, Jill.'

'I don't mind bread. It's your dinners!'

'It doesn't mean just bread, child. It means there are people starving so we should be glad of every crumb of food we get. We're the lucky ones.'

Jill hitched herself up onto tiptoe so that she could see inside the saucepan. 'Ugh. I don't feel lucky.'

Bill heard the second post land on the doormat. 'Come and collect the post, Jill.' He'd probably saved her from a sharp slap. She ran to the hall with him and picked them up. Two government envelopes, and one from Dad. That would cheer Mother up.

'Post, Mother.'

She read out Dad's news. 'More dismantling and reorganising, he says. No date for his demob yet. Jill – Daddy says to be good. Bill – he suggests you join a Scout pack.' She opened the other letters. 'Oh. You've got to re-sit the exam for Wandsworth Grammar school next week. The LCC don't recognise that test you took at your elementary. We must make sure you have two pencils with sharp points.'

Exam. He didn't mind. It would be interesting to see inside the school, and he wanted to see who else went for it.

He reached for his jacket. 'Can I get off to Alan's now, Mother?'

'Yes, you deserve some free time. Here's a shilling. That should be enough for bus fare, sweets and emergencies.'

'Thank you!' How super that Mother let him go out now.

He ran first to the hall in Wiseton Road to see when the Scout pack met. Jim had said he'd fallen foul of Boss Wright, the Scoutmaster – a little matter of missing sixpences – so Jim wouldn't be at Scouts, but some of the others might be, and anyway it would be fun.

There weren't many people catching the Thornton Heath bus so he was able to get the front seat up top. It was super looking down on everything and exciting to be meeting Alan. There was so much news to exchange. Alan had said he'd wait at the clock tower stop. Bill had to watch out for a church, a crossroads and then the road with the clock tower. They were going to walk round the pond and get some sweets before walking up to his home for dinner.

Alan was standing right near the clock tower looking like the Macleans advert, all smiles and good health. Bill leapt off as soon as the bus stopped. 'Like your blazer!'

'It's for my new school!' Alan was in very good spirits. 'I had to re-sit the exam but I've got a place at the school I wanted.'

'I've got to re-sit next week, Wandsworth Grammar.'

'I know it. They play rugby there, like at mine.'

'Rugby! I don't want to go there if they play rugby!'

Alan shrugged. 'Doesn't matter. As long as there's a decent field and sports master, it'll be fun.'

Bill didn't answer. Football was far too important to be just fun. Was it worth bothering with an exam for a school that didn't have football?

Alan led the way to the pond and they jogged around it as he chatted on about everything he'd been doing since they'd last seen each other – two whole months ago.

'Have you been bored?'

'No time. Shopping in the mornings. My Uncle Ted's back. He's not – very well; my grandparents aren't either. A V2 just missed them. I'm going up there to help, gardening and that. What about you?'

'I've been working on our allotment, and I ride around on my bike while Mum's at work.'

'Hasn't she given it up now war's over?'

'No. Civil servant, she's always done it.'

When they reached the sweet shop its jars were mostly empty. Alan pulled out his coupons. They could only buy boiled sweets and wood chews. 'See who can keep chewing the longest!'

'Yes, even when all the taste's gone and there's just wood.'

Alan's father had just been home on two weeks' leave. 'It was spiffing. We played cricket and went to the

Geology museum and a race track and swimming, but now he's away again. Diplomatic work, like I told you before.' Alan turned his mouth down.

Bill said, 'I can't imagine my dad doing any of that stuff with me.'

'What will you do when he's demobbed?'

'Don't know. I would like to go to his Court, see the villains, if he'd take me.'

'That would be spiffing.'

'Specially as Mr Durban works there too.'

'Mr Durban of the Cossack sabre?'

'Yes. The shashka,' he breathed.

'Did you tell him about the Russian book in the Manor library?'

'No. We haven't been round there yet, and I can't risk showing him the story you wrote out for me until I can get up there on my own. I've hidden it somewhere no-one will ever see it – in my dad's law volume, one on the highest shelf.'

'Why?'

'Because when Kenneth moves in, he'll suck up to everyone. If he finds out about the shashka he might try to get it for himself.'

'Why should he?'

'Just because he wants to take over everything I have. He used to take my toys. He took all my friends that first evacuation when we were away and he stayed behind. You remember how he was with Jill and Mother when they were billeted at the vicarage – like he was their boy, and I was just someone they visited?'

Alan scratched the back of his neck. 'But this time, he'll be far too busy settling in. Look. Don't show too much interest in the Durbans when they're mentioned, then he won't know it's important.'

Alan always said sensible things. Bill picked up a thick twig and poked at a broken boat some child had abandoned. 'It'll be awful sharing my room with him and putting up with his sarky remarks.'

'He's not so bad.'

'You don't know. He was always trying to be nice when you were around.'

'Just don't rise to it when he riles you. I mean, you're big enough.' He put a hand on top of Bill's head and laughed. 'Anyway, Kenneth might be painting all the time, too busy to follow you around.'

'I'll suggest it!' Bill managed a grin.

'Come on, let's see what Mum's made for dinner.'

Alan's house in Norwood didn't have any others joined on either side, and the garden went right round it. The straight path to the front door had a line of oval pebbles keeping clumps of flowers in their beds. 'I did those,' Alan said proudly as they went to the front door.

Indoors, Mrs Routledge was making a special pie. 'In your honour, Billy. We're so pleased to have you visit. I'm only sorry my husband's not still here to meet you. We've often talked about you.'

'Really?' How super, the Routledges actually talking about him!

She had put some cheerful music on the gramophone. It stood in the lounge but could be heard all round the downstairs. Alan lifted the lid to show him the record twizzling round and the little dish for used needles. There were cupboards with doors underneath for storing the records.

'This is super, Alan. My dad would love one like this!'

'Go along into the dining room, if you're ready,' Mrs Routledge called.

They went in and sat down at the table. It didn't have a tablecloth, but mats on its shiny surface. A photograph on the sideboard showed Mr and Mrs Routledge with their arms around a young Alan, who was holding a large ball.

It looked as if they'd just come back from a happy time in the park.

Bill pointed to it. 'How long ago was that?'

'Before our second evacuation. Must've been early that summer, 1940, before the bombing started.' They grimaced at each other, remembering the air raid warnings.

Mrs Routledge brought in the pie, smiling. She didn't seem bothered about having another boy to feed. Her face was calm as she spooned out some carrots, beans and mashed potato onto each plate from the flowered serving dishes. Why was she different from Mother? Dad would say they were both the same class. They both wore pretty jumpers and skirts and no hair rollers under a scarf like many ladies had. And Mrs Routledge had an even bigger house to keep clean without a home help. She smiled across at him. 'You must be glad to be home at last, Bill! Such a long wait. I brought Alan back the day after VE Day.'

'Mother had to finish war work. She was really cross about it.'

'Oh dear.'

'She says a woman's place is in the home.'

Mrs Routledge nodded. 'So many people think that; mostly men.'

Perhaps he shouldn't have spoken out, since Mrs Routledge had stayed working.

She held the vegetable dish. 'Have some more beans. Since he got home, Alan's been quite a gardener. I doubt if they're as good as you had in the village; the soil is poorer.'

Bill felt his throat tighten as he thought of doing the vegetables at the Pawseys. 'I'm doing some digging for my grandparents, but Mother doesn't have an allotment. It's not her sort of thing.' Bill forked up another mouthful of mash, all smooth with no lumps. 'This potato is lovely.'

'It would be lovelier for some butter in it. I do miss that.'

Alan said, 'I've been to see my new school. There's science with laboratories. There's a gym with wall bars and a horse, and proper playing fields. We didn't get any of that at the elementary, did we?'

Bill thought of visiting Kenneth's exhibition. 'No, but I saw it at the Priory Grammar – you know, that school Kenneth went to. Now he's got a place at Dulwich College.'

Mrs Routledge's eyebrows went up. 'Goodness, he's a very lucky boy. How special!'

'Is it?'

Alan put in, 'Bill's got to re-sit for the grammar next week.'

'Ah. No problem, then.' Mrs Routledge piled another helping of pie onto Bill's plate. 'I'm sure you'll do well.' There wasn't any pudding but Mrs Routledge gave them an apple each to take into the garden.

'Let's go.' Alan took him round. There was a slope for rolling down; around a corner there were circles with rose bushes in them, and some way down a path, an old swing. They each climbed up one side of it then tried to touch hands when they stretched forward. Afterwards, they clambered into the swing, Alan sitting on it and Bill standing, with his feet either side. 'We're nearly too big for it!' They swung to and fro, looking out over the hedge and commenting on any aircraft coming out of Croydon airport. He was the happiest he'd been since being torn away from the Pawseys. It was ages since he'd played like this.

They went inside again and up to Alan's bedroom, where there was a huge bookcase filled with books.

'You lucky thing! Bet you won't read them all.'

'You can borrow some if you like.'

'Gosh, thanks! Let's see what you've got. Any Biggles? I love those.'

When it was time to go back. Alan put a couple of Biggles books under Bill's arm and some comics.

'You're a sport, Alan.'

Downstairs, Mrs Routledge held out a large volume. 'Bill, I remembered how keen you were on photography. This is a professional manual my husband needed once, but no more. You'll make good use of it, I'm sure.'

It was full of pictures and diagrams. She was so kind! 'Thank you ever so much.' He took it carefully. 'Without that film you got me last year I wouldn't have been able to take photos of our last days.'

'I'm glad you did. You'll have to bring your album to show us when you come next.'

'I will!'

'You can be studying this manual before school starts and you get loads of homework,' she smiled as she showed him to the door.

On the bus home Bill looked at his manual instead of out of the window. It had lots of chapters with small writing, as well as diagrams. He'd really need to work at understanding it if he was going to be a proper photographer.

Chapter Eight

The post lay fresh on the kitchen table, Aunty's familiar handwriting on the top envelope. Mother tore it open. She no longer used the paper knife with its ivory handle, but then she no longer sat at her desk in the garden room to open her post. She kept to the smallest area so she had less housework. He watched her read the letter, knowing what it would say.

'Aunty says they'll arrive back Thursday, early afternoon.'

Bill nodded, ignoring Jill's squeaks of delight. He put his chin on his hand letting his fingers slide up to cover his miserable mouth. Kenneth was coming.

'I think the front room's all ready for her, but goodness, you'll have to get your bed out of your room. The bunk beds must go up there today!'

'Yes.' He must hide his misery from Mother. He wouldn't be able to cope with her hostility too.

'They're coming straight here, taking a taxi from Clapham Junction. Doreen can't face going to her house, understandably. It would bring home Uncle Frank's absence all too strongly. The new owners are having most of the furniture, but she's arranged with Quilters and Co. to bring her favourites here. Those should arrive this afternoon, so make sure you're around to help move it in.'

Bill cleared his porridge dish away. 'I'll go and find some tools for taking my bed apart.' At the open cellar door, he pulled a hammer, screwdriver and wrench from the hanging post Dad had made. They were all covered in dust, showing how long since they'd been used. He couldn't go down the steps for a rag; the light bulb had gone. They needed a new bulb and a large torch so that he could see to fit one. He ought to make a list of these jobs.

He gave a shake of each tool to send the dust into the gloom of below. That would have to serve.

Jill followed him when he went upstairs looking excited. She was so stuck on Kenneth after five years of living right near him. He'd seemed like her brother, not Bill whom she only saw on visits. How Kenneth had enjoyed taunting Bill by encouraging Jill to avoid him!

Jill danced around Bill's feet. 'I can't wait to see how you'll both fit into your room. Will you quarrel? I'm going to listen outside your door and tell Iris if you do.'

So it was more that she was curious! He turned away from her. 'We shall be all right.'

'But I bet you will quarrel. Mummy won't hear. I shall. I'll hear all the cross words.' She puffed and crossed her arms across her chest importantly. 'Iris wants to see Kenneth.'

'Well she can. Take him down to her house for tea. Grown-ups always like Kenneth, I'm sure he'll get invited.'

Jill wouldn't notice, but Bill heard his sharp tone clearly enough. *I'm getting to sound like Mother. Perhaps I am like her. Is that why people like Kenneth better?*

Jill elbowed him in the ribs, squeezing into his bedroom beside him. 'Iris wants to see his paintings. He'll probably pin them up on the bedroom walls. They'll be all over your bedroom.' She waved expansively to the bare walls.

A grunt escaped through his gritted teeth. That was a new thought. He liked the walls as they were now, plain, so that his hanging aeroplanes were what you saw immediately you opened the door. He pushed Jill gently onto the landing saying, 'I've got to get my bed to bits and clear wardrobe space for Kenneth now,' and shut the door behind him.

He spread out his arms, bi-plane style and twizzled around, liking the little wind he caused, a whirlwind of private space.

His room only had a wardrobe, a chest of drawers and the toy drawer under the bed. If Aunty sent a chest of drawers for Kenneth, there wouldn't be much room beside the bed. They couldn't have one side of the room each, only a section of floor and half the windowsill.

He hoisted the mattress off the bed and leant it up against the window, then bent down to see how the bed might come apart. He tried the screwdriver and then the wrench but the nuts under each bed corner were as tight and closely fitted as Kenneth was in Aunty's heart.

If only Alan was here, this was the kind of problem they'd sort out together. He could hardly ask Mother! He'd have to go next door to ask Mr Bentham for help. He went downstairs again, not in the best mood.

Mr Bentham came to the front door looking friendly. He was quite happy to follow Bill up to his bedroom, leaving his wife trying to find seaside accommodation. 'We just want a week by the sea now the barbed wire's off. But all the rooms are still taken by servicemen, Americans a lot of them, waiting to be transported home. I'm fed up with hearing "No vacancies" everywhere. The Missus is telephoning, non-stop.'

After some puffing and blowing over the bed frame, he said, 'There's no way of taking this apart, Bill. We'll have to man-handle it down the stairs in one piece. Put the mattress back on top.'

It wasn't easy, but once they'd negotiated the sideways turn for getting through the front door, they took one end each and walked it from Primley Road to the second-hand store, resting every few yards.

'Suppose they won't buy it? We'll have to lug it all the way back.'

'No worry of that, son. There's plenty will snap up a good solid bed like this.'

They struggled on to the shop and sure enough, a woman asked to buy it before they'd even got fully inside. Mr Bentham did the talking and then handed the money to Bill. 'Right. Let's get back.'

Bill took a last look at the blue bed knobs, the stripy mattress, hating the idea of some other boy lying on it. It was another part of him being given away. He was having to keep leaving things behind, and face things he didn't want to happen. He sighed. In October, he'd be thirteen so he must have more grown up thoughts.

He brought Mr Bentham indoors for a cup of tea. 'The bed's sold, Mother,' he called out.

She tripped into the parlour. 'That's good. Mr Bentham, you're a tower of strength. Let me pour you some tea. I'm sorry it's a topping-up of the pot, so it might be rather watery.'

'Never mind, Mrs Wilson. Hot and sweet, if you've got any condensed milk, have you?'

'I have, and I think I can find you a biscuit.' She went to the forbidden tin embossed with Father Christmas of 1936. The biscuits for very special occasions were kept there. She brought out a wrapped chocolate wafer. Luckily Jill was out at Iris's or her eyes might have popped out of her head, and who knows what words from her mouth.

Bill sipped his tea. 'The bed's gone, and here's the money for it, Mother.' He pulled it out from his pocket.

'Hooray. That's a help. I don't know what may need buying when Aunty and Kenneth arrive.' She passed the plate with the chocolate wafer. 'Please. My widowed sister-in-law is moving in, Mr Bentham, and her son of thirteen. Artistic and quiet, you won't need to worry about noise. You must remember Bill and his football? How I didn't go mad with the sound of it bouncing against the wall! No more of that; he'll be playing football down at the common now he's a big chap.'

'Boys will be boys, Mrs Wilson.'

'Luckily, Kenneth is different. How is Mrs Bentham?'

She listened to the Benthams' difficulties with gaining seaside accommodation. 'Nothing's easy, is it?'

She took his empty cup and saucer. 'The bunk beds are waiting in the sideway, if we could prevail on your kind help again, Mr Bentham.'

Chapter Nine

Bill drove the last screw into the gate hinge and went indoors to put the tools away.

'There you are, Bill,' Mother called from the garden room. 'I thought you were still at Nanny's.'

He went in to her. 'No, I got back a while ago. I've been mending the gate.'

Watching her tidying the bookcase, he said carefully, 'I could borrow some books for Grandad from Mr Durban if this is a good time to go over.'

She straightened up. 'Perhaps it is. I'm certainly missing adult conversation. I'll ring.'

He waited in the doorway while she phoned. Mother was smiling as the receiver tinged on its rest. 'Mrs Durban was delighted to hear from us and she's invited us down this afternoon. How nice!' She went to the stairs. 'I'll just go and tell Jill.'

He waited for an argument. Jill wouldn't want to join them. She'd want to go to Iris's, or Dawn's, a girl only four doors up whose mother had already invited her in for orange squash and biscuits.

Mother came back downstairs wearing a smart outfit, one she'd had before the war. 'She's begging to go to Dawn's instead. Should I make her come with us, do you think?'

'No, Mother, let her go. She won't remember the Durbans and she's excited about having other girls to play with at last.' He felt like Dad or a teacher, telling Mother about how things were for Jill.

'True. She has been a bit starved of other children's company. There were so few opportunities for her while we were marooned in the depths of the country. You and I will go alone, then.' She was probably relieved not to drag a moaning Jill along. That hadn't gone well at Nanny's. Also, he knew how Mother liked spending time with other women, and without children.

Jill lingered halfway down the stairs, ready to pout if Mother made her come with them.

'Very well, Jill. Come down and we'll see if Dawn's mother will have you for the afternoon.'

Jill's face changed from cloudy to sunny and she let Mother tidy her curls without a fuss.

'You'll have to behave well or you won't get asked again. Dawn's a private school child, remember. Make sure you're polite and not too noisy. We'll collect you when we get home.' She stood at the hall mirror to pin on a jaunty hat that matched her suit.

Jill gathered her two dolls and skipped out of the gate, Mother in tow. Bill waited until the front door conversation with Dawn's mother ended and Jill was taken inside. He pulled his jacket on and shut the gate. This was going to be a good afternoon.

He and Mother set off down Primley Road. Last time they'd gone to the Durbans, he'd walked behind his parents watching Jill's pram wheels. He hardly came up to Mother's shoulder then. Now they walked side by side, and he strode along feeling like the man with Mother, until she asked him to slow down. She had her high heels on. He took her arm saying, 'I'm as tall as you, now.'

She half smiled, half grimaced. 'Yes. You certainly are. Do you know, we could have taken the bus. We always had the pram before, so had no choice.'

'Actually, it's nice walking. I like going over the bridge.'

They paused a moment when they got to it, watching some children poking around the river edge with their sticks. She laughed. 'I remember seeing children doing that when I was a girl. I doubt if I was allowed to, but I believe there was one time I did.'

So she had once been disobedient, like Jill! They walked on, chatting almost like friends. It had never been like this with Mother before. He let go her arm as they got to the Durbans' road. His heart thumped rapidly at the sight of the familiar line of houses. He let Mother ring the ding-dong bell.

'That used to be your joy when you were little, Bill.'

It must be Mrs Durban opening the door but her face was not as smooth and lipsticky as he remembered.

'So lovely to see you, Letty.' Mother stepped forward.

'Marcia! Welcome back. My goodness, is this really Billy…?'

'Bill, Mrs Durban,' he nodded, as Mr Durban came forward to shake hands.

His eyes went straight to Bill who felt his cheeks tighten around a wide grin. Mr Durban, his own grown-up friend, his ally. 'Bill now, is it? My word!' His warm and firm hand thrust forward. 'Hello, a larger Bill. All grown up, I see.'

He turned to Mother. 'Well, Marcia, very glad to see you again. How well you look. And it won't be too long before Bert's demobbed and back with us, I'm sure. Category B.'

'Mopping up operations, he calls it. It surely can't last long.'

'Definitely not, or Judge Ware-Simpkins will be writing to his commandant, demanding Bert's presence. We struggle to manage, without him.' He led the way down to the lounge where everything seemed untouched by the war. The chairs were flowered and comfortable, the pictures were the right way on the wall, not turned backwards against windows to black out any light.

Bill was so busy reminding himself of the time Mr Durban had told him the shashka story that he missed the initial to-and-fro of the catch-up conversation. He latched on at the point where Mrs Durban was saying, 'You'll be out of practice, Marcia, feeding a grown son.'

Mr Durban turned to give Bill a grin.

'Not that easy,' Mother put in worriedly, 'a boy his size. It's true I'm not used to it. And Jill's got so fussy. The food problem is so much worse in London.'

While the adults discussed the shortages, Bill surveyed the hallway and landing. He was waiting for a door to open, for Angela with her blonde curls and neat white socks to trip in.

Mrs Durban went to the kitchen. 'Do you drink tea, these days, Billy?' she called out. 'Or do you still have orange squash?'

He tried not to scowl. 'Tea, please, Mrs Durban.'

'I expect you're waiting to swap all your news with Angela,' she said as she brought in the tea tray. 'It's so long since you've been here. You've had a great chunk of your lifetime away. What a lot you'll have to say to each other. She'll be home from work soon,' she said.

'Work!' He accepted one of the biscuits, which were disappointingly plain.

Mr Durban said, 'Yes. She's finished School Certificate and will start evening classes at college in September. She's landed a good job at the bank.'

The women looked at each other with a little nod and Mrs Durban poured the tea.

Mother said, 'Good prospects.'

Mrs Durban said, 'It gives her time. A while in business does no harm before she starts walking out with someone. Early days yet, I think.'

Mother nodded, sipping at her tea. 'I wouldn't want a girl of mine walking out when she was only sixteen.'

Walking out! The last time Bill had seen her, Angela still had dolls on her bed. By the time he was biting his next biscuit, the grown-ups were discussing the run-up to the next election.

'Herbert will hate not being here to vote, but he'll tell me how I should. The newspaper says. *Vote for Him*, and they mean our husbands, stuck overseas and not able to put their cross where it counts. Still, there's surely no question of the result after what Mr Churchill has achieved for us. It's inevitable he'll get in.'

'Don't be too sure,' Mr Durban lifted a warning hand. 'Churchill's as popular as ever, as a person. As a politician, putting this country to rights – I don't know. Most people will vote with the need for housing and jobs in mind, I think.'

Jobs. Jim had one, Angela had one. Ted didn't have one, couldn't have one yet. As Bill finished the last of his tea and took another biscuit, the front door slammed and a cheerful voice called out 'Hello!'

'Here she is,' Mrs Durban beamed. 'Come and see the Wilsons, Angela, back home again. Isn't that nice?'

A strange woman in a tweed skirt and shoes with heels stepped into the room. She walked over and shook hands with Mother. Her hair was fastened into some kind of knob at the back of her head with a big wave at the front, and it looked as if she had lipstick on.

Bill was sitting on the pouffe with his mouth full of biscuit. She stared at him, then gave a small smile.

'Hello, you. Back from your adventures? You've changed more than I'd expected.'

She was the one who'd changed more! It took him a few moments to finish his mouthful, and to take in that this was still Angela.

'Yes.' He should have stood up. Too late now, and the low pouffe didn't make it easy.

Angela smoothed her wave from her forehead as she answered Mother's questions about her job, perching herself on the sofa beside her father. 'Yes, I am enjoying it really. Sometimes it's a bit scary. The Manager is quite old and can be crotchety if any of us make mistakes. But the other girls are nice and we help each other out.'

'And with your wage you can buy yourself little things,' Mother said.

'Yes! Clothes, if Mum and Dad share rations with me. I'll go without butter and bacon to get another pair of stockings. I'm fed up with painting a brown line down the back of my legs. But I got this blouse last week from Allders.' She moved her shoulders from side to side. 'If only there was more choice.'

The women grimaced to each other. 'Or even the right size!'

Angela turned to Bill. 'Well, Billy, are you going to tell us all your adventures?'

'Yes, have you been running wild in the country whilst we've all been hiding in air-raid shelters?' Mrs Durban asked.

'Running wild. Some get all the luck, isn't that so?' said Mother.

Mr Durban looked carefully at Bill. 'I expect he's glad to be home. It must be difficult for returning youngsters to know where to start – telling five years of news.'

'He wrote little letters to people,' said Mother.

'Yes but it's not the same. I want to hear all about it,' Angela said. 'Bet you had fun, Billy.'

'He's *Bill* now, Angela. See how grown-up he looks?' Mr Durban said to her.

'Yes. He'll have lots to tell us.'

Mother leant back in her chair. She crossed her legs and gave a tiny yawn. 'Of course I've heard it all, so are you going to take him off for a natter, Angela, while we adults chat, or are you too grown up for him now?'

Angela didn't look at Mother. She stood up with a flounce and said to Bill, 'Come along, then.'

He heaved himself out of the pouffe, feeling clumsy, and followed her out of the room, his eyes on her legs which did have lines up the back, painted on like she'd said.

He hovered near the closed door of the study. Did she know he was waiting, was she deliberately making him wait?

'Come on, we'll go to my room.' She tripped upstairs and opened her door. Her room looked different now, no sign of toys. There was a pink gauzy thing hanging up, a film star poster from a girls' magazine and on the dressing table, a little mirror behind a tray full of bottles and sticks.

She saw his glance. 'Mother says I may use cosmetics if I apply them lightly. Pond's powder cream and lipstick.'

'Oh. Are you wearing them now?' Her lips did look pinker than he remembered.

'Yes. Do you like it?'

He shrugged and looked away.

'It's a new lipstick. I bought it on payday. I wish I could have my room that colour, like the ones American girls have; pink and green and pale blue.'

They both glanced at the utility paint on the skirting board, shiny brown, like everyone's everywhere in Great Britain. He waited. Angela plumped up a cushion on her bed. She sat down. 'Have you missed me?'

He said, 'I've been longing to come over again.'

'I know.'

'So...' he said, still standing, waiting for her to lead the way back to the study.

'So,' she said holding out her arms to him. 'I said you'd grow into a handsome man. Another year or two, and then...'

He gawped at her.

Angela put her head on one side, smiling. 'You said you'd been waiting.'

'For the sabre. To see the sabre.'

She sat still. At first he wondered if she'd understood him. Then his heart lurched in case there was no shashka any more. She gave a slight flick of the head. Then she stood up. 'That sabre. Huh, stupid. You just want to see the sabre? Come on then, let's see the wretched thing.' She stomped off and left Bill to follow, bewildered. *She* was the one who'd shown him it back before the war, the most special thing she could think of. She led him down to the study, not even glancing to see if the grown-ups noticed, and opened the cupboard. There it was, still in the same place. He bit his lower lip. Would it really be the same as he'd remembered it or just a rusty old blade in a torn scabbard? But even at first sight he could see the hilt was as handsome as his memory of it. Angela drew it from its shelf and laid it on the table, not across her hands. She didn't look at him, but put her hands on her hips.

'One Cossack sabre. Okay?'

Now it seemed more a punishment than a treat. And it wasn't even secret. She left the study door open and called out, 'I'm showing him that sabre, Daddy, all right?'

'Be careful, then.' Mr Durban didn't seem to mind.

Angela took the shashka from its scabbard, not particularly slowly. He followed the movement, his eyes searching for detail. The blade was tarnished, the letters too difficult to distinguish their shape properly. The studs had been polished, though. As his eyes followed their design, he could see flecks of colour reflected in them from the curtains. He thought of the next war and imagined Kenneth ogling the blade, then trying to get it from him. He saw himself slashing his way through the fields with his shining blade, holding it aloft and Mr Durban saying, *I'm too old for war. This shashka needs a younger man, someone who has proved his bravery and can draw it clean from its scabbard. I have no son, so, Bill...*

'I suppose it's all right if you hold it, now you're older.' Angela picked it up and put the hilt in his hands. 'As long as you don't muck about with it.'

He picked it up reverently. This shashka had been given to Mr Durban at the point of its owner's death. It could kill many men. He held it against his right hip, feeling its weight. He paused a long time, then placed it slowly into its scabbard. In Mr Durban's story, the cannons had stopped its success. This war had been all bombs. The next war would have even bigger explosions, not swords or sabres for this soldier or that. He held the shashka out to Angela.

She took hold of it as if it was a pan handle. 'Satisfied?' she said, her mouth a purse of pique, '*Bill*.'

He watched her shut it away again. Mr Durban would be so interested in the Cossack story Bill had waiting for him.

When they returned to the lounge, Mrs Durban was talking about cutting some old curtains up to make skirts. 'The material's too good to waste and there's certainly enough to make three. Angela, you and Mrs Wilson are more or less the same size, so we can cut out a pattern twice more. Come on, we're going to decide on patterns. I've got a Vogue and two Simplicity.'

'I prefer Vogue, but I've never risked making anything alone. It's my sister-in-law who sews,' Mother said as they disappeared through the door.

Now there were just the two of them. Bill turned to Mr Durban who smiled in a *Men Only* way. 'Well, Bill. It's been a long hard time. We have missed you. How does it feel to be back in Wandsworth?'

'Funny, sir. And it's all different.'

'Different, yes.' He turned his mouth down. 'So much damage. It's strange for me, too. Time on my hands instead of rushing off for fire patrol or lookout after work.'

'It must've been bad during the bombing. I've been round looking at the bomb sites.'

'Well, don't go on them. There's always the chance of an unexploded bomb. We were lucky. No hits in this road.' He pointed to his ARP helmet hanging on the wall. 'Just decoration now, thank the Lord. Tell you what, though. I'm going to make that snug,' he pointed to the small adjoining room which had a desk and chair in it, 'into a war mementoes room. I'll have the helmet and operational maps on the wall, albums of photographs on the table. My items from the Great War as well.'

'So the shashka will be there?'

'Yes, the shashka will be there.' He nodded, his expression showed that he knew how important it was to Bill. 'And things from this war, too.' He lit a cigarette and bent forwards to search Bill's face. 'So, changes around here and even more changes for you. Your father wrote me about Kenneth coming to live with you all.'

'Like another son.'

'That must be difficult for you.'

Admitting to *Yes* would be disloyal, but *No* would be a lie. He swallowed and said nothing. Mr Durban would probably understand.

That was more than Bill did about Angela, he was thinking, as the women's footsteps sounded on the stairs. Why had she been so friendly, and then moody about nothing?

Mr Durban stood up. 'Sounds like you're going to be taken off home.' He led Bill into the hall where Mother was putting her hat back on. 'Come again, Marcia, before my leave ends.'

'Thank you, and you must meet my sister-in-law and Kenneth, my artist nephew, once they've moved in.'

Mrs Durban said that would be charming, and Angela was nodding. He felt cross with Mother for mentioning it.

He was cross with Angela too, but he still couldn't wait until he saw her again.

Jill was hot and excited when they called to collect her. From the sideway of the house they could see the girls climbing over discarded boxes in Dawn's back garden and jumping off the top ones. Dawn's mother brought Jill out, laughing. 'Here's your pickle, Mrs Wilson. She's been great fun.'

'It looks as if she's been rather a bother. Thank you so much for having her. Very kind. We'll be glad to see Dawn at our house, too.' Mother turned away, her glare at Jill hidden from Dawn and her mother.

'What a mess you are,' she said as soon as they were out of earshot. 'Come along home for a good wash and a quieten down. Why is it that unless I watch you the whole time you behave like some wild peasant? If only I could get you to a private school like Dawn!'

Jill made googly eyes behind Mother's back as Bill pulled her along.

Mother's perky hat and matching jacket seemed to signal to him, *best be quiet,* so he didn't stick up for Jill.

Chapter Ten

Thursday arrived far too quickly. Bill lay in bed savouring his last moments of being the only boy in the house. It wouldn't be long before he was showing Kenneth where to put all his things. Would the top bunk would be better than the bottom: Kenneth clambering over him, or having to clamber over Kenneth? How he'd hate feeling Kenneth's movements above him, but was it worse knowing that Kenneth could feel his below? Whichever bunk he chose, Kenneth would want that one. So he'd choose the top bunk. Kenneth would demand it, Bill could give in and end up with the bottom bunk. He'd see less of Kenneth on that one, for he could slide out of bed first.

He got up, smoothing the sheet and tucking the whole lot in tightly, so that no-one could see which bed he'd occupied. He left his room with a long glance. He'd never have a bedroom to himself again until he left home.

He kicked himself on the back of each calf because he'd had over four years to face this. Dad had announced directly after Uncle Frank's funeral that he now had two sons, that they'd all live together. Yet away in the country, with the war going on and on and London so far away, this had seemed unreal. Happy at the Pawseys', he'd so wanted it to be.

He nearly slammed the bathroom door. By the time he'd washed, Mother was down in the kitchen. From the smell as he sidled in, it was clear that she'd burnt the porridge. It wouldn't be Jill's dish the black bits landed in. He wouldn't say anything, for how could this morning be worse?

He'd swallowed his last mouthful when he heard Aunty's *Cooee* through the letter box. He couldn't face going to open the front door because it wouldn't just be Aunty standing there but Kenneth too. The doorbell rang and he let Mother go.

He stood up. The time had come to face that Kenneth would be part of his family every single day, and in his bedroom every single night. Soon he'd go upstairs and help Kenneth fill his side of the wardrobe with his neat clothes, his side of the windowsill with his books, his under-bed box with his art materials.

Aunty caught sight of him hovering near the hallstand. 'Billy! Come and give me a hug.'

She deserved a welcome. He didn't want her to be sad about not having her house or Uncle Frank any more. He came forward for the hug, nodding to Kenneth as best he could.

'You're so huge,' she giggled. 'Surely it's only two months since I've seen you, and you're even taller than before.'

'Yes I think I am, Aunty. And I'm *Bill* now, you know.'

Aunty made big eyes at Mother. 'Fancy that! We shall have to watch our step with two new men to rule us. Bill absolutely towers over us.'

Kenneth slid one shiny shoe to stand on its toe across his supporting foot, like a film star. He raised an eyebrow and turned down one side of his pinkish mouth, showing what he thought of an extra-large twelve-year-old.

Bill tried not to scowl.

Mother was already in the front room directing operations. 'Bring everything in here, boys.'

Kenneth began to push the smaller of Aunty's two suitcases into the front room. 'Here you are, Mama.'

Mama! How stupid that sounded! When had Kenneth stopped calling her *Mummy*? It must be something he'd started at his grandparents in Northampton. It might be French or something foreign. Mother had an old, old doll she sometimes let Jill touch. If you swung it forward and back, it said *Mama*. He'd like to say 'Dolly voice' to Kenneth but he shouldn't when he'd only just arrived.

Kenneth placed a small bag into the room and flicked his head at the large suitcases. 'Big boys carry big suitcases, Bill.'

This wasn't the time to take Kenneth on. He took the suitcases in and undid their straps.

Mother directed. 'Over there with that, Kenneth. Bill, put those down. Aunty can unpack later when she's had a cup of tea. You'll have to put up with our curtains, Doreen. They're probably not what you'd choose but at least they're not—'

'Not blackout,' Aunty joined in. They laughed. It was an easy sound, at least on Mother's part. So Mother didn't mind Aunty sharing her house as he did about Kenneth? Aunty was smiling, but she usually was brave.

What about Kenneth? Dad had sold their house because Aunty needed the money to live, so Kenneth had lost his whole home, not just his bedroom. Bill stole a glance at him. Mother and Aunty were chatting as they put things away, paying the boys no attention. Kenneth was lolling against Uncle Frank's mahogany tallboy which now stood where the armchairs had been. He was looking at furniture from his old home squeezed now into Bill's. His mouth was set. Then he caught Bill's glance and his expression became smooth.

He took a little breath and spoke in a snide, sing-song voice, 'Come on then, Bill-y. Up to th-the aewoplanes, just like old t-t-times.'

Immediately Bill was furious with himself for not taking the aeroplanes down, even the best one that had always hung from his ceiling.

'You can c-cut that out.' He stopped himself. There was a lot more he wanted to say but he'd only stutter more if he went on. It was a flipping nuisance; he'd hardly been troubled by the stutter for ages.

He led the way upstairs, letting Kenneth carry his own cases. He gestured to Kenneth's side of the wardrobe, 'That's your half.' He'd wait a few moments before tackling the bunk bed confrontation. 'Why don't you unpack? Your chest of drawers came, see. Make yourself at home.' He tried not to sound sarcastic. 'I've left you this half of the windowsill.'

Kenneth ran his finger along Bill's treasures on the right-hand half, as if planning how to use his own half. He took off his jacket and hung it up.

Bill said, trying to sound nice, 'Which bunk do you want, then?'

Kenneth clicked open the catches to his suitcase and drew out two beautifully folded shirts. He looked up. 'Which do you prefer, Billy boy?'

'Top, really. That's best.'

'Is it really? I'd better have it then, if that's best.' He pulled out another hanger from the wardrobe. 'Shall I keep these folded or hung up?'

'Either.' Bill bit back his moment of satisfaction and climbed on the chair to remove his aeroplanes. 'I was just about to do this when you arrived.' He held them carefully as he stepped down. 'Be back in a minute.' He took his aeroplanes down to the cellar where they'd be safe. He'd sorted the light problem yesterday, so now he could see where things were stored. He found an empty box and placed the aeroplanes carefully in it. There was a roll of string hanging from a hook and scissors on the bench. Dad was well organised. He made his aeroplanes safe, tying the string round the box using double knots. Nearby, another box had a newspaper neatly folded on top. He saw the word *Disaster*. It made him pull the paper out. It was a report of the Balham bombing. The picture showed the bus that Uncle Frank had been on, its front stuck down a hole with its back end poking up. He shuddered. Even though Uncle Frank was a bully, no-one deserved to die that way.

He read on. It got worse. The bomb had crashed through the gas and water pipes, both cascading onto the poor people on the platform. They hadn't a chance of surviving. But the story described how the bus driver escaped with minor injuries. He had been alone on the bus. There hadn't been any passengers! So Uncle Frank must have been on the platform. Dad must have lied about what happened. He swallowed. Dad lying? He squatted down, trying not to get dust on his clothes, folding the newspaper up carefully. He'd better put it where Kenneth would never see it. Dad would have had a reason for lying – like wanting to save Kenneth, even Aunty, from knowing the worst. Dying on a bus above ground didn't sound as bad as being trapped way below it with tons of gas, water and rubble smothering you.

He stood up. For once, there was something he knew that Kenneth didn't, but he wasn't glad.

He sniffed the dank air in the cellar remembering those nights when they'd huddled together, scared stiff. They were lucky they hadn't been bombed. He climbed back up to the daylight. He was lucky. He hadn't lost his father. He'd lived happily with the Pawseys while Kenneth and Aunty were stuck in the home of some spinster relative of the vicar's. He'd never visited their billet, but if it was like the vicarage, it probably had texts on the wall telling you about *Sin, God's love* and government reminders about *Doing Without*.

He plucked a couple of custard creams from the kitchen table as he passed through. Kenneth liked those biscuits. He'd take them upstairs for him.

Chapter Eleven

'I must say it's a shock,' Aunty said. 'All that hero-worship and now we've let Churchill go.'

Mother raised her arms helplessly. 'It's so difficult without Herbert here to guide me, but I'd have thought it inconceivable that Churchill would lose.'

'Remember, Aunty,' Kenneth broke in, 'the paper says that a hero's all very well for war, but no good for peace.'

Bill said nothing. He'd always wanted to be a hero. Now he'd have to think again. Peace was important.

He'd endured twelve days of having a cousin living with him. Things hadn't been too bad. Kenneth generally came up to bed after Bill, and got up later, so that they weren't in the bedroom together much of the time. Kenneth could also slide into Aunty's room for privacy. The trouble was, there was no room where Bill could be free of Kenneth.

Luckily, Jill took a lot of Kenneth's attention. She'd brought Iris round to admire him. 'He's a painter, just like I told you, Iris. Look!' and they huddled round Kenneth, one either side while he painted or drew. He pretended to take little notice of them, but his smirk showed that he liked their attention. This was a help. He wouldn't risk losing their admiration by being nasty to Bill.

Because Mother relied on him to fix things and for shopping, Bill could avoid Kenneth most of the time in the day. But when Mother took Jill to see Nanny and Grandad, Aunty and Kenneth went along too. Kenneth didn't hang back like Jill. He was more than happy to be centre stage.

Bill squatted beside Grandad as Mother began, 'You remember Doreen, don't you? You may only just remember Kenneth.'

Nanny came forward and held Kenneth's hands. 'Oh I do. It was so lovely seeing the little boys together when Kenneth first moved to live near. Billy always wanted a brother.'

Bill watched Mother's face tighten. She wasn't pleased at the reminder. 'All right, all right. I did have a second child to please you all, remember.' She turned to Jill. 'And here she is.'

Jill cringed back behind Kenneth. Nanny went on, 'And here you are again, Kenneth, so Billy has a playmate now that he's home at last.'

While Nanny patted Jill's head, Grandad leant forward to shake Kenneth's hand.

Kenneth smiled, pulled chairs out, passed cups around, picked up papers that had fallen beside Grandad's chair, and all the things that grown-ups think make a lovely person.

When Bill was there to help the following day, Nanny stopped pushing the carpet beater over the mat to praise his cousin: how bravely Kenneth was dealing with losing his father, how thoughtful, what a support to his mother, how sweet with Jill. Bill took the carpet beater from her hands and took it apart, emptying the dirt. Grandad and Nanny didn't know what Kenneth was like!

Worse waited for him when he got home. Aunty had found a part-time job in an accountants'. The firm had known Uncle Frank. 'Bill, you'll keep Kenneth company, won't you? You can show him where to shop, how to queue. He hasn't done shopping before, but he can help you.'

Kenneth moved his shoulders slightly and widened his eyes with his head on one side. Bill knew what that meant: he'd only make a gesture of doing it to keep Aunty happy.

Sure enough, when Bill showed him the shops the next morning, Kenneth looked at the queues of women with their prams and shopping baskets and said, 'That's women's work, or for little boys.'

Bill ignored that. 'Come on, Aunty told me to show you about the shopping. Here's the list. Look. First the baker's, then the grocer's. See, that's the longest queue today, which means they might run out if we leave it too late.'

Kenneth stood alongside Bill, leaning on one foot, then the other, like people do when they're really bored.

'You need to look out for sudden queues. That'll mean there's been a new delivery of something useful. Last time it was tin openers at the hardware store, and I had to be pretty quick to get the last but one.'

'Exciting for you.'

'All right, sarky, but think how you'd feel if you couldn't open any tins.'

After the baker's and grocer's queues, the butcher's stretched so far along the road that Bill sent Kenneth to do the greengrocer's. 'I'll wait for the meat. You take the list and this basket. Go on.'

Kenneth slouched off with a bad grace.

With the mince and the liver resting on top of the second basket, Bill got to the greengrocer's just as Kenneth came out. He peered in the basket. 'Where's the cabbage?'

Kenneth said, 'Horrible stuff. I forgot it.'

'Flipping heck. Now we'll have to queue all over again. We need it for dinner.'

Kenneth sighed. 'The sun's too hot on my head to be standing out here. You don't want me to faint, do you?'

'You look all right to me.' But it would be awful if Kenneth fainted. What would he do?

'Go on, Bill. You're much better at this sort of thing. It's more sensible if you do the shopping.'

'So what will you do? I do the jobs around the house and I have to help at Nanny and Grandad's. You have to do *something*.'

'I can look after Jill. Keep the mothers happy, that sort of thing.' Kenneth wandered over to stand at the Spread Eagle pub, because of its shady archway.

It was flipping annoying, but Kenneth was pretty useless. Bill queued for the cabbage in a bad mood. Worse still, when they were walking home, Bill with the heavier basket, Kenneth started asking awkward questions.

'Why do you need to help your grandparents?'

'They're old and not well.'

'So? They've got Ted.'

He didn't answer.

Kenneth nudged him hard in the ribs.

'Ow.'

'Jill said Ted's loopy. Too loopy to help his parents, is he?'

Bill turned on him, scowling. 'Jill's a naughty girl. That's an awful thing to say. He's not loopy, just convalescing.' That mightn't be true, but it sounded good. He'd heard the word in the shopping queue. 'We unpack now.' He pushed Kenneth into the kitchen, their baskets scratching against each other.

'Big day for you, Thursday,' Mother was polishing the silver.

'What, Aunty Marcia?'

'Not you, dear. Bill. His resit exam at the grammar.'

Kenneth gave Bill a pitying look that suggested *Fat chance you've got.*

Bill had more or less forgotten about it; it was still holidays. 'Veg goes in the basket in the larder, Kenneth.'

Kenneth took the cabbage in loose hands while Bill unpacked everything in his basket.

Mother said, 'I wonder how difficult the test will be. Education is so different, now these secondary school changes have come in. When I went to Larchmere Girls' High we had Literature, Arithmetic and Nature Study, Elocution, Needlework, Deportment.' She turned to examine Bill, as if he'd suddenly been switched from grey to coloured. 'You're a practical sort of boy, aren't you, Bill? Good at fixing things, not intellectual like your father or Kenneth.'

He caught sight of Kenneth pressing his lips together and inward, as if he must be modest about being more able, more everything than Bill.

Kenneth said, 'Would you really like to study Latin and calculus and physics, like me?'

'How can I know? I've never tried any of them. What is Latin for, anyway?'

A smug smile spread over Kenneth's face.

'Your father needed it for getting his position in the Court,' Mother said, 'but I can't see you going in that direction.'

'I was going to ask Dad if I could go and see the Court with him.'

Kenneth's left hand came up and touched his nose. His upper lip lifted. Bill longed to thump him.

'I mean, what you think you'll do when you leave school?' said Mother. 'That's the point.'

'But I'm not thirteen yet. I don't know what there *is* to do.' This was making him cross. How could he decide things like this? Kenneth hadn't had to; the Priory school had arranged everything for him. But of course, *he* did know. He was going to be a painter, an artist.

Mother held up a just-ironed shirt. It already had its name tape on the inside of the collar. *Kenneth Wilson.* 'And there'll be the problem of uniform.' She picked up Jill's skirt and sprinkled it with water. The iron hissed as it tackled the creases.

'Your father won't want you with the hoi polloi. If you don't pass to the grammar, it'll have to be St Werberg's. Those boys have nice manners, I remember.'

Bill was relieved when the subject was interrupted by Aunty coming in, smiling broadly. 'What do you think I've got?'

Kenneth shrugged. 'New socks?'

'No, it's something to open.'

'A mammoth box of chocolates, oh ha ha ha.'

Aunty smiled in a knowing way. 'Yes dear, chocolates would be completely impossible. But wait there.' She stepped out into the hall and brought back a large box with American stamps on the top and the red capitals C A R E.

Mother squealed, 'Doreen! You dark horse. Treasure. When did this come?'

'First thing. That's the advantage of sleeping in the front room, I get to see the postman first.' Aunty put the parcel on the table. It seemed heavy. 'Look, boys, a food parcel!'

Bill cheered. 'American food. How spiffing!' The box was big enough for everyone to have a good share of whatever it was, ham, biscuits, and surely there would be chocolate too!

Mother passed Aunty the scissors. 'Is this from Dwaine, bless his heart?'

She nodded, and started to open it. 'Isn't it exciting, Kenneth? Who knows what you'll find.'

It was *terribly* exciting waiting to see inside the package, but Bill just longed to watch how Kenneth would manage to resist its treats.

Kenneth cast a superior glance at the package. 'Are you suggesting that the Yank has sent me something?'

'Don't call Dwaine that! How disrespectful.' Aunty's hands hovered over the top of the box. 'You're going to be very glad of this, I promise you.' She tore open the box and pulled out some tins exclaiming at each one's label: 'One pound of steak and kidney! One pound of beef and gravy!' She pushed a tin over to Bill, and one to Kenneth, who left it where it was. 'Corned beef loaf!' she went on. 'Bacon, apricots, raisins!'

'Tinned peaches!' Bill put the large tin to his lips.

Mother's hands groped inside the box. 'Tea! Bless the man. Evaporated milk.'

'And sugar and rice,' Aunty started to put things on a large tray.

'And a very large bar of chocolate.' Bill looked across at Kenneth whose eyes were fixed on the treats, despite himself.

Chapter Twelve

It wasn't the first time that the doorbell had rung and Kenneth had got to it first. Bill could hear his beastly polite-boy voice chirping away before the voices came into the hall.

Kenneth put his head round the parlour door. 'There you are, Bill. This gentleman's come to speak to *you.*' The emphasis was meant to show how unusual this was.

Bill came out. 'Hello.'

The man held out his hand. 'Colin Donnington. My mother told me about you.'

Kenneth was still in the hall.

Bill led Colin quickly back into the parlour. 'Glad to know you. Would you like to sit down?' He turned to shut the door, but Kenneth was already through it.

'I'm Kenneth Wilson, Bill's cousin, brother really.' He sat down opposite.

Colin turned to him with a smile. 'I didn't realise.'

Bill scowled at Kenneth. How could he find a way of getting him out? 'How about making Colin a cup of tea, Kenneth?'

'I would, but I think we're out of tea. I saw Mama cleaning out the caddy.'

Colin raised one hand. 'Look, don't worry for me. I'm not a great tea-drinker.' He turned to Bill. 'Ma told me Ted's back. Smashing to hear there's someone else from the regiment nearby. Where can I get to see him?'

'He's back living at my grandparents. I'll take you round.' Bill stood up and opened the door. 'It's not very far.'

'Smashing.' Colin followed him out. 'He got demob way before me. He wasn't in the same battalion, but my mate was. He knew Ted.'

Kenneth's voice came from behind them, butting in. 'Ted was invalided out. Got sent to a military hospital.'

'But he's been out of hospital a couple of months now,' Bill put in quickly.

'There were loads of injured in our battalion all the way up to Italy.' Colin was setting a smart one-two pace down the road.

Bill met his pace and turned to Kenneth. 'We're going to Nanny's. No point in you following us.'

'I might as well come too. I'm not doing anything special.'

'I go to do their chores. Are you offering to help?'

Kenneth didn't answer but came to Colin's far side. 'Italy?'

Bill strode faster, catching hold of Colin's sleeve. 'Ted hasn't wanted to talk about the war. I only know he served in Africa.'

'Right. We moved on from there to the Med. Sicily, then Italy. Got harder then.'

'We'd love to hear about it, Colin.' Kenneth was almost running to stay in the conversation.

Bill said, 'Better to wait till we get to Ted. We turn right at the bottom of the road.'

'Okay.' Colin's fast pace, left-right, swinging arms, reminded Bill of Ted, still yet to go to war, demonstrating his marching in Nanny and Grandad's garden. He strode alongside Colin hoping Kenneth wouldn't keep up. 'Do you know why Ted was sent back to England?' he asked in a low voice.

'Bullet in his back, removed at field hospital first.'

'In the back! You mean – he was running away?' Kenneth squeaked breathlessly.

Bill swallowed a gasp. This was terrible. Was this why Ted wouldn't talk? Bill looked ahead where the shire horses plodded along to deliver the barrels of beer. 'Look at those horses, Kenneth. You could paint them.'

He nudged Colin's arm. 'That wasn't why Ted was sent to hospital over here. It was his nerves.'

'Oh right. Yeah, some of the blokes got hysterical when the enemy were at close quarters. That sort of thing couldn't be handled, not in action.'

Kenneth was like an irritating puppet. 'Hysterical?'

'Shut up, Kenneth.'

Colin stopped walking. 'Listen, lads. You've no idea what it was like. Anzio, Salerno and Monte Cassino. We'd done well in North Africa; left Tunisia, defeated the Huns in Sicily. We were ready for a break. But no, we landed in a flipping storm. So there we are, marching through the mud, days and weeks struggling uphill to gain each position, shell fire around all the time. The regulars knew how to handle it, not the ordinary squaddie. One battle, two. Weeks of it, low rations, streaming rain, no change of clothes, delayed mail, shell fire or grenades landing every which way. It doesn't take much more to break the spirit.' Colin started walking again.

'Ted's spirit was broken?' Kenneth's bony knees poked forward as he loped along, his mean face alight with eagerness to suck up the worst news. He had probably never enjoyed exercise so much.

'He'll have done his best,' Bill growled. 'Isn't that so, Colin?'

Colin nodded. 'Surely. In most platoons it's only a few men do the real fighting. Most follow the fighters, if things go well. Some run away. They're kept in line by the older chaps, but when the captain's killed, the next in line isn't usually trained to lead. He dithers. There can be panic. I wasn't in the same platoon but probably when he was hit, Ted thought he was done for. The bullet was in his backside, that was easy for the doctors to fix, but say he lost his bottle, seeing his mates killed around him – well! Some blokes went plumb crazy under heavy fire, especially when it was coming from close by.'

'Crazy?' Kenneth's lips were pulled back like a weasel's.

Colin pressed on. 'It's one possibility. If he didn't let up, the doc would've passed him unfit to fight. Mentally.'

'Mentally,' parroted Kenneth, still puffing.

How he'd love to pummel Kenneth until he was as flat as a pancake! He touched Colin's arm. 'We'd better be getting on.' He shoved his hands in his pockets, his eyes on the ground. What was Kenneth going to do with all this secret information? Loudly, so that Colin didn't miss it, he said, 'Kenneth. You'd better not tell any of this to Mother or Aunty, right?'

Kenneth's face became full of concern. 'No, mustn't upset the women, of course.' But there was something in his tone that suggested he had plans to broadcast it.

'Or anyone at all, mind.'

Finally, Kenneth dropped behind, unable to jog any further. He began to wheeze and for once, Bill was glad.

Once they were ahead he asked, 'Will he get better, Colin?'

'There's supposed to be help with whatever problems you have. There was a film about it for returning servicemen.' He waited for the panting Kenneth to catch up. 'You'll have to do more PT, mate, get fit.'

They were silent until they reached Nanny and Grandad's road. 'It's just up there,' Bill pointed. 'We won't knock. Ted's not expecting to see anyone from his battalion. I'll go round the sideway and tell him, then bring him out.'

'Righto. We can go down to the High Street for a pie and pint, a good old natter will cheer him up.'

Bill blocked Kenneth from following him. 'You stay here, Kenneth. Once Ted's come out we can go in and do Nanny's chores.' That'd stop him! He ran down the sideway. Making a brief turn back, he saw Colin leaning on the gate, and Kenneth, like a long-term mate, leaning on it beside him.

Ted was having a cup of tea in the kitchen. He looked alarmed when Bill told him about Colin Donnington waiting outside. 'I don't know anyone of that name.'

'Colin's our Home Help's son, just demobbed. He was in another platoon but he's keen to meet up with you. Come on. He wants to go for a pie and a pint.'

'That all?' Ted looked relieved. 'Right.' He found a jacket on a hook by the back door and followed Bill round the sideway.

It was lucky that Ted seemed fairly okay. Bill watched as the two men shook hands and went down the road together. Kenneth had already turned to go into the house.

Bill called after him, 'All ready to get on with some chores, Kenneth?'

Of course, that didn't work out. Kenneth was already in the sitting room with Grandad when Bill went through the back door.

'It's nice to see you again so soon, Kenneth,' he heard Nanny's voice. It sounded warm.

'And nice for me to see you.' Kenneth's voice rang out down the passage. 'Ted's found a soldier pal. They've gone down to the café and Bill's just about to do some chores.'

'We both are,' Bill growled, but no-one paid any attention.

'So frustrating for you, Grandad, to be stuck in here,' trilled Kenneth. 'Perhaps I can entertain you.'

"Grandad?" Kenneth had his own grandad. What a cheek!

'I was wondering if you'd like me to sing for you?'

'My, my, that'd be a rare treat.' Grandad had perked up.

'Your aunty Marcia has told us about your lovely voice,' Nanny added.

Bill stood in front of Kenneth. 'Shall we do the dishes first, Nanny?'

'Thank you, Bill,' was all she managed as she sat back to listen to Kenneth, standing with his back against the fireplace. The sun shining from the left-hand window highlighted his curls, his cheekbones. He loosely folded his hands and lifted them to his middle. He cleared his throat. 'I'll start with something cheery, "Widecombe Fair".'

Bill went straight to the kitchen and started on the dishes. Last night's tea hadn't been cleared away. Ted had obviously started, but the cheese was still on the table, not that there was much, and the plates were only half stacked. Potato peelings were blocking the sink. By the time he'd tidied up and washed the last dish, Kenneth was on to his fifth song.

'Really lovely, dear,' Nanny was saying as Bill came back to ask where he'd find a clean tea towel. 'In the third drawer down, Bill. You are such a help.' Then she turned to the shining face of Kenneth.

'Oh Danny Boy,' his voice rang out. Bill felt slightly sick at the sight of Kenneth's scrawny neck, his lips curved to gain exactly the right sound. But the plaintive tune and the soaring notes were so super that he left the door open to listen. He jolly well wouldn't let Kenneth know he liked it. He found a clean tea towel for the last dishes.

Clearing up had taken too long to do anything else. It was time to get back home. He saw a load of dry clean washing thrown into the basket any old how, and bent to fold each item. Suppose Colin was wrong about Ted? It was only what his mate had told him. Bill badly needed to discuss it with someone he could trust, like Mr Durban.

Kenneth came in. 'Should we get back, if you've finished this clearing up? Can you get me a drink, orange squash preferably? My throat's parched after all that singing.'

Too cross to answer, Bill pointed to a glass then to the larder door. After a distinct pause, Kenneth found the squash and poured himself a drink. Bill watched his beastly throat move as he glugged it. 'And remember – no mention of Ted's war to anyone, mind.'

Kenneth shrugged. 'Who's interested? Not me.'

They went home, not speaking. However hard Bill tried to listen to the bicycle bells and distant rumble of trains, the wretched 'Danny Boy' kept playing in his head in Kenneth's trilling voice. He imagined himself grown up still having 'Danny Boy' ringing in his ears and the sight of Kenneth's pulsating throat always in his head.

Chapter Thirteen

It was Aunty's turn to cook and serve dinner. She was putting food on everyone's plates with jerky words and movements. 'Bit more? Gravy? No greens? You must.' She seemed agitated.

Mother didn't notice. She was intent on finishing the meal quickly because she needed to buy new shoes. 'I'm off, wish me luck!'

'Can I come?' Jill whined.

Kenneth offered to take her to the park. Bill scowled and started packing up the plates. Kenneth wouldn't want to do the dishes.

'Bless you, Kenneth!' Mother said as she disappeared through the door.

With the house empty of any sound but washing-up, Aunty confided, 'Bill, I have to tell someone. You'll be the first to know.' Her hands came out of the washing-up water and waved around, drops splashing on the lino. 'This morning's airmail—' her breath came in a rush, 'Dwaine's sure he'll be demobbed in the next few weeks, and afterwards, he says he'll be securing his income so that he can marry me. Imagine!'

That would cause some ructions. He said, 'That's super, Aunty. When – I mean, how?'

'He'll come over here for a few weeks. If we still get on, then we'll get married. I'm hoping it won't be too long. All I've had since he went is that photo you took of him, Bill. To think of a time when I'll see him every day!'

'We can show him London; he'll like that.'

'Yes. I'm so excited, I'm all in a tizz. And scared, because I have to prepare Kenneth for Dwaine coming, and he's going to be f—'

'Fed up, yes.' *Furious* was what they were both thinking.

'So if you can do anything,' she plunged her hands back into the hot water, 'anything to talk him round, I'd be so grateful. I mean, with everything being so different for Dwaine, all our English ways, we don't want an atmosphere at meal-times and that sort of thing.'

'No. But, Kenneth won't listen to me of all people!'

'Oh he respects you so much, Bill.'

He smothered a bitter smile.

'You're so steady, so reliable. I'm so hoping he'll listen to your reasonings, boy things, whatever you discuss up there in your bedroom.'

Poor Aunty, she hadn't a clue! She wasn't there in the silences while he and Kenneth avoided each other.

'Shouldn't I take over the washing up for a bit, Aunty? Your hands are all red with the washing soda.' Anything to change the subject.

Dwaine would want to take Aunty off to America. That's what had happened to Mary, Mrs Youldon's sister. She'd gone to America to get married, and was still there. Aunty would never leave Kenneth. He'd have to go too. Yippee! But it would be very sad to lose Aunty.

She passed him the last dish to wipe. 'You'll chat about it, you two boys, won't you? And you'll be in support.'

'I should think Dad will pronounce on this, Aunty, when the time comes. He's top dog.'

'Yes, when he comes. I mean, clearly Dwaine can't arrive first.' Aunty dabbed her red hands on the roller towel, looking embarrassed. 'It's difficult, Herbert not having met Dwaine yet – and Frank being his brother...' Her voice tailed off.

Bill put an arm round her waist. When Jill was born, Aunty had been a comfort to him and now he was the bigger, stronger one, even if he was still in short trousers.

'Dwaine promised he'd come for you, and now he's keeping his word. I like Dwaine a lot, and I'll tell Dad that when I write. But you'll have to break the news to Kenneth. Otherwise, if I say anything tonight he'll think I've read your letters!' He moved away quickly as Kenneth came into the kitchen.

'Five minutes on the swings, and Jill wants to come home again. The real reason she asked to go out was that she could see Dawn. She's gone in there for an hour. Will you collect her?'

'You can, Kenneth, can't you?'

'No, I will.' Bill gave Aunty a look that was meant to convey *Tell him now* and he made a point of going out noisily so that Aunty would know that she could speak to Kenneth privately for as long as she needed.

He took a long run, keeping to the park instead of the common. He needed to think and didn't want to bump into Jim. Being with him was a risk. They were too different these days. It was exciting about Dwaine coming. For him it would be a treat, and Alan would be cock-a-hoop. But for Kenneth – he couldn't pretend that it was just a pen friendship now. Aunty would have to come right out with it. She wanted to marry Dwaine.

His stomach leapt. Then Kenneth would have a new father! Surely, he wouldn't need Bill's any more? Dad would get so cross if Bill asked him, but at some point, he could ask Aunty about that. Dwaine visiting – how would Dad react? He'd never had Aunty and Kenneth sharing the house before, let alone a man he'd never met. And would he mind Aunty being sweet on a man that wasn't Uncle Frank?

Mother was already home and in high spirits when he jogged back for tea, and there was no sign of Kenneth. Mother had actually found three pairs of shoes in her size to choose from! She described each in detail to Aunty, who had to admire the pair Mother had bought, so he

108

couldn't tell whether the conversation with Kenneth had gone more or less all right. Aunty was obviously avoiding telling Mother about Dwaine until they could speak in private. He'd better go for Jill now.

She said, 'Kenneth's gone for Jill, so you don't need to after all, dear.'

He soon came in with Jill, whom he'd struggled to get out of Dawn's, and she chattered all through toasting the bread so that no-one could get a word in edgeways. Usually, she wanted a turn at holding the toasting fork, which meant someone holding her arm to make sure she didn't burn herself. This time, she was too busy saying what her dolls had done, how she and Dawn had made them clothes out of leaves and plasticine.

'You've got half of it under your nails!' Mother complained. 'And it's not your bath night.'

Bill sneaked a look at Kenneth as he bit into his toast and dripping, but his expression didn't give anything away. Had Aunty actually told him?

It wasn't until bedtime that he faced the problem. Aunty gave him a long look as he said Goodnight, a look that probably meant *Please say something to help.*

Kenneth had already gone up, saying he was deep in a book about Henry III he'd got from the library.

When Bill came in from the bathroom, Kenneth was up in his bunk, his nose in his book, but he must have been waiting for Bill, because as Bill climbed into bed, he began to talk – a very rare event in the bedroom. He obviously didn't guess that Bill knew about Dwaine because he spoke with an announcer's voice. 'Bill. I must inform you that Mama's friend, the Eyetye, is proposing to come to this country. To this house, if you please.'

Bill allowed a pause to suggest surprise. 'Well, that'll be good. He might bring American things to show us.' Best to help Kenneth look on the bright side.

'He could bring the Statue of Liberty and I wouldn't be interested. I shall be tremendously busy with my school by the time it happens. If it happens.'

'What do you mean – if?'

'Don't you think Dad will forbid it? The Yank in his house? No, Duh-waaaine will have to stay somewhere else, and hopefully it'll be too expensive. I doubt he's a man of means, or a man of much at all, once out of his uniform.'

'We don't know what his work is. I remember Mrs Youldon saying he only joined up after becoming a widower.'

Kenneth snorted. 'Wife probably died of boredom.'

Bill persisted, 'Aunty will enjoy some company. I mean Mother's got Dad, and she…'

'…hasn't got my father. You needn't rub it in.'

Oh dear, this wasn't the kind of conversation Aunty had hoped Bill would have. He was meant to get Kenneth to accept the idea of Dwaine so that everything ran smoothly when he arrived. 'He'll know lots of things we don't. He could be a good friend for us, for you.'

'More likely we'll have to teach him civilized English ways. And if I want to know anything, I'd hardly ask him! I shall have an excellent school to inform me. As for friendship I have you, don't I?'

Bill stiffened. Lying below Kenneth, he couldn't see from his face whether he was being sarcastic. He must be, surely! Bill made a last attempt. 'If Aunty's happy, it will be nicer for you than if she's unhappy.'

There was a long pause. Bill wondered momentarily if Kenneth had dropped off to sleep.

Then in an anguished, grating tone Kenneth said, 'I shall call on help from Dad. We'll see how happy he is about his brother being replaced by some ignorant GI.'

Chapter Fourteen

The weather had turned dull in tune with Bill's spirits. The clouds seemed low enough for him to punch in their sides. He'd have to be off to Nanny's in a minute. She needed extra help because Ted was in bed with an ear infection. He pressed his lips together. The chances were that when he got there, she and Grandad would be swooning over Kenneth's lovely singing.

In the scullery, he finished sorting the good wooden pegs from the ones whose ends had broken. 'You need about a dozen new pegs, Mother. I've thrown away more than that.'

'Mend any of them where it's just the metal bent out of shape, will you?' Mother let the clothes airer down and started hanging the wet clothes over the wooden slats. 'For all I know, the hardware shop will be out of them. Just find the clothes horse, Bill. I think there are two, in fact. There's far too much washing to fit on the airer. I wish I'd left the sheets on the beds for another week if it's going to rain.'

'It is,' Kenneth's voice informed them from the kitchen. He had his paint box open on the table. He unrolled a length of the old wallpaper that Bill had just brought him from the cellar. 'I'm going to try to paint the rain.' He cut off a large piece of wallpaper and pinioned it down with four breakfast cups. The surface wasn't really smooth and he stroked it, tutting to himself. 'While you're in the scullery, Bill, get me a jar of water, will you?'

It wasn't much more to ask, but still jolly irritating. Why could Kenneth sit amusing himself with his paints while Bill had to do boring household chores? He brought the jar of water and banged it down in protest as he went to find the clothes horse. He knew his mood was not about the weather and the chores, but about Kenneth.

He found one clothes horse in Mother's bedroom. He took it downstairs and saw through the window that it was now raining hard. The smell of wet clothes filtered from the scullery into the kitchen. Kenneth had moved off and left his work unfinished. He often painted one part and let it dry before adding another wash or some details. His paintbrush, washed and dried, lay beside the wallpaper and paint box. It would be so satisfying to smother the picture of the rainy garden with black paint and gash huge crosses across the delicate work. His hand prickled, but of course he didn't do such a dreadful thing. He put the clothes horse beside the remaining wet washing.

Mother nodded towards the dry washing that Aunty had just ironed. 'Thank you. Take your clean sheets from the ironing pile, please, and Kenneth's too.'

He took the sheets upstairs. As he opened the bedroom door there was a quick movement. Kenneth stood up and turned. Bill held out the sheets and looked hard at him.

'All right. I was just – you know, finding a safe place for my special things. Somewhere you won't poke into.'

'I wouldn't.'

Their eyes met and their gaze held.

And suddenly there it was between them, the knowledge that Kenneth had stolen Bill's precious photograph of the sabre, that time, years ago, when it was hidden in Bill's special place in the base of his bed frame. He said, 'Whereas *you*...'

Kenneth's chin went up. 'That was ages ago. And you still remember. So you see why I mustn't risk you getting your own back.'

'I'd have done it by now. I don't pry into people's private stuff, or steal. What would you have that I would want, anyway? A special paintbrush?' Bill could hear his voice hard and sarcastic. He didn't like sounding this way, but Kenneth was making him into a nastier person.

Kenneth opened the folds of his sheet and started making up his bunk. 'You're not worth bothering with, not worth listening to.'

Bill dumped his own sheet onto his bunk and left the bedroom. He'd do it later when Kenneth wasn't there. Let Kenneth hide whatever stupid thing he had in some secret place. Bill truly didn't care. He ran downstairs where Jill and Dawn were dithering by the back door with their dolls' prams. 'Is it going to stop raining soon, Bill?'

'Don't know, girls, but doesn't look like it. Sorry. Tell Mother I'm off to Nanny's.'

The clouds were clearing, although not enough for the sun to shine warmly. Bill could have taken the girls to play in Nanny's garden. That way Nanny and Grandad could get to know Jill better. There was much more space there for throwing a ball or pushing their prams. He had thought several times about taking Jill. He was her real brother, after all, although he'd be in terrible trouble if he said that.

It wasn't the rain, but Ted that stopped him taking Jill round there. He came out with things that little girls shouldn't hear: *Darn it; Damned if I will* and even *Shitloads of shit.* The worst of this was that he wasn't saying it to anyone you could see, and you couldn't tell what he was saying it about. That was scary. Jill had already called him 'loony' before they'd even got back to Wandsworth, so it was too risky to bring her without Mother. He ran down the sideway and pushed the back door open. 'Nanny?'

She came through from the parlour, a duster in her hand. 'Hello, Bill, dear. Ted's up and about but he's left some digging unfinished in the garden, tools lying around. He's a bit down. His ear's better but they've said he's not fit for any work yet.'

'That's rotten luck. You were hoping he'd get a little job nearby. Until he's ready for his proper one.'

'Yes, we were.' She sighed. 'His old job, that's out of the window. I can't see Ted getting back to anything responsible for quite a time. And at nineteen, he was onto such a good thing at his office. Grandad says Ted's chances of getting back in that sort of position are poor. While he's been away serving his country, his place has been taken by a man who's over fifty. So many men are wanting work and there's many more to come. What the government can do, I really don't see. We thought if Ted came back alive he'd get a big welcome, not left here to wash dishes and manage a bit of garden.'

He'd better not show Nanny how glum he felt about Ted too. He said, 'I thought seeing Colin might cheer Ted up.'

'I'm not sure it did. We were glad Colin looked him up, but Ted was very quiet when he came home afterwards. Just sat in the lounge, smoking. He doesn't even seem to read anything. Grandad keeps trying to get a conversation going.' She sighed again. 'But the rehab office have got Ted got a new appointment. I think it's only to do with jobs, not for someone who helps with... Ted's sort of illness.' She didn't say what the illness was. Did she know it was mental?

'Where is it best to start helping?'

'Dig us another trench, dear, will you? I asked Ted to start one but he hasn't finished. It'll be quicker if you do it. We need to plant as much as possible. Next door kindly gave us all these starters – there's beetroot, lettuce, onions, radishes.'

Bill took the bowl with its promise of autumn and winter vegetables and went into the garden. It wasn't raining and Ted was standing at the bottom hedge, smoking.

Bill waved. 'Coo-ee. Shall I go on with that trench, Ted?'

The spade was lying half in and half out of a two-foot hole. Ted picked it up and started digging. Bill thought it best to leave him while he was actually getting on with something, but after a few spadefuls Ted ambled forward. 'Digging trenches. Just what I came home for!' His voice was raw.

Best to change the subject. 'Did you like having Colin to talk to, Ted? Did you spend a nice long time together?'

'Nice bloke. We had the same rotten time, though he seems chipper enough now he's back. Probably because he's got a spanking new job in Streatham. Nearly as good as the one I had before they sent me off to war.'

Bill started digging. What was best to say? *Keep your sunny side up. There'll be bluebirds over, the white cliffs of Dover.* He said, 'I bet you learned a lot of new things. Colin said you had months of training. It'll come in useful, won't it? When you get back to work, I mean.'

Ted laughed an awful laugh. It was like a choke in a black tunnel. 'Oh yes. Learned a lot, I did. This is what I was taught, Bill. See if it'll come in useful. Watch.' He picked up the garden fork and ran down to the bottom of the garden. Sheets and an eiderdown were hanging on the washing line. Ted bent low and thrust the fork towards them threateningly, then turned, and rushed screaming and yelling towards Bill who backed rapidly up the steps and into the flower bed at one side.

Ted turned round and made another dash to the washing line. 'Yaaaaah.' He thrust the fork with huge force to each sheet and, then bending low with the fork held full length before him, rushed at the eiderdown and ran it through. 'Yaaaaah, yah, yah, yah.' It hung limply, four great gashes open to the wind. Small white feathers escaped wispily to the sky.

Ted's yelling was enough to bring the whole street running, but no-one came. He walked forward, unsteady, his hips and legs so skinny. 'That's what I learned, see. With a bayonet. Come in useful, will it? I killed one Jerry and left another twitching. Enemy shooting down on us from all around, four of my mates wiped out. We had to retreat – bodies lying all around us, men we'd ate with and run beside.' His face was pasty, glistening.

Bill stayed backed up behind the steps, his feet pressed into the flower bed. He was very scared, but he needed to protect Nanny and Grandad. He put out his arms to either side, but Ted wasn't trying to get past him.

Ted threw down the fork. 'Don't you fight, Bill. Don't go to war. It's barmy.'

Bill held one hand up as if pressing the idea away. 'No. I won't.' He risked taking a few steps forward. Ted didn't move, so he rescued the fork and poked it deep into an innocent pile of soil.

Ted straightened up but his eyes were glazed and his eyelids twitched. 'Now I've shown you the sort of things you'll be expected to do, perhaps you won't sign up. They mustn't recruit you.'

'No.' He needed to calm Ted down. 'The war's nearly over, Ted. Soldiers are coming home now, not being recruited.'

Ted wasn't listening. He went on, 'No more signing up, see. Bert understands. He's a pacifist at heart.'

'I know.' But Dad had said he would do his duty, even so.

There were several silent minutes before Bill thought it safe enough to pick up the bowl and show it to Ted. 'Look, we've got to put these in, beetroot, onions and things. You need these growing. There's not enough food, without.'

Ted's hands didn't move towards the bowl.

'Will you do a bit more digging while I start putting these in, then?' Was it safe to turn his back on Ted and bend down or would he be a target?

Ted nodded. 'Okay, if I must,' and picked up the spade, but gently.

Starting at the finished end of the trench, Bill started planting the carrot tops. He felt shaky from Ted's outburst. What on earth would Nanny say about the eiderdown? Did she have another?

Thank goodness she hadn't seemed to hear, for everything was normal when he got back indoors after planting out the vegetables. He should say what had happened, but it would upset her and Grandad. He hesitated at the front door, but couldn't find the words. He shouted *Goodbye* and ran down the road. He might be able to talk to Mr Durban about Ted. He wasn't going to tell Mother. You didn't worry women with men's troubles.

Chapter Fifteen

The really heavy rain saved itself for August 1st, the day of the exam. Mother fished his raincoat out of the under stairs cupboard. 'It doesn't look as if you've worn this for a year.'

'I haven't.' He put his arms in it. 'It doesn't cover my knees now. I'll look silly.'

'Well we haven't anything else so you'll have to wear it.'

'It's all right,' Jill said, pulling at the hem. 'It covers your top half.'

Mother took her umbrella from the elephant's foot stand. 'Jill, you're to stay indoors with Kenneth until I get back. All right, Kenneth?'

'Yes, Aunty.' He turned to Bill and said quietly, 'Good luck. Remember that WRITE has a W in it.'

Bill glared at him.

Jill said, 'Does it? It doesn't sound like it has.'

Bill saved his worst expression until he was at the front door behind Mother. He turned and stuck out his tongue as far as it would go and turned again to meet the drenching rain.

Once they had sloshed along the pavements to the school, Mother got him signed in and then hurried off, almost hidden under Dad's black umbrella. 'Come straight home once the exam is over.'

It was jolly uncomfortable sitting with wet legs in wet socks and looking out of the large dusty windows until all the exam papers had been handed out. The school building was impressive but he could see that the field had no football posts. Mother thought he wasn't brainy like Dad or Kenneth, so why struggle to answer loads of exam questions?

On each desk there were three white leaflets. When they were told to start, Bill saw there were loads of questions. The first leaflet was English, then next one was Arithmetic and the other paper was called Verbal Reasoning, but it was just puzzles. Surely those weren't important? He pushed it to one side. He did some arithmetic problems and part of the English while the points on his two pencils were sharp, but when his pencils got blunter it was more difficult to ignore his wet socks and the idea of having no school football ever.

After the set papers, there was a break when they had a glass of weak orange squash and were allowed to talk to each other. Most boys were saying how nervous they'd been, so it wasn't a very jolly chat.

Afterwards, he was interviewed by a senior teacher and invited to ask questions. He asked if the school had photography lessons, and the teacher looked surprised and said there were not.

So when the letter came a few days later saying he hadn't got a place, Bill didn't mind.

'Oh dear,' Mother said, holding the letter. 'Your father will be disappointed.'

He folded his arms across his chest. 'Surely it doesn't matter. You said I was more practical!'

'Yes. Well, it'll have to be St Werberg's. Only a short walk. It's even on the way to Nanny and Grandad's.'

That was useful, but the main thing was that St Werberg's played football. Bill went to sit in the parlour until dinner-time. He would study his photography manual. No-one had said how much homework you got at St Werberg's but he wouldn't chance it. With his luck, there could be loads.

After a while, he heard the phone bell, then Mother talking, then a pause. 'Yes, Letty, that would be lovely.'

He was alone, so no-one could hear his groan. It would be an invitation to bring Kenneth to the Durbans,

Mother's fault for saying he was moving in. Angela and Mrs Durban would definitely make a fuss of him, because he'd lost his father. How rotten it was going to be, seeing Kenneth suck up to all of them. He slammed his manual onto the wireless top and came out to see if dinner was ready.

There was no Jill to lighten the conversation over the dinner table. She was at Iris's for the day. Aunty came in a little late. She'd finished work at twelve thirty. 'Sorry, Marcia. I did hurry.'

'Mama, you look flustered.'

She patted Kenneth's hand. 'Home now, dear.'

Over the spotted dick, Mother said, 'We're invited to Fulham tomorrow, Doreen. The Durbans. I said you didn't work Fridays. Peter Durban works at Chambers with Herbert. Letty's very nice, you'll like her. They're keen to meet you, and Kenneth of course.'

'That'll be nice.'

'I'll leave Jill at Dawn's again. She'll only be a nuisance – the journey, and then no toys or children there.'

Kenneth's spoon was in the air, his chin raised. 'Mr – D – who did you say, Aunty Marcia?'

'Mr Durban. It will be nice for you. Their daughter, Angela, has just left school. Such a pleasant girl. She plays the piano.'

Kenneth's face was tight, alert, like the dogs used to look when Mrs Pawsey was scraping a bone for them.

'Durban,' said Kenneth almost dreamily. 'I've heard that name.'

Surely he couldn't remember? It was years ago that Bill had almost let out where his secret power came from, when he boasted that he knew about soldiers in the Great War in Russia. Kenneth had pressed him and pressed him to say who'd told him, and when Bill wouldn't, Kenneth had asked Mother the names of any men Bill knew. That was ages ago, around the time Uncle Frank died.

Bill kept his face stiff and tried to look as if Kenneth's words were unimportant, just as Alan had advised.

But that night, when Bill had his face to the wall ready for sleep, a quiet voice came from the bunk above. 'Mr Durban. That's the man that told you about the dead bodies in the snow, isn't it? I'm looking forward to meeting him.'

Bill didn't answer.

'And Angela. She's the one who likes Shakespeare.' Kenneth's memory was amazing. Why were Bill's secrets so super important to Kenneth?

He attempted a little snore, hoping Kenneth wouldn't know he'd even heard his words.

But Kenneth went on in a whisper. 'Of course, I doubt if you'll study Shakespeare when you get to your local school. But Angela and I will have that and the piano playing to talk about.'

Bill gritted his teeth silently. How on earth was he going to stop Kenneth smarming his way into the Durban family?

Chapter Sixteen

'It's best we catch a bus,' Bill said. Otherwise the mothers would walk together and leave him to walk with Kenneth.

Aunty was glad. 'Yes, let's. I have enough of a walk on work days, and I'm never sure how far Kenneth can get without tiring.'

Kenneth had slicked back his hair and was wearing his best jersey, the one Aunty said the vicar had admired. A long walk would do him a lot of good, but he spread his pained expression around so that everyone felt sorry for him. Luckily, the bus was empty enough for them to sit separately. Bill pointed things out to Aunty on the way to avoid having to talk to Kenneth.

Once they'd alighted in Fulham Broadway, Bill strode ahead towards the Durbans' road. It felt important to be the one to ring the doorbell. He was their real friend.

As the front door opened Kenneth tried to link arms with Bill, to look like a dear brother. How *odious*, but Bill couldn't wriggle away without putting himself immediately in the wrong.

Mother stepped forward. 'Here we are, Letty. Can I introduce Doreen?'

While the three ladies were making introductory remarks, Bill tried to sidle past them to talk to Mr Durban but he was shaking hands with Aunty and asking a few polite questions about settling in. She introduced Kenneth who was at his most charming. They'd hardly got as far as the lounge when, holding open the door for the ladies, Kenneth found an opportunity to shine. He set his eyes on the piano. 'What a lovely piano.'

'Thank you, Kenneth. It's for Angela.' Mrs Durban smiled proudly. 'She's just passed her Grade Six, even though she didn't quite manage a merit.'

Bill had never discussed piano playing with Angela although they were such friends.

'Such a benefit to a girl to have something to offer in marriage, when the time comes,' said Aunty. 'Music is something wonderful to share. Kenneth sings, you know.'

Kenneth turned his best smile onto Mrs Durban, a dimple showing on his left cheek.

'Yes, beautifully,' Mother added.

Bill frowned at the floor. Did she really need to join in?

Mrs Durban was delighted. 'Really? He'll have to join a choir here.'

'I should so like that, Mrs Durban,' he said.

She went to her desk to look for a list of music societies and wrote down information about a choir in Wandsworth.

Aunty took it. 'Oh, that is kind. We'll be glad of this, won't we Kenneth?'

Angela came in just then, and attention turned to her. She was so taken up by the grown-ups talking to her and about her, she hardly looked at Bill.

Kenneth went to the piano and looked at her music. He knew the right questions to ask, talking about Bait Hoaven and other strange foreign names Bill hadn't heard of. The talk was all about music, singing and societies. Soon Bill was mooching in their garden on his own while Angela was playing the piano and Kenneth's treble soared over the remains of the Anderson shelter. His voice should flipping well have broken by now. Bill's was husky already and Kenneth was nearly fourteen. It would be smashing to say 'There's something wrong with you', but he couldn't risk it. Kenneth was so often poorly, suppose there really was something wrong with him?

At tea-time, he went indoors with half a hope of cakes, but Mrs Durban hadn't any flour left to make any, so there were only buns. 'I'm so sorry. I never seem to keep within our ration. I'm always running out of everything. It makes me realise how very much we had before rationing came in.'

Mr Durban said, 'We can't grumble. Going without our luxuries is nothing in comparison with the thousands starving in Europe.' There was a silence while everyone nodded. Recently, newspapers had shown wafer-thin children in Germany and Poland.

Aunty passed a half packet of tea to Mrs Durban. 'Almost as precious as gold,' she laughed.

'Are you sure you can spare it? I can't deny it's so welcome.'

'I got it in Northampton where my parents live. It's not so hard to get things there.'

'Well, thank you.' Mrs Durban gave it to Angela. 'Pop this to the kitchen, dear, and put it in the caddy.' She turned to the teapot and began to pour out while Bill handed round the plate of buns.

After tea, the talk was about Japan and how long it was holding out, delaying the real end of the war. This was the point at which Bill and Angela should disappear to play Ludo, but she was tidying the sheets of music on the piano.

Kenneth was leaning forward, his full attention on Mr Durban and the newspaper he was holding up.

Aunty said, 'We keep hearing about Allied attacks, but the Japs don't accept they've lost, it seems.'

Mr Durban folded the newspaper onto the side table. 'Well, ladies, I think we have to be patient for another three or four months. The blighters will have to give in eventually.' He pulled out his packet of Craven A.

'Their stubbornness is causing so many unnecessary deaths,' said Mrs Durban.

'Yes, but as we step up the attacks, hopefully we really will see the end of the war before Christmas.' He clicked his lighter and the flame punished the cigarette end. Bill kept his eyes on its glow.

'I read in *The Times*—' said Kenneth.

Bill frowned. 'We don't take *The Times*.'

'I use the library. Don't you?' That surprised tone was a wretched sham, and if they'd been alone together it would have deserved a shove in the stomach. It was all right for Kenneth, taking it easy. Bill was too busy with chores at home and at Nanny's to sit in the library.

Kenneth turned to Mr Durban. '—that it was a mistake to put Labour in power before the Far East is conquered.'

'The US won't let up, and neither will we, you'll see. But, it's good that you keep yourself informed, Kenneth.'

'Until Dad gets home, one of us has to stay informed at home.' Kenneth spread his hands as if he was managing all the information Mother and Aunty had available. He leaned forward a short way so that a long piece of hair fell over his forehead. This meant he could push it back with one delicate hand. Bill saw Angela watching the small movement. Ladies liked that sort of thing but it made Bill want to spit. Kenneth sat back. 'So I always read the main feature and Letters to the Editor.'

Mr Durban nodded approvingly. 'Angela, you should take a leaf from Kenneth's book.'

She gave a pat to her pile of music. 'Far too busy with work, Daddy. The newspaper's so big and you get cross if I crumple the pages. Anyway, what do I know about Japan? It all sounds horrid and I just want the war to be over, over, over.'

Mrs Durban put a hand over Angela's. 'We all do, dear.'

Aunty sighed and nodded. 'We're all sick of it. It will be so marvellous to get things back in the shops: proper food, clothes, everything. Once the war's really over.'

Kenneth nodded, as if he was her teacher or something. 'Patience, Mama.'

Mr Durban didn't seem to notice how sickening Kenneth was. 'Good lad. That's the way.' Anyone would think Mr Durban had forgotten it was Bill who was the boy he knew and liked.

When the time came for them all to go, both Mr and Mrs Durban said how much they'd enjoyed meeting Aunty and Kenneth. Even Angela smiled at Kenneth and said she'd liked playing the duet, before she said goodbye to Bill. He and Angela hadn't had a moment to themselves but she didn't mention that.

'Well, wasn't that nice,' said Mother as they went home.

'A lovely visit,' said Aunty.

Bill stuffed his hands in his pockets and Mother didn't even notice. Altogether, it wouldn't be surprising if they were all invited again before Bill had a chance to pop down on his own. When would he get a chance to talk about important things, like his own shashka story? Suppose Mr Durban stopped liking to see him and wanted to hear Kenneth sing instead?

Chapter Seventeen

Saturday morning pictures had been super. Roy Rogers was fighting a great mass of Red Indians lined up on the dusty rock. They looked so scary, dipping their arrows in poison. Then they pulled their bows, and all the arrows went flying through the air! But Roy Rogers escaped and later, he won. Everyone cheered.

Aunty had given him the sixpence to go. 'You deserve it, dear.'

Kenneth said, 'I'm not interested in sitting with a lot of rowdy kids.' He hadn't done any chores, so he didn't deserve it anyway. He'd not said a word during dinner.

Now Aunty was writing to Dwaine. Bill could guessed that from Kenneth's black expression as he strode out of the front room and straight out of the house, slamming the front door behind him. Bill peeped out of the small hall window to check that Kenneth was actually going up the road.

Mother was also out, visiting her dancing friends and had taken Jill with her.

The feeling of freedom was wonderful. But was Aunty upset about Kenneth's temper? Because Bill had been the one who'd introduced Dwaine to Aunty, there'd always been a special feeling between them. Now it was even greater, with Kenneth so furious at the idea of Aunty having any man friend.

Bill slipped into the kitchen and poured her a cup of tea. He took it in to her, to show he was still on her side. As far as Kenneth was concerned, 'Daddy', Uncle Frank, was supposed to last all of Aunty's life even though dead. It wasn't fair. Kenneth had a new father – Dad – so why shouldn't Aunty have a new husband?

Afterwards he went up to his bedroom, a rare chance to have it to himself. He pushed the window open wide to let the essence of Kenneth blow away in the light breeze. The extra chest of drawers made it too squashed now to hold his arms out wide and pretend to be a Spitfire, or twirl around to see how fast and long he could do it without being dizzy. He couldn't do that anyway with Kenneth around to sneer and make superior comments to the mothers. He could shut his eyes to the pile of Kenneth's books and painting things on the windowsill, and to the sight of his clothes hanging in the wardrobe. But he couldn't escape the smell of the medicines Aunty gave Kenneth: Vick if he had a cold, bitter drops for Vitamin D, cod liver oil for health, Virol for strength, and sickly liquorice stuff to be regular.

Bill leant out of the window and breathed the outside air. No sign of Kenneth either left or right along Primley Road. This was his chance. Leaving the window latched open a little, he bounded downstairs, two at a time, another thing he couldn't do with either Mother or Kenneth around. Now, most importantly, they wouldn't see him go to his special hiding place: the largest, highest law book in Dad's study, too boring for anyone to want to read, even Dad, otherwise he wouldn't have it on a shelf too high to reach.

He put the Windsor chair before the fitted bookshelves, and stood on it, then pulled out the tome. Inside were the letters he'd had from Mrs Pawsey, and Mrs Youldon's postcards. Behind them were those handwritten sheets from a Manor notebook: Alan's careful copy of the shashka story. Although he was keen to go out, he couldn't stop himself reading the story again, pushing his head into the pages that still held the slight chestnut smell of the Manor library. One day he would go back there and beg to see that book again. He knew the first sentence by heart. 'The new Cossack, strong and dark, mounted his horse, ready to embark on a raid in a distant land.'

He put the chair back, ready to leave. At last he could tell Mr Durban about the Russian book and perhaps slip in a question about Africa or soldiers escaping battles without Mr Durban realising he had Ted in mind. He slipped on his jacket, too short in the arms these days, but it covered his shirt, which wasn't clean on.

He set off towards Putney Bridge, and soon found he was panting although he wasn't running. His chest was thumping too. He was anxious about Ted, and about Kenneth pushing himself into the Durbans' home.

How long would it be before Ted got back to normal, and what could anyone do about it? Mother was worried about food, clothes, and housework she wasn't used to. Aunty had just started her part-time job and had her mind on Dwaine. Anyway, Ted wasn't her brother. Nanny and Grandad were old and ill and didn't seem to know what to do about Ted. Until Dad came home there was no-one who could help and meanwhile beastly Kenneth might tell everyone about Ted in a sneering way.

When he got to Fulham, Mrs Durban came to the door, allowing a wisp of stewed lamb smell to escape. 'Ah Bill, we've just finished dinner. We've all been out today so we're late eating. If you're hungry, I think there's just a little mutton left and two dumplings.'

He saw Mr Durban approaching, his newspaper under one arm. The smell was wonderful but he couldn't eat yet. 'No thank you, I'll be having my tea...' He left his voice in the air hoping she'd realise he was here for a chat with her husband.

'I'm afraid Angela's out at Guides. She heads the pack these days, very important,' Mrs Durban smiled.

'Yes. I'm joining Scouts. Dad said to.'

'I can entertain our Bill,' said Mr Durban in a rescuing voice and Bill followed him swiftly into the lounge.

'Anything special today?' It was like an invitation, suggesting that this would be one of many private visits Bill might make. Mr Durban put his newspaper on the table and tapped it. 'You know what's happening, of course? Japan.'

'About them holding out?' He didn't really know much more but he didn't want to sound ignorant. 'I remember the Japs bombing Pearl Harbor and then the Yanks coming into the war.' He smiled at the memory of the GIs in the village, what fun they were, the sweets and gum, the dances for ladies.

Mr Durban slid a cigarette out of its packet and flicked his lighter. 'The Japanese onslaughts have been lethal. And now it's payback time.' He drew a breath and the end of the cigarette glowed a bright red. 'I believe there's going to be a huge reprisal.'

'Reprisal?'

'Reprisal means getting back at the enemy with a vengeance.'

Bill nodded. He sometimes wanted to get back at Kenneth with a vengeance. 'But the war is finishing, isn't it?'

'Japan has to fall before war's really over. But it will. Their last day of action is coming. Then the many servicemen they're holding prisoner can be released. We want them home just as much as our men in Europe.'

'Yes. I want Dad back. Things won't be right until he is. There's all sorts of things to be sorted out.' His voice trailed away.

Mr Durban nodded slowly several times.

'Aunty's having a romance with a Yankee soldier and he'll come one day to collect her. It was me who introduced them.'

'You sound proud of that!'

'Well, Dwaine's really nice and other ladies were having fun and Aunty was sad after Uncle Frank died.'

'Yes. A very tragic affair. So you wanted her to have some fun too?'

'Mm. And not be lonely.' He thought *and to have a nice new husband, not like bullying Uncle Frank.* But that would have been an awful thing to say. Bill looked down. 'But Kenneth isn't glad.'

'Understandable. Imagine how you'd feel if your father had died.'

Bill blushed and hurried on, 'Anyway, I thought when you and I were alone I could tell you what I found out when I was evacuated, a bit about the shashka. It's sort of a secret that we discuss it, isn't it? I haven't told anyone I've seen it, except my best friend, Alan. And Angela, of course. But she doesn't know the shashka story, does she? Because it's not a story for women.'

Mr Durban's face might have had a smile or that could have been his lips gripping the cigarette. 'So what did you find out down in the country?'

'Read, actually. Alan wanted to cheer me up when—' he stopped. He mustn't let Mr Durban know that the precious photograph of the shashka had gone missing, '—when I was a bit miserable,' he finished. 'At the big Manor where Alan was billeted there was a library; a whole room of books on shiny shelves from down low to right up high. Alan got help to find something old about Russia, and there was *Russian Classic Folk Tales. Extracts.* It was on this yellowy paper with crinkly edges; only a few pictures, black line ones, small. *And:*' he took a breath, 'there was a story about the Cossacks. Alan and I read it over and over, lots of times. It said the sabre that killed in a specially brave fight was called a *shashka lixodaika*. There,' his words had been coming so fast, 'I've practised saying that so many times especially so that I could tell you.'

'I'm impressed, Bill. Spoken almost like a Russian.'

'Actually, Alan wrote it down, and we both practised it. *Shashka* is like a reward name that other sabres didn't have.'

'Ah, interesting. A special name, as if it's a person. They do that with the bravest bulls in Spain. Spanish bullfights, you know.'

He didn't know. They could discuss that another time. 'Therefore,' a grown-up word to make Mr Durban attend, 'because – your sabre (he nearly said "our") is a shashka, it must have killed someone after a fierce brave battle. You kept seeing huge battles, didn't you? And in that last one, the Cossack who gave it to you owned it, so he will have been very brave.'

'He was.' Mr Durban waved a flat hand downwards.

Bill slowed down and caught his breath. 'But at the end of the story, it said that the shashka would have a terrible future. What did that mean, sir?'

Mr Durban took another pull at his cigarette and blew the smoke out towards the open window. The smoke joined the clouds lowering over the garden. It was going to rain. 'Let's think about that a moment.'

Bill watched the cloud of smoke disappear, but its smell remained. It was a different smell from Dad's tobacco smoke, and different again from Mr Pawsey's Old Holborn. He said, 'I wonder if I'll ever find out why the shashka had a terrible future.'

Mr Durban finished his cigarette and stubbed it out on the Bakelite ashtray, grinding it hard as if it had done something wrong. 'All weapons are dangerous, and some are so dangerous that we shouldn't touch them without supervision. Just think. A rifle and most guns have safety catches. A sabre, now, that's dangerous every moment it's out of its scabbard.'

Bill looked at the floor. Angela had let him have it out of the scabbard. Mr Durban might tell her off if he knew. 'That story we found. I read it loads of times. It was about

132

the olden days, way before the Great War. Your story was at the beginning of it, wasn't it?'

'It was. 1914. Cossacks, horse-back forays, hand-to-hand fighting. I think we've seen the end of that.'

'Yes. It's all bombs, now, isn't it? Hundreds and hundreds of thousands.' Bill thought of the hundreds and thousands on Nanny's iced cakes before the war; how they'd melted like the bloodied bodies sinking into the Russian snow that Mr Durban had talked of.

'Mass killings, yes. Governments want to save their country from being invaded, but in the fields and trenches and mountains, who knows if the poor servicemen really understand what they're fighting about.' He gave a sour laugh.

'Yes. War's so very bad when you're in it that it wouldn't be terrible for a soldier to turn away to escape it, would it?'

'Run away from enemy fire? If soldiers really ran away, they were deserters. Punishment by death, often.'

Bill felt a pain the back of his eye sockets. 'Death!'

It is a fearful thing facing the enemy under fire, but that's what we come into war to do. To save our country, not run away.'

'Even if a soldier had been in lots of battles already, and the next was just too awful?' Bill's throat seemed to be in his mouth and his stomach in his shoes.

'The regiment stands together, you see. They don't turn and flee, unless the order's given – RETREAT!' His voice rang out making Bill's head turn sharply to the window in case Mrs Durban was obediently rushing into the garden. 'Otherwise, the regiment stays put. That's what training is all about, Bill. You learn to obey orders, support your mates, stay with your regiment.'

'What if a soldier is ill?'

'A trained man has a duty to do his best. That's why soldiers are heroes.'

Bill kept his eyes on the ashtray. The ground-out cigarette was a crumpled black mess that needed clearing away. He must quickly change the subject; Mr Durban had begun to look at him too closely.

'The Cossack always fought on to the death, didn't he? I remember you telling me that. This book we found was more than a hundred years old. It had leather covers with ridges outside and coloured wavy lines inside. I can even remember some of the words, I read it so often.'

'Fascinating. I'd like to have seen it myself. I wonder whether I can get hold of a copy, or something like it.'

Bill pulled his prize piece from his pocket. 'Look, Mr Durban. I saved it to show you. Alan copied it all out for me on Manor notebook pages. Smell! It's his best writing and it took him ages.' He held out the pages proudly.

Mr Durban took it. 'What a good friend! Let me see,' and he began to read closely.

The new Cossack, strong and dark, mounted his horse, ready to embark on a raid in a distant land. Beneath him, the kazachii ybraynii sedlo, *a saddle decorated with the booty of Grandfather's previous raids and pillages. Now his old life of idle freedom was behind him together with his adolescence and he must accept his responsibilities as a member of the group. Thus he would be identified as a man.*

Last night, the songs round the campfire had described the possibilities of death and glorified the brutality of war. Death would be an honour! He threw out his chest. He was young, death just could not happen. A sword that managed to kill him would be honoured with the name Shashka lixodaika, *the name which identified it as legendary for downing an invincible Cossack warrior.*

He already had a shashka *himself. He put one hand on its hilt as the sun hinted a presence on the horizon. He* sniffed the air, fresh with the scent of feral cat, ripe for the hunt.

If he was the grandson of a rabble-rouser, one of the motley escapees of the political and penal systems of Polish Ukraine seeking the freer frontier, he was, above all, a Cossack. His grandfather's generation had developed military prowess to defend themselves against raids, and thus his father had been raised. Like other Cossacks, Father had learned a nomadic lifestyle to avoid enemies. He lived in a constant readiness to fight. So impossible was it to settle, farm and feed themselves this way, they depended on fishing, hunting but mostly pillage. The spoils displayed on Grandfather's saddle symbolized the honour of a Cossack warrior.

He had only known his father part-time, for Cossacks must leave their wives and children the moment duty called to embark on raids. But during those times at home before his honourable death, Father was memorable. He starred in all aspects of Cossack culture – the haunting folk songs, wild athletic dancing and dramatic, aggressive horse-riding.

Eventually the Tsar employed the fearless Cossacks to defend Russia's borderlands and it was in such a way that Father died. His compatriots brought him to the family for his final hours, enough time for him to croak his wish to his only son.

'Take this shashka, son of mine, and let it only leave your hands in those of your son, or in death, of a noble warrior as brave as you must become. Mind its path, protect it well. It will inflict the most terrible wounds.'

After his father's death, he put it to one side, had wild times, passionate times, ruined his mother's hopes of his heroism then sped back to renew them.

And now, the camp fires dead and his comrades mounted beside him, it was time to ride forth. Ahead of him, twenty years and many skirmishes on, would be the

Great War. But for the shashka, a much longer history awaited its terrible potential.

Bill let him read uninterrupted, his mind on the dreadful words *punishable by death*. Would many other soldiers know that Uncle Ted had tried to run away? Wasn't getting a bullet in his backside enough punishment?

Mr Durban reached the last page, shaking his head slightly. 'Well, I never, Bill! How wonderful to have found this.'

'Yes. It's my secret treasure.'

'Then keep it somewhere safe. I'd dearly like to have my shashka's full history. The shashka is the most valuable thing I own, not only its antique value, but—'

'—your own story; when you were just a school leaver!'

'Yes, indeed. What an adventure! How can I ever forget the shashka's owner and having him give it to me!'

'Well, you deserved it for trying to rescue him.'

Mr Durban smiled. 'I'm no kind of hero, but like your father, just turned to the job when needed. Now that I have more time, I might seek out a military expert in Russian weapons, to fill in more information when everyone's demobbed. The best chaps from the universities are still in service. Life's been difficult at home without our best brains available.' He began to talk about how difficult it was to find someone to fill in for Dad while he was away, someone who had the right knowledge.

Mrs Durban came in with a tray of tea. 'It's a fresh pot. You'd like a cup of tea, Bill?' and as she poured out, added, 'We were pleased to meet your cousin. So nice that he's musical. Someone for Angela to play duets with. Here's your cup, dear. I'm sorry there's no sugar.'

He nodded, trying not to look too glum, and slid the story sheets back into his pocket.

Chapter Eighteen

As he got close to home, the sky was hanging in a threatening manner over Primley Road. He took the rest of the road at a fast run. He joined Aunty and Mother in the parlour with relief that he'd got there before the rain.

The front door opened before he'd hardly said *Hello*. That would be Kenneth. He came in with library books and the loaf, which he put on the table with a noble expression. He'd shopped!

'You're just in time, Kenneth, dear. And you, Bill. Just escaped the downpour.' And she was right. The sky seemed to split apart as she spoke, and a loud bang made them all jump. Rain hit the window at an angle, sounding angry and aggressive.

'Goodness,' said Mother. 'More like March than August.'

There was a bright flash, and after a few moments, another boom. 'Lightning.'

Jill ran in and put her arms round Mother. 'I'm frightened, Mummy. Put your hands over my eyes!'

Fierce raindrops bounced off the surface of the concrete yard, hard and high, with a regular drumming sound.

'Ooooh,' Jill kept her head buried in Mother's front, and Aunty patted her hand.

'It can't hurt us, ducky.'

Kenneth had picked up his paintbrush and was trying to paint the bouncing drops, each with a little overhang and a speck of light at its top. 'It's too dark!' And it did look like night-time rather than early evening. Beyond the window, the sky lit again, this time brilliantly.

'Cor! I'm going to watch it properly from the garden room,' Bill said. 'It's not often we get a really big storm.'

Kenneth followed him, holding a tray of his painting things. There wasn't a table in the garden room so he put it on the bookcase. Bill went to the French windows where he could look up and sideways, left and right. The flashes came one after another, then dramatic zig-zags slashing through the navy blue sky, lighting it up more colourfully than ever the searchlights had done. The garden became vivid, yellow one minute, orange and scarlet another and a backdrop of a deep mystic purple. Boom. It was as though the thunder was announcing the light show.

'If only I had some film in my camera,' he couldn't help himself saying, even though it was Kenneth standing with him. 'This might never happen again.'

'If only I had indigo and carmine red. I can't paint this without the right colours.'

Bill found his head nodding in sympathy.

They carried on watching, the storm continuing and even intensifying, one or other of them letting out a 'Phew' or a 'Golly' as a shard of orange hit the ground or slashed the sky. It must have been an hour before Mother called them for tea. Until then neither of them had moved.

It was odd, he and Kenneth had never felt so close. Yet, as they went towards the parlour for bread and dripping and a currant bun, the fury of the sky and the deadened thuds of thunder seemed to signal that something dreadful and dramatic was going to happen.

Chapter Nineteen

Mother came into the kitchen looking serious. 'Where's your mother, Kenneth?'

'Reading a wretched airmail in her room.' Kenneth was examining both his shirts on the ironing pile. 'Mama will need to turn my collars. Look how worn they are.'

Bill snorted. The comment wasn't meant for him, but Mother had a faraway expression and didn't answer. Instead she said, 'I think the end of war may come earlier than we'd expected.'

'Why?' For once Kenneth didn't insert his superior knowledge.

'I've been listening to the news.'

'What's happened?' Kenneth pushed his face towards her as though she had wilfully kept him from information.

'The Americans have dropped a bomb on Japan. A huge one, apparently.'

'Many killed?' It sounded as if Kenneth was keeping a tally.

'I couldn't take it in. The newscaster said a great dust storm was covering the city where the bomb was dropped. A town called Haro or Hiro – something. Bill, run next door and see if the Benthams have a newspaper.'

When he came back with it, Aunty had finished her private time with her airmail and was just coming into the parlour.

Kenneth held out both his shirts toward her. 'Look at these collars, Mama. You really need to mend them or something. By the way, the USA has dropped some great bomb on Japan, but you probably know that from your Yank friend.'

Mother said quickly, 'I think it's that atomic bomb.'

'Oh my goodness,' Aunty sighed. 'This Japan business!' She took out her small scissors and started removing the stitches from around Kenneth's blue and white shirt collar. 'Is it too much to hope that the Japanese have given in?'

Bill spread the newspaper over the parlour table and Mother leaned over it. The front page announced, 'The Bomb that Changed the World' and showed an enormous cloud in the shape of a mushroom standing in an almost blank landscape. He couldn't stop a huge breath whistling out.

'Look at that, Mama!' Kenneth sounded impressed. He read out 'Japs told to quit.'

'Just like the wireless announced,' said Mother in a small voice.

'Horrific,' said Aunty. 'Much as I hate the Japs, I hope the women and children got inside their homes fast enough. That dust in their lungs – it could be a killer.'

'That'll put paid to Japan,' said Kenneth. 'I'd like to hear their fighting talk now!'

Mother was trying to read the detail. 'They don't know the casualty level or the damage. The dust is covering everything.'

Bill said, 'How will people be rescued?' but the phone rang and Mother hurried to answer it.

'I don't understand. I thought we were holding off from invading to avoid civilian casualties. Now they'll be huge' Aunty put her scissors down and stretched forward to turn the page, Kenneth's shirt still in her hand. She started to read silently, Kenneth and Bill looking over her shoulder. Most of the article was about how enormous, how much bigger than anything before this bomb had been.

Mother came back. 'That was Nanny, Bill. Ted's not too well and they need you to sleep over. Did you know he was ill?'

Bill swallowed. Nanny must have found the eiderdown. He'd counted on Ted clearing up the feathers and getting rid of it. Or had the neighbours told her about the yelling in the garden? What was best to say? 'He wasn't that well, Mother, but I don't know what's wrong.' That was true enough.

'You'd better go upstairs and pack overnight things. Is there anything we can spare them to cheer them up, Doreen? My mother shouldn't be having this extra worry on her hands.'

'How about some Jenner's Soyacream? It's supposed to be good for health and energy. Vitamin B, I think. I've got a packet in the back of the larder.'

'Thank you. You know, I *said* Ted was run-down. Didn't I say that?'

Aunty nodded. Her expression showed that she'd guessed something different was wrong with Ted. She made room for Mother beside the open newspaper. 'What a world this is coming to, Marcia.'

Bill didn't think extra vitamins would help Ted but Aunty was being kind. He went to find the Soyacream. Horrible stuff. At least he didn't have to eat it. Then he hurried upstairs and put a change of clothes and his toothbrush in a carrier bag.

'Good riddance,' Kenneth muttered as Bill left, the mothers still bent over the table.

Was he talking about the Japanese victims or Bill? Probably both. Bill slammed the door behind him and hoped Kenneth would know that was for him.

Chapter Twenty

The doctor had already visited Ted when Bill arrived, but it hadn't changed anything. Ted was mooching around in a shirt and pyjama trousers, trying to help and not finishing the jobs he started.

It was hard, trying to talk to Grandad cheerily with Ted in that state and the worrying news on the wireless. Nanny was too upset to speak about the eiderdown, but Bill saw the remains in the dustbin, and the bulgy canvas bag in the parlour where she was saving its feathers.

At night, Bill slept on the spare bed, which was in Ted's room. This meant he heard and saw Ted's dreadful nightmares. He sat bolt upright and flailed around with his arms, shouting out, swearing and even making crying sounds. The first night Bill rushed out to get Nanny, but she told him, 'Just wake Ted up and tell him he was only dreaming. It often happens, dear. He can't help it.'

Bill woke him and tried to calm him down, but Ted didn't seem to hear anything he said. By the morning, Bill felt tired through, then it was the same the following night.

Nanny used his help to get Grandad down the stairs. Leaning on Bill's arm, Grandad whispered, 'It's perhaps a bit safer to have you alongside rather than Ted, at the moment.'

'How did you manage before he came home?'

'Slept on a camp bed downstairs for months. I don't want to be forced back to that. It's not like my own bed.'

'What's going to happen to Ted, now?' Bill asked, once Grandad was safely settled in his easy chair. Until today, the sticks, the medicine bottles and being stuck in the chair had turned Grandad into a remote figure. Now he was more like an equal.

'The doctor said there's a place Ted can go to during the day, some days, not all. He'll be taught things to make, probably. He has to wait until there's a vacancy.'

'Will that make him better?'

Grandad moved his lips to and fro as if he was chewing a toffee. 'It's always better to be occupied. He can still help us out at home when he's at his best.'

Bill really didn't want to mention the eiderdown incident, but someone ought to know how wild Ted had been with the fork. 'Did the doctor think Ted should be digging the garden?'

Grandad nodded. 'It's all right if he does a bit, even if little comes of it.' He stretched his top half. 'Lordy, I'm stiff.'

'Grandad, have the Japanese given in yet?'

'No, they haven't, stubborn fools. Wouldn't you have thought that great bomb would have done it? They've only themselves to blame when they get truly clobbered.'

Nanny came in with a cup of tea for Grandad at that point and Bill went to start peeling vegetables.

Next day, the sun was bright but not beating down too strongly. Nanny wanted the lawn mown. He pulled off his V-neck and shirt so that he could feel the warmth directly on his back. It was comforting, and bare-chested, he felt like a proper workman. The smell of cut grass made everything feel fresh. He couldn't believe in atomic bombs with this smell and this blue sky.

Ted wandered out.

Bill called, 'Can you pull the deckchairs out of the shed, and help me get Grandad outside? It would be nice for him to sit in the sun for a change.'

'They're a bit done for. Not been used for ages.'

'Can you fix them?'

Ted went to the shed.

Bill enjoyed making the stripes on the lawn with the mower. They weren't as neat as the farmer's ploughing back in the village but it started to get the garden into some order. He stopped to pull lumps of grass from the blades and surreptitiously check on Ted.

Ted opened one deckchair out and twisted a screw, then sat in it. 'Just testing. This one's all right now.' He moved the wooden notch to its next position and lay back. 'It's nice.'

'You will do the other one for Grandad, though, won't you?'

Nanny came down towards them, walking carefully on the uneven stone path.

'You should go home, now, Bill. You've been such a help, but your mother will want you back and we're all right now for a bit. Aren't we, Ted?'

'I've fixed one of these deckchairs, and I'll do the other in a bit.'

'I thought we could get Grandad to sit out here, Nanny.'

'Ted can do that. I'll see that he does. You come inside, Bill.'

He followed her indoors. Nanny found three shortbreads from a tin on the high shelf in her larder and wrapped them in greaseproof paper. Goodness knows how old they were. 'One for you, one for Jill and one for Kenneth. There you are, dear. And there's your overnight bag.'

Bill called *Goodbye* and started off down the road with relief. When he was little it had been a great treat to be going to Nanny and Grandad's, and really thrilling if Uncle Ted was there. Nowadays it was rather awful.

When he reached Primley Road, the postman was just ahead of him. He was quite old and the heavy bag on his shoulder bent him forward. Bill ran to take their post before he got to their gate.

'That's saved me a few steps, young'un. Here you are,' and he held out a few envelopes. One was from Dad.

Bill rushed indoors with it. Dad wrote as often as he could but they hadn't had a letter for a couple of weeks.

'Ah you're back, Bill.' Mother was in the hall, dusting, and Kenneth was on a step-ladder dusting the high part, the top of the dado rail. 'Nanny rang me. She said things are calmer.'

Kenneth looked down. 'Calmer? Who isn't calm?'

Quickly, Bill held the post up between Mother's face and Kenneth's. 'Letter from Dad! Perhaps he's coming home?' He almost pushed the letter into Mother's hand.

Kenneth stayed where he was up the step-ladder. Bill saw that by peering down, he'd be able to read the letter over Mother's head.

Mother was reading quickly through, peering at tiny writing up the margins where Dad had saved paper. At the end, she turned back to the beginning. 'Get down, Kenneth. I'm to discuss this with you both.'

They all went into the parlour, where Aunty was sewing.

'Herbert's written, Doreen. You're to hear this too. He says,

I want you all to know. The bomb dropped on Hiroshima was mammoth and I cannot imagine the extent of death and injury. Any published figures are unlikely to be accurate. I want the boys to think seriously about the wrong of hitting back with ever more powerful weapons. Retaliatory force - where will it end?
We've been told the explosion spread far and wide. Those within its reach will have been most horribly burned. The fumes will be noxious. Therefore, there must be dreadful consequences even for those who survive and deaths will surely continue for years as result of this atrocity. Needless to say, it's the civilians who suffer, the families, babies, innocent of any part

146

of their mad masters' machinations. I am not in tune with the edict "Kill them all, for God will know his own". In fact, since God accepts ALL as his own, the comment - translated from the Latin - is nonsense in religious terms also.

I would not be able to write this letter such if the war in Europe had not ended, for the censors would destroy it, and probably my good service record too. In any case, I am no longer 'serving' as being a soldier is so horribly described (serving to kill, which is not, of course, God's purpose). I am now temporarily helping the Education section prior to my demobilisation. We are told this demob will happen on a certain date, and it does not. We wait upon another date. Some go, some stay, and while this inefficient mess is being sorted out, I make myself useful to the many who need the education they have lost for the war.

Meanwhile, my words to the boys will not wait. I wish them to consider the dreadful massacre that has occurred before newspapers and schools encourage them to rejoice when the Japanese military sign a peace treaty, as of course they must. We all desperately want an end to world war, but this way cannot be right. I do not want my sons to believe in mass destruction or to applaud it. So I trust you to read this to them while you have their full attention, Marcia.

My love to Doreen, whom I trust is well settled in our front room, to dear little Jill, and to the two growing boys who will shortly be considered ready to hold a gun. Let their minds reign supreme! And my true love to you, Marcia, "holding the fort".

Herbert. X

'Dear Herbert,' said Aunty. 'Such a pacifist! What a dreadful day it was for him when he was forced to take arms. Especially after being assured that both he and Frank were in reserved occupations.'

Mother was still gazing at the letter. 'Yes. If poor Frank had been spared, it would have been far easier for him to be called up. He was all for fighting the enemy from the beginning.'

Kenneth came down the step-ladder. 'Aunty Marcia! How can you suggest Daddy should have been called up when he's dead?'

Mother put an arm around his shoulders. 'I am sorry, Kenneth, dear. It is so hard for you. I only meant that your father wasn't a pacifist like Dad.'

And neither is Kenneth, Bill thought.

'True.' Kenneth shook his head slightly from side to side as if acknowledging each father in turn. No-one had ever spelled out the difference between the two fathers before. Kenneth's chin went up. 'It is such a well written letter, one I'd be proud to show my future masters if it didn't criticise war.'

Bill stepped in front of the step-ladder. 'Dad wants us to be thinking about all the people who died and whether such a bombing is right.'

Aunty said, 'Let's see what the effect has been on the Japanese military, and whether they'll sign the treaty now. It's nearly news time.' She opened the parlour door and the crackle of the wireless began. 'Come and tune this, one of you, will you? I never seem to get it right.'

Bill turned the knobs until the voice became clearer. The pips sounded.

Mother was re-reading Dad's letter. Perhaps there were private bits she hadn't read out loud.

Then the news began with a shock announcement. A second atomic bomb had been dropped on another Japanese city.

'Another!' Mother exchanged an anguished glance with Aunty.

As the size and extent of it was being spelled out, Kenneth screeched, 'Serve them right! Now they know what it's like to be smattered into bits. The Japs are done for!'

Aunty put a hand over his mouth. Her eyes were screwed up. She and Kenneth would be thinking of what happened to Uncle Frank.

Mother gasped at the wireless's words. She bent to the wireless, trying to hear more clearly. 'Twenty thousand times greater,' she muttered.

Greater than what? What on earth would Dad say about a second A-bomb? Bill stayed in the parlour doorway, one arm pressed on either side, as if holding it up. Dad had said the first must be killing thousands. Now it would be thousands of thousands.

Kenneth pushed Aunty's hand from his mouth and leant back against the table with one foot across the other in his film star manner. His chin was lifted, almost as if he didn't need to hear the news because he had found the solutions to everything.

Bill had to get out. He needed fresh air. He needed a long time outside. As soon as Mother turned off the wireless, he strode down the hall to the front door. 'Won't be too long,' he called, shutting the door before anyone stopped him.

He'd run. He'd run anywhere to breathe easily and not look at Kenneth or hear all the war words. He didn't want to think about people being blown up, burnt or what happened to them if they survived. It was horrible to think that Andrew would never walk down the road, that a bomb had fallen on him and his mother; that one had nearly got Nanny and Grandad, changed them and made their lives miserable; that thousands of Japanese survivors would be full of – what did Dad say? – nocksous fumes. Then, think about Ted! Even without injuries that you could actually see, war could make a man ill and batty and not able to work. Even without joining the army or helping it in any way, even being a baby, you could be killed in war. He'd always known that, of course, but this Japan stuff was forcing him to think of it all, and his chest heaved, as though each breath was desperate.

The street was too crowded for him to run and as he passed a dustbin, he saw yesterday's *News Chronicle* on top. He took it, turning back to find the front page. It was more detail about the first A-bomb. The colonel who'd dropped the bomb on Hiroshima said it went down like a clap of thunder. 'Hiroshima disappeared in cloud, boiling smoke and flame.' That colonel must have known what he was doing to the people underneath! But that wasn't mentioned, only his award, which he got immediately afterwards. The article went on to report some other colonel who saw the bombing from a distance saying it was 'awe-inspiring and magnificent'. His tummy churned at the words. Those colonels were so disgusting. If only Dad could have spoken to them before they dropped the bomb. He stuffed the paper down inside the dustbin and jogged on until he reached the common, then he ran fast. He ran along the main path, dodging around prams and slow walkers. He ran through the trees until he reached a deserted path, and there he ran his hardest until his breath came fast and loud. He ran as far as the lake. That felt better. He stopped under a group of trees and bent double.

The smell of the grass was fresh and good. He stayed bent over, but looked upwards through the tree tops and between their leaves where the sky showed bright blue. He was so lucky not to be in Japan, and he was glad he had a father who hated the bombing.

Chapter Twenty-one

It had been a long run and the overgrown grass had made it harder. He straightened up once he'd got his breath back.

A couple of kids dodged around the trees near him. 'Watcha. Got any chewing gum?'

'No, sorry.'

'Aw.' They ran off, disappointed.

Being at Nanny's the last three days had stopped him from going to Mr Durban's. Now he simply must, to discuss what Dad had written. If he'd heard Kenneth's last hateful words, Mr Durban wouldn't be so keen to advise Angela to 'take a leaf out of his book'.

Alan would say it wasn't Kenneth's fault. Awful things had happened to Kenneth's father, and when you got hurt you always felt like hurting back. He knew that; he and Kenneth used to do hitting back when they were small. Only it always felt like him, Bill, getting hurt the worst and no-one sticking up for him.

He left the common and crossed Gants Hill between the buses. The water under Putney Bridge was smutty and grey, the blue sky showing in fits and starts between clouds. Would Mr Durban be in?

By the time he arrived, after his long run and the walk from the common, he was very thirsty. Mrs Durban opened the door to him and took him in the kitchen. 'Bill, you look over-heated and dusty. Come in here and have a drink.'

He drank the glass of squash gratefully and so quickly, that she poured him another.

'You have got a thirst! What have you been up to?'

He had so much to say, but they weren't things you really talked to ladies about. War, bombing, being blown up, Kenneth getting round people, Ted being batty. 'Nothing. Just running on the common. I've been away a couple of days. To help my grandparents, you know.'

She screwed the top on the squash bottle. 'Good for you. I'm sure you are a help, especially with their trouble over Ted.'

His head snapped upwards in a query. Then he put his glass down carefully. What did she know? 'Did Mother telephone you?'

'No, dear. Your cousin came round the other day to bring something for Peter.'

Kenneth had come round on his own! Brought something for Mr Durban!

'He was chatting to me and Angela afterwards. So sad that your uncle buckled under the strain of battle. I'm sure he's not the only one.'

Kenneth had come round here on his own, and then told about Ted! Bill could feel his teeth grinding in an effort not to spit and snarl. No-one should know! He hated Kenneth. It wasn't his information to spurt.

'I can see it's really upsetting for you. Kenneth said that Ted was a favourite with you before the war. But cheer up, dear, I'm sure there will be help for him.'

She found two ginger nut biscuits but he couldn't eat them. He had to sip the last drops of orange to stop his lips wobbling. He could throttle Kenneth. Nothing would get his words back. Thank goodness no-one knew about the eiderdown. He wasn't ever going to tell anyone.

As her mother left the room, Angela came in. She looked pretty. 'Hallo, Bill.' She put a hand on his shoulder. 'Oof, you're hot. I can feel you burning through your shirt. What've you been doing?'

She was sounding like her mother. He said again, 'Running.' It was embarrassing talking to her, now that she'd heard about Ted.

'Do you like my outfit? Do you recognise it?'

He blinked hot eyes and looked at her properly. She was wearing a silky blouse and a cotton skirt. 'Should I?'

'Your mother's skirt. We cut it up to make me and Jill blouses. Don't you remember her wearing it?'

He shook his head.

'Boys! These little green flowers are pretty, aren't they? Has Jill got hers yet?'

He had seen Aunty sewing. Perhaps that was what it was. 'I think Aunty's working on it.'

He heard Mr Durban's cough, but he hadn't come in.

Angela twirled around. 'This skirt's not very full, but I'm saving up for one that makes a balloon shape when you twizzle round. It takes lots of material.'

Didn't she know what had happened to Japan? Or did Mrs Durban hide news that was too horrible for her to know? At least she wasn't saying anything about Ted. Perhaps she'd been too busy thinking about skirts and twizzling to pay attention to what Kenneth was saying.

But she went on more seriously, 'I'm going to start evening classes in September. There was a notice up in the library. English Literature. I always loved English at school. Kenneth and I were talking about it, and all the famous authors. He knows a lot, although he's younger than me.'

Bill stood up. It was just like Kenneth had threatened. He and Angela had lots they could talk about. But she wouldn't like Kenneth if she really knew him. Didn't she remember back before evacuation when he'd told her some beastly things Kenneth had done? She'd said then that he sounded mean. And he was, he really, stinking well, was.

Now, standing beside Angela, his eyes were level with the roll of hair over her forehead. He could smell a sweet soapy smell. Shampoo. She was too nice to be friends with Kenneth. He bit his lip and looked towards the hall. 'Is your father busy?'

153

'No. Just reading the paper, I think. Go, then, if you're bored with me.' She stepped away.

He always seemed to be saying the wrong thing, but he went anyway, and put his head around the door of the lounge. 'Mr Durban?'

Mr Durban lowered his newspaper slightly, 'I heard your voice, Bill. Had some squash, have you?' and then he went back to reading.

Bill sat himself on the sofa at right-angles to him, ready to get an idea of what Mr Durban thought about Japan. He waited.

Mr Durban went on reading, almost as if he'd forgotten Bill had come in. Was it because of what Kenneth had told him about Ted?

While he waited for Mr Durban to finish his article and turn his attention towards him, Bill looked around the room. The snug door was open and he could see some books, an album, a couple of framed pictures in a pile on the mahogany side table. The plan for a memorabilia room was underway. His glance swept over the newspaper Mr Durban was reading to the side table beside him. He couldn't prevent a gasp. On top of a book about tanks, there lay a photograph of a Cossack sabre, the sabre, the *shashka*. It was the same as the precious photo he'd lost. 'You've got another photograph, the same!' He hadn't meant to interrupt but the words were out before he knew it.

The newspaper lowered. Mr Durban glanced down at the photograph and turned his head to Bill, his smile – was it a smile – just a flat line with a quirk on one edge? 'No. It's the one I sent you, if you remember, and which you apparently didn't want any more.'

Bill shook his head as if to shake the puzzle out of it.

'Young Kenneth kindly brought this round for me. He noticed my name on the back and thought I might want it. He found it in your waste paper basket.'

No! So Kenneth had kept it all these years and then brought it round here! How dared he do such a thing! And to make Mr Durban think Bill had thrown the photo away! 'I didn't. I kept it safe for ages, it was precious and—' It was too embarrassing to explain how he'd hidden the photograph where he could reach it in the night, so that he could wave it like magic when things were miserable to make himself brave. '—then it ... went.'

Kenneth stole it. That's what he wanted to say, but was it right to tell on someone, even if they'd done something wrong? He'd never been a tell-tale-tit, people hated tell-tales. The furious feelings in his heart and his tummy were so enormous that he couldn't go on. He needed to explain how he wouldn't *ever* have thrown the precious photo away. He licked his lips, trying to find the words.

Mr Durban had turned back to his newspaper. 'It can add to the display in the snug,' he said, almost to himself. He turned the page.

For a while Bill sat on, wanting so much to speak about what had really happened, but too afraid now of tears coming, because he couldn't shout out that Kenneth was a thief and a traitor. It was difficult to say anything, especially as he'd have to interrupt Mr Durban when he was concentrating on reading.

It felt as if half an hour had passed, but it might only have been minutes, before Angela came in. 'Would you like to come to the pet shop with me, Bill? I have to get some Macleans paste and a bar of carbolic soap for Mummy, and the pet shop's next door. They have some new rabbits, so sweet.'

She was still at the door, and with Mr Durban's face still slanted down to the newspaper, it was easiest to go with her.

He got up, slowly, hoping Mr Durban would look up and say he must stay longer for a chat, but he didn't.

'Goodbye, Mr Durban,' he said in a choked voice, and then, 'I didn't throw it away,' but the words seemed to land in the cushions of the sofa and he could hardly hear them himself.

'Coming?' Angela said, cheerily. And then, as their front door closed, she said, 'Daddy's deep into the world situation. Dreadfully serious.' She almost skipped out of the gate but her heeled shoes slowed her. 'Do you realise? After today, everything will change. The war's really, truly going to be over.'

His war wasn't. He tried to keep calm but the fury kept rising from his tummy to his chest and through the top of his arms, his shoulders and into his mouth. He wanted to shout and punch – almost drop a bomb. Everyone in the road looked normal, but he wasn't. Things were not all right.

Angela was chatting happily about how it would be now the war was bound to end. I'm so looking forward to the end of queuing and having things – like bananas. I can just about remember them. I don't suppose you can?'

Bananas? How could he think about anything but what had happened to thousands of people, and what Kenneth had done to him? He must have answered for Angela went on,

'No. You would have been too young to remember the last ones.'

At first he thought she was talking about the last people dying but then caught the rest of her sentence.

'…didn't like that little tiny bit on the end, but I would definitely be eating every morsel if I got one now.'

After a pause she said, 'You don't seem happy about war ending. Don't you believe it? It really will be at an end now, you know. Daddy said so, after this morning's news, and he's always right.'

He kept his silence, and Angela bent down to stroke a little dog that was passing. 'I'd love a pet, wouldn't you?

Perhaps I can have one now. Perhaps Mummy will let me have a kitten. You can help me choose one. Then we'll go back and tell her about it, and beg. The shops are only a bit further.' She stood still a moment, and turned to him. 'Why aren't you talking?'

He ground the heel of his shoe into a hole in the pavement, this way and that. Angela had been a good friend all these years. Could he trust her with what had happened? He tried, 'What would you do if someone had done something really bad to you, like lying about you, or being a traitor?'

'Like Germans spreading propaganda? All lies. That's horrible, I know. Daddy said both sides did that sort of thing, it was necessary.'

'Great Britain did? No!'

'Yes. It was like a weapon. But Mummy doesn't agree that *All's fair in love or war*.'

'He didn't like that thought. Nothing was fair in war. But what about a traitor…?'

'Horrible again. We had them. Lord Haw-Haw, for one, and he's in Court now. Soon he'll be in prison, I bet. Come on, the pet shop's here.'

He turned away. It was no good, he wasn't going to get a useful answer about dealing with a liar at home; his roundabout questions were no good. He would talk to Alan.

Meanwhile, he'd have to look at rabbits and kittens and pretend he was all right.

Chapter Twenty-two

Scuffing his shoes as he made for home, Bill saw that the soles were loose and his toes were curled up. He needed a new pair of shoes, or even boots. His toes were trapped by the toe caps, trapped like the whole of him. He looked at the bombsite beside him. He was like that blade of grass under a pile of fallen bricks and debris, one small green tip trying to become tall and straight. He wanted to be Mother's right-hand man, he tried to be the best help to Ted, Grandad and Nanny, and to prove himself a hero to Mr Durban but he had a traitor in his home and what could he do about it without being a tell-tale, and causing more problems?

Angela would be back at her home begging for the white and brown kitten she'd fallen in love with. Mr Durban would be putting the shashka photo in the snug, believing that Bill had thrown it away. Kenneth would be warbling his songs, head in the air, top dog with Aunty and now with Mr Durban too. How he'd be crowing to himself, beastly Kenneth. How spiffing it would be to push his stupid head into a dustbin. He kicked every fag end he saw into the gutter and pretended it was Kenneth.

When he got home, Aunty was getting the tea. It was beans on toast, one of his favourites, but that didn't change the way he was feeling.

Jill didn't notice his mood of course. 'Beans on toast, Bill. Mummy's out. Gone to her friends and they're going dancing. She was wearing a pretty dress.'

'Pretty old,' Aunty smiled.

Kenneth sat at the table, fingering his knife and fork while humming a melody. Its trilling notes were like a taunt.

Bill sat down with a thud.

'You're late,' Kenneth said.

Bill couldn't trust himself to look at him.

'Not answering?'

Bill glared, his eyes feeling like glowing embers.

'What's wrong?'

'You know.' The words spread slowly over the space between them like a poisonous stain.

Kenneth's face showed some alarm. 'What?'

Jill giggled. 'You're going to quarrel. I can tell.'

Bill couldn't say he'd been down to the Durbans, revealing that he went there alone. Even Mother didn't know. He drummed his fingers on the table while Aunty was out in the kitchen. He wanted the drumming to sound like Africans in the jungle before they did their war dance.

'Am I supposed to have done something?' Kenneth brushed the stupid lock of hair from his forehead.

'You know what you've done.'

Kenneth raised an eyebrow, but he was looking uneasy. Even Jill had gone quiet.

Aunty came back and served out the beans. 'At least the juice from the beans means we don't notice there's no marg on the toast. I've done a nice big plateful for all of you.'

At first, Bill thought he wouldn't be able to swallow but as he saw Kenneth's tension, his fury began to die down. Kenneth knew Bill had found out something, but he didn't know what, or which. There were lots of nasty things he could have done. That would make him nervous. He'd worry about how much Bill knew, and what Bill might do back.

He put his fork into his beans and lifted his knife just above the toast, then cut it very deliberately as if causing it the maximum hurt. Kenneth would be watching. Hopefully, Kenneth was afraid.

The beans were good. Aunty didn't overcook them like Mother who had the juice bubbling until it tasted stewed and the beans went to mush. He took another mouthful, aware that Jill was peeping at him and then Kenneth.

Aunty leaned over the table. 'Have your glass of milk, Kenneth. You know how important it is for your health. I don't want you back in bed with a bad chest, now.'

Kenneth drank and didn't argue. Was he getting worried?

Bill ate a few more mouthfuls. 'The beans are nice, Aunty.' He sat up straighter and smiled across at Jill, an idea coming to him. Of course – if Kenneth thought Bill had told Mr Durban about the stealing, then he jolly well would be worried. He'd done the deed while Bill was away and relied on not being found out.

He allowed himself a slight smile as he cut the next mouthful. Kenneth would be noticing.

Kenneth would worry that Mr Durban would tell Aunty. How awful for the perfect Kenneth to be in trouble! And Mr Durban worked with Dad. Kenneth would be scared of Mr Durban telling him. Dad would certainly see stealing the photo and pretending to return it as very, very wrong. Not behaviour he'd want in his new son.

The beans were going down very nicely. Looking across the table, he saw that Kenneth's plate was still quite full.

Kenneth always told tales so he'd assume that Bill would tell on him too, like he'd assumed Bill would nose into Kenneth's secret stuff. Ah! He took a sudden breath and nearly choked on the next bean. *That* was what Kenneth was hiding when Bill burst into the bedroom; the photo was one of his secret things! No wonder he hadn't wanted Bill there. He felt his chest swell and his shoulder blades against the chair back. It felt so powerful knowing things, and working out things, that he didn't have to stifle fury any more. He polished off his remaining beans. 'Thank you, Aunty.' He took his cup of tea and his share of the broken biscuits. He passed one with cream on it to Jill. 'Did you go to Iris's today? Can you skip with both feet yet?'

'Silly. You can't do skipping with one foot. Boys are rubbish at skipping.' She nibbled the last of her biscuit and nudged Kenneth. 'Slow coach. You're still on your beans. I'll eat your biscuit if you don't hurry.'

Kenneth forked up another small mouthful and didn't answer.

After tea, and the clearing up, Bill didn't go outside as he usually did, but hung around looking at the books Alan had given him. He knew that Kenneth wanted to borrow them but now couldn't risk asking.

Kenneth went into the dining room. Bill followed, putting his books on the sideboard, closing the curtains, by which time Kenneth had slid out and Jill had come in to play with the line of china dogs on the windowsill.

Bill then left for the parlour, walking softly. Behind the door, Kenneth was turning the pages of a years old *Readers' Digest*. Bill called out, 'Jill come in the parlour, your snap cards are here.'

Kenneth put the magazine down quickly, pretending to tidy it into the pile of papers before going out. He went towards the front room for sanctuary, but Aunty stopped him as she walked in there herself.

'Don't come in just now, Kenneth. Let me have a bit of a lie down, my headache's come on again.'

Kenneth heaved a sigh and went into the kitchen.

After a moment, Bill followed.

Aunty noticed. 'While you're in the kitchen, Bill, could you fetch me the aspirins, please?'

It was quite fun, in a dark way, finding an excuse to be in each room in turn.

Eventually, when Aunty was safely in her room, and Jill upstairs, he went to corner Kenneth properly without interruption.

These moments had made him feel much stronger, less trapped. He couldn't take away what Kenneth had done, but he could deal with the wrong.

He strode into the garden room where Kenneth was standing at the far end, studying some sheet music. He'd joined the choir that Mrs Durban had told them about, and these were the songs he had to practise.

Bill stood by the reclining chair, watching. Kenneth couldn't pretend he was just leaving the room when he had the music in his hands. He kept his eyes on it as if he hadn't heard Bill come in. He traced the notes with one lily-white finger, mouthing 'semi-breve, diminuendo'. Dim something he'd be, if Bill really got going on him. But words would be enough. Bill stepped back to the door and shut it, very firmly. It made a loud enough click. He stood against it, straight and upright, feeling his shoulders and the muscles of his calves hard against the door.

Kenneth raised his eyebrows at the interruption and moved his finger to the next block of black wiggly notes.

Bill let his voice carry across the room. 'So what will everyone think of you now, Kenneth?'

Kenneth didn't look up, but his finger stayed pinioned to a big note with an empty middle. *'What?'* he said in the kind of voice he'd use to a small child or imbecile.

Normally, that would feel intimidating to Bill but it didn't today. He just hmmed, as if considering his words.

Kenneth was sounding rattled now. 'What? What do you mean?'

'Does Aunty want a thief and a traitor for a son? Will Dad be proud of you when he gets back?'

Kenneth looked up, and his face paled. Now he'd know what Bill had found out, but he wouldn't know how. Bill would leave him guessing. That felt good. He folded his arms over his chest and stayed with his back against the door. It would look as if he was preventing Kenneth from escaping. Kenneth might be expecting a thumping. He certainly deserved it. Bill let the seconds pass, and enjoyed the tick of the mantle-piece clock. Tick, tock, tick. How threatening it sounded.

Kenneth turned a page, avoiding Bill's gaze. 'I've no idea what you're on about. I'm trying to practise.'

Bill waited.

Kenneth put the music down. His hands were clenching. 'So, um, what—'

Are you going to do, was he thinking? Bill let him wait a moment longer before saying, 'So you won't want to be visiting the Durbans on your own, will you? In case stealing is mentioned. Better to have Aunty there to protect you, and Mother chatting away, so that the subject doesn't come up— if you want to go to Fulham at all, that is.' He turned and opened the door, walking out very deliberately, leaving it open.

How satisfying! Kenneth had done something really dreadful, thinking he wouldn't be found out. Bill had shown him up and paid him back without thumping him, without even telling a lie about how he'd found out. He'd left him scared that Bill would tell the grown-ups. AND, he'd scotched Kenneth's attempt to sidle into Bill's own special place. The rat wouldn't want to risk going to the Durbans on his own now. Tonight, at bedtime, it would be Kenneth in bed first, pretending to be asleep.

He told Alan all about it next day, phoning when everyone else was out. He was glad to hear Alan shocked.

'Golly! That's dreadful. I wouldn't have thought Kenneth would be so slimy.'

'Yes. Think! Hiding it all through evacuation and bringing it with him – waiting four years for the opportunity.'

'Bad enough stealing it in the first place. He is a rotter, after all.'

Bill told how he'd dealt with Kenneth. 'He's got the wind up now.'

'You did well. But what he did was so odd. Was he paying you back for something he was upset about?'

Bill hadn't thought of that. 'Upset? He's only upset about Dwaine coming over. And that's more to do with Aunty.'

'Dwaine! Is he really coming? That'll be smashing.'

'Yes, super. I'm going to let the Pawseys and Mrs Youldon know. They'll love to know Dwaine's coming.'

'But Kenneth won't.' Alan put in.

'No…' Suddenly, Bill realised the connection, 'Yes!' He punched one fist forward. 'Of course! *That's* what Kenneth is punishing me for. He was always furious about me arranging for Aunty and Dwaine to meet in the first place. So! And now he's counting on Dad scotching Aunty's plans to have Dwaine here.'

'Your dad's going to have a lot on his plate when he gets back! Shame it's not now. We're getting ready to celebrate VJ Day, are you?'

'What? Have they signed, the Japs?'

'Mum says they have no choice. Wait till the news. Then there'll be another great party on the common.'

'That'll be spiffing. Do you think there'll be a funfair?'

'Probably. And after that, new school the following week, Bill. Are you excited?'

He wasn't. It was embarrassing to let on that he'd deliberately failed to get a grammar school place. He'd leave Mother to tell Mrs Routledge about St Werberg's. He shrugged. 'I'll let you know after I've tried it.'

Chapter Twenty-three

Summer was over, together with the excitement of the real end of the war. Bill had been in the crowd cheering the King and Queen. Aunty had enjoyed the VJ Day holiday so they'd all gone to the festival on Clapham Common. Now it was Autumn, the news had got miserable again.

Kenneth crowed when he read that the Japanese war minister had killed himself. 'That's what they do, the Japs. Either win or do yourself in.'

Mother and Aunty shushed him. They were worried about the Lend-Lease being ended by America. 'Herbert says Britain will be bankrupt. That will mean even less food and goods. No wonder the government gave us all a holiday and let us celebrate.'

'Party then Poverty,' Aunty said.

Kenneth raised his chin. 'Ending the lease without notice. Now you know what sort of country America is, Mama.'

'You'll feel differently when the next food parcel arrives, Kenneth.'

Bill privately wondered if Dwaine might arrive first, his suitcase full of goodies.

Mother waved towards the near-empty larder. 'Goodness knows how we'll survive if the shortages get worse.'

Bill shut his eyes and tried to remember a plate full of roast dinner. Poor Jill was too young to know what a decent meal tasted like. Now she'd have to suffer school dinners for the first time! She'd find out that there were far worse meals than Mother's. She was already full of misery because she'd never gone to school before. At her village the vaccies had to be taught in people's houses. The thought of real school must be scary for her.

Kenneth was the most cheerful of them all, still uppity because he had Dulwich College to look forward to.

Bill had no idea what St Werberg's would be like. He'd never known anyone who went there. Somehow, he didn't care. It would be all right, and he'd have football at last.

At the start of term, he filled his satchel with a pencil box, a handkerchief and a new notebook. St Werberg's wasn't far to walk so he wasn't hurrying.

Upstairs, Mother was struggling with Jill who was determined not to start school.

'I won't know what to do. I don't know anyone. I've never been to school before, I won't go-o-o! She was scared to bits.

Behind him, Aunty was in a fuss. She couldn't take Kenneth for his first day because of work. Kenneth smoothed his collar for the third time and did up all the buttons on his striped blazer. He had long trousers, lucky devil, with sharp front creases down them. 'The firm could have given you the day off, Mama, for something this important.'

'So sorry, dear but you do know which bus to take to Dulwich, don't you? Make sure you drink your milk at break. Have you got all your things?'

What a fuss! Kenneth would be fourteen in November!

The front door opened wide, Jill's sobs floating out. Kenneth left in one direction in a flurry of Aunty's fussing, and Bill left in the other, swinging his satchel. Just ahead was a boy in the same uniform. He vaguely remembered him from junior school. He fell in step with him and they went on together.

St Werberg's looked rather grim, with cement flaking off its arches and danger notices where the surfaces needed mending, but at least it had a decent football pitch.

It was also part of the way to Nanny's, which would cut down the time it took to get there after school.

A teacher in a black gown came out and gathered people into groups. Most of the boys had been there a year or two, but some were back from evacuation like Bill. He was directed to an upstairs classroom, its windows set too high to see outside. 'No-one enjoys lessons but we put up with them,' the boy sharing his desk told him. 'It's boring but not beastly.' And Bill soon found he was right.

The dinner was almost the worst he'd ever had, so it was good to hear moans all around. The other boys were friendly enough and he soon found that, like him, they just longed to be outside playing. He'd definitely be all right when they found out he was a whizz at football.

That night, when Alan phoned to exchange news he seemed sad that Bill wasn't at a grammar.

But school was all right. He did his lessons and they weren't difficult, and made sure he played lots of football. Only History was actually interesting. It was taught by an old man who told them stories about kings, abbots and cardinals instead of making them read from the boring textbook.

For football, there was one actual lesson a week, two practices and a chance of being picked for the school team. That was one thing Bill felt he could be sure of.

At home, there was less nastiness. He saw less of Kenneth, whose journey from Dulwich took some time, while Bill went to Nanny and Grandad's to help out after school. In the evenings, Kenneth was too full of the wonderful things he was doing at Dulwich College to bother about Bill. Altogether, it was easier to avoid each other now. Bill was too busy to get down to the Durbans hardly at all, so it was a relief to know that Kenneth couldn't, even if he'd dared to, for he had choir and travel and after-school *societies.*

Bill only had Scouts, though that was pretty good. It was quite fun working towards badges as well as playing a bit more football after Scouts had finished. He had a school-friend to go to Saturday morning pictures with, and Alan to meet on some Sundays.

He was worried that he wasn't at Nanny and Grandad's for long enough to be really useful. Meanwhile, nothing had happened with the Rehab Office for Ted, so he was more fed up than ever.

One afternoon after school, Bill bumped into Colin. He was wearing a jacket that was quite smart, brown but scratchy.

'Colin!'

'Watcha, young'un,' he said, pointing to Bill's uniform. 'St Werberg's is it? Right near our place, but you haven't dropped in.'

'Sorry. I will, but I go to my grandparents after school, and one evening I have Scouts, and there's homework and chores at home.'

'Phew, you're busier than me, a working man. I've just been picking up a fridge part for my boss. Normally, I get home quite late.'

'Are you busy in the evenings? Is there any chance you can get round to see Ted again? Nothing's happened and it's a bit of a problem.'

'If I can help, I will, mate.' Colin fell in beside him. 'Shall I walk up to Primley Road with you while you tell me what's what?'

'Righto.' They walked in step while he explained how Ted was. He ended, 'You might help with that rehab thing. Nothing's been done for Ted.'

Colin nodded. 'Typical. It's not right. I'm going to get into politics now we've got Labour in power.'

'How do you do that?'

'Go to meetings, complain, stand up for the lads. There was supposed to be help on hand when we got demobbed.'

'Will there be help for Ted? He's a super chap, really. He did handstands and card tricks before he went to war. And he was always joking. I want him back like that. Everyone does.'

Colin laid an arm across Bill's shoulders. 'It's tough. He's not the only serviceman come back a different person.'

'But will you go up to see them sometimes, after you finish work? Ted may cheer up, seeing you,' His voice tailed off, 'sooner or later.'

Colin's lips were pushed forward, like someone solving problems. 'There is a way this could work for all of us.'

'How?'

'You've seen how cramped Ma's place is. I have to sleep on the settee and it's a small living room anyway. Apart from her bedroom, the scullery and privy, it's all we've got. When Dad died, Ma had to let out the upstairs and my old bedroom with it. So now I'm back home, it's made life difficult for her, though she's glad to have me.'

'Yes.' It was true that Mrs Donnington's home was hardly big enough for one.

'So,' Colin took a breath, 'if you could persuade your grandad to let me do out their box room, I could rent it off them. It would be a bit of money for them and I'd be around to help with Ted after work.'

Bill nearly jumped in the air. 'That'd be spiffing! Sorting the stuff in the box room would give Ted something to do. I'll ask them tomorrow. I go up almost every day.' He stopped.

'What?'

'But if you find out more stuff about Ted and what happened in the war, will you tell me but NOT Kenneth?

He sneers about my uncle, and I don't want Mother to know what happened, or Nanny.'

'I see. You're a real old protector, aren't you? Big for your age and grown-up with it.'

He felt his cheeks flush.

'So. If you're going to your nan's tomorrow, I'll wait to hear what she and your grandad say, eh?'

'Right you are.' Bill turned into the gate of forty-three, smiling.

Colin hitched his jacket further onto his shoulders and raised a goodbye hand. 'See you in a day or two, then.'

At last there was some sort of solution. Colin would help Grandad move about, keep an eye on Ted, find out what rehab help there was.

He went inside to get Mother's help to persuade Nanny and Grandad that it was a brilliant idea.

Chapter Twenty-four

Dad had missed Bill's birthday and Kenneth's, and now it was December. His last letter said that he would be properly demobbed before the end of 1945, but hadn't given a date for arrival, so no-one was expecting him this Tuesday evening. Bill was on the stairs fixing one of the stair rods when the doorbell sounded twice. Kenneth's warbling paused. 'Who's that at the door?'

Bill had been trying not to listen, let alone admire Kenneth's choir practice, so he concentrated fixing the stair rods. They kept getting loose. 'I can't get the door, Mother, I'm holding this rod in place.'

'Coming,' Mother called as she came out of the parlour, irritated that her wireless programme was being interrupted. 'Another wretch doing his ring-and-run-away, no doubt.'

Round the Horne boomed down the hall together with her sigh, while Kenneth shouted out, 'Is that him? Is it Dad?'

Did he have a sixth sense? For at that moment, the front door opened with a key. And it was him.

'A bell to announce, a key to open. You didn't expect me so soon, Marcia?' Dad stepped inside, a raincoat over one arm, his swollen kitbag preventing the door from shutting at first.

'No,' Mother squeaked. 'No! But it's wonderful.' Mother's hug and kiss only stopped when Aunty rushed to hug Dad too.

'Oh, Herbert! Home at last! Lovely!' Then she ran back into the kitchen to put the kettle on. She must have held Jill back because Jill's squeaks of excitement didn't get further than the door.

Bill put his head through the banisters and took a long look. It was very odd to see Dad in khaki uniform wearing ugly black boots that turned up a bit by the toes. He was like an actor stepping off a newsreel; only newsreels always showed soldiers with a wide smile making the victory sign. Those were missing on Dad.

Kenneth had glided rapidly to the landing but Bill made the rampant stair rod a barrier. He pressed his face to the banisters, blocking Kenneth's way. He wasn't going to let Kenneth be first this time. Anyway, they shouldn't interrupt Mother and Dad just yet.

After they had kissed and hugged again, Mother held Dad at arm's length. 'I'll have to learn to know you all over again.'

'I know, dearest, I know.'

Bill knelt still, ignoring Kenneth's pushes from behind. It was exciting, Dad arriving, but he hadn't lived with Dad since he was seven, or even been with him more than the odd two days at a time. Things were going to be different at home now. It felt like a loss as well as a gain. He was the one who'd been Mother's handyman, the person she looked to when things went wrong. He wouldn't be important now, with Dad in charge.

Mother's smile made her whole face glow. She looked Dad up and down as if to make sure he was there. 'Thank goodness you're home at last. Thank goodness you're in one piece.'

She shouldn't have said that because Uncle Frank was in lots of pieces. Had Kenneth heard? Luckily Aunty was still in the kitchen.

'Indeed I'm fortunate to be so. And how well you look, Marcia.' He smiled and held her by the tops of the arms. He turned to the boys coming down the stairs, one behind the other. Somehow, Kenneth was now in front.

'Hello, boys!' Dad stepped forward to shake Kenneth's hand hard and long. 'Are you settled in here,

Kenneth?' He put his hand on Kenneth's bony shoulder. 'I hope you feel fully at home? Yes? *All things must change, to something new, to something strange* – Longfellow. Studied him yet? There's a copy of his work on the garden room bookshelf, I recall. Ah, we shall be all right, shan't we, son?'

'Hello, Dad.' Bill came forward as Dad turned to him. Now their eyes were at the same level, which was a shock. Dad's were hazel coloured. Bill hadn't noticed that before. He must get his own green eyes from – not Mother, hers were dark, dark brown. A tiny shudder went through him. It was Uncle Frank who'd had green eyes.

Dad was looking Bill up and down as he shook hands. 'So here I am, back again to family life. It's been a long time since you galloped up the hall on that wooden horse, isn't it?'

A giggle sounded behind. Kenneth was paying close attention and would rag Bill about that for sure.

'Made yourself useful since you've been home, Bill?'

He nodded, not sure what to say.

'Good, good. *Choose the life which is most useful and habit will make it the most agreeable*, Sir Francis Bacon.'

One saying for each of them. Bill grimaced at the habit of living with Kenneth. It wasn't agreeable. 'Change to something strange' was nearer the mark.

Now Jill pelted down the hall. 'Daddy, it's me. Here I am.' And Dad had to catch the flying leap she made towards him.

He held Jill up high. 'So my little lady, not so little nowadays, isn't that so?' He placed her down gently to stand beside him. 'And heavier than my kitbag, which is certainly saying something. What has your mother been feeding you on? Roast lion?'

She giggled and held hard onto his arm. How strange for Dad to joke. So, Jill wasn't going to have the sayings to puzzle over; no quotations for girls.

Kenneth was smiling but silent. Bill looked at him out of the corner of his eye. What was he planning about Dad's presence? Oh heck. He'd be thinking how to get Dad to prevent Dwaine from coming.

The kettle boiled and when they crowded into the kitchen, Aunty had already roughly laid a table for speed. Bill's lips felt dry and he couldn't stop his hands fidgeting. Jill was at Dad's knee fiddling with his badges, then one part of his uniform, then another. The two mothers gabbled away with all the news until Dad held up both hands. 'Tea first, say? The cup that cheers.'

Mother inclined her head. 'Of course. So much to say, so much to hear about, Herbert.'

'We're all energized by the arrival of our hero,' Aunty turned to the boys, 'aren't we, boys?'

But Bill was as silent as Kenneth, who was probably thinking about his mother's hero in the USA.

After two cups of tea and a Bath bun with a scrape of marg, and the shortest reference to the fact that he had been serving in a major war, Dad stood up and stretched. 'I must unpack my kitbag. It's stuffed full of washing (Mother groaned) and a couple of souvenirs.'

'Oooh,' Jill pulled at its strap.

'Wait, young lady. Most of it is very dull indeed.' He began to pull out the contents. After the clothes for laundering and his soap bag, Dad pulled out a large fat rolled package, wrapped in brown paper. He turned down his mouth as he looked at Mother. 'Now, dearest, you will hardly recognise me if I wear this ill-fitting suit. We were offered the following: a flat hat or flat cap. A clear choice there! A double-breasted pinstripe three-piece suit, or trousers and jacket. The suit sounded good but they failed to warn us of the limited choice of size. You can tell what I think of it from the fact that I chose to return home in uniform.' He threw back his head and laughed, not sounding like himself. 'And guess what, round every

174

corner some spiv offering good money for the suits. They'll sell them on the black market, of course. Nice profit.'

'That's dreadful, Herbert! The government are trying to fit servicemen out properly.'

'And what's a chippie or decorator going to do with a three-piece pin-striped suit? Go to a funeral, that's about it.'

The women shook their heads at each other, tutting.

'I'm also the owner of two new shirts with matching collar studs, the least awful tie I could find, a pair of shoes that almost fit, and that raincoat,' he jerked his head towards it, lying across an old *Sunday Chronicle*. 'And I get to keep the kitbag and anything of my own I managed to salvage. Lucky me.'

Kenneth actually swapped a glance with Bill, one that recognised the sour tone of Dad's cheery words.

Mother said in a housewifely voice, 'Well, Herbert, someone will be glad of the pinstripe. Obviously someone in your position couldn't sell it to a spiv. You don't have to wear it. Luckily your own suits are still hanging in the wardrobe with fresh mothballs inserted in the pockets. You'll soon be looking your old self.'

'And old is how I feel, let me tell you.'

He delved into the depths of the kitbag and handed over two pairs of gloves. 'One pair each.'

Mother and Aunty took them, looking impressed. 'Thank you so much. They're very fine.'

'Strangely, good shops in France don't seem to be suffering the shortages you have been talking of, and clothes are not on rations there, either.'

'Well!' said Aunty, stroking her gloves. 'The French caved in and let us fight without them, and now they're better off than we are! A fine state of affairs.'

Dad pressed bloodless lips together and nodded. He pulled a knobbly parcel loosely wrapped in brown paper. 'Here, Marcia. Booty.'

Jill crept near as Mother unwrapped it, but then sank to her knees disappointed.

'I don't quite know what we'll do with these,' said Mother doubtfully, turning over the carved wooden bottle stoppers in one hand. 'It's not as if we were drinkers.'

'At least they haven't been taken off some poor dead soldier,' said Dad. 'I found them in an abandoned inn. I thought they were rather decent. And here's some food.' He placed some army tins on the dining room table. 'Bully beef plus some unmarked surprises. Not caviar, but still welcome in these harsh days of rationing, isn't that so?'

'Definitely, Herbert.'

Bill waited for the quote, but Dad was now pulling out a lengthy piece of white material. 'You'll be able to make good use of this, Doreen.'

Aunty squealed. 'You've managed to save your parachute!'

'Yes. Although everyone was told to turn them in, I reckoned I'd earned this. We were dropped a trifle short so we came down in a forest. I narrowly missed being the fairy at the top of a tree.'

Kenneth laughed, his voice trilling up and down. It was certainly rare for Dad to crack a joke.

Aunty was running the white stuff through both hands. 'The silk is wonderful for ladies' clothes, Herbert. Clever you. The things we can do with this, Marcia!' She probably meant *I*. After all, Aunty was the one who cut and sewed. The material went on and on unfolding itself from the kitbag as she pulled.

'Wonderful. It's so smooth. There'll be enough for gowns, nighties, petticoats for both of us,' said Mother holding a section up to her face.

'I like that stuff, Aunty. Let me feel.' Jill scrunched up the material in one hand.

'We shall get you a pretty blouse out of this, dear,' Aunty nodded to her, 'as well as our ladies' things. What riches!'

Jill held onto Dad's arm until he pulled out some ribbons and some elaborately decorated postcards. 'I got these somewhere in Holland. You see, little missie. I didn't forget you.' He straightened up, bringing the almost empty kitbag onto his knees.

'Now boys, under these socks, for which you will be very grateful this winter, there's something else for you.' He placed several pairs of khaki wool socks on top of Aunty's mending basket. She would darn the toes to make sure they lasted longer. 'I managed to get you a book each. Not easy, I can tell you. There's a German grammar and a Dutch history. Who would like which?' He held up both volumes.

It was so disappointing. Other boys' fathers had brought back all sorts of goodies. 'Thank you, Dad.' Bill was in no rush to take either book. Kenneth could choose. There was little chance Bill would be learning German or Dutch at school.

Kenneth put a hand on each cover and stroked them. 'Lovely leather. May we look inside?'

Dad held them forward with a satisfied smile. 'I guessed these would please someone scholarly.'

Kenneth opened each book part way. 'Look, Bill. Such soft paper and it's lovely print. Which do you like best?'

Bill shrugged. Why play Kenneth's beastly game? He jolly well knew Bill wouldn't be interested in foreign language books, whatever their pages were like.

Dad still had both large hands opened flat, supporting the books. 'Very nice, Dad,' Bill said, to be safe.

Kenneth turned to him with a sweet smile. 'Then, Bill, do you mind if I take the German? I can start learning the

177

grammar before the others at school. They offer German in the fourth form, Dad.' Kenneth took the grammar text in one hand and passed the smaller book to Bill.

He took it, closed. 'This will be useful if I'm parachuted into Holland during the next war.'

Aunty squeaked, 'Ooh, Bill. Don't say that, dear. Another war!'

Dad was looking at Bill closely. Was it a surprise to him that his son was using sarcasm? 'Hmm. We're going to take many years to get over this one.'

'Otherwise, Daddy would have given you the parachute,' Jill said brightly.

Bill suppressed a chuckle.

Kenneth put his heel on Bill's toe, pressing down hard, while at the same time turning the pages of his grammar religiously. Bill extracted his foot but said nothing. Now was not the time for a good kick on the back of Kenneth's calf, nor for highlighting Kenneth's sneaky attacks.

Dad asked, 'How's Ted, dear?'

Mother's mouth turned down a trifle. 'Things were dire when we got back and I didn't know how my parents would manage once Bill had school again, but now they've got a lodger, Mrs Doddington's son, and that's made all the difference. Colin was in the same regiment.

'The Doddington boy. He must be, what, in his twenties now?'

'Yes. My parents like him. It's worked out well.'

'Before that, Bill has been round almost every day helping out. Quite a godsend,' said Aunty.

'Well done, Bill. *We do not so much need the help of our friends as the confidence of their help in need.* Epicurus.' He turned to Mother before Bill had worked out the meaning. 'I shall go round, see what I can do for Ted. I'm well aware of having had a light burden during my service and even then, would like to forget what I've seen. Ted had a hard innings. 'These boys,' he waved a hand at them. 'Young men to be. Thank the Lord they were too young to serve. Now that I'm home I must involve myself in their schooling.'

He looked round the kitchen as if he'd never seen it before, and then at him and Kenneth as at items in a museum or a library. 'So Kenneth has a place at Dulwich College. Fortunate, very fortunate.'

'Yes, we're so lucky,' Aunty smiled. 'I did nothing! After VE Day, the head of Friary Grammar contacted the headmaster of Dulwich College on Kenneth's behalf, anxious that he continued with the same advantages he'd been enjoying there.'

'No entrance exam?'

She shook her head. 'Although that is normally essential, it seems that admitting "a student with exceptional artistic talent" was possible. That's as I heard it. I think it was Kenneth's work in the Priory's exhibition that did it. His paintings did seem to be the star attraction. But it's so lucky to get a scholarship when Dulwich College needs restoring. After the big fire there, the parents have to pay increased fees! £18 a term now!'

'Good heavens!' Dad's eyebrows jerked upwards.

'So we're feeling so proud of Kenneth!'

Kenneth was leaning against the wall, one bent leg crossed over his supporting leg, in the way he often did. It looked neutral and superior. Bill hated the pose as much as Kenneth's smirk, a half smile, with one side higher than the other.

'What an excellent opportunity for you, Kenneth. Are you enjoying it there?'

'Wonderful, Dad. The masters are top-hole. The science is so exciting, I adore Latin, and the Art is absolutely fine, which is the main thing for me.'

Dad nodded, and his pleased expression stayed put some moments.

Bill waited for the inevitable.

'And Bill?' Dad turned towards Mother. 'How has school worked out for you?'

'It's all right, Dad, I mean, good.'

Dad continued looking at Mother. 'So – St Werberg's.'

'Yes. I didn't want him with the rough children at – you know where.'

'I assumed Bill would go to Wandsworth Grammar.'

'The school only came back from Surrey this summer, and now they're amalgamating with the Central School. I thought that might bring the tone down. Anyway, he sat an exam and didn't do well enough, I don't know why.'

Keeping his eyes on the floor Bill justified the poor exam attempts to himself. He'd lost everything else by coming back to Wandsworth, so he needed to keep football even if he went to a school that wasn't as good as a grammar.

'St Werberg's boys are always so polite. We used to share lessons with the top year when I was at Larchmere Girls, and ballroom dancing.'

Dad didn't look impressed at the thought. 'But academically?'

'Bill seems to me a practical boy, all the things he's fixed in the house and garden. I did write to you all this.'

'You did, Marcia, yes. And it's a great pity I wasn't home in time to sort this out. But I dare say you're settled, Bill? What do you think about the school?'

'It's all right, Dad. Football's super. I play left wing and I score lots of times.'

'Well enough. But the work, the actual reason you attend school?'

'I enjoy not having to write essays all the time,' Bill said, trying a bit of cheek since Dad had been making jokes earlier.

Dad's eyebrows beetled up towards the ceiling. Another saying was coming. *Whoever neglects learning in his youth loses the Past, and is dead to the Future –*

Euripides. And it would be too much to hope that you know who that is, so I will tell you he was—'

'A Greek playwright,' put in Kenneth. 'Our English teacher adores him.'

Bill saw Dad's eyes brighten.

He shrugged before he could stop himself. His own English teacher had enough difficulty getting the boys to stay in their seats during the lesson. Bill struggled to think – had he heard of any playwright? Only Shakespeare – and that was through Angela.

'It would have been lovely for the boys to be together,' said Aunty. 'Bill is clever as well as practical.'

Dad corrected her. 'No. You just heard him. He doesn't like writing any more than drawing. So he's different from Kenneth, and academic work might be wasted on him.'

'Never mind, old chap,' said Kenneth, placing a hand on Bill's shoulder.

He heaved it off vigorously.

'So protective,' said Aunty. 'Don't shrug Kenneth off, dear.' She gave Bill a mildly resentful glance. It was a beastly shame, Aunty deserved a nicer son than Kenneth.

Bill waited to hear Dad's plans for him, but Jill clamoured for Dad's attention, clambering onto his lap, full of chatter. 'Daddy, Daddy. I am one of the best readers in my class and I only have to share a book with two others.'

'I'm more worried about Jill,' Mother said. 'Forty-one in her class and she cried every day for her first two weeks.'

'Thank goodness she's not a boy,' said Dad.

Bill went to the hall to take his jacket off the hallstand. He could call on Colin, or someone from school, but his hand stopped halfway to the pegs. It was Dad's first night home. He shouldn't go out. He left his jacket hanging beside Aunty's mac, Mother's shopping coat and

Kenneth's blazer. They needed more hooks now Dad was home. Would it be him who banged some up? He mooched back to the kitchen.

Mother was saying, 'If we'd known the date of your demob, Herbert, we'd have had a special meal ready.'

Aunty flapped her hands. 'Go and sit in comfort, all of you. I will find something. We saved the peaches and evap. from Dwaine's parcel, and I think there's jam for our bread.'

'Ah, Dwaine. We must have a talk about him, Doreen.'

Aunty blushed, and as Mother pulled Dad into the garden room, Kenneth added, 'Yes, Dad, that's important.'

Kenneth had now dropped his film star pose and sidled nearer to Dad. 'They play cricket at Dulwich, but I haven't any whites.'

'We must get you some. You haven't had a sport before, Kenneth. That's important. Frank would have wanted that.'

Everyone's eyes turned downwards.

Bill's did too, so that he was looking at his shoes. If Kenneth needed cricket whites, gosh, Bill badly needed football boots. How would he ever get to play like Stanley Matthews in ordinary boots? He blurted out, 'Uncle Frank liked football. He might have wanted me to have proper football boots.'

'Like the ones I gave you,' Kenneth put in quickly. He wouldn't let anyone forget the one nice thing he had done for Bill.

'They were super, but my feet have grown so much since then. It was two years ago.' His voice trailed off. 'May I have football boots, Dad?'

'Succeed in your studies first, Bill. Play comes later.'

Kenneth nodded as though he was one of the masters. 'Yes, Bill. Like how I have to learn my declensions before I go to choir on Wednesdays.'

Bill gritted his teeth. Moving well away from Kenneth, he said, 'You never got to see my bravery medal, Dad. I'll just go upstairs and get it.'

Once in his room with the door shut, he gave way to his fury. He felt like kicking the wall, and ripping the wretched Dutch book in half. He put it on his bookshelf to be safe from his feelings and went to his secret place to get his medal out. He wasn't innocent any more, like at the Pawseys' where he'd relied on his bed base as a hidey hole for the precious shashka photo. Kenneth's theft demonstrated that Bill needed to be more cunning.

He went to the wall. Aunty had put one of Kenneth's paintings in an old wooden frame for Kenneth to hang up. The back had several layers of card behind the painting because of the thickness of the wood. Kenneth would never think to search for Bill's treasures among things of his own. He slid the cardboard aside and took out the medal, its stripy ribbon band a little faded now. The medal wasn't secret, but it mustn't go missing like the photograph.

Perhaps Dad would tell everyone about it, boast about it, even. Kenneth had excellent paintings and would be bought cricket whites, but he hadn't won a medal and he wasn't even brave at all.

Chapter Twenty-five

Sunday. No school, no football. Kenneth warbling some kind of chant in the bedroom. The cellar door open. A draught along the hall. The weather was cold.

He peered down into the cellar. Dad was removing all signs of their wartime shelter and checking the level of their coal. Bill moved off to find Mother.

Well out of Dad's earshot, Jill was whining, 'When can I go to Iris's again? We'll be good. Please, please. I like her better than any of the girls at school.'

Mother made a face at Bill as if she expected him to help out. 'I'll phone Iris's mother, Jill. Perhaps she'll be able to come over here. So shh now. Run and play outside.'

'It's co-o-old!'

'Upstairs, then.'

'That's cold, too.'

'Just put on a second cardigan, then, and stop making a fuss.'

Christmas was coming soon and there was no sign it would be jolly. He thought he'd better get his own request in quickly before Dad came up from the cellar and asked to see his homework. 'Can I go to Alan's?'

'*May*, not 'can'. Go on, then. But get back before dark.'

He pulled his new school mac on, and slipped out before Dad emerged from the cellar.

When the bus slowed to a halt, he could see Alan waiting.

'My dad's back,' Bill shouted as he leapt off the running board. 'Got home last Tuesday.'

'Super. Bet you're glad.'

They trotted side by side alongside a row of trees whose colour had turned to a brittle brown. All the other trees were already bare.

'Is he okay about Dwaine coming?'

'I think so. Kenneth kept making pointed remarks, hoping Dad would scotch the idea. When he didn't, Kenneth whinged about it being inconvenient for Mother. Dad's discussed what's appropriate with Aunty. Dwaine isn't to stay at our house, but nearby, so Aunty is reading accommodation adverts all the time now.'

'That'll be tough with everyone who's trying to get a room. Mum says the *Share Your Home* drive is a nightmare. There isn't enough accommodation.'

'Kenneth will be flipping thrilled if they can't get anywhere. I'm looking at all the cards in the shop windows. Someone left a newspaper on the bus and I tore this advert out in case it will do. *Well-furnished, every convenience, suit person out during day, use of bath (geyser).* Sounds okay? And Dad said he'd talk to likely people. He has contacts.'

'And he's on leave with nothing much to do. Where did he serve?'

'Holland. France. He didn't say much but I don't think he killed anyone. He wouldn't.'

'Any souvenirs?'

'Bottle top things, carved wooden figures with cork underneath. Mother wasn't very pleased because she and Dad don't have alcohol, except at Christmas.'

'I was meaning for you.'

Bill almost growled. He stopped by a bench. 'Ha. I'll show you if we sit down a minute.' He sat and opened his satchel. 'Jill got ribbons, our mothers got posh gloves from France as well as the parachute silk for making petticoats. Kenneth and I got boring books. We were supposed to choose which one of two. Kenneth was pleased, of course. He had the grammar because he's

185

starting German, so that left this for me.' He almost threw it onto Alan's lap. 'Not Russian history, but Dutch. Double Dutch to me,' his laugh was hollow. He hated himself for saying it but the words spat out. 'Other boys at school got sweets and toys and all sorts of things their fathers brought back for them. And Dad was so interested in Kenneth's new school he hardly bothered with me.'

Alan was opening the book and examining it, page by page.

Bill went on. 'And look at the stuff your father brings back! Foreign comics, that spicy sausage, the wind-up boy that walks, and I bet that's not all.'

Alan looked embarrassed and hunched his shoulders. 'I know it doesn't seem fair, but perhaps this book is valuable. Look, it's signed and it's by a professor. Do you know what I think?'

'No, what?' Bill could hear his voice sounding sulky, like Jill when Mother said she had something nice for dinner. Jill never agreed that it was.

'You know knights?'

'Uh?'

'Knights. To be a knight you have to have three things, and I reckon you've got two now. The first is the sword of a brave man. The second is a book written by a learned man.'

'Is it? Interesting.' Bill stopped huffing and complaining. A sabre was a sword and its owner had been brave. But it would take some miracle for Mr Durban give it to him. *Bestow* it. If ever. He did have the wretched learned book. 'And what's the third thing?'

'A flower from a faithful lover.'

Bill pushed him in the ribs, laughing. 'Oh yeah! I don't know any girls, except Jill and her kid friends. We don't even have girls at school.'

'You'll have to wait until there's dancing in the top year. If it's like our school, you do it with the top class of the girls' school.'

They shoved each other, laughing and rolling over the frosty grass together.

Knights! Bill remembered how often he'd got *Tales of King Arthur* from the library before he was evacuated. 'I used to imagine being Lancelot, handsome and gallant, the bravest knight of all.'

'Not a good choice! Lancelot went on to steal Guinevere's love.'

'Really? That's awfully rotten. Then I should be Arthur himself, the only one who could pull the sword from the stone. I used to dream about it, only it was never the sword that came aloft in my hand but the shashka.'

Alan shoved him in the side as they both burst out laughing, and Bill shoved him back.

'Do you think I'm daft, thinking about the shashka so much?'

Alan knelt up, brushing the grass from his smart blazer. 'I hadn't thought.' He paused, obviously thinking now. 'It's just part of you, same as Biggles was part of that boy, Marley, remember him?'

Bill frowned. Marley was a dolt who ran about wearing old sunglasses, mounting the fence, pretending to climb up into the cockpit of his plane. 'I don't want to be a kid just pretending,' he said.

Alan clapped him on the shoulder. 'We found some real history, remember. You can find some more now, at school or at the library. You can become an expert about Cossacks and their sabres.'

Bill felt a grin start at the sides of his mouth. That was more like it. If he became expert, all the more reason for people (Mr Durban) to realise that he, Sir William of Wilson, was the rightful owner of the shashka in the future.

Chapter Twenty-six

There was a New Year's Day postcard from Mrs Youldon on the mat. It was the first with a 1946 postmark. He hid it in the pages of an old *Boy's Own* so that he could read it over and no-one know. He knew it annoyed Mother that he kept in contact. He turned a page of the comic as he perched on the edge of a chair to be nearer the small fire in the parlour.

A bitter wind whooshed in as the front door opened and shut. Kenneth came in from the library wrapped in about six scarves. He stood rubbing his hands by Bill's chair so close that it was obvious Bill was supposed to move from in front of the fire. Since it was only a few days since Kenneth had been in bed with laryngitis and a high temperature, Bill thought he'd better move. He put his *Boy's Own* under one arm and stood nearby. It was jolly cold.

Aunty hurried in with a mug of hot cocoa. 'Here you are, Kenneth. Sit and drink this slowly, and not too close to the fire or you'll get chilblains.'

Kenneth huddled himself into the chair, grasping the hot mug, while Aunty took his scarves into the hall.

Bill snapped, 'You could at least have hung those up!'

'I've brought you a library book, so stop complaining. *Robinson Crusoe*. About time you read something more challenging than a comic.'

Bill took it and slipped his comic inside the front cover. The story did look interesting, not that it reduced his anger at Kenneth's jibe, though he should be used to that by now.

Before they could get into an argument, Dad came in, also rubbing his hands. 'Make the most of the fire, boys, there's not much coal left or even Coalite and we've reached the limit of our ration.'

'How bad?' There'd been ice on the inside of the bedroom windows for over a week.

Dad jabbed at the newspaper notice.

'"*You may not obtain more than 8 cwt coal including Coalite between January and February.*" Ha! and your total can't be more than thirty-four hundredweight over the twelve months!'

Kenneth looked up with a pained expression. 'We'll just have to pray that the weather thaws, then.'

It would be nice to retort, 'You can always return to your sick bed if the house is too cold,' but Dad was standing too near, rifling through the library books Kenneth had brought in.

'*Life of Byron*, Kenneth. We must compare notes. And for Bill? *Robinson Crusoe*. Good choice. Now, Bill – did you know that Daniel Defoe (Foe was his real name) was virtually the first novelist?'

Bill shook his head. He'd never heard of Defoe, *Foe* would have interested him more.

Kenneth's body blocked the warmth from reaching Bill. Better to go for a run and leave Kenneth to hog the only fire in the house. Or should he go up to Nanny's – unless Dad had just been. 'Have you been visiting Ted, Dad?'

'I have. I do what little I can.'

'He's in a bad way, isn't he?' said Kenneth in an old man's gossipy voice.

'Not good, I'll allow. When Colin's at work, I think the grandparents struggle.'

Kenneth leant towards Dad. 'Poor things. I shall go one Saturday and give them a little concert. They enjoy my singing.'

'They do.' Dad nodded, one hand stroking his chin.

'I feel a bit sorry for Bill,' said Kenneth, as though Bill were not immediately behind his chair.

Dad raised his eyebrows questioningly.

'I mean, we have no madness,' he coughed to indicate he must find a better word, '*mental* problems in our side of the family, do we, Dad?'

Dad turned, and now he wasn't pleased. He sat down on the worn leather armchair opposite Kenneth. 'A few years older, Kenneth, and you could have been up a mountain or hunkered down in a trench, hungry, muddy, wet, suffering what Ted suffered, facing the constant bombing around you, seeing death, day after day. Don't be surprised if that's had an effect on decent men, probably many hundreds of decent men. We don't know. But combat stress is not madness.'

Kenneth's face tightened and he readjusted it to look sympathetic. 'No. It's tremendously tragic, of course.'

Bill hid his grin. At last Dad had seen how mean Kenneth was and had corrected him! He wanted Kenneth to know he'd heard. 'Dad, I'm just off for a run if you've been to Nanny's.' How Kenneth would hate him witnessing Dad's put down.

Dad softened it immediately. 'The Odeon National Cinema club have a nationwide painting and drawing competition for children up to the age of fifteen, Kenneth. There's a good prize.'

Kenneth swung his body around. 'Should I enter?'

'You should. *Draw or paint anything relating to the sea or the Merchant Navy.*'

Bill went for his coat and balaclava. 'I'm going now. I've got football practice later, Dad.' How would Kenneth know about the Merchant Navy? But, then, he really could paint just about anything.

It was four o-clock when he got back from football practice. Kenneth emerged from the dining room. 'Try to clean yourself up, dear chap. I am having school friends to tea any minute and I would prefer not to introduce some ruffian as my cousin.'

Bill clenched his fist deciding what he could say and what he couldn't. *This is my house. This was always my home before you got here.* It was like having constipation, being the boy who hadn't taken his Syrup of Figs: so much to come out, and so much held back.

Mother came in with a cake that must have been baked with the precious American sugar and the week's egg, as well as a lace cloth for the dining table. She said, 'Run along and get washed, Bill. Isn't it nice that Kenneth has Dulwich College friends that will come to an ordinary home?'

Did she really think it nice? To be safely neutral he answered, 'You're doing them a fancy tea. They should be glad.'

Mother smiled, a smile with lips as hard and smooth as old marg. 'That's not the way the world works, Bill.'

In fact, Kenneth's friends turned out to be perfectly decent, polite to Mother and Aunty and quite friendly to Bill. After tea they even helped clear the table before going into the garden room to play Monopoly with a set that Dad had borrowed specially from someone at his work. No-one had done anything like that for Bill when Alan visited.

Then, as January took hold, Bill had no time to think about niggles over Kenneth. When the snow fell and stayed on the ground, crisping up with worsening temperatures, the boys at school were thrilled. The prefects allowed snowball fights within reason. Then the snow was so high that it came over the tops of wellington boots and stopped the fun. There was a lot of shovelling in the freezing roads and paths; he was often called on to do it.

As the cold went relentlessly on and on, the difficulty of getting food supplies meant dinners were even worse than before, so that people were bad-tempered with hunger.

At home, there were not enough clothes to keep warm, not enough blankets for the bitter nights. Dad didn't dare use up the last of the Coalite, but eked out the supply with coal dust from the far reaches of the cellar. It was only enough for the boiler, so only the kitchen had any heat. This made every day totally wretched, and ice coated the inside of the bedroom windows.

Worse, Mother caught 'flu and then Kenneth fell ill. Even Bill felt anxious about Kenneth's hacking cough and the doctor could not call; he was too tied up with emergencies and heavily pregnant mothers. Aunty, and then Dad, had very heavy colds. Bill ventured out in wellington boots and all three of his jumpers under his coat to shop for what he could find, and then to take hot drinks to everyone as well as fragments of food. If only he could cook! Soup was what people needed and he didn't know how to make it.

Kenneth had grey dents in his cheeks and was coughing too much to hold the mug of Bovril Bill had brought him. Bill pulled the blanket from his bed and wrapped it round Kenneth's shoulders. 'What medicine do you need? I don't want to worry Aunty. She's asleep.'

Kenneth shook his head. 'Best not bother. It's too hard on my stomach.'

Each day, Bill scraped out a hole from the ice on their window and peered out, desperate for signs of a thaw. Each day the cold remained, or got worse.

The wireless told of extreme weather country-wide. The sea froze over in Minehead! Bill remembered that was a long way south.

The electricity cuts for five hours every day continued even now, as if the government didn't know that everyone was freezing. It was almost a relief to be out of the house, so despite everything, he did get to school.

On the long-awaited day of the thaw, he got home to find Mother on her feet again and Dad huddled in a blanket in his study. Bill went into the parlour still in his coat and balaclava to start his homework, and found Kenneth there, up and dressed.

'I've made you something,' he said. 'Sorry it won't warm you up much.'

It was a still life drawing of a red mug, steam coming from its top. Bill did actually feel warmer from looking at it, and not just because it looked so life-like.

Chapter Twenty-seven

'If this last winter was the worst I've ever known, I think spring 1947 will be the best!' Aunty was looking pretty in a lemon coloured blouse she'd found in the church Bring and Buy sale.

She delved into her pocket and waved an airmail over the kitchen table. She'd obviously waited to tell her news until Dad had left for work and Kenneth to the library. 'Ten days and Dwaine will be here! It's been such a long wait.'

Mother said, 'Goodness! Will he? Let's have all the details.'

'He's arriving on the *Queen Mary*, leaving New York.'

Bill asked, 'Is that near where he lives?'

'No, it takes a whole day on the bus to get there. Imagine that! The bus goes through four states!'

Bill thought of the bumpy coach that had taken him and the other children from the evacuation train to the country village hall. How terrible to be stuck on a bus all day.

Mother obviously thought the same. 'What a journey, Doreen! And think, that's what you'd have to do if you went there.'

'He'll stay a night or two there before embarking, so he can do some shopping.'

'And then a week or so on the sea passage?'

'Yes. I'll go to Southampton on the train to meet him. Even that's an excitement for me.'

'Will you come straight back, I mean he'll be tired and perhaps travel sick?'

'No,' she blushed. 'We will stay at a hotel for two nights before coming home.'

It was lovely for Aunty to have all this to look forward to. Before he'd even thought about whether they would be sharing a bedroom, Mother giggled and gasped. 'Staying over, Doreen! What shall I say to Herbert? Won't he think it risqué?'

Mother's face had an expression he'd not seen before. It was a mixture of envy, embarrassment and shock.

Aunty tossed her head. 'It will be totally decent. Dwaine is a gentleman. She leant forward. 'Marcia, I'll be able to wear my new dress. It was worth every one of the minutes I queued for it, or was it hours! If only I could travel first class so that it won't get grubby in the train!'

Bill knew the dress was pale blue. It would be a risk to wear it. Every time Dad went on a train he needed a clean shirt the next day. His collar and cuffs had black stains by the time he got home. London was so dirty, and it was worst around the rail stations. Aunty needed to look her best for Dwaine's arrival.

'Oh Doreen. Take your old mac to cover it until you get there. I wish I could get to wear a new dress and stay in a hotel! Count your fortunes.'

Aunty laughed, a trill like Kenneth's soprano. 'I do, but I must warn Herbert and then—' she sighed '— Kenneth. Even though he's still so pleased about his painting competition, I'll have to choose my words carefully.'

Kenneth had won second prize for his Merchant Navy painting. Disappointingly, the money went into National Savings Certificates for him. It could have bought a cake or something that they could all share. About food, yesterday morning's news headline had made them all feel worse, 'Austerity Must Continue'.

Kenneth should jolly well accept the Dwaine situation. He'd tried his best to poison Dad against him and had gone into the study with Dad several times. He must have lost the argument, for Dad had arranged Dwaine's accommodation with the Benthams next door. He'd told Mother and Aunty, 'The *Share Your Home* scheme means people like the Benthams with a good house and no dependants would have some stranger billeted on them, so they're jolly glad to have a lodger that you two know.'

Bill rubbed his hands. It would be super-duper having Dwaine. There'd be an excuse to go to the West End. He'd get Alan over and they'd take Dwaine to play football up at Garretts' Green, perhaps even to watch a match at Chelsea!

He came to from these thoughts to hear Mother and Aunty exchanging excited comments about clothes, and places to show Dwaine. The chat went on and on, until the front door opened, and they all fell silent. It didn't take long for someone to go to the library.

Mother stood quickly, saying, 'He's back. I'll leave you to it, Doreen. Best if I'm out. I was going to do the shopping now, anyway.'

Bill slipped upstairs. Poor Aunty, it wasn't going to be easy. He sat on his bunk. Aunty's voice sounded from downstairs, calling Kenneth into the parlour. Safe from interruption for a while, Bill bent down and got his camera from under the bed. Last time he'd used it was when he'd run round the village snapping his memories. That was months and months ago and he still hadn't had that film developed. He had no new film, of course, and no money to get one. Perhaps he could get a paper round or errand boy's job. He was thirteen, after all, although in the bread queue, women were complaining that the demobbed soldiers were taking anything that was on offer, even boys' jobs.

He opened the camera, cleaned the lens with his breath, dusted the concertina bits with his hanky, and closed it again before putting it back beneath his bunk.

His album sat tied into its own box on his side of the bookcase. Because Kenneth sneered at pictures that were photographed, rather than painted, the album was fairly safe from his prying fingers. Bill opened the cover. His photos were stuck with the black photo corners his village science teacher had given him. Some had lost their glue so that photos wobbled between perhaps two corners instead of four.

On the first page were the pigs, Laurel and Hardy. They'd been so important in his first months of evacuation. He missed them even now and the memory hurt; the awfulness of seeing Hardy's nose, lifted up towards him as if in prayer before they were driven towards the butchers that dreadful day, their very last. It had been even worse when it ended with the empty pen and the shocking news of Uncle Frank's death. Worse still when Kenneth had to stay with him while the mothers went to the funeral. He shuddered. And the scene after the funeral! That had been a truly terrible few days.

He turned a page. Sally and Timmy. Mrs Youldon had been so thrilled with the photo. He smiled at the little ones' faces. When he'd shown them, how amazed they were to be in a photograph! It was the first time they'd actually seen their own faces, for their cottage didn't have the luxury of a mirror.

The next page held photos of dear Mr and Mrs Pawsey, so comfortable and safe. He sighed, longing to be with all of them right now.

He turned a page. Not all his important people were in the album. He needed photos of Ted, Nanny and Grandad and the Durbans, and, if he could get it, a new one of the shashka. There were a lot of blank pages waiting to be filled. He closed his album carefully, before Kenneth came upstairs.

He hadn't thrown away his one photo of Kenneth. It wasn't in the album. He hated the thing, and kept it separate. He'd only taken it because Dad insisted he take one of Kenneth. He could throw it away, of course, but when it was developed, the chemist had said how good it was. Kenneth hadn't wanted to be photographed while he was feeling so sad after Uncle Frank's death. When Bill lifted the camera, Kenneth threw his hands over his face and the window light made them shine.

Now that he'd learned so much from the photography manual Mrs Routledge had given him, he could look at it with new eyes. The photograph was like a – Bill couldn't think of a word. It was like a piece of art itself. You could even see all the paintings Kenneth had done, pasted behind him on the wall. Bill looked at the photo as if he didn't know the pale boy, his curls falling forward on his brow, whose white hands, the sunlight streaming through them, were like angel birds spread in front of his face. Bill had hidden this photo at the back of the pack but now he felt a thrill to have taken a photo that told a story. Anyone looking at it would ask questions. This was the sort of thing they put in *Picture Post*. He would keep it safely, and if he met a proper photographer, he'd show him; but it wasn't a photo to be put in his album with all the people he loved.

He put the Kenneth photo in an envelope under the album at the bottom of its box, which he secured with a length of hemming tape, making a double bow.

Aunty must surely have done her telling by now. He put his head round his bedroom door in case there was any shouting. There wasn't. Kenneth had known Dwaine was coming. Just like Bill had known that Kenneth was moving in last year. Kenneth would have to face it, and get used to having Dwaine around.

Bill rubbed his hands. There was so much he wanted to show Dwaine. He could take him to see Ted. They might even talk about Africa. But what would happen when Dwaine's stay ended? A sad postcard at Christmas told him Mrs Youldon's sister, Mary, had been whisked away across the Atlantic by her GI, and Tim had added little pictures of the steak, ice cream and washing machine she'd be enjoying.

Bill stepped back rapidly as Kenneth stamped up the stairs and into the bedroom. 'Oh you're here.' He flopped onto Bill's bunk without asking. 'Did you know the Yank is already on his way here? Dad's just too lenient. Anyway, the US of A won't let him be away for long, and Great Britain won't let him stay here for more than a short visit.'

'Perhaps he'll invite you both to America. Dad said he wasn't short of a penny – dollars, I suppose.'

'If Mama lets him talk her into going to America, she needn't think I'm going too. I shall stay here with you lot. Dad'll speak up for me, I know it.'

It was an awful thought: Kenneth but no Aunty. Bill took a moment to think of the right comment. 'You know, Dwaine could be a really good friend for you. Remember how he praised your paintings when you had your school exhibition at the Priory? He might get his rich friends to buy your work.'

Kenneth snorted. 'Rich friends! He works in some kind of factory. Probably left school without any qualifications.'

The sound of the front door opening with a key announced Dad's return home. Bill stifled a sigh. *Thank goodness.* 'Let's go down and see Dad.'

'Yes, let's,' Kenneth added menacingly. 'We'll see what he has to say to Mama staying with the Yank in a hotel, even if they do have separate rooms like she says.'

Chapter Twenty-eight

It was such an excitement, the day Dwaine came to Wandsworth. Aunty had been nervous about Kenneth causing an atmosphere. No-one wanted the visit spoiled. He wouldn't dare to be rude or sarcastic when Dad was around, but there would be many other opportunities.

Luckily, Kenneth was in bed ill again before they arrived.

The whole of that first week, Kenneth was tucked up with the curtains drawn keeping his suffering to himself, while downstairs the house almost shook with the thrill of Dwaine. They didn't usually have visitors, and never one from overseas!

Dad was quietly welcoming. If he minded about another man taking Uncle Frank's place, he didn't show it. It helped that Dwaine was very respectful.

The parlour felt too small to contain Dwaine and his fine suitcase and carry bag. They all helped carry everything into the garden room where Dwaine pleased Mother straight away with his, 'Say, Ma'am! This room is grand; real stylish!'

Jill was soon perched on Dwaine's lap. He opened his suitcase and shared out all sorts of goodies; tins of meat, a little dress for Jill, candies, art pencils for Kenneth. Best of all, six rolls of film for his camera! Six!

Aunty hung on Dwaine's arm, beaming. She must have told him the make of his camera, nice Aunty.

Mother had made cakes, specially, and the extravagance didn't matter, because there'd been sugar in Dwaine's suitcase too.

After tea, Dwaine brought out postcards of his home town, Savannah. Everyone hung over them, amazed at its beautiful gardens, fine squares, everything looking so clean.

'Have you got seaside?' Jill wanted to check all the possibilities of the place.

'Yep. Sea, and river. Savannah's got most things.'

'I'd like to go there.'

'Guess you'll have to wait till you grow up, little lady.'

Bill smiled to himself as he turned over Dwaine's pictures, one by one. There wasn't going to be much here that Kenneth could sneer at. Dwaine didn't "work in a factory". He had been a supervisor in a tool-making business before he signed up for military service. He was a skilled engineer and wouldn't be out of a job. It was the law in Georgia that servicemen returning must be allowed their old job back.

'That's the trouble, here,' Mother said. 'The men are coming back to nothing.'

Bill said, 'Ted can't get his job back.'

'Poor Ted. He wouldn't be able to cope with it, anyway,' Mother turned to Dad.

Dad leant forward to Dwaine. 'Ted's Marcia's brother, East Surrey regiment. He served in much the same places as you, but he had a very bad experience in Dunkirk first. He hadn't got over it when he had to serve again, even though it was some months before they got sent to Africa.'

'And now in no state to work. His nerves, you know,' Mother was going on.

'Gee, that's too bad.'

'Yes. He's lost his chance of a good income. I hope you're in a stronger position, Dwaine.'

Dwaine stretched his shoulders into an expansive shrug. 'We-ell, I've been away four years, not getting the promotion I would've done if I'd stayed home. And war's made me grow some, if you get me. So I reckon it's the neat thing to set up on my own now.'

201

Dad was interested. 'Is that what you've been arranging before coming over?'

'Dead right, Bert: a business loan from the government to set up my own workshop and employ twelve men – ex-servicemen, preferably. Folk'll always need tools and I'm the guy to design them. I'm the guy to train the men, 'n all. I got the building, got the equipment, all fine and dandy. It'll be swell. So it's anchors away when I get back to Georgia.'

Dad leaned forward, blocking Bill's view of Aunty's sparkling eyes. 'This is a fine project. So many men need just that chance. It's clearly a very sound venture with your experience behind it. What was it Einstein said? *Try not to become a man of success but a man of value.* I think you're emulating that.'

'Say, that's real decent of you.'

Aunty was all puffed up with pride. So 'emulating' must be a praising sort of word.

By the time Kenneth was over the flu, or bronchitis, or whatever it was this time, Dwaine was part of the home as if he'd always lived here, and it was Kenneth who was more like the visitor.

Aunty didn't know who to fuss over first when Kenneth was well enough to come downstairs. Dwaine was at his nicest, and Kenneth's sore throat stopped him from saying much. If he rolled his eyes when Dwaine was speaking, it could be put down to his feeling poorly, and anyway, it was Dwaine who was the centre of attention. Kenneth didn't like that, but even he was glad of the treats: in his case, the art pencils Dwaine had brought.

Every time Dwaine spoke, Jill hung onto his words, wanting to hear him say things in 'his funny voice' over and over.

'Say, maybe funny for you, little lady, but all folks talk like that where I come from,' he told her.

Bill loved the sound of the place he came from, as well as having him around. It was impossible to have 'an atmosphere' with someone who was always cheerful, never critical, always ready to help.

Mother had been at her nicest since Dwaine's arrival, only worrying about the poor fare every meal-time once his tins had been used up. 'It must be awful for you, putting up with our meals. The newspaper tells us we get only half the food that Americans are used to, but the Ministry of Food say we're lucky.'

Bill could see that meal-times were a shock to Dwaine, although he was polite about it. 'You Brits are certainly suffering but don't fret. I got my brother Ernie to send another of those food parcels. I guess it'll arrive before we all starve.'

'The Benthams are dreading the day they lose you. They say it's taken the rough edge off their days.'

'Gee. That's nice. It's sure nice for this Yankee to be made welcome in a true British home.'

Dwaine was a blessing to Nanny and Grandad, too. He'd only been in Wandsworth a few days before he caught up with Bill halfway down the road. 'Guess I'm a-comin' with you, buddy. Doreen told me what you're doing for your old folks, and I guess they could do with another man's heave-ho.'

'That'll be super. They'll love to meet you. They might not have met an American ever before.'

When Bill took Dwaine inside he could see it was certainly an excitement for them. Dwaine had some Hershey bars that he put on the table near enough for Grandad to reach.

It wasn't the only visit Dwaine made. Ted was brighter having Dwaine's company, and much more gardening got done. But if they chatted about the war, they didn't do it where Bill could hear.

Alan came over to Wandsworth as often as he could. He'd always loved to be with Dwaine. The three of them went down to the common, with Aunty watching on a bench as they played ball and compared British and American rules.

It was like a competition with Aunty, who could collar Dwaine's company first and longest. Kenneth couldn't have liked this, but he didn't act up. How could he be the only dreary face in the house? Altogether, it felt as if a golden ball had descended on Primley Road, lightening and brightening everyone around.

One evening when Dwaine had gone next door for the night and Kenneth was still not back from choir, Dad settled back in his chair. 'Well, Doreen, I think you're sensible to give your friendship time, rather than rush into anything.'

'Yes, Bert. It's lovely to have a man friend after being alone these last years. We get on so well, but I am taking things slowly, as you say.'

'That's good. You didn't know him for very long in the village; it wasn't in your normal home circumstances and there's been such a long gap since then.'

Aunty took up her knitting, this time a V-neck for Dwaine, although he surely didn't need any more clothes. 'I'm a widow. I recognise that some people would feel I should stay that way. My parents are of that mind. Of course I still miss Frank and the tragedy of it doesn't go away, especially poor Kenneth losing his father but...'

She stopped there, so no-one learned what might come after the *but.*

Bill risked Dad noticing that he was still there, hearing all this grown-ups' talk. 'Actually, Aunty, how did Dwaine lose his wife? Was it an accident?'

'No, dear. A heart complaint, poor thing. She was ill in hospital for some weeks before she died. Very tragic.'

'There's a commonality in that, of course,' said Dad. 'It helps the relationship that you've both been through a similar tragedy.'

Aunty nodded sadly.

'It will be a huge adaptation for Kenneth to make if you do go, although a wonderful opportunity. However, he's not fifteen for another six months and what about his Higher School Certificate?'

Aunty said, 'Dwaine's made several enquiries about his education. There's even a fine university in Savannah.'

Dad nodded. He gave a lot more advice, almost as if he was Aunty's father. It was strange for Bill to be present. Fancy Dad having such a conversation in front of him! In the past, voices had dropped or stopped when he was near. Serious conversations happened when children were in bed. Now they were often happening in front of him.

Dad didn't talk like this in front of Kenneth, even though he was older than Bill. Yet he often took Kenneth into the study, somewhere that had always been Dad's private place. They talked about books together, like a twosome.

When Aunty went to get the cocoa, Bill went with her. She was always the safest person to discuss things with. 'Dad never used to say important things in front of me. Is it because he forgets I'm there?

'Oh, Bill,' she put an arm round him. 'You're steady, dear, like a big bear, nearly adult. I think your father trusts that you'll never say a word out of turn, so he speaks freely in front of you.'

He didn't feel like an adult but didn't want to admit it.

Kenneth got home before the cocoa had cooled.

'How was choir, dear?'

'Quite taxing, Mama.' He held out a sheaf of music. 'All this to learn,' but his face was shining. He loved his singing. They must have choirs in Savannah, though.

'Herbert thought he'd seen you coming out of the Evening Institute.'

Kenneth flicked his hair back, and said airily. 'Maybe. I have friends who take evening classes. It's worth finding out the classes they have on offer.'

Friends, choir, Dulwich College, Art lessons: so much Kenneth loved. It must be awful for him, dreading the moment Aunty said 'I've decided that we're going to leave on the next ship.'

By the time of high summer, Dwaine had gone. He had to travel back to start his new business. He comforted Aunty with 'Just a few months, and I'm coming back to collect you, honey.'

Jill cried for a whole day when he left, Bill and Alan were down in the dumps, but it was worse for Aunty.

'It'll be dreadful waiting until the moment is right,' she confided to Bill.

'Dwaine won't let you down,' he said. 'America is waiting for you.' Was he a rotten person at heart because the thought of Kenneth's departure made him glow with sheer joy?

Chapter Twenty-nine

Jill was pouting. She had grown out of the pretty dress Dwaine had brought over from America. 'It will be ages and ages before we see him again.'

'If we ever do,' Kenneth added.

'And I haven't got another one. And it's too hot to wear this skirt.' Her bottom lip stuck out. Tears were coming.

'I shall have to sew a flounce on the bottom of the dress, Jill. You know that Dwaine had to travel back to start his new business, but he'll be back.' comforted Aunty. 'You heard him say so.'

Kenneth gave a rotten imitation, 'Say, honey, just a liddle why-le, and guess I'm comin' right back ter collec' yer.'

Bill butted in to save Aunty's feelings. 'We're all missing him. I've got some paper you can write to him on, Jill, and some transfers and glue to decorate the page. Come on.'

'Goody.' Jill followed him out of the room.

Despite his sarky remarks, Kenneth had seemed to be accepting Dwaine by the time he left. Or it could have been the food parcels and treats that made the difference. Then, because Aunty hadn't gone with Dwaine – "too soon" – Kenneth had been more relaxed, and he hadn't been ill for weeks.

Bill hadn't relaxed, for Kenneth kept his sarcasm anointed like the Red Indians' poisoned arrows: aimed to hit the vulnerable spot.

Recently, this was about girls. Bill did like girls, but didn't really meet any. The one time girls from the neighbouring school joined St Werberg's boys for a geography film and lecture, they just giggled. No-one managed to talk properly with them.

Kenneth, however, was smoothing his hair with water these days, and boasting about girls he knew from choir 'and other places' but he wouldn't say where these were. Sometimes he even got into trouble for being late home in the evening. Afterwards he'd wink at Bill. 'Worth a wigging for the time I've had!' leaving Bill to wonder what sort of thing he'd been doing.

'You must be green with envy, Billy-boy.'

'You're fourteen and a half. I expect I'll have girl-friends when I am.'

'Ha! It's going to be years before any of us (annoyingly, he meant himself and the parents) can civilize you sufficiently to approach a girl. Look at those great knees and bulging pockets!'

'It's not my fault we don't have long trousers at school. And you could jolly well stick up for me when I ask for them for out of school.'

Kenneth snorted and turned away, as if Bill's words, let alone his wishes and feelings, were way beneath him.

Bill could have hit back by referring to America but he didn't. It would be hard enough for Kenneth when he was forced to go. It was only a matter of time.

Time passed, months, in fact, and Aunty still hadn't mentioned going to America. Somehow, Bill had expected that she would announce a departure on Kenneth's fifteenth birthday: she would give him the bad news softened by balloons and brown paper parcels. He was wrong. Aunty just took Kenneth for a trip to the National Gallery, with tea in a Fullers' tea-shop afterwards. Kenneth painted a picture of it for his Art homework and it got an A+.

Now it was near the end of autumn term when days were shortest and tempers with them. Bill was so often hearing about Kenneth's achievements that he hadn't thought much of his own, although he had been thrilled to captain the football team. It was a tremendous shock, although of the nicest kind, when the headmaster called him into his study and told him he and the staff had selected him to be a senior prefect, and if he did well, he would be Head Boy next year when many of the fifteen-year-olds would leave.

He left the study in a glow. It was simply spiffing to know he had the teachers' good opinion. Prefect!

And it was a wonderful feeling, having that news to announce at home. It would even things up a little. Kenneth always had art competitions he'd won, or school studies to tell Dad – History, Biology, Latin and World Affairs. Bill just seemed to have *lessons*. They weren't particularly difficult but not very interesting, so it was always Kenneth and Dad in conversation and Bill left with household jobs. But now Kenneth wouldn't be able to sneer at him. He was at the posh school, but he wasn't a prefect.

First off, Bill stopped at the nearest telephone box to ring Alan. He'd be really pleased. He broke the news and sure enough, Alan's whoops and whistles sounded down the earpiece. 'Hooray. Three cheers, Bill. My mother will be pleased. Everyone will look up to you now. Even Kenneth will sit up to hear this!'

That would be good! As Bill stepped out of the kiosk, a sliver of sun hit the glass windows as if it was waiting for him. Football Captain wasn't the kind of honour to excite his parents but surely senior prefect and Head Boy would? He let the sun warm his neck for a moment before he ran home with his news. Tonight he'd phone Mr Durban with it.

Instead of using the sideway, he rang the bell at the front door like a visitor. Mother opened it and before she could complain, he stood high on the step and announced,

'Good afternoon. This is the future Head Boy of St Warburg's arriving!'

'Really, Bill? *Really?*'

'Well, Senior Prefect for now, but Head Boy next year if I do well at it.'

'That's wonderful! Doreen, Jill, come out here!'

Aunty hugged him when he repeated his news and Jill leapt up and down. He couldn't wait for Dad to get home. He'd surely be very proud. Appointments were what he really valued.

But it was Kenneth who got home next. He came into the parlour weighed down with a satchel full of homework.

'Guess what, Kenneth. Bill's been made senior prefect and will be Head Boy next year!' Mother said.

'We're so proud,' Aunty added.

Kenneth's face tightened, his eyes flickered but with only the smallest pause he directed a small smile at Mother. 'Isn't that excellent, Aunty Marcia. Something to cheer you up.' He opened his satchel, busily, and brought out some sheet music. 'I'm going to be busy tonight preparing for the school concert. Since I'm the soloist for the Purcell, I have the responsibility of learning the music before all the others.'

'The soloist, Kenneth?' Aunty squealed. 'What I secretly longed for. The music concert, Herbert will love that. We'll all go, won't we, Bill?'

'Of course,' he said, making his way out of the room and upstairs.

He sat in his bedroom on his own while Kenneth warbled snatches of Purcell downstairs, timing it to catch Dad's ear immediately he arrived home. Bill's own news could be discussed over the tea table, perhaps.

He waited until he heard Dad come in and the snatches of music stop. He ran downstairs for tea and sat himself opposite Dad's chair.

Laying the table, Aunty was saying brightly, 'What have you got there, Kenneth?'

'Birthday cards.' He pulled a pile of them out of his satchel and put them on the sideboard where there was already an envelope for him, probably from his grandparents. The pile must be from boys at school. Strangely, they liked him there, all right.

Dad was hitching his trousers ready to sit down. 'Fifteen coming up soon, eh?'

Was Dad going to talk about school leaving age, and going to America?

Kenneth smiled. 'Quite a nice haul of cards, don't you think? I'll open them on my birthday itself.'

'I like balloons better than cards,' Jill said. 'Can we have some on Kenneth's birthday?'

Kenneth stretched. 'It's the present that matters.' He cast a quick glance at a wrapped package on the sideboard.

Bill knew that Aunty's present was a hardback book of special Art paper. Bill had found a shop in Clapham that had some tubes of paint from before the war. He'd bought the two colours, indigo and red carmine, that ones Kenneth had wanted the night of the storm. When he saw them, perhaps Kenneth would turn into a nicer person.

As if he'd read Bill's thoughts, Kenneth turned to Dad. 'Do you know, Dad? Bill was made a prefect today.'

Chapter Thirty

June was Bill's favourite month. He liked hot weather, and there was swimming twice a week at school, plus a camp at Scouts some weekends. The winter had been so vicious he thought he'd never take sunshine for granted ever again. It had been grim, and Kenneth's constant illness as result of the extreme cold worried Aunty to death. It was probably the reason she still hadn't taken the huge step of telling Dwaine she was ready for America.

On several occasions, Bill had been the only member of the family fit to do anything, 'flu and head colds worsening the suffering of a scarcely heated house and a snow-bound environment. He hadn't felt really well himself until April, and it was a helpless feeling seeing the rest of the family ill.

After a late spring, just as the headmaster had promised last autumn, he was made Head Boy. Striding into school, he sensed some importance, even if this was a shabby building with struggling staff. He was allowed to use the school library whenever he liked. This meant he could do his homework there in peace, instead of sharing table space with Kenneth and suffering his sneers about the simplicity of Bill's studies.

Aunty and Mother had just left to take Jill to see a dancing festival so Bill was enjoying some peace alone in the parlour. He wrote June, 1947, at the top of a fresh page. He was compiling scores for Arsenal's last hundred matches. There'd be some badge at Scouts he could put the information towards.

Kenneth pushed the door open. 'I'm going to do this weekend's homework in here, so don't interrupt me.'

'I was here first.' Should he take his scores upstairs, or would Kenneth follow? He bent his head over the notebook and hoped it would look like some maths.

Kenneth collapsed onto the sofa and put his feet up. That wasn't allowed, but Dad was at the Conservative club. Bill wrote down a few more scores and pretended not to notice. It was getting near the end of school year, Kenneth was taking School Certificate this month and Aunty needed to make her decision. Kenneth had been increasingly tetchy lately, as if it was all Bill's fault.

Sure enough, Kenneth started to bate him. 'Maths is it? Probably what I covered in my first year. It's not like a grammar school, yours,' he said, pulling out his copy of Victor Hugo and his Latin declensions from his satchel. 'No fine traditions. I suppose I've benefited from those in both the establishments I've studied in.'

Bill let a moment pass and closed his notebook, ready for the off. 'You'll have left school soon.' He didn't say, 'left the country', but that's what he meant, and Kenneth would know.

(*Kenneth in America, earning his own living starting at the bottom; and no Kenneth here; Dad with only one son. Me.*)

'No I won't have left school. Sixth form at Dulwich College for me. I discussed it with Dad last night. He says he's glad to support me until I graduate from university.'

Kenneth often lied. 'University! I thought you'd go out to work this summer hols (*go to America*). You'll be sixteen in November. You could've worked last year. I've had to.'

'Go out to work? What, like a coalman or bank clerk? No, that's what you'll do when the time comes, unless you want to hang on as a paper-boy with your seven and sixpences. You're not destined for university, are you?'

But you're destined for America. Bill stopped himself from saying it.

'That's why they've made you Head Boy, sort of compensation.'

Bill stood up and turned his back to stop himself putting a fist in Kenneth's face. It was time to get down to the newsagents, both for bundling up the day's stock and to manage his temper. Strange how he worked six days a week at the crack of dawn, whereas Kenneth earned his pocket money just by collecting golf balls on a Sunday afternoon, yet they ended up with the same money. It really wasn't fair! Kenneth snaffled lots of his Art stuff from school so that he had cash left for luxuries, whereas films and processing ate up nearly all Bill's money.

He shoved his notebook into his jacket pocket and looped his camera strap around his neck. 'I'm off. Keep your mean comments for your school friends – if you have any left.'

He loped down the road swallowing his anger. At the corner of the road, he hesitated. Did he have enough time to drop in on the Durbans between bundling newspapers and tea? It was always a tricky decision: if he stayed to eat with them, he would have to announce to the family where he was; if he kept quiet about it, he had to be back in time for tea. He might just photograph people piling off the bus instead.

His camera spent most of its time around Bill's neck. He was up to Chapter Eleven of the manual, and trying different photograph techniques. He photographed buildings, animals, too, if they appeared in the street. Although he found it a bit awkward, he'd also started to photograph people.

One of his new excuses for popping in on the Durbans, these days, was to get Angela's help with this. He needed to experiment with the light and shade of a face, he said, and no-one else would have the patience to sit for him. Even if Angela didn't believe that, she did enjoy being his model. He could see that, by the way she arched her back and turned her face up, or to the right, or just as he asked.

It was true that he needed to improve his portrait pictures. One day he would be a real photographer and Mr Durban said it was portraits that people came to a photographer for. People wanted mementoes. But the main reason for taking photographs of Angela, and he was embarrassed to admit it, was the thrill of getting close to her.

Although he was three years younger, Angela had always been quite huggy with him. At first he'd found that very embarrassing. It still was, but he liked it more each time, looked forward to it – even longed for it; the smell of Pears soap, the close-up of Pond's lipstick, the soft curl of her hair. Angela was the only person who made a fuss of him, although occasionally Aunty gave him a hug. He'd always had hugs from Mrs Pawsey. Now all he had were her letters. And Angela was a young lady, someone who might go on dates. He decided to go up there later. An extra hour sorting newspapers at the shop meant extra money, and by the time he got back, Kenneth might have gone out.

Even though Kenneth had sneered at what the paper-round earned, putting the shillings in his cashbox was one of Bill's greatest satisfactions. Even the sight of the black oblong tin with its narrow red stripe could cheer him up on a dark day. He'd been saving for two things: more film and processing money, and a present for Angela. Dwaine's six films had been used up long ago, and he couldn't very well ask for more. Dwaine would need so much money. A passage to America was about £100, and if Dwaine came here to collect Aunty, three tickets would cost a fortune!

How often did Kenneth think about all this? Was he telling the truth about Dad keeping him here to take his Higher School Certificate? Bill wasn't going to risk asking Dad in case he'd expect *him* to study for it, too! That would be awful, for he'd set his heart on being a photographer. Mother said to keep that to himself until Dad decided on Bill's future. 'He might well have firm ideas for someone who's a Head Boy.'

Chapter Thirty-one

Bill folded the newspapers for 15th August 1947, ready for delivery. They were so light, now that they could only be four pages long. Rationing was a flipping nuisance. Milk allowances had been cut and he hated drinking tea with only a splash of milk. Kenneth, of course, had the usual amount because he needed it for his health.

But nothing could stop Bill feeling cheery. He loved the hot weather and he had enough money to go swimming. Everything felt rather exciting. Princess Elizabeth was getting married. India had its independence. He knew what wanting independence felt like. A country must feel it a thousand times more. The newsagent's wife couldn't stop talking about the royal wedding, how it would be a grand affair, golden carriages, beautiful dresses, processions. It would certainly brighten up November. Even Dad had agreed that they would all go, and camp overnight in the street, if necessary.

Aunty wouldn't see that great day. She had just given in her notice at work because, at last, Dwaine was on his way to collect her. She'd whispered to Bill 'If I dare go,' and he'd put an arm round her and said, 'You should, even though I really don't want to lose you.' She'd already given her clothing coupons to Mother, saying she'd be able to buy better in New York and without needing coupons.

Would this mean the back of Kenneth at last? No-one was saying anything about him going, although he was past school leaving age now. He'd gained excellent School Certificate results, surely good enough to get into a college, or whatever they had in Savannah? The new school year would begin at Dulwich College next week. He asked Mother if Kenneth was enrolled on a course in

Savannah. She just answered, 'Don't tempt Providence, Bill.'

He wouldn't trust what Kenneth said about staying, and he couldn't tell from the way he behaved. He'd been wearing a supercilious expression and smarmed-back hair, and had whisked out after breakfast, most of the holiday. Was he going to go to America with Aunty or not?

Bill would take School Certificate himself next year, then he'd leave school and somehow train to be a photographer, whatever Dad's plans. But today he had something special to do.

Everyone was out: Dad at the Conservative club, Jill at Iris's, Kenneth at cricket, Mother and Aunty at a Bring and Buy sale. He ran upstairs to put on his first pair of long trousers, the best thing that had happened for simply ages. Thank goodness Dad hadn't made him wait until he was sixteen like many boys! It was a sort of reward for becoming Head Boy.

Bill looked in the long mirror on the landing, at the satisfying spread of grey covering his knees and shins. Surprising how different long trousers made you feel. Outside, the August sun was blazing a fierce invitation to do something out of the ordinary, and he would!

Today was the day he'd take Angela her present. He could pass it off as a thank you for posing for all his photographs. He'd thought hard about what to buy. She was always longing for something new. Her tastes were a bit above him. She was a proper working woman, after all. She wore nylons, lipstick and the New Look. She wasn't keen to play Ludo or Backgammon any more, or even Draughts. Even though they didn't share interests, she was the most important thing for him outside of football and his camera. He so wanted to be the one to provide the latest thing she yearned for.

Her most recent desire was for a pin-up photo, a big one, of Gregory Peck, and she wanted it framed. You could get them signed from this fan club. A boy at school had told him about it, but it was ever so expensive, and then there was the frame to buy.

It had taken him weeks to save enough for it. Every time he put his shillings and pennies in the right-hand side of the cashbox he thought of Angela's face brightening when she saw it and perhaps her arm around his shoulders. She'd be so pleased, that she'd probably kiss him. Sometimes he thought of that in bed at night, and it made him quiver. He rehearsed the scene. After he'd given her the photo and she'd put it on her wall, he was going to ask her to the pictures. He actually only liked cowboy films, but whatever was on at the Odeon, it would be super sitting beside her, walking in with her, just the two of them.

Kenneth had taunted him that Bill couldn't approach any girl, but he knew Angela liked him and she always had. Even though he'd be going out with a family friend, it would still be a date.

He'd collected the precious poster from his school-friend yesterday and hidden it in the study to join his shashka story behind Dad's Annals of Law.

He went to the kitchen for a Bovril sandwich before getting ready to take the poster over to the Durbans. Angela didn't work on Saturdays and he wanted to catch her in before one of her girlfriends called. He ate his sandwich, making himself chew slowly so that he didn't get hiccups. Then he checked that he looked his smartest before stepping out into the sun. If they hadn't given in over the long trousers, he wouldn't have the confidence to start on this now. You can't go dating in short trousers.

The sun shone down so brightly on him that he had to remove his jacket. His shirt was clean on that morning and was the greeny one that Angela had said matched his eyes. She'd noticed his eyes!

The poster safely under his arm, he swung his jacket chirpily as he walked up the Durbans' path. He rapped on the door and Mr Durban opened it.

'Hello there, Bill. Come on in. I've just been organising some old snaps you can advise me on.' He led the way to the living room where magazines and knitting suggested that Angela and her mother were not far from home. He continued into the snug where the photographs were spread out over the desk.

'You can see I've made progress. Now these, photographs from the Great War are irreplaceable. I'll put most of them in the red album, but which shall I get enlarged? I want two or three framed for over here.' He pointed to the bare patch on the wall where his war-time duty rota had hung before.

Bill's eyes were on the other wall. The shashka now hung there, resting on two brass hooks. The curved mirror opposite magnified and framed it; the bright sun outside caught the silvered hilt and reflected a spot of light onto the desk.

'I know what you're looking at. The shashka looks good in its new place, right?' He turned to a sheaf of large photographs. 'Here's a photograph of the Middlesex marching back home. Here's the ARP wardens at the hut, remember them? This one's a photograph of the King and Queen when they visited the Balham bomb site.' He drew breath sharply. 'Sorry, Bill. I was forgetting your uncle Frank was in that number.'

'Yes,' said Bill thoughtfully, his eyes still on the shashka. 'It does look really good there. Better than some tommy gun with only one round of ammunition.'

Mr Durban laughed. 'Right. You can remember the 1940s Home Guard then?' He spread out the photographs to cover the whole width of the table. 'Which of these then?'

Bill picked two. 'These are sharp enough. I'd enlarge these two.' He rocked on his heels, ready to stroke his chin like his father did, waiting.

'If you're waiting to ask where Angela is, she's out shopping with her mother, but she's coming back first on her own. She'll be home soon. She said she was expecting someone.'

He drew a sharp breath. 'Did she really?'

'Yes. I thought it was someone from her evening class but I should have guessed it was you.'

So she more than half expected him, and he hadn't even brought his camera with him!

'Thing is, I've got to be off and out now. Home Guard Social Club, a special meeting. But you make yourself comfortable while you're waiting for Angela. Why don't you have a look at my albums?' He nodded to the albums on a shelf. 'You needn't think you've seen all of them. There's even a photo I got from my father. He served in the Boer Wars.'

'Gosh. I'd like to see that.'

'Black album, fourth page, I think.' Mr Durban went back to the lounge, put his jacket on and straightened his tie in the mirror. 'Toodle-pip. I shall leave you in charge of the house. Angela won't be long.' He swept out, clipping the front door behind him.'

Bill watched him fondly. No fire patrol, no doodlebugs to dodge, no ARP hut, just memorabilia and photos. It was good that war was over.

He pulled out the oldest looking album and took it into the lounge. He arranged himself on the sofa, giving a twitch to his trouser legs before he sat, just like David Niven. He'd practised that a lot of times since he'd had them. He stretched out his legs, proud of the trousers, and the length of them. He propped the poster against the sofa and looked at his watch, his last birthday present, more for style than to check how long Angela would be. If she was expecting him, she couldn't be long. He arranged his position so that he would be facing the door when she swept in with her little bags and strappy shoes.

The doorbell rang. Not Angela – she surely had a key. Bother – it might be one of her friends. Should he wait until they went away? It rang again, loudly; ding dong. He'd loved that sound when he was a little boy; it was darned annoying now. It came again. He was the only person in the house so he'd better answer it. It was nice to be trusted with the responsibility of the Durban house. Just like a son, an in-law or something. He got up and strode to the door, opening it confidently, ready with his advice to call back another time.

The door opened onto brilliant sunlight which momentarily blinded him. He blinked. Kenneth stood there, immaculate in cricket whites.

'What are you doing here?' Bill said, filling the doorway. It surely must be an emergency for Kenneth to risk coming here. 'Do they need me at home?'

'I haven't come to see you, stupid. I've come for Angela.' He peered around the side of Bill's bulk.

'Angela!' Something leaden thumped in his chest. 'What on earth for?' He must get rid of Kenneth now. He said, 'They're all out.'

'That's all right,' said Kenneth blithely. He put two tapered fingers on Bill's chest and pushed him aside. 'Angela said she might be a bit delayed. She told me to come in and wait. So I will.'

She told him? It couldn't be true. Was *this* the person Angela was expecting! Surely he'd scotched Kenneth's keenness to come down here ages ago? He paced down the hall after Kenneth. All the jauntiness and sunshine in Bill's heart sank to his boots, or rather the same old school shoes, earthier and clumsier than Kenneth's trim white lace-ups.

'No-one here, Billy boy? Left you to, what, wash the dishes? That's what people have you to visit for, isn't it? I shall wait in the lounge.'

Kenneth deserved a thrashing. If only he dared! He looked at Kenneth's back. Aunty had spent hours knitting that white cable-stitch V-neck. It certainly looked good over Kenneth's perfectly white shirt. He couldn't have made many runs.

Kenneth turned a smooth face to Bill. 'Twenty-four not out,' he said almost companionably, as if reading Bill's mind.

As they went into the lounge, neck and neck, Bill noticed that Kenneth was carrying a cardboard tube.

'What's that?'

'None of your business, matey. But I don't mind telling you. It's a pin-up Angela's been wanting for ages.'

'How do you know?'

'It was mentioned in evening classes,' he said airily.

So that's where Kenneth had been, those evenings when he was late home. Had Angela really told Kenneth the things she longed for? 'Gregory Peck?'

'Yes, as a matter of fact. Gregory Peck. Her heart-throb. So far. But perhaps that'll change after what I've got in mind for her today.' He gurgled in the back of his throat.

'But Angela's *my* friend, the family are my friends. You can't muscle in like that.'

'Oh no?' Kenneth snorted delicately. 'What's to say that they don't want me as a friend, a musical person, a Dulwich College student?' He looked around the lounge as if choosing the best place to drape himself. Then he spotted the opened snug door.

'What's in there, then? Haven't seen that. The old man's study?'

So he couldn't have been here much before. 'No, it's Mr Durban's private room. You shouldn't go in there!'

223

But Kenneth was already inside the snug. 'Not here to see, is he?'

Bill followed anxiously. 'Don't touch any of that. It's his memorabilia.'

'Displayed for people to see and admire, surely.'

'Not without permission.' Bill grabbed his arm, but Kenneth shook him off and left him to watch as he moved around softly, picking up one item, peering at another, sliding aside the albums to look at the photographs on the table and finally, dreadfully, looking up at the wall and the shashka.

'Hmmm. That looks brutal.' He placed his long fingers delicately under its curve and lifted it down.

'DON'T you dare!'

Kenneth placed it on top of the spread-out photographs. 'There. A nice little trophy of the—? Well it won't be our war, will it? Which war did this killing object come from, I wonder?'

'Stop it! It's very dangerous. You mustn't touch.'

'And you'd know, of course. From the person who told you all about the Great War, the bodies in the snow?'

Everything he had, everything he did, everything he wanted, Kenneth pushed himself into. And now he'd bought the special poster for Angela. He certainly wasn't going to get the shashka. Suppose Kenneth persuaded Mr Durban that, as Angela's boyfriend, he should take possession of it, hang it over his bed even!

Kenneth rolled back on his heels. His laugh was like slop water down the drain. 'Your face!'

He walked in a circle around the table, pulling out a photograph here and there, looking at it sneeringly and putting it down again. The shashka lay on the photographs, its hilt glinting as the sun streaked through the window beside them. Kenneth stroked the pattern, silver reflected on his fingertips.

Suddenly the small room seemed stifling in the heat, overfull with people. They should get out, get out quickly. Bill gestured with a wild arm to the lounge.

'That's enough. Come out. We shouldn't be in here.'

Kenneth folded his arms, staying put. 'You go then. Angela will be showing me everything in a minute, when you've gone to whatever you do on your miserable Saturdays.'

Bill moved nearer to the table, his eyes on the shashka. Angela wouldn't be showing Kenneth that, she couldn't. 'I'm in charge of the whole house in Mr Durban's absence. Mr Durban said that. Go out.' He must keep everything safe.

Kenneth wasn't moving. He hummed a little tune very quietly with a mocking tone, *Run rabbit, run, rabbit, run, run, run,* the song they'd had to sing at junior school to practise hiding from the bombs. At the same time, Kenneth drew out the shashka from its scabbard almost blinding Bill with its reflected sunlight.

'STOP!' Bill gasped, grabbing the hilt from Kenneth who at the same time bent forward in order to hold onto it, using his left hand to wrench it away from Bill. The shashka leapt upwards in Bill's hand meeting something hard. Kenneth screeched and Bill crashed it back down rapidly using his full force to bring it to the table and safety, but Kenneth's right hand was there, clenched around the scabbard.

Whether the shriek came first or the blood, Bill didn't know, but before he'd registered that it was Kenneth the shashka had hit, a fountaining spurt of blood was before his eyes and it took several seconds for him to realise the shashka's blade was now pinning Kenneth's hand to the table, and had almost severed it below the wrist. The shrieking was so terrible that he didn't hear the front door open and Angela's frantic footsteps running towards them. He stood in the same spot, terrified to move for fear

225

the shashka would do worse work, seeing nothing except the brilliance of blood.

He saw Angela take in the sight of him holding the shashka and start to scream.

'Billy! Let it go!'

He looked at his hand on the hilt, a foreign thing, then at Angela as her bulging eyes swivelled to Kenneth, his left hand stuffed in his mouth, blood covering his face and his hand pinioned to the table. He saw the little heels of her shoes as she pelted straight out of the open front door, screaming for help.

Bill let the shashka fall where it would and Kenneth fell in synchrony, his cricket whites merely a canvas for the crimson display. The knitted V-neck was smothered in blood. Aunty would never forgive him; she'd never get it white again. There were specks, a spotted line, a little lake and the main feature – an arm ending in blood, the hand hanging from it with its long, helpless fingers.

And then there was airiness in the little room, silent inside except for a light gasping from Kenneth's mouth.

Blood was ruining Mr Durban's Afghan rug. Kenneth was unconscious. He should do something, mop up, tourniquet or – he hadn't done war wounds in Scouts. This was more than bloody, like when bodies littered the earth. His feet wouldn't move. His hands stayed halfway in the air, useless. He tossed his head from side to side. He must do something.

Rushing feet into the room took responsibility from him. A man, neighbour, passer-by, knelt down by Kenneth. Another man was running to the kitchen, bringing tea towels. A tablecloth was bound round Kenneth's arm, a cushion under his head. Bill couldn't look directly, he might be sick. A minute, an hour? Then, Angela, still screaming under her breath, came leading men with armbands, who took over. They leaned over the slumped figure, clicked open their first-aid boxes, lifted

Kenneth, his legs dangling, one man's strong arms under the damaged arm.

He had a glimpse of shocked, intent faces as they carried Kenneth away, ignoring Bill. But Angela, leaving with them, turned at the door. Her stunned gaze penetrated him like the tip of the shashka.

He was left alone, and the space was terrible. He crouched down, covering his whole head with his arms.

Suddenly the man, the neighbour, was back beside him, pulling at his arms until he unfolded them, pulling him up from his crouch. 'I know you, don't I? Often round here, I've seen you. An accident, wasn't it? Surely an accident. You, a boy like you, you wouldn't have done that on purpose?'

Bill's mouth was dry and his throat closed up. No words would come. His head was hung so far down he could hardly shake it. The floor seemed the safest place to be. He wasn't here. He couldn't be here.

The man pulled him to his feet, still grasping him by the arm. 'You're in a state. We'll go into my house, wait for someone to take you home.'

But as they moved away from the Durban's front door, a police car drew up and its occupants ushered them both indoors again.

Chapter Thirty-two

SOUTH LONDON COURIER
The newspaper that gives the full story

September 5th 1947

LATEST:
Wandsworth Boy Assaults Cousin with Cossack sabre!

William Wilson, fourteen, swiped his orphaned cousin, fifteen-year-old Kenneth Wilson, with a fearsome sabre snatched from the wall of a family friend's room, severely damaging the victim's eye and right hand. Doctors say that Kenneth, a talented artist, has no hope of regaining the use of either eye or hand.

At the South Western Juvenile Court, the accused youth pleaded Not Guilty, claiming it was an accident. The victim, too ill and traumatised to attend Court, also told his mother and investigating officers that it was an accident.

The magistrate heard evidence from family members and friends and considered the medical reports. Police evidence about the scene of the assault, and interviews with Wilson, formed the major part of the hearing.

It was clear from the scene at the house of Mr P. Durban, that a tussle had occurred. The weapon, an ancient sabre, had been taken from its place on the wall. Evidence showed that only two people had been present in the small room. William Wilson had suffered no injuries himself. He had been a poor interviewee with little to say for himself except that it was an accident.

The victim gained a scholarship to famous Dulwich College just after VE Day. His Headmaster, Mr P.E. Cambridge, described Kenneth Wilson as a very artistic, sensitive boy with delicate health. He was fully expected to make his name in Fine Arts having shown unusual talent from an early age. Mr Cambridge expressed extreme shock and dismay at what had happened to Kenneth.

Mr Herbert Wilson, coincidentally employed as Chief Clerk to the County Court for the last nine years, gave evidence as the father of William, and uncle and acting father of Kenneth. Tragically, Kenneth's own father, Mr Francis Wilson, tax inspector, died in the Balham bombing of 1940, Mr Herbert Wilson then taking on Kenneth as a second son.

When questioned, Mr Herbert Wilson admitted awareness of some past tension between the boys. However, there was no recent sign of discord in the home. The boys had different interests, were at different schools and kept themselves rather separate from each other. His son had never been involved in a previous incident of violence.

William Wilson's Headmaster, Mr A. F. Rundle of St Werberg's School, said that Wilson was a good student, never in trouble. Other boys looked up to him. He had been appointed Head Boy, chosen by the staff for his reliability and common sense. In 1941 during his evacuation, Wilson had shown bravery in saving a small child from drowning. He was a large, strong lad who excelled at football.

Asked whether Wilson had ever needed correction for his behaviour, Mr Rundle said he had not. At his school, bullying or assault is severely punished. Mr Rundle stated, 'I hate saying this, but what this boy has done requires a birching.'

Evidence from Miss Angela Durban, who came upon the sorry scene shortly after the assault, revealed that the two boys were rivals for her attention. After the assault she discovered two identical pin-up posters that both boys had brought her that day.

Mr Peter Durban told the court that the weapon hung in his study. Leaving for a meeting, he had left the house temporarily in the charge of William Wilson, a very frequent visitor there. He expressed the view that William was very unlikely to have initiated a fight.

There was no witness to the attack.

Was the frailer Kenneth in fear of his cousin in whose home he now lived? Mr Herbert Wilson was unable to confirm or deny the possibility of intimidation of Kenneth by William.

When examined, William Wilson admitted he had not been happy when Kenneth became part of his immediate family. He admitted to discomfort with Kenneth's presence in the Durbans' home that fateful day. He remained unable to describe the tussle during which the sabre caused Kenneth's severe injuries. He agreed that he was holding the sabre when he saw the blood spurt out.

On balance, the magistrate felt reluctant to accept either boy's claim that the wounds were accidental: the injuries were too severe. The motive of jealousy suggested itself. William Wilson, though the younger boy, was larger and much stronger and may have seen Kenneth as an invader in his home.

William Wilson was convicted of assault causing grievous bodily harm. The background information and context of the incident suggested that this was an assault made in temper.

Despite William Wilson's former good conduct, the magistrate concluded that a sentence was required.

For such a serious assault with its devastating consequences a penal term was appropriate. Wilson should be sent to a Juvenile Detention Centre or Approved School where he could receive education and moral guidance. There he could reflect fully upon his offence and consider how best he could redeem himself in the future.

He should spend a minimum of six months at such a Centre, with a review of his behaviour and progress before release.

Chapter Thirty-three

'You'll have to wait until an Approved School place becomes available. Autumn's always a busy time.' The man was a policeman, taking him in a van away from the Juvenile Court.

He'd arrived in the dark and so had no idea of the size or the shape of the place, but he was at a remand centre, kept separate from whoever else was imprisoned there. There were occasional shouts, words he'd never heard before but obviously swear words, and there were bars. Briefly, he imagined he'd been left in the zoo.

When things were not happening to him, when he was not being told what to do, Bill sat on his bunk, its thin grey blanket reminding him of the time he was first evacuated, the first time he'd felt abandoned by his family. The humilities and discomforts that so shocked him then, were nothing in comparison with now. He knew he could survive discomforts and hardship. It was his thoughts he struggled to survive.

From that one moment when the sun shone viciously on the shashka, he could only think in fragments; each sharp and painful. He thought of them as scenes. That's how they came in the night. Then in the morning he'd know they were not scenes from a nightmare, but from real life.

There was nothing in his life now that wasn't awful, unless it was terrible. He couldn't *not* think however hard he tried, so he switched scenes, going from one to another before any could become too vivid and hurt him so much that he doubled over.

Sometimes the officers would ask if he had stomach-ache. He nodded. He had everything-ache.

How long was it between the accident and seeing his parents? He didn't know. It felt like a week but it might have been next day. He held his head. The first scene was coming:

Scene A – Afterwards. The scene has Mother in a doorway holding Jill's hand, pushing Jill behind her, saving her from contamination. His mother looks at him with horror in her face as if she's never seen him before, not known him, not belonged to him. She says something, some things, but he doesn't hear: her expression shrieks louder than any words. Then Dad comes into the scene. He's coming into the room, in his work suit, the best one with stripes, but his shoes aren't shined. Where was it, that room? It wasn't in a police station but it was bare, with hard chairs and a table where other bad people like Bill had sat and carved signs and letters.

He's sitting, his eyes level with the table's edge where all the carvings are. He can only see one through his blurry eyes, a Chad with the bubble, *Wot No Sympathy*. Then through a grey sound-mist of cleared throats and scraped chairs, there's Dad saying his words. He may have given one of his quotations. Bill hasn't taken it in.

Dad doesn't make Bill look at him or sit any nearer. 'You realise why you can't come home? Even if it wasn't for Jill's safety' – he swallows the word and changes it to – 'well-being, it's Kenneth. We have to be there, visiting him. Later, when he comes out of hospital, however long that takes, everything must be right for him. He mustn't have any fears or anxieties. Home must feel safe. He needs the right atmosphere, no stress, no sound of raised voices, no arguments, nothing like that, given all he'll have to adapt to, with what's happened to him.' His voice tails off, pauses, then lurches into a shout of pain. 'Unforgivable!'

Bill's body jumps, his knee bashes against the table edge.

232

'My brother's boy, the pride of his life! I promised to look after him as my own and it's my own that has nearly killed him,' the voice subsides to a whisper, 'and killed what was best in him.'

Bill's shivering. The room's empty but for the chair and table. A person entering, takes his shoulder, pushes him towards the door, away, somewhere. The voices behind him fade to agonised whispers.

Another scene, was it the same room? If not, it's closely similar. Police talking. Bill's retained nothing else of the scene, only the sense of internal horror.

Bedtime is the most desirable part of his day but then there's the tossing and refusal of sleep to come. When it does, in his dreams, the cold, damp forehead signals Scene H.

Scene H is Hospital, Dad marching him down towards a glass-topped door. Jill is sitting with a *Girl's Own* open on her lap on a hard wooden chair in the corridor, looks up, eyes widening. She mouths 'Bill!' almost to herself.

Now he's in the ward. White curtains surround several beds but there are none around Kenneth's. Bandages, tubes, bottle and enamel pan sit on the bedside cabinet. Mother, Aunty are on either side of the bed.

Dad pushes him forwards towards the lump in the lower part of the bed. Bill can't make himself look at any higher part where the tubes and bandages are.

Dad's hand hard in the small of Bill's back, his voice soft, 'Kenneth, my boy. Bill's come to say how – dreadfully sorry he is. Are you willing to hear him?'

No sound from the bed, except a slight rustle of bedclothes.

The hard hand pushes. A choke's got Bill's throat, his cheeks are red hot but his whole body freezing cold. He can't look, he won't. Another choke, another push, then he manages, 'I'm d-dreadfully sorry. It was – you know it was – an accident.' And in a tiny voice, '…Kenneth.'

Silence from the bed.

Aunty breaking down, running outside.

Dad shoving him in the back, getting him out of the ward, into the corridor. Jill running away.

Aunty pulling at his jumper, her whisper becoming a scream, 'His beautiful face. And his hand, his drawing hand, Bill.'

A windowsill, hands over his ears, his face, forehead pressed to the windowpane. The cold damp of it.

He wakes, stifling his own scream.

Scene B is Blood. This can start at any time. He has to screw up his eyes to make everything blur so that he can't see things clearly. Blood trickles down the windowpanes when it rains, onto his porridge instead of milk. At night, blood from Kenneth's hand mixes with the bodies around Ted in the sea at Dunkirk, with the soldiers bombed into the mud of Italy, the fields of Russian dead where Mr Durban is given the shashka. It slashes at mounted Germans whose arms or ears fall off gushing blood, the same scarlet hue as the fountain from Kenneth's wrist, pooling around those whitening fingers.

P is the Police scene. A large policeman stares at him over a table. He's been talking. Saying something, then, 'There's a social worker coming for you, because your father thinks it would be better.'

Bill stands up, of course he does, when she's shown into the room but he keeps his eyes on her clothes. It's dangerous to look at anyone's face. The dark-haired woman is plump, wearing clothes that Mother would never have worn even for war work in the garage. Her jacket doesn't do up and the hem of her skirt is wavy. Aunty would say that she hadn't turned it up well. Dad would say she wasn't turned out well.

'William Wilson, is it?' She is speaking to the policeman who opened the door for her, as if Bill isn't reliable enough to answer to his own name. Probably criminals pretend their names are something different. Criminals lie.

The policeman nods. 'The dad's on his way. The mum's at the hospital with the victim's mother. The kids are cousins. *Dad*,' his voice gains a heavily sarcastic note, 'is Clerk to the Court.'

'No! A pretty pickle!' She nods, and the policeman leaves her to it, to Bill.

'William. I'm Mrs–' (*Lunt, Lamb, Lowe - does it matter?*) 'You can tell me anything that troubles you. I come here for young people who don't have a parent with them. Feel free to talk to me.' (*She might be smiling. Smiling!*) 'It'll be me who takes you to your placement.'

He stares at the table. Someone's carved a cross on it with a dagger.

He can't remember the rest.

Scene R. Road. There must have been something which happened between the remand centre or police cell, he doesn't know which, and the dormitory, but all he remembers is the Road. It's long. Driving along it is the dingy woman who sat in the empty interview rooms with him, talking, expecting him to talk. Bill doesn't look out of the windows to watch the dirt of London become seductive countryside, but focusses on her pudgy hands controlling the car, in charge of what must happen.

An hour, or maybe a month, passes.

She speaks, a man's voice in a stocky woman's body: 'We're here, William, Brigville School. Stiff upper lip. It'll be all right. It's not as tough as a Borstal. Luckily, you're too young for that. The Approved School has football, you know.'

He didn't know, doesn't know anything. He'd never heard of Borstal before it was mentioned in Court. It could have been a pig pen for all he knew.

The long roadway, the large fine building, reminds him at first of the Priory Grammar School where Kenneth had his Art displayed. His first and last display. A shudder goes through Bill. It loosens his shoulders.

The car stops. The woman opens his car door. It had been locked. 'Come along.'

He climbs out stiffly. Outside it's bright sun, but cold, very cold. When had it stopped being summer? Blue sky surrounds stark trees, their vicious arms pointing to the sky. They sway in a keen wind, sigh to him, *Look what you've done. You know who's looking down on you. God. Jesus. My son died for you, suffered on the cross. He bore the wounds for you.* He shudders. *My son, my son.* Uncle Frank in bits, knowing what Bill's done to his son, waiting to mete out the punishment.

He comes to. This is real, he's not in a nightmare. S is something ahead of him, unknown. S for school, *Approved School,* approved for boys as bad as he is. This is not a scene, it's a sentence. His.

Attend! He told himself to pay attention. Unlike his school, this building was surrounded by high walls. A wide path led towards the arch and through to the large front door with a glass porch the size of a greenhouse but with a desk and hatch instead of plants.

The social work woman marched him on, the gravel crunching under her feet like discarded bones. 'Up these steps, now.'

He looked at the brick arch. Behind it, well set back, a wall of windows and a huge front door. Far to the right a cemented area surrounded by fencing. Wire stretched high towards a mean sky, whose blue was smeared with grey, like Kenneth's rough paper where he cleaned his paintbrush.

Right now at St Werberg's, boys would be sitting at their desks learning French verbs. Bill's name would be scrubbed from the register in thick black ink. In the playground, they'd whisper about their ex-Head Boy, ex-football captain.

'Any questions, before we go in?' Unlike his school, this building was surrounded by high walls.

'When will I be going home?'

'That will be discussed in the next few months.'

'Months! Are my parents going to visit me here?'

'You will have visits. Don't expect any the first week or so, though.'

They walked up the flight of stone steps between pillars and towards doors. Inside were men, hatches, shiny wooden tables, papers for the woman to sign, corridors. The woman stopped at a windowed counter, spoke to someone, showed documents.

She stayed beside him as he was taken to Reception.

Another man inside spoke quite a lot, but Bill didn't take in anything until he said, 'So what have you brought with you, Bill?'

He'd been too overwhelmed to think about what might have come with him. For a dreadful moment he thought there might be a bloodied shirt, like evidence of his crime. Somewhere, he had been provided with a small case (was it from home?) that he hadn't packed himself. When it was unpacked at the desk, he was amazed to see his Dutch history book in it. His hand shot out towards something he knew, a hand that surely didn't belong to him.

'No, we'll keep all this for the moment.'

Apart from a sponge bag, his possessions were labelled and taken away.

'You'll get them back.' The man turned to the social worker and they spoke to each other, or was it to him? He felt in his pocket. At least he had his bit of green and white napkin.

The wavy hem moved nearer to him. 'William, I'm going to leave you now. Mr – the name sounded and

237

immediately disappeared from his mind – will get you sorted out. I'm sure you'll want to do well here. You must do your best. Make things up to your poor family. Perhaps I'll see you when you finish your term.'

She put a hand on his shoulder. It felt kindly enough, but meaningless.

Then she went, her footsteps sounding rhythmically down the length of the corridor. A door slammed behind her, keys jangled. The day was shut out.

'We'll get you installed, then.' The man opened the door and led him down the corridor and to a wooden staircase. There was now an upstairs part. He had to undress, shower, put on their clothes, the school clothes, muddy brown Brigville School clothes. And they didn't fit.

'Can I keep my handkerchief?'

'Yes, we won't want that.'

With relief, Bill squeezed his handkerchief tight, knowing the napkin piece was safe inside it.

The man took him to another room, furnished, this one: a desk, easy chairs, framed photographs on the wall, a shield. The man said, 'William Wilson, sir,' and went away.

Bill stood at the desk. Behind it, a teacher, head teacher, social work man, he didn't take in who he was, spoke to him about reforming boys' ways; turning from the bad towards good, education, training, discipline, rules, sanctions. It was probably wise and important stuff, but it didn't make sense to him because everything was like a dreadful headache that stopped you attending to anything else.

There was something about bullying, but since he hadn't been a bully or even been bullied much, it wasn't relevant to him, was it? Other boys something or other. Yes, he had heard their voices down the corridor.

The man ordered him to think hard about what he had done, how he must knuckle down, change. He rang a buzzer on his desk.

Back came the other man to take him down another corridor. There was a dormitory, empty of boys. 'They're at supper.'

His bed was next to the door. Beside it, there was a box for his things, empty. 'Now you know where you'll be. But tonight you sleep in here.'

Down the corridor was a small room with a small table, a hard chair, a towel hung over its back. He put his sponge bag down.

'We'll keep you apart for the moment. Just stay in here tonight, get used to being here. We'll put you with the other boys tomorrow. There'll be lessons. You'll learn to fit in.' The man left him.

Later, he was given a meal, a comic. The day ended, eventually, and the dark night began.

Chapter Thirty-four

In the morning he was taken to the shower area, then a dormitory where eleven other boys were making their beds. 'This is Bill Wilson. Help him settle in.'

The boys were being supervised so they said nothing, but their eyes said everything. He saw curiosity, dislike, aggression and challenge in their expressions. Settle in? How was he going to ask the way when he got lost in this place, or if they could pass the salt in the dining room? What would they be like, once there was no supervision?

He soon found that there was always supervision. He didn't have to ask for what he needed. The tin dishes held what they must eat. He didn't have to ask any questions. They were told exactly what to do. It wasn't a dining room, but a room for eating, with a hatchway to the kitchen. Boys talked, but didn't laugh. An officer walked around the benches.

Afterwards, there was lining up. They filed outside. The order came to spread out. Each boy stretched out his arms, making sure he couldn't touch the next. A whistle blew. Exercises began, a teacher demonstrating in front. Feet apart, feet together. Arms up, arms down. Apart, together. Apart, together. Up, down. Up, down, faster, faster, faster. Exercises stopped at two blasts of the whistle for lining up again. The line marched indoors, along a corridor with whitish walls and sick green paintwork.

'Morning lessons,' the boy next to him whispered.

'New boy?' the supervising officer came alongside. 'Spell *lesson*.' He waited. 'Correct! What is elevenpence ha'penny plus threepence?' He raised an eyebrow. 'Correct. You're in here, then, top class,' and he opened the end door of three.

'Posh, ain't yer,' whispered the boy again, turning into the first door.

Sheets of printed sums were on the desks inside the room Bill had been assigned. A teacher pointed to the desks, said, 'Sit' and told them to work in silence, but most boys disobeyed. The work was easy and he finished quickly, putting his hands on his lap.

'Don't do that, stupid!' the boy next to him muttered. 'You'll only get given more.'

Before he could pick up his pencil again, the teacher handed him another sheet of sums.

Later, the teacher put a map on the board and talked about it. Bill thought about the boys at St Werberg's and how far away they were now.

He began to revisit the Court scene in his head, what the magistrate said and perhaps that social work woman had repeated, something about his 'term'. A boy at breakfast had asked how long Bill was in for. For the first time he focussed on that idea, *term*. It was six months. When would six months end? He didn't know the date now, so couldn't work it out. Looking around at the bare beige walls, glossy with layers of bad paint, he could see that calendars were not the sort of thing that would be pinned up. There wasn't even a picture, only the times tables on a piece of cardboard and a list of the English counties. He struggled to think of the last time he had known the date. He couldn't remember when summer holidays had ended. Had he started the Autumn term at school? Who was Head Boy now?

The teacher was asking questions. He didn't know any answers.

'Have you been listening?'

'Yes, sir.' A lie. He was a liar now. But he needed to know when he would be leaving here. He needed to have a date in his mind. It was very important. He put his hand in his pocket, to feel the piece of napkin.

'And where is Egypt?'

Bill pointed to the map.

'Next to—?'

He couldn't say which country sat next to it, but none of the other boys could either.

'I've just been telling you all these countries, boys. Sit up! Listen!'

The lesson went on, and Bill still hadn't managed to calculate what date he'd leave here.

After a lunch slopped into those tin dishes that would have appalled Mother, they were allowed in an outside area with wire on top of the walls, where a ball could be kicked around. He joined in, but the game was just an opportunity for boys to thump each other under cover. Old scores were being settled and new ones set up. Larger boys eyed him before kicking out at his shins. It was to see what he would do back. He was glad when the whistle went.

Back in the classroom, there was an officer in charge instead of the teacher. He pointed to their chairs and said they could write their letters.

Bill began to write eagerly, *Dear Nanny and Grandad*, but then dropped his pencil as if it had cut him. Mother's hushed tones came into in his head, 'I shan't tell my parents, Herbert. I can't. It would kill them.' Where did she say that? The hospital, the court, the interview room?

His hand pushed his pencil away. The news might kill the Pawseys too. And Mrs Youldon wouldn't want Sally and Timmy to know about such a thing. Who would understand how *that* could happen by accident? How could he write to anyone without telling them where he was, and why?

Mr Durban was the only one who knew, but he'd never want to even think about Bill again. The awful thing had happened at his house. The rug! It had been ruined; blood staining the precious photographs on the table; the memorabilia room left in chaos. At the Juvenile Court, Mr Durban was criticised for leaving his sabre on display. He'd had to admit under oath that Bill had been 'very taken' with it. The magistrate had changed that to 'obsessed' and made Mr Durban agree. The Durbans would all hate him. Bill couldn't possibly write to them.

He looked at the empty sheet of lined paper.

'Jeez, I can't spell neither,' said the freckled boy next to him. 'Just write what it sounds like. A lot of the boys here are illiterate. We're the bright set. Anyway, the officers censor everything you write, so you can't say what you really mean.'

Bill twiddled his fingers under the desk. Who could he write to, and what could he say? 'What sort of thing are you writing then?' he asked the boy.

'I'll write slogans, and some of them will get through. I'll write my news in between them, and my mum'll work out what's happening. Like she writes bits between silly sentences to let me know the latest about the uprisings.'

'Uprisings?'

'Sure – I'm only here to stop me taking part in them. I'm Irish, can't you tell?'

He did have a funny accent that was a lot nicer than Cockney. His face was jollier, too.

'So I'm a political prisoner, not a criminal like you lot.'

Criminal! That's what he was now. 'Is everyone here criminal?' Some of the boys were small and didn't look evil.

'Some are just absconders but there's thieves and murderers, too! Him at the back with the black hair and eyebrows.' He gave a cheery wink. 'Done his Ma in with a brick. And I got wind that you done near that with a sword.'

'No!'

243

'That's enough. No talk of your offences. You know the rules.' The officer walked slowly between each of them with the measured step of a policeman on his beat, his footsteps keeping time with the thump of Bill's heart.

Bill shook his head, the only gesture he could make to show the boy he wasn't a murderer.

The officer's tread, one, two, one, two, stopped beside him. 'You not writing, lad? I heard you were one of those who could.'

Bill picked up his pencil again and twiddled it until it became hot and damp in his hand.

'I don't know who to write to,' he muttered to his neighbour.

'Just anyone, or it's a cert you won't get any letters back.'

The only person he could risk writing to was Alan. He might tear the letter up; he might never reply. He could hear Mother in his head again: 'Everyone we've ever met will read those newspaper reports'. Alan's mother would have seen the newspaper. She'd be horrified. Alan would never, never be in this kind of trouble. But if Bill said it was an accident, Alan would know that it was. He scribbled away at length pretending he and Alan were together. At the bottom he wrote, *Please, please, answer. Tell Mrs Youldon I'm away at school and ask her to tell Mrs Pawsey that.* (That was best and true-ish.) Else they'd wonder why his letters had stopped. They'd think he'd forgotten them. He kicked the heel of one boot into the front of his foot several times. It hurt quite a lot and he deserved it.

Somehow, a week passed, or maybe two. He was now a Brigville School boy. On a pouring wet Tuesday, normally when fierce Mr Sandson (nicknamed Samson) led vigorous PT lessons outside, they couldn't go out into the paved yard and the letters were handed out. One came for Bill, his first. Alan had replied! The letter was short. It had already been opened and one sentence blotted out with a thick blue line.

Alan wrote that he was still Bill's friend, but wasn't allowed to write again until Bill had completed his sentence. At first Bill thought Alan was joking about missing a full stop, but then he remembered that 'sentence' was the thing he was 'serving'. That meant being shut away with other bad boys, where no-one could see him. Alan said he missed him. It was the only bright spot since all this terrible stuff started. Alan said he hoped Brigville was 'not too bad' and that there were decent history books in the library. 'Remember knights.'

He almost smiled. It was a coded message. It reminded of a good, laughing time when Alan told him a good knight needed the three things: the brave man's weapon, the wise man's book, the flower from the faithful lover. That Dutch history book was in the case Brigville had shut away, too wise for an Approved School boy. He wouldn't touch any kind of weapon now, however brave its owner, and he'd never have the flower, for who would love someone like him?

He kept the letter in his pocket with the piece of green and white napkin. Even though it was short, just knowing that Alan was still friendly made the following days bearable, and the idea of reading up about knights gave him something new to think about.

Many boys were hardly able to read or manage anything as difficult as long division and so most daily lessons were of little use to Bill. After many lessons sitting blankly with his finished work, he was provided with a stack of books and left to get on with things himself. Eventually he plucked up courage and asked for a text book on photography.

'When you've earned enough privileges.' Several books were put in front of him. 'You can have these textbooks to study.'

Bill read through the books as if they were set lessons. He actually missed those hours of studying at St Werberg's. These books had been donated, their previous owners sometimes named on the inside cover. They were a strange mix, none of them books for children. *My Travels through Kurdistan*; *Handicraft for Beginners*; *Business Administration*; *Poems to Comfort the Bereaved*; *A History of England, Book II, Tudors and Stuarts*; *Cats and their Care*; *Steelwork in Sheffield*. There was nothing about knights.

In the evening free hour, before supper, he read a library book, *Missing Chums* or *Dick Tracy* and pretended he was at home in the parlour. But the click-click of table tennis and the raised voices of boys waiting their turn to play as well as the frequent tussles and fights made that difficult.

As well as lessons, meal-times, exercises, the rota of tasks, there was football. After the first joyous moment of his foot touching the ball, the roughness of the game and the need for constant intervention of the supervising officer meant he couldn't pretend he was back playing with his friends at St Werberg's. After a few more evening games, the officer tapped him on the shoulder and told him to 'give the others a chance'. After the game ended, he said to 'forget being a star'.

So now football was something else where Bill might do the wrong thing. Until then, he'd always gone full out to play his best.

Visits were allowed after the initial month. It was another trauma; to have to face Mother and Dad for the first time since Juvenile Court.

The room that visitors saw was the neatest and cleanest in the school. There were some easy chairs as well as several small tables with hard chairs around them. He had made himself as smart as he could in the dreary brown uniform and paced in behind the other boys who had visitors.

Dad had chosen one of the tables to sit at. He was looking straight ahead. Mother sat close beside him, holding onto his arm and it was some moments before their wary glance at the boys entering the room latched onto his face.

He came forward and sat opposite them in the third chair.

'Are you well?' Dad said.

Bill nodded. 'Yes, thank you.'

Dad, perhaps *Father* now. *Dad* was surely far too friendly for a boy like Bill to use? Dad sat with his feet firmly planted either side of the table's metal legs. Was he assessing how far Bill had reformed?

'You're doing lessons.'

Nod. What point was there talking about Business *Administration* or *Steelwork in Sheffield*, books that now formed his education?

'Do they talk to you – about what you did? The wrongs you have to think about during your time here?'

Swallow. 'Yes.' There was Mr Jones on a Wednesday who saw him on his own, and the religious assemblies covered most sins.

Bill had rehearsed a list of worthwhile tasks he had performed to convince his parents he was reforming, but now the words wouldn't come out.

'You look well enough,' said Mother in a tone that suggested that he shouldn't. 'There's enough to eat, then?'

'Yes, thank you.'

'You realise the whole thing has been in the newspapers, especially after the Hearing. There have been Letters to the Editor, even articles about it.'

Bill hung his head, imagining everyone reading about it, everyone he knew, his parents knew. How they would have hated it.

'It's been the most dreadful time of our lives.'

'Yes,' he choked out. 'Dreadfully sorry.'

There was a long pause, an expectant one. Before this visit he'd worried about what questions he might risk asking. He longed not to ask any, it would be best not to know the answers, but then they'd say he didn't care about the consequences of the accident, that was called an 'offence' here. The real question: *How is Kenneth?* was obviously ridiculous to ask. Such an everyday question was probably denied to him forever, for the answer would never be *Very Well*. But he must ask something. He opened his mouth. Before he could get the first words out, Mother leaned forward over the ink-stained table top.

'You realise that people blame us?' Her eyes were watering.

It was terrible to see that. She was properly upset, not just being upset like when Uncle Frank had died. He tried to take in what she had just said. Blame. But that was what he had. Blame was his.

Dad put one hand over his beard as if to protect it. He was going to say something, quote something. But no, he gave his own words. 'The theory, for what it's worth, is that when children go wrong it's because of faulty parenting.' He looked around the room as if it was the Court, with benches of people waiting to hear the words of the judge. 'What a travesty of understanding! However, this view is what your mother and I are faced with. Despite my position as a senior officer of the County Court, I am derided behind my back, looked down upon by those much lower in social class.'

Bill stared hard at a point somewhere below Dad's beard, glazing his eyes deliberately, willing them not to fill with tears, his ribs pushing at his chest.

Dad's finger jabbed towards him and wagged once, twice. 'You should be made aware of this theory. You may wish to contradict it – at least in your own case.'

He must answer. With the right words. He choked out, 'I'll say it's not your fault.'

Mother's voice was clear enough for other parental heads to turn, 'No, indeed.' She turned to Dad, as if it was he who needed the explanation. 'He was evacuated for years, that's what I explain to people. I had no influence.'

A tea trolley rattled along the corridor. Teachers would be given tea and a slice of dry fruit cake. Soon afterwards, boys would file to the dining room for bread, margarine, a hard-boiled egg and an apple. Brigville School was careful to provide for the boys' health.

'No influence.' Bill tried to absorb what was being said and not being said. Mother was blaming Mrs Pawsey for influencing him?

'Indulged. That's what you were at that place.' Mother spat confirmation of his thoughts.

Dad's beard was being stroked into place by his large hand. It had become a character in its own right, like a crown on a king, or a cap on a dunce. Dad's voice emerged above it. 'That ruined your character, apparently. Under the surface. We'd never have known. The school thought you reliable, made you a prefect even! Head Boy!' He snorted. 'They never knew either, never noticed a thing. No sign of this – canker.'

Canker had been mentioned in the cat book, but Bill couldn't remember quite what it was. He pulled his earlobe, which was flaming hot. Weren't earlobes the things that police looked at to see if you were a criminal? They could get hot, red, give you away.

'And we didn't notice, Herbert. Did we? We even though him reliable, Doreen did too. She trusted him even more than I did.'

Was he supposed to hear this conversation? Was he part of it? He shifted his feet. Size ten now. Shoes had been provided when he'd arrived, so Mother needn't know just yet. His size had always upset her.

'I ask myself, would I walk down the street with you now? No, I wouldn't!' Mother moved her hand from Dad's arm and folded both hands on top of the table. She was wearing gloves. 'And what have you got to say? Sitting there silent! Don't you want to ask our forgiveness?'

He'd wanted to ask if he'd be coming home soon. But now he saw they wouldn't want people seeing him in Primley Road, the reminder that Mr and Mrs Wilson had a son with a bad character.

He stuttered a start, 'If I w-walk along on m-my own …,' then managed, 'When I'm finished here, am I coming home?'

Dad coughed and fumbled for his handkerchief. He blew his nose.

On the easy chair nearest to them a woman was saying, 'Yes, Robbie's had his party, but you'll be having yours when you come home, lovey. Promise.'

It was a sudden reminder. His birthday was in October. Wasn't it October now?

Mother twitched. 'At home, it's a matter of Kenneth needing one of us all the time, being there.'

The beard shifted a little. The voice came through it. 'Decisions must come later. In the light of events.'

A bell sounded as if to emphasise his non-words. Dong, dong, dong.

Chairs scraped on the floor. Visitors were preparing for their sad goodbyes, choking back their tears, or in Bill's case, their release.

Dad stood up, placing his chair back under the table with precision. Mother was occupied in handbag rearrangement and negotiation of the fifteen steps to the door.

Bill couldn't manage to come out with the, *Will you come again?*

Mother said, 'Goodbye, Bill.'

Other mothers, fussing, 'Be brave, dear. We miss you so much.' One wiping her eyes. 'I'll write often, lovey pet.'

Other boys were saying, 'Don't go yet.'

A son, mother, their hands clasping, 'Be a good boy. It won't be long.'

Dad lowered his head towards Bill, allowing him a shared breath of tobacco smell, '*Ordinary people merely think how they should spend time; a man of talent tries to use it.* Schopenhauer. I have always tried to guide you with moral thinkers.'

'Yes, Dad, I know.' He had, he always had.

'So spend your time well, and thoughtfully.'

Spend? Surely it was *serve* your time. The door closed behind Dad, the last parent to leave.

Chapter Thirty-five

He knew it was his birthday when the post was given out. Dad had forwarded two birthday cards to him with his own, a photograph of Wandsworth that stated *Greetings*. Even Dad couldn't imply that today would be a happy birthday. The second card was from the Youldons and the third from the Pawseys. There wasn't one from Nanny and Grandad. The tin tray had a slice of cake with jam in it for tea.

October ended, the weeks after it rolled by, then the winter began. Because of the electricity cuts and the vicious winter of the year past, a dread of its repetition prevented the whole school from thinking of anything else. Christmas Day jollities were minimal and Boxing Day was the coldest day of all.

When February brought snow, the early thrill of being allowed out to build snowmen soon waned when they came indoors to the failed heating. Shivering in classrooms was like a new punishment that the grown-ups had to share.

The teachers, wrapped in scarves and blanket wraps, peering through balaclavas, were in the worst of moods. They said they could hardly face 1948, for they'd remember winter 1947 for the rest of their lives.

'So will we!' murmured the boys who'd been there the longest, 'and not just for the cold.'

For Bill, the Brigville routine kept things manageable. Everything was thought out and Bill just had to do it all; obey.

When he sat on his hard bed at night facing the door, he went through all the awful things in Brigville life: the bullying, the punishments, discomforts, friendlessness, isolation from all he'd known, it was the lack of any

252

personal possessions that felt worst. He'd been lonely and sad before, but not guilty and without absolutely everything he owned except the scrap of napkin he kept hidden inside the day's handkerchief.

In evacuation, he'd comforted himself with a photograph of the shashka. Then it had been stolen from him. Next it was used to try to turn Mr Durban against him. Then the shashka itself had turned against Bill. It had fulfilled the dreadful prophecy written in the ancient book.

What could comfort him now? Only his camera, with its one promise of a future beyond dread and shame. Photographs were in black and white; something you could understand. How long a wait before he saw it again? Or would Dad throw it away as a punishment?

After his second review, Bill was interviewed by the governor about his future. All the boys were encouraged to think of an occupation they could work towards once they were released. The Brigville School concern was that they shouldn't continue a life of crime. 'When you're released, we don't want you back here, and you don't want prison as a future.'

The Governor, as the boys liked to call him, had Bill brought into his study. He discussed the wounding, the damaging of Kenneth, the effect on his life, on his parents' lives, on Aunty. Bill kept his hands clasped behind his back, his eyes on the floor where he pressed his heavy regulation shoes down as hard as possible to prevent him swaying to and fro. He nodded from time to time, to show the Governor his understanding, his agreement. He stood as he'd learned a guilty man should.

'Right. Now, before your offence, Wilson, I gather you were studying successfully at school, expected to get leaving exams, then move on to some sort of professional life like your father. When you leave here you will still be fifteen. Many boys leave school on their birthday but technically you're not too old for the end of that last school year, School Certificate year. However, it might be difficult to get a school to take you. Your reputation will go before you.'

Bill had never considered returning to school as a possibility. All his focus had been on surviving the experience of Brigville. He hadn't dared to look ahead. He almost laughed at the idea of returning to St Werberg's – a preposterous notion. He could go to work. He'd shown himself to be useful but what employer would take him, and where? 'Sir, am I to go home?'

The Governor placed his hands on his desk, about two foot apart from each other. His nails were square and beautifully kept. 'When you've finished your term? I assume so. What do you mean?'

'My parents may not want me. I mean, they have Kenneth living with them.'

'Ah.' The skin above his eyebrows was loose enough for folds to come and go. They did so now. 'Well. There are hostels for boys like you. Have you thought about your future?'

'No, sir.' Since he'd been here, Bill had only thought about leaving each day behind.

'I want you to think now. You will have to earn your living as soon as possible. What do you see yourself as doing?'

Relief. That question was easy. 'Before this happened, sir, I was hoping to be a photographer. I need to practise. I have a camera and manuals, but they're at home.'

'I'll contact your father. You realise that you cannot use a camera here, but I'll allow you to have the manuals. When they are brought, you can study them after classes each day.'

His parents were due to visit in a few days' time. Would they agree to bring the manuals? The visits were something to dread. By now, the shame of what had happened, the suffering Bill had caused to each member of his family had been so thoroughly rehearsed with him that he knew it better than times tables or French verbs. And yet he didn't know it at all. Words such as guilt, pain, suffering, anguish, embarrassment, endurance, shame, responsibility, were said over and over, but never an incident or example that would make these real to him. He was expected to know, without being told, what those words meant was happening. Were people shouting at Mother in the street, bullying Dad in the Court? What dreadful things were being done by doctors to Kenneth? He didn't know any incidents, yet he felt he was perspiring his family's pain and shame through every one of his pores. Aunty was never ever mentioned. She must hate Bill so much, her fury too intense for even Dad to risk telling him about it.

Although he'd been told that Approved School was his punishment, the visits were actually far worse. As excitement rose among the boys, even a 'Yippee!' when the announcement came: 'Visiting Time', Bill lined up with dread, envying the boys with no visits who sat on their beds with morose expressions.

Yet, on the day of the next visit Bill saw immediately that Dad had brought the manuals. He placed them on the desk.

'Thank you. Thank you very much.'

Bill knew they meant nothing to Dad, no more than if they had been *Robinson Crusoe* or *Biggles Flies Again*.

'I gather you're allowed to study these after lessons?'

'Yes. It's like an earned privilege.'

Mother said, 'Just as well to keep your head in a book. You can't risk making friends with these boys. Such a dreadful influence.' She'd never understood loneliness. He'd been lonely at home when he was very little and wasn't allowed friends home. He'd felt lonely that first evacuation when she didn't find where he'd been billeted, and the second time when she let him be billeted away from the rest of them. He missed his friends, especially Alan. Even if the boys here were rough and dishonest, he needed to be friends with at least some of them.

'I dread to think what you'll be like when you get out.'

Dad added, 'I trust you're reflecting on those matters that you need to change in yourself?'

'Yes. We get told that sort of thing most days.'

'Because you have to think of that time when you're no longer at Approved School.'

'I do. The Governor is allowing me to study my photography because that's what I'm going to do when I get out – be a photographer.'

Mother looked stunned. 'That seems a long way ahead.'

Dad said, 'You can't just begin a career as though nothing has happened. You'll need to be accepted by some sort of employer, and that won't be easy. The first thing is your base. After your sentence has been worked you'll need a base.'

'To live?'

'Yes. Somewhere.'

That meant, not home.

He didn't take in the rest of the halting conversation. He tried to remember the chapter he'd reached in the photography manual. Something to do with arranging the light.

When the bell went he was sure he heard a joint sigh of relief pass between Dad and Mother. It was time for them to line up with the other parents, none of them acknowledging the others, shuffling out like refugees from the normal world.

'I shall study about light and shade,' he said to their retreating backs.

'We must be willing to let go of the life we planned so as to have the life that is waiting for us,' E. M. Forester,' said Dad.

They said their goodbyes and left Bill to consider each of their few words and all of their meanings.

Chapter Thirty-six

The officer turned the key and the first door opened. They walked together down the corridor, out of step. This man wasn't one of the teachers, those who set exercises, talked about how to do better, how to make changes, but one of the supervisors who checked boys were in the right place, or broke up fights, chased after anyone stupid enough to run away and held a boy down if he had to be caned. Bill had always avoided this man, for he looked as if he really didn't like boys at all.

The man paused before the second door, clicking his keys in his hand. 'This is it for you, then, Wilson. An out.'

Bill shuffled his feet. The shoes were too shabby for the miracle that had happened to him, too shabby for words. Surely, when he saw him, his rescuer would change his mind.

'You're a lucky blighter. Not just because someone's willing to take you on, but because of your age. A few months older and you'd probably have had a birching for your offence. Birching is *real* character building. That would have cooled your temper. I reckon the magistrate up your part of London has gone soft. We've never had an offence in here like it! Next time...' His voice trailed off with almost a snarl. 'Reckon you'll do it again?'

Bill took a step back. 'Of course not! It was an accident.'

A snort. 'Yeah! I was told. With a sabre. Just appeared in your hand like magic, a sabre. Did for the kid's eye and hand. Your cousin, wasn't it? Accident? Yeah! Marvellous.'

The man turned the key. It was twice forwards, once back. Then the door opened, all the great thickness of it, cranking to the outside. Sunlight, of a sort, fell in. There was glass in the porch window where it said, *Reception* and lower down, *Please show identity document*. Bill could just about remember arriving here. The calendar looked the same, plain, white, the top sewn onto a cardboard backing, but it wasn't. It now said, March 1948, the first time he'd seen a date since – when? He looked around, as if the woman who'd brought him might materialise. She'd stopped at this porch, that came before the corridors, the taking away of things, the undressing, the school clothes.

Now he was wearing his own clothes. The small case and all its contents had been brought to him before he left the dormitory and the bed near the door for another boy. A boy coming to an Approved school for boys who were not approved of.

His clothes felt tight, formal. He had once worn these things, and when wearing them, he'd done a terrible thing, made a terrible accident happen to Kenneth. He looked down at the blue-green jersey which Angela had liked him in. Now she wouldn't. It would always remind her of what he'd done. His grey trousers, his first and only long ones, ended above his ankles. He could see marks where he'd knelt on Mr Durban's floor, even specks of blood, Kenneth's blood. He'd been allowed to keep the school shoes since his own no longer fitted. He walked them forward, bringing to the exit the huge feet for Mother to hate.

Papers, keys, signings. That's what the porter was doing at the reception hatch when he came. But now he was moving to the outer door, swinging it open, telling Bill not to come back. 'The gentleman's waiting for you in his car.'

An open door. The pillars, stone staircase. Outside. Nothing in between him and the swathe of grass behind the gravelled road. Air, sky, space.

It seems very bright, though it's cold and the sky's grey. Bill screws up his eyes, dazzled. A voice comes through the faint sunlight.

'Bill! Come on, lad, I'm here now.'

It sounds kind and it's familiar. So is the jacket. That comes nearer to him until he can touch it. Like a small child, he holds a piece. He's seeing whether it's real. Behind him, papers have been signed, official words spoken, but it doesn't matter because he's standing on the right side, the outside, with Mr Durban next to him. It really is Mr Durban. All that the Governor said had come true. Mr Durban is collecting him, giving him a home.

They walk to the gate. Mr Durban lights a cigarette. Bill breathes in the smoke hungrily, so very long since he's smelled it, Craven A. He swivels his eyes sideways, gets a view of his rescuer, his oldest friend.

Mr Durban's got a car now. It's black. He opens a door and touches Bill, pushes him into the passenger seat.

The smell of leather is overwhelming. The dashboard is familiar. The car's the same make and model as the woman's car that brought him here.

Mr Durban slides into the driving seat.

Bill hangs his head. How can he say a whole lifetime of Sorry? He chokes out, 'I'm really sorry.'

'It was my fault, Bill. Mine. I shouldn't have had it there, or left you alone with it in the house. I got into terrible trouble.'

He remembers, coming out of the Court, as he was put in a bare room, Dad's voice, raging, 'You never told me! If you'd said he was obsessed with the wretched thing, I could have dealt with him.'

'It was an accident,' Bill mutters, pathetic even to himself.

'I know. And Kenneth said. A terrible accident. But—'

There's the <u>but</u>. Bill's had time, months of hours on his own to think of the <u>but</u>. The magistrate sentenced on the basis of the <u>but</u>, the secret thought 'but I hated Kenneth at that moment. He was always taking everything, like my friends, Jill, the photo, Angela, and he was taking the shashka.'

It was the shashka that took the wounding thoughts and made the frightful incision. Bill can still play football, still take photographs, while Kenneth—

'What can I do, now?'

'To put it right?' Mr Durban takes a cloth and rubs the windscreen free of smears. 'Lead a good life. Your parents want that more than anything. You must be rehabilitated. I've got the responsibility for that now.'

'But Mrs Durban?'

'She's agreed and it's all been arranged with your family. You're to live with us.'

'In your house?' *He'd imagined some bare room or two that Mr Durban would supervise, not a house. Not his house, the place where it happened! How could Mr Durban let him through the door again?*

'You'll have the spare bedroom.'

'Angela—?' *Angela would never want to see him again. That last look as she turned back to him before she left the bloodied lounge, following the stretcher with Kenneth on it. An image of her face, shocked beyond words, blasts him between the eyes.*

'She's in Nottingham. An opportunity came up at the bank. We encouraged her to take it, her mother comes from there. So Angela won't be at home. When she wants to come back for a weekend, well, we shall have to see. Let's sort that out when it happens, not now.'

'But you shouldn't have to,' *Bill's voice trails away.*

Mr Durban puts his hand on Bill's, almost in it. It's the first gesture of affection Bill's had for over six months. He flinches.

261

'Remember, I always wanted a son. Remember, I told you when you were a nipper that I'd have liked a son just like you.'

Bill shakes his head, very slowly, as if confusion might flake away and lightly descend onto the car mats. 'Not like me.'

'Like you will be. Let's get you out of here.'

He starts the car and it moves away down the long, long road.

Bill turns and sees that from here there's no sign of what goes on in that fine building, Brigville School. Now the detail of detention is too far to be detected by the naked eye. He screws up his eyes hardly believing that he is being drawn away from it, further and further. He sees it glide into a distant perspective. The large gates and monstrous brick walls grow smaller. He keeps his eyes on them until they are just a black fleck on the grey horizon.

Chapter Thirty-seven

Bill blinked hard. When the car was well clear of the Approved School environs, he could dare believe that this was not a dream. Mr Durban *had* come to rescue him.

The car slowed down and Bill saw woods and fields passing on either side. Although the sky was low and grey and the trees hardly one bud more than bare, the scene was as fresh as if he'd never seen countryside before. Mr Durban opened his window and Bill breathed in deeply. He smelled pine, flowers, grass. The field beside them stretched on and on until it reached a row of trees in the far distance.

'Is there anything you'd like to do before we get back? I know it's going to be difficult, seeing it all again.'

Bill had his hand on the door handle. 'I'd like to run.'

Mr Durban got out promptly. 'You mustn't...'

'I won't – I mean I'll come back.'

'...mustn't go far.'

He was out, into the field and running at full tilt, catching his breath and feeling his limbs stretch to their full extent, his shoes hitting the grass softly, rapidly. He felt like a cricket speeding along, invisible to any predator. He ran and ran until his lungs pained like thumps in his side, then he turned, held Mr Durban in view and loped back.

He got back into the car and said nothing.

Mr Durban drove straight to Fulham.

Bill couldn't avoid seeing the streets and buildings become more and more familiar. By the time they got back to the scene of his crime, he found it difficult to walk up the path let alone go through the door. It opened before he could back away and Mrs Durban stood there. His armpits dampened as a trickle of cold sweat made its way down his sides. What could he say? Slowly he approached her with his hand held out. He quite expected her to smack it away but then his brain reminded him that coming here had been arranged with her agreement. How long would he be staying for? Would he see his parents here? And what would happen to him afterwards?

Mrs Durban smiled at him. She said only a few words before taking him upstairs to the guest bedroom past Angela's slightly open door where flashes of pink gauze taunted him. It was only now that the question forced itself upwards. 'What was Kenneth doing visiting Angela that day?' How could he be stupid enough to speak that thought out loud!

'They were at the same evening class, English Literature. Don't you remember Angela had started them?'

But Kenneth didn't need evening classes. He had Literature at Dulwich College. Those evenings when he wetted his hair smooth, brushed his shoes, looked in the hall mirror, was it Angela he was going to meet! He shook his head. He couldn't cope with that idea as well as facing the enormity of moving in to live here.

Meanwhile, Mrs Durban had opened the guest room door. 'This is for you. I think you'll be comfortable in here.'

It looked blissful, a room with only one bed and no bars. 'Thank you,' was quite inadequate for how he felt.

The plain bed had a tartan blanket tucked tightly over the sheets. There were two Biggles books on the bedside table, and a lamp. A familiar suitcase stood on the floor. It was the one he'd taken into the front door of Primley Road when they first got back from evacuation. The suitcase must have been left here or passed to Mr Durban by Dad. It would have more clothes. He put his Brigville bag beside it and put his hand in his pocket. The piece of napkin was still safe.

'Look, Bill.' A cork board had been pinned on the wall. 'For your pictures, we thought,' said Mrs Durban. 'Your photos.'

She'd remembered his hobby!

They went downstairs, Bill silent, fearing sight of the snug. He was sick with the kind of fear he had when opening his eyes after nightmares to see whether the horror was real. But the Durbans had shut the snug door and it remained shut.

In the dining room they sat around a cheese and onion pie and a bowl of salad. It was the first time Bill had eaten off a plate since the accident. He felt awkward and clumsy, like the half-clothed vagrants had been at the vicarage where Mother had been billeted.

Mr and Mrs Durban spoke as if Bill was a full part of the conversation, about the journey, their relief at some sign of sun, the management of cooking times because of the electricity cuts, the roadworks approaching the bridge.

He had difficulty swallowing, yet every mouthful made him full of appreciation. The food was wonderfully different from the Approved School's. He finished the plateful.

Afterwards, they cleared the table together. Mrs Durban checked the onion soup that was simmering ready for lunch the next day. The aroma was strong enough to sting his eyes. She put on a half-lid and the sweaty smell followed them as they moved away to sit in the lounge.

Mr Durban lit up a cigarette. Bill breathed in the smoke, wanting to feel a part of that, floating away to safety. He knew this was a preparatory pause. He looked at Mrs Durban to see what was coming.

She spoke kindly. 'You're fifteen, Bill. School leaving age, although if nothing had happened you would have continued at St Werberg's until the summer of this year, if not longer. You will have missed getting your School

Certificate. Perhaps the education at Brigville was limited?'

He nodded. Care of cats and travelling in Kurdistan didn't seem very useful.

'Perhaps you should attend school in Fulham.'

He hunched down in his chair. 'I can't.' Where would he tell teachers, boys, he had been at school?

'No? We must see.'

'No-one will have me now, Mrs Durban,' he muttered.

'You can call us Letty and Peter. We're going to treat you like a grown-up in the hope that you'll be one. A good one.' She looked at her husband, a comforting figure in his sports jacket and corduroys.

He puffed away, his smoke rising and twirling. 'The thing is, Bill, we're in loco parentis now. That's what's been agreed.'

His parents didn't want him home. He knew that. He wasn't going to ask what *in loco parentis* meant, it might be too awful. It sounded like one of Dad's sayings. *Loco* suggested being sent on a long train journey. How long was he allowed to stay here? What was Dad wanting him to do, where to go, after this? He kept hunched into his seat, as if the slightest movement of a muscle would make things more dangerous.

'You know I'm a long-standing friend of your father's. He's in a very difficult position. He has responsibilities to you, but also to Kenneth, in lieu of Frank.'

Mrs Durban added, 'Too difficult, the two of you in the same house.'

Bill nodded slowly. Dad had given him away; he could feel it. Mother had too. Although she wasn't Uncle Frank's blood, she preferred Kenneth. She'd never wanted a boy, not Bill's sort of boy and certainly not what he had become. She hadn't wanted one in the beginning when she was ready to have babies. She didn't want one now, but she could handle Kenneth's sort of boy, quiet,

266

artistic. And now he was an invalid, needing to be quiet, he would not be like a boy at all.

'Dear, I don't think you're listening to me,' Mrs Durban – Letty – chided him. She'd carried on talking and he hadn't taken it in.

The thing was, he wasn't used to a woman's voice these days.

'Sorry.'

'I was saying that because it was in our house the awful thing happened, and it was Peter's sabre, we felt a long way responsible.'

Mr Durban said, 'We discussed this, coming here. As the magistrate pointed out, I was responsible.'

Responsible. Such a heavy word. But he, Bill, was the one who crashed the shashka down, no-one else.

Peter screwed out his cigarette into the wooden ashtray that had the big-beaked bird joined on one side. It looked down with disdain at the damaged stump of the cigarette. 'Try to pay attention. This is important, Bill. Now that you're here, you're safe. You've got us to stand beside you. What we're trying to say is that we have the task of setting you on your feet, and that means telling you everything that's happened since Juvenile Court. All right?'

'Yes, sir.'

'Don't "sir" me. Letty's said, you can call me Peter. This is all very hard, but before you go to bed tonight I want you to be completely clear about everything.'

Bill nodded, *Peter* not finding an easy way to his lips. He blinked, telling himself to pay attention, focus on what was being said. After all, there was no-one to shout things now. It did feel strange to be without the shouts, the orders, the clanging, the quantity of footsteps. There would be orders, though, there were bound to be.

Peter Durban began.

267

Bill was glad he didn't have to say anything. To avoid trouble, he had rarely talked more than the necessary sentence, the Yes, the No, the three bags full, for months. He didn't think his throat was up to much more. He was waiting for the bad news. There were bound to be bad things about Kenneth, about everything at home, things lying in wait for him, awful things that he was going to be forced to face. He must listen, it was important.

'You should still be at school, really, but I agree it's too difficult,' Peter was saying. 'Your parents feel your name is still too notorious for you to attend a school locally, even in Fulham. There is also Jill to think of.'

Jill! What would she be thinking? She'd never be allowed to see him again. His last sight of her had been a bewildered face, pushed behind Mother.

'It became terrible for her at school. The things children said to her, so they thought it best if Jill went to boarding school, away where no-one would know.'

A whispered 'No' escaped his lips. It wasn't fair that Jill had to go away. How she'd cried those first weeks at junior school, where at least she came home for tea, slept in her own bed. She would hate to be on her own. Who would tie her hair ribbons, find her skipping rope when she left it around? He slumped further into his chair.

Peter was saying that there had been a collection locally so that Kenneth could have private tuition until he could return to Dulwich College. It had funded a visiting tutor for Kenneth to catch up all the time he'd lost while in hospital. He had his Higher School Certificate to worry about. He needed that before the possibility of university could be considered. Individual school friends were helping with his study notes, for writing with his left hand was a slow and frustrating task, and he was having difficulty adapting emotionally—

Bill looked at his own hands, ones that could write any time he wanted.

'—to the damage to his eye and drawing hand,' Letty continued Peter's theme, 'so that he can't now be an artist.'

Bile rose to Bill's gullet. This was what he had forced himself not to think about, he just couldn't think about. He turned his head away from both of them.

Peter ended her point, 'Yes. So your father has to do his best to educate Kenneth for other things.'

Other things? Bill felt his neck where his Adam's apple had been poking out more and more, recently, and sometimes hurt badly, like now. What other things could there be? Kenneth loved Art.

'You're probably wondering why I say "your father" and don't include your aunt... weren't you?'

He hadn't been wondering. Aunty wasn't ever mentioned and he'd got used to that. Dad was always the one to decide things.

The small silence signalled that Peter wanted a reply. A couple of bicycle bells sounded outside on the road. Such a sound seemed so unusual that Bill started, his head lifting to the window then dropping. In the months and months since he'd heard a bicycle bell, ordinary life had been going on outside. He became aware that Peter was looking at him expectantly.

'Your father, not your aunt.'

He felt blank. Aunty.

'You need to know that she has taken all this very badly. She tried hard at first, when Kenneth came home, to do everything for him, look after him.'

Aunty. That awful cry 'His beautiful face!' shrilled through his brain. She would have worked really hard, looking after Kenneth. She would have been so upset by his bleeding, crying all the time at the sight of him. She'd no longer be the friend who had a soft spot for Bill. Her kindness would be gone.

'Look at me, Bill. It's best you know everything straight away. We all decided this. It's very hard, but you have to face it full on, and then go forward.'

Peter Durban paused and Bill could only see kindly concern in his face. He nodded his readiness.

'She had a nervous breakdown. What had happened to Kenneth wrecked the excitement of Dwaine's arrival.'

Dwaine! How had Bill forgotten he was on his way from America that fateful day. He would have arrived to find everything awful.

'When he arrived, your aunt collapsed and needed treatment. Dwaine was all for taking them both off back to the States, installing Doreen in his new house, getting Kenneth top treatment there at his own expense...'

Wondrous! Dwaine would fix everything, make Aunty happy, cure Kenneth, far, far away in America.

'...But Kenneth wasn't well enough to go. I think you knew that he didn't want his mother to marry Dwaine. He told her to go to America. Doreen couldn't cope with the problem. All the plans to go had been decided before Dwaine arrived, and then—'

'She really went to bits,' Letty put in before Peter's hand stilled her.

Bill had to look down, hiding his eyes which had filled. He'd so wanted Aunty to be happy when he introduced her to Dwaine.

'Dwaine had come with only enough time to arrange the passages to New York. Either Doreen had to go, or he had to go back alone. Your father thought Doreen would fare better with a man to look after her. With your parents already caring for Kenneth, and his hospital treatment under way, she decided to marry Dwaine, which meant leaving with him.' Peter paused. He looked over to Letty.

'It was arranged that Kenneth should remain with your parents. That's what he said he wanted, but he can join his mother in America whenever he chooses.'

Kenneth wouldn't choose that. He'd prefer to be in Bill's house, in Bill's room, with Bill's sister, Bill's parents. Bill clenched his fists beneath the curl of the armchair. Yes! And it was his own fault.

'Do you understand all this, dear?' Letty said, leaning forward to him. 'It's so much to take in, isn't it?'

So much. So awful, all of it. He took a deep breath. He could smell the onion soup, wafting from the kitchen, stale, sweaty, stinging. He managed to stammer out, 'Is Aunty all right now?'

'Dwaine's looking after her,' she said. 'Your father says he's a strong, kindly man. And she will be having a good life in America.'

'She's already gone!'

Letty nodded.

'But I didn't say Goodbye, I haven't… I mean I couldn't…'

'Say you're sorry properly? She'll know.' Peter rubbed one side of his face. 'Whatever else, they do all know that you didn't mean to do this. Even Kenneth says it was an accident.'

Bill desperately needed to be on his own. He wouldn't be able to hold back his tears much longer. He needed to cry and cry and cry out with his shame and misery for in all the months since it happened, he'd hardly shed a tear.

Peter said, 'We're nearly finished with all this and then you can go to bed. I can see you're really tired and overcome, but you need to know the whole picture so that you aren't left confused and without knowing the situation. Things are not all bad, Bill.'

He set his jaw and nodded. Surely he'd heard all the worst by now.

'Since your father has Kenneth's problems to manage, through no fault of his own, it's been decided that we will take on the responsibility for you. You will live here until you're ready for work. We will give you a new start in life, and you'll do your best to improve and rise to the challenge.'

'I will, I will.' Was that all he was going to be asked to do? Work, try hard? That was easy.

'And when you're on an even keel, in work, earning your keep, your father thinks it's only right that Kenneth should decide what retribution he wants.'

A shudder went through Bill despite himself. 'Retribution?'

'You don't know what that means, that word? It's like a correction, a putting things to rights. It used to mean a vengeance but that's not what your father meant, of course. He feels you owe Kenneth something you can do or provide that will improve his life: a small thing, if you think how it's been so terribly damaged.'

Bill understood. He nodded with the truth, the fairness of it. Dad knew what was right. He just didn't know Kenneth.

Chapter Thirty-eight

Although Bill, heavily blanketed, had saturated the pillow slip with his tears for what felt like hours, he found he'd slept long and soundly. It must have been the comfort of the bed, the room all to himself. Church bells woke him, a comforting, pure sound. It was a Sunday.

Despite the awfulness of the information Peter and Letty had given him last night, it felt good to be here, the soft bed comforting him into a new stage of his life. He sat up and drank in the smell and sight of the fresh dew on the garden outside his window. A bedside clock informed that it was nearly nine. Goodness! He would have had breakfast, done PT and be ready for lessons back at Brigville.

He washed, and hurried down to breakfast and found a conversation going that was wonderfully trivial and normal. Peter and Letty smiled, nodded and continued their discussion of the prefabs going up near the common, the tasks of the day, the problem of wandering dogs in their garden. It was a comfortable discussion. Once it was clear that last night's subjects were not going to be raised again, his stomach began to relax.

He helped Letty clear the table. There was another painful thing he needed to know. He'd better get it over with, while she was busy with dishes and putting things away, not sitting looking at him.

'Letty, did Angela like Kenneth best?'

'She'll have liked him differently, Bill. They used to have a cup of tea after class, in the café opposite the Reading Rooms. She had told me that week that she thought Kenneth might ask her for a date.'

I was going to ask her that! he stopped himself from blurting out. Angela had never told him, all those times he'd photographed her, that she was seeing Kenneth. He made his words come slowly, 'Then, after – afterwards, did Angela visit him?' Would she even come back and start dating Kenneth as soon as he was well enough to go out?

'She didn't keep in touch after the first visit. She couldn't cope with the way he looked. She felt so bad about that, because she should have been one of his supports. But he had school friends, and soon afterwards, she met Vincent.' Her voice tailed away.

Vincent? Was he someone working in the same bank? Had he gone to Nottingham with Angela? It didn't matter now. Angela was a distant figure altogether.

Letty turned to him. 'Have you unpacked?'

He hadn't thought about it. He hadn't packed the suitcase himself and so it didn't feel like his own. He went upstairs. *Angela and Kenneth.* All that time, when Bill thought Kenneth was still avoiding the Durbans, he had begun a secret friendship. He'd been paying Bill back for that time he'd made him feel small, after the theft of the photo. It didn't matter to Kenneth how long after an event it was, he paid Bill back. And now, when what Bill had done was as serious as it could possibly be, how awful might the *retribution* be? And it might come after years. He would never feel safe.

It was no good panicking about it. He had to think of the *now*. The *now* was challenging enough. He was supposed to be unpacking.

The suitcase held clothes that smelled of Primley Road, clothes he needed. But under them it had his precious camera! He picked it up and hung it round his neck, back where it belonged. There was his photograph album tied safely in its box, his football boots – too small now – a couple of his favourite books and the Head Boy badge. Dad or Mother must have bothered to pack these for him. They had thought about what he might need or want. That small germ of thoughtfulness was a comfort.

He turned to his soft overnight case with its horrible memories of Brigville. It had his photography manuals and the Dutch history book Dad had brought from the war zone. He emptied the case totally, and screwed it into the furthest corner of the wardrobe.

When everything looked tidy, he opened the bedroom window onto the garden where he and Angela had once run, where the Anderson had stood. He breathed in the sweet air. It smelled like spring and it would be spring next month.

Downstairs, Peter was moving towards the back door. He gestured for Bill to join him. They moved outside where it was chilly but bright. They strolled up the path as the church bells chimed. He said, 'I love Sundays. I had too many years when I still had to work on them, not to appreciate the leisure now. Home Guard duties and catching up with work or sleep, that's all over, thank goodness. But let's move on with your concerns.'

Bill fell into step with him. It wasn't difficult; they were much of a size.

'I don't know what we're going to do about friends for you. That is, your old friends. Your father thought it best you didn't contact anyone from St Werberg's.'

Bill nodded glumly.

'And it's not very helpful to stay in touch with any friends you've made at Brigville.'

'There aren't any, really.' He wouldn't tell Peter about the misery of isolation because of being different, the wariness between the boys, the hum of resentment and aggression in their movements, the viciousness ready to surface at any lapse in supervision, the knowledge that his false reputation as a swordsman, near murderer, was likely to shatter at the slightest confrontation. Some boys, like the Irish lad, were friendly enough for conversations or board games, but there were no real friends.

'So, you're not in touch with anyone from before?'

'I can be now! There's Alan!' Alan had said they'd be in contact as soon as he finished his sentence. 'Near Thornton Heath, Norwood, he lives. Alan's the friend I had in evacuation, we were billeted together. He knows about – what happened. I wrote to him from Brigville and he wrote back once. He will be all right, I think. His parents – I don't know whether they will have contacted my family.' He heard his own enthusiastic tone fade.

Peter stopped beside the garden shed and leant against it. 'We'll have to see if it's appropriate to see Alan; if it's not going to cause anyone any distress.'

Bill looked down, the heaviness of the previous evening returning. Mrs Routledge would probably have telephoned Mother early on, to sympathise. What would she think of him? How could she want Alan to stay his friend?

They went indoors and Bill asked for notepaper. He wrote to Alan, not saying too much about Brigville. The censoring couldn't be forgotten even though Bill knew that wasn't there anymore. Would Alan write back as he'd promised?

He sealed the envelope and looked at the notepaper's next blank page.

'Should I write to Aunty? Could I?'

'Write and wish her every happiness in her new life.'

Every happiness! *Some* happiness, more like. Unless he wrote *Sorry* five thousand times over every inch of the card, what else could he say? How stupid a thing to say, *Sorry*, knowing that her son could never be *un*damaged.

Alan wrote back. He said they'd get together in his school holidays. That was marvellous. But even after three weeks, no answer came from Aunty. He wasn't surprised.

She'd never forgive him. Did she have some happiness? He imagined Dwaine escorting Aunty in his gentlemanly way to a large American car; or at home, opening the door of a huge refrigerator loaded with food. 'Let's eat, honey,' he'd say. Dwaine would make sure Aunty was all right.

Peter walked Bill down to the local football club on the Saturday. 'The juniors meet here at ten. I've explained to the coach that you're just back from boarding school and that you're keen to play in any position.'

Bill took a huge breath and felt it surge through his chest. It would be wonderful to play football properly after the constant fouls in the Brigville School games.

'You sign on with the juniors today, and who knows? Wouldn't it be superb if you managed to be selected to their training scheme? Fulham are working their way up to the first division. Think of that.'

Bill's thrill subsided at the words *sign on*. 'But Dad said everyone will avoid me once they know my name.'

Peter held his arm. 'There is something else important that Letty and I haven't discussed with you, yet. We thought it best to tell you in the context of something positive.'

What now? What else did he have to face? Had the whole bunch of junior footballers been warned about him?

'Because of that very difficulty, your name being in the newspaper, your father and I thought it was better if you were known as Bill Durban. We can't do that if you went to school or college, because of your birth certificate. But otherwise, shall we do that for the present? It saves you being bothered with any questions.'

It was like a thump in his stomach. Dad didn't want him to be a Wilson any more. A new surname. Whatever name they called him, he was the boy who dreadfully damaged his cousin.

Chapter Thirty-nine

It would have been easier to stay in the Durbans' house and garden and not see anyone, but Letty said that the weekly football game and Wednesday evening training were important for him socially. She'd suggested Scouts, but he felt too old somehow. Fulham Scouts might want to check how he'd got his badges, and those would be under his real name.

He did play football enthusiastically, but didn't chat in the changing room or see the other boys in between training sessions and matches. He knew they thought him boring. He didn't mind. It was safer.

During the day he did some gardening and household jobs. Letty was out and left him to himself, which was what he needed. Sometimes, he went into the kitchen and watched her make soup or stews. He liked the cooking smells and it might be useful to know how to make some meals for himself. Suppose Letty got ill? He would be able to step in and help out.

In the evenings, after supper, Peter helped him with his studies. 'I'm not a mathematician but this is what you might need in the real world ahead of you; keeping accounts, devising a budget, knowing what things cost.'

Bill found he was expected to read the newspaper fully every day to keep up with what was happening in the world, as well as listening to the six o'clock news on the wireless.

Otherwise he wrote out information from Peter's books, luckily more interesting and comprehensive than what was available at Brigville. There was a whole set of encyclopaedias that Letty said had cost the earth. They had been a wedding present from her parents. Bill taught himself facts about countries, products, population, culture; and about animals. One day, under K in the encyclopaedia he saw something about knights. For the first time he could follow-up Alan's suggestion, as long as it didn't involve swords.

He soon found the code of chivalry, and he wrote it down twice, once in his notebook and once on separate paper. It felt important to have something to show Alan, even if it wasn't as good as a School Certificate.

Peter got textbooks in physics and chemistry from a second-hand bookshop. 'You can't do experiments but you must learn some of the things you've missed in your schooling. Chemistry's involved in photographic work, the processing.' That made sense to Bill so he took especial trouble to learn what he could.

When he'd finished all the study Peter had set, or in gaps during the daytime, Bill studied his photography manuals. The problem was, he needed film to practise what he was learning. He certainly couldn't ask Peter for film: the Durbans were doing so much for him already.

But then, the miracle. The post on a Tuesday brought a package from Alan. Inside there were two films and the Vacuee card game. They'd played that in evacuation. Because he was alone in the hall, he twizzled around twice. Film at last! Now he could put some of his study into practice. The Vacuee game was precious because it was like saying, *Remember those old times*. Alan would have meant something like that when he sent it. Mrs Routledge must have allowed him to. It was a great relief that she didn't want Alan to keep away from him. The best thing of all was knowing he was still a friend, whatever Bill had done. The Routledges would be very shocked by what had happened but they would know, surely they'd know, that Bill had never meant to damage Kenneth? He kicked at a ruck in the mat. He'd like to tell himself he never meant to hurt Kenneth, but in his heart he knew that he had wanted to hurt him – just not with the shashka, and certainly not seriously.

He took his treasures upstairs and found his camera, ready to wind in a film. He'd use it carefully, not waste a single snap. The chapter he'd reached in the manual was about photographing a person who was speaking, to avoid the posed effect. He'd like to photograph Alan, if he was going to see him.

He went back downstairs slowly. Peter was at work, but Letty was in the kitchen. Before he could think of visiting or meeting a friend, there were further things he had to face – those questions he'd never asked – because knowing the answers would have made Brigville unbearable. Now he'd better approach each question carefully. He'd found out why Kenneth was here that dreadful day. He'd found out about Angela. There was a worse question he hadn't asked yet. He was like a soldier testing for a bomb, risking that it would blow him to bits.

With Letty's back towards him as she stirred mince on the stove, he ventured the hope he could never quite put out of his mind: 'Letty, with the hospital treatment is Kenneth's hand... on the mend?'

She twisted around so rapidly that a strand of her hair flew sideways. 'On the mend? Bill! You surely know? They must have told you months ago.'

He shook his head.

She sat down at the table and waved him to sit opposite. 'Bill, I think you must have been told, either by your parents or the headmaster at Brigville.'

'Was I?'

'And you've somehow put it out of your mind. Kenneth's hand had to be amputated.'

His own hand flew to his mouth, the back of it pressed against his teeth. 'Cut off?'

She nodded.

No! The hand had been bleeding loads but the ambulance men would have bandaged it. He knew it was very badly damaged but surely it was still there, in its bandage, a sling perhaps.

Letty leant forward searching his face. 'Sometimes when we're very shocked we stop ourselves facing the truth. You know you damaged Kenneth very severely.'

'Yes.' He nodded, looked at the floor, looked up again. 'Yes, I know.'

'Well, Kenneth's hand is gone. He is being fitted for a prosthetic hand.' She said slowly, 'That means a false hand.'

False hand. He tried to imagine it. So far he'd thought of Kenneth not able to draw because of his hand in a sling, and hurting still, but not of having *no* hand. He felt terribly sick. He might have to dash to the cloakroom. But before he could do so, Letty went on.

'And his eye. You do know that his eye can't get better, don't you? He's lost the sight of that for good. There is no treatment that can repair the damage.'

He stared at the kitchen table so hard that it expanded and swayed in front of him.

She stood. 'I'll make you a strong sweet tea. You've had a shock.'

It was as if it had just happened. As if he'd come out of the snug with all the blood on the carpet and a doctor had said, *Look what you've done. Your cousin has no hand and his eye will never see again.* All he'd seen of Kenneth after the accident was that one time, in hospital, just a lump under the covers, silent. People had spoken of damage, pain, suffering, disaster, injuries, but they hadn't said what Letty had just told him. It was only now that he knew what he'd really done to Kenneth.

That night, he was slow to go to sleep. He heard the telephone's ting as Peter picked up the receiver to dial a number. Another Brigville boy had told him how to work out who was being telephoned: 9 9 9 was all of the clicks all of the way, three times – easy! And any number you could work out from counting the clicks after the first three, which would be the exchange name.

His door was not completely closed. He shouldn't listen, but he couldn't stop himself. He counted the clicks for the exchange name, then three, eight, one, one – home, his old home.

Peter's voice, muted, announcing himself. Something about a file and a new entry on the Court list, a pause, then, 'Yes, he's doing quite well.' Pause. 'Yes, the name problem appears to have been accepted. And what's the latest your end?'

A long pause. Peter tutting, 'Did he? With the same consultant? Yes, I see. Poor chap! Dreadful.'

Another wait; hm hmming. Then, 'The problem, this end, is that Bill hadn't realised the extent of it. Letty had to spell it out, unequivocally. Didn't you say, when he was at Brigville?'

Pause.

'You didn't? No, it doesn't seem that Brigville did. Or if they did, Bill must have been too traumatised to take it in. He certainly knows now. We've tried to be very direct with him from the start. The best way, don't you think?'

Pause.

'Yes, I agree. He is buckling down to things, but it's going to be a time before he's ready to go out into the world in any form.'

Bill slid back into bed. He'd been leaning out, listening. That wasn't what a decent sort of chap should do. How could he be any sort of decent chap ever again? He'd served the time the magistrate had ordered, but it hadn't put things right. It wasn't ever going to.

Next morning, Peter opened up the Kenneth subject over breakfast. 'Your father and I spoke on the telephone last night. He's off to Lincoln this morning, the assizes timetable, so we shan't see each other for a few weeks. I told him you're settling down, studying. I needed to ask him about the visits.

'Dad and Mother coming here?'

'No, their visit will be later.'

Letty passed him the toast rack. 'Better that visits are somewhere neutral, Bill.'

Peter said, 'I was meaning Kenneth's visits.'

All the bones in Bill's head felt they were expanding and pushing their way outwards. 'Kenneth!'

'Yes. Kenneth will decide when he wants to see you.'

'Not yet!'

'No, not yet. But it must be planned for.'

He hadn't planned, hadn't expected ever to visit Kenneth. He pushed the toast rack back to Letty. Toast would choke him.

It was later that week when Peter said the Routledges had agreed that Alan could meet Bill. 'It will lift your spirits, and get you another step back into the world.'

'Are you sure it's all right?' The thought of going to Norwood, just as he used to, was exciting but rather scary.

He felt nervous throughout the bus journey to Thornton Heath. It would be awkward at first. What was he going to talk about? He and Alan couldn't ignore what had happened.

Alan was waiting at the clock tower, like all those times before the trouble.

Bill went up to him slowly. 'Thanks ever so much for the film and the game.'

Alan said, 'I thought you might like them.' He led the way. 'Might as well go to the rec.'

The day was cloudy and grey. Once they would have run, but now they walked in unison, not speaking, past the pond and across the grass. They sat on the swings, since no-one else was there.

Bill gave a quick glance sideways at Alan. It had been a whole year since they'd seen each other. They'd never been so long apart. Now it was like looking at a before time, like going back to the village or like arriving in back Wandsworth after the evacuation.

'You look pretty well the same to me,' Alan said. 'Except for your clothes.'

'I grew out of most of them while I was inside. Letty, Mrs Durban, got me these. We had an awful uniform at the Approved School, short trousers, scratchy, colour of shit.' He paused. He'd never have used that word before Brigville. Now it felt like a normal word. They'd better get the subject over with. 'You'll say I deserved it.'

Alan was straight. 'Probably not. You've always said it was an accident. I suppose it could've happened to anyone if they were messing about with something lethal like that. You just shouldn't have been.'

'But it was Kenneth took it down from its place, pulled it out of the scabbard. I tried to stop him. He knows that.'

'I know you'd never have hurt someone on purpose, even Kenneth. But you were crazy to get hold of the shashka. Still, it was hard on you, sending you away. Perhaps a birching would've been easier.'

'Yes. Then it would have been over with. Whereas, you wouldn't normally speak to a boy from an Approved School.'

Alan shrugged. 'It doesn't stop us being friends. We always have been.'

'Thanks.' Bill's feet went forward a little way, starting his swing. Having his old friend back was a huge thing. Alan was someone who really knew him. He was the friend he'd had in evacuation with the kind of freedom you just couldn't have in London. Bill had been so long without any freedom. He threw his legs forward and made the swing go high. 'We two got through the whole war together,' he shouted. Do you remember that first night, when Mrs Y showed us the privy?'

Alan swung up to meet him, laughing. 'And that rotten tin potty under the bed!'

'And being hungry all the time!'

Alan grinned. 'There were good things, too. We made things better for Mrs Y, I reckon. Not just the billeting money, but playing games with Sally and Tim. That helped her. She said as much when I went down there.'

Bill swung higher, remembering the rope round the post in the road. 'Playing out' had been so shocking to his mother. And now, being at Approved School would be so shocking to Mrs Youldon and the Pawseys. As he and Alan passed mid-swing he said, 'They'd all want to forget me if they knew this stuff.'

'Never. Think of your bravery award.'

'Anyone would've done that.'

'I don't think so – not in freezing water, when you couldn't swim. Another person would have gone for help, like me. You were the Youldons' hero.' Alan stopped his swing. 'Especially Sally. She's waiting until you eventually go down.'

'Really!' That was a warming thought, that she remembered him as a hero. Bill brought his swing to a rest and turned to face Alan properly. Alan's letter had said that he'd just passed his School Certificate. 'Congratulations on the exam.'

'It's the school's doing, really.' Alan pointed to his blazer badge with its Latin words.

'Don't know Latin.'

'It means: *Good Education leads to Success.*'

'I'm going to have to succeed without,' said Bill. In the old days they would have drawn a Chad on his wall –

285

Wot, no education – and rolled about laughing. It wasn't funny now.

'What are you doing about studying?'

'Peter sets me tasks, and there's the encyclopaedia. That's where I found this: The Code of Chivalry. There weren't many books at all at Brigville, so I couldn't follow up your hint about knights but I have been looking at Peter's. I don't understand all the words. It's from the Middle Ages. Look.' He pulled out the sheet he'd prepared.

To fear God and maintain His Church
To serve the liege lord in valour and faith
To protect the weak and defenceless
To give succour to widows and orphans
To refrain from the wanton giving of offence
To live by honour and for glory
To despise pecuniary reward
To fight for the welfare of all
To obey those placed in authority
To guard the honour of fellow knights
To eschew unfairness, meanness, deceit
To keep faith
At all times to speak the truth
To persevere to the end in any enterprise begun
To respect the honour of women
Never to refuse a challenge from an equal
Never to turn the back upon a foe

Alan looked impressed. 'Pretty strong advice. You can imagine the knights avowing it all, holding their chalices.'

'Who's the liege lord?'

'That'd be Peter, where you're living.'

'Wanton?'

'Careless.'

'Pecuniary?'

'Don't know. Look it up in the dictionary.'

'I have been trying to do some of those things listed.'

'You are a bit of a knight; I've always known that. Come on.' Alan led him to a cafe and ordered tea and buttered buns. He read the list again. 'It's good you found this. It's a bit beyond me, but well worth talking through with Peter.'

'Never turn the back upon a foe. That means, not neglecting Kenneth, doesn't it?'

The tea and buns came before Alan found an answer. He said, 'What do you reckon you'll do now?'

'I'm still going to be a photographer; I haven't changed my ideas. Tell your parents I've been studying that manual all the time, even at Brigville. Now you've sent me film I can try some of the things out, the techniques.'

'Such as?'

'I had been trying portraits before this happened.'

'Portraits?'

'Angela sat for me,' His stomach lurched. She never would again. 'And I didn't ever guess that she was seeing Kenneth every week after night school.'

Alan frowned. 'So there was something more behind what happened?'

'I've told you all about it. Peter says I must look to the future now. But I'm worried about it. I don't go to school, I won't have exams, I only go to football club and that's it. I'm just studying indoors.'

'Goodness, you've got to get out! I'll come over when I can, but Higher School Cert has lots of homework. Look, have another bun. Let's eat up then have a kick around on the common for a bit. There's some chaps I know who'll likely be playing.'

Alan, and all he stood for, was like a tropical island; calm, in a raging sea.

Chapter Forty

Bill slid into a deckchair glad that there was enough warmth to sit in the garden for a while after work. It was wearisome at Whitley's of Fulham and dark in its storeroom, but stacking the hardware in the back was about right for a strong lad with no school leaving exams and a bad record. He was lucky getting any sort of job considering the length of the queues outside the labour exchange.

He'd been working part-time there for five months. Would he still be doing this at sixteen, at seventeen, his high spot in the month meeting up with Alan, seeing his successes. Would football on Saturdays be his only weekly pleasure?

He looked up at the trees, remembering that time of the A-bombs, feeling lucky to see blue through the branches, that he wasn't in Japan when the A-bomb dropped, that he had a father who was a pacifist. He must hold onto Letty's advice to keep hold of his ambitions, and just use Whitley's as his first step into outside life.

He'd finished Alan's two films a long time ago, and was saving up for another. There was something in Chapter Eighteen of his photography manual that he wanted to try out: getting a transparent effect on objects. That was going to be a challenge.

Peter came out of the French doors, back from his Wednesday evening club. 'Hallo, Bill. Brighten up, I think I've arranged you an apprenticeship.'

His deckchair wobbled as he stood up sharply. 'Instead of working at Whitley's?'

'Yes. Gibson, an arty type at the philosophy club has a photographic studio at Clapham. The chaps say he is well respected. I've told him of your passion, and he's going to give you a trial.'

'Does he know about–? Do I have to say?'

'No. And he wouldn't be interested. He's a philosopher more than a photographer.'

Bill almost danced into the house. The beginning of a proper career! 'Thank you so much, Peter. That's spiffing, simply spiffing! I'll give it my very best.'

'I know you will.'

Bill took the bus daily. Mr Gibson, in a ginger suit with a collarless green shirt beneath it, met him at the door of the studio. 'Hello, Bill Durban. I hear you're keen. Good. Two weeks' trial, okay? Eight thirty to five thirty, Monday to Saturday, except half day on Fridays, free from one p.m. Duties: number one, study my works of art,' he waved a square hand to the window display, 'and number two, just make yourself useful.'

The studio was a one-man affair. Passers-by mostly came in for a one-off portrait. Mr Gibson didn't do weddings. 'Can't stand the affairs. Having the happy couple in the studio is the nearest I'm going to get to marriage, thanks very much.'

He was a modest man. Looking through a range of the standard photographs, Bill saw the odd artistic study, such as a man at dusk, disappearing into the distance, just a small pool of light from the gaslight above. There was the occasional portrait that caught the eye, a child with an adult expression, a dog looking up at its master. Bill knew he'd be content learning photography here.

As Peter had indicated, Mr Gibson didn't bother him with any questions about school or past events. Bill made himself very useful, arranging the equipment so that it was easily to hand, bringing tea promptly between sittings, taking payments from customers, and giving change with no mistakes.

There was the front room where orders were taken and money paid; the studio with its big lights and camera set-up, and down below, the darkroom with open dishes on the table, bottles of chemicals, and negatives pegged on a line, rather like washing. He meant to learn every tiny thing he could.

They didn't work inside all the time. Even the first week they attended an important auction and an acrobatic performance at the theatre, both tremendously exciting after Bill's last year. It was Mr Gibson under the photographer's hood, of course, but Bill watched the techniques and asked questions when Mr Gibson was free.

Sometimes a customer brought an animal to be photographed. Bill might have to walk a dog around the block before it posed. Mostly, he had the clearing up to do and the sweeping. Afterwards he'd take the bus back home and could pepper the conversation over tea with something interesting for once.

After Bill had arrived punctually every day for the two-week trial and brought a cup of tea at regular intervals to the back studio, the trial ended with a two years' apprenticeship. 'There'll be a better wage in Year Two if you're competent by then.'

At last there was something to smile about. As Bill Durban, photographer's assistant, he could feel a different person, a worthier one.

Mr Gibson was appreciative. 'You make a mean cup of tea and don't keep me waiting for it. No, joking apart, I can see that you have a real passion for photography. I don't. This just earns me money sufficient for my passion – I collect Toby jugs; ugly, some say, but there's no greater excitement for me than finding the next one. I like going to auctions, wherever they are. You'll be the real photographer eventually. By the way, I shall provide all the film you need.'

'Gosh, really! That'll be a tremendous help.'

'Yes, you'll just show me all the photographs you take. That way, I can check your progress and guide you. You get free processing, of course. In fact, you'll be doing most of the processing for me once you've learned how to do it properly.'

Having film was a wonderful bonus. Bill could properly experiment without worry over the cost. He went back to Peter and Letty that evening with a lighter heart.

'Well done on completing the trial period,' said Peter.

'Things are moving forwards for you, you see,' Letty smiled as they settled into the comfort of the evening.

He nodded, feeling a rare grin spread his cheeks and he looked around at his new home as if he had only just moved in.

The carpet where they were sitting was cream with a green and maroon pattern that repeated itself only four times. Letty's shoes had a pattern of tiny holes and she had fastened them with a neat double knot. The cushion beside him was a tapestry pattern, and the walls were papered with pale green, with light beige flowers. It needed re-papering, but the pattern was gentle. All this had been around him for weeks, and he was only just noticing it.

Peter said, 'It's good to see you more confident. Now we must work out a budget with you.'

Bill's pay at Whitley's' had been so tiny that Peter told him to keep it, so that his empty pockets at least had bus fares.

'Now that I have a regular wage, I can give most of my pay packet for my keep.'

'We'll take some, and part must go to your father towards Kenneth's keep, but you must be left enough for essentials. When your earnings go up, you'll be able to contribute more.'

It was a relief to be paying his way and something towards Kenneth's costs. 'I'll feel better now. I ought to pay more. I know Aunty sends money for Kenneth, but there's Jill's school fees. She wouldn't be at that school if it wasn't for me.'

'Don't feel too bad,' Letty said. 'Your mother had been wanting Jill at a private school ever since she found that Dawn was attending one.'

Bill remembered all the tears when Jill started at the local primary, the shock about having forty-one children in her class. He squeezed his nails into the palms of his hands, praying that she was happier at her new school.

Peter said, 'This feels like a success for Letty and me, you know, starting you on a photographic career. We will gain great satisfaction over fledging you into the world as a useful citizen.'

There was a cosy silence as Bill took this in. There'd been a time, a long time, when he'd dreamed he'd inherit the shashka because he was Mr Durban's son. Now that he really was Bill Durban, the last thing he wanted was the shashka, and until this moment, all he'd felt was misery that Dad didn't want him as a Wilson anymore. That had hit hard, but being a Durban was very good. "Bill Durban" was his face for the world now.

'Could I make a telephone call?' He'd waited so long for this: a good time to phone Mr and Mrs Pawsey. He had some explaining to do, but he wouldn't lie. He could talk privately in the hall while Peter and Letty listened to the wireless. He watched Peter bend down to turn it on.

He didn't need to look up the number, it was in his heart as well as in his head. He dialled with a sweaty finger, praying Mrs Pawsey would be in to answer the ring. In his mind he could see the very phone in her hall, imagined it vibrating as it rang. When her voice sounded, he only managed to blurt out, 'Hallo, it's Bill.'

'Oh Lordy me.' She called out to Mr Pawsey. 'It's our Bill phoning, at long last. What a treat it is to hear you, that's for sure.'

'I have been wanting to phone for ages.'

'Isn't your voice so deep, my love?' she remarked in that way he remembered so well, a question instead of a statement. 'Let's see, are you still at school?'

'No. I'm nearly sixteen. I'm a working man.'

'Well, I'll be blowed.' She went on in a flurry of chat.

It was so wonderful to hear her delight and her string of questions that he could manage to say why he'd been out of touch for such a very long time. 'I did something really bad, and that stopped me telephoning before. I'm putting things right bit by bit.'

'That's good, Bill. Didn't I know there must be trouble?' She was too nice to ask awkward questions about it. 'And what are you doing now?'

'I'm going to be a photographer, and it's Mr Pawsey's camera that made it happen.'

'My, won't he be pleased?'

Soon it was his turn to ask questions. Having Mrs Pawsey talk about the village, giving the sense that everything was pretty much the same there, except the dogs had got too old and had died, and there were now two new ones – he could hear some barking.

'Aren't they going to love meeting you, tails a-wagging?'

He said, 'When I'm a real success, I'm coming down to see you.'

'Then I shall have to get your bed made up. Don't leave it too long. And let's have a letter, occasionally.'

Now he had the awkward task of telling her that his address, his very name was different. 'It's best I explain when I see you.'

She went quiet at that.

He went on, 'But will you tell Mrs Youldon I'm in contact, and give them all my love.'

'Won't I just, Bill. And we'll be waiting the day till we see you.'

He came back into the lounge just as *Twenty Questions* was finishing.

'I can see that was a good call from the smile on your face,' Peter said as he switched off. 'I'm glad. You need to keep your spirits up.' He rubbed his knuckles and leaned forwards. 'Now – a harder subject to consider.'

Things could never be nice too long! Bill tensed, and prepared himself.

'Seeing your parents.'

That hadn't been mentioned since the first day he'd moved in. He'd thought that at least Dad, Peter's friend, would come here; the families had often exchanged visits before the *event*. The last time he'd seen his parents had been at Brigville. If the atmosphere was the same, he could see that Letty wouldn't want that awkwardness in her comfortable home.

He pressed his fist into his other hand. 'How is it best for me to see them?'

It was clear from Peter's expression that a visit had already been arranged. Peter didn't look at him but into space, as if seeing the event at the cinema. 'Once a month, your parents will meet you at the Corner House, Oxford Street.'

Did he have to meet them there? He wasn't even used to going into the West End.

'It's easy enough to find.' Peter gave him clear directions.

Then he realised he had visited this Corner House, it seemed years ago now, when they were showing Dwaine the West End. They had gone inside, for Dwaine had been impressed by the decor and all the different restaurants on four or five floors, some with musicians. Kenneth had been thrilled by the lithographs on the walls. There'd been a picture of a pier at Herne Bay and Kenneth was excited because the artist, Mr Goss, had been born in Dulwich.

'It's such a grand place to go into on my own.' And then he'd have to face his parents as people from his past. It was as bad as suggesting he put on his old St Werberg's uniform and walk in as if he'd never left.

'A nice place where lots of people go. A meeting around tea, that's probably best. Your father's arranged to be free on the fourth Friday afternoon of every month.'

In the days that followed Bill found it difficult to keep his mind on his work. On the Friday, he set off after his half day at work. Every stitch he wore was clean on, and he'd been to the barber's in his lunch break the day before. Surely his parents would be pleased to see him now?

The bus inched along between the mess of blackened buildings. The ugliness of Stockwell, the sad and decrepit Elephant and Castle where there were so many grubby people in such dirty crowded roads. He wouldn't have liked to walk along them, especially in the dark. The men in ill-fitting clothes looked as if they were just waiting until they could get drunk. They hardly noticed the women with their battered prams overfull with children whose faces needed a thorough wash.

At last Hyde Park appeared with its welcome green swathe. He got off there so that he could take deep breaths of good air before walking alongside the car fumes to face his parents. At least he had progress to report. Last time they'd seen him he'd been in the Brigville uniform, humiliated to be back in short trousers so soon after the joy of his first long pair, the pair he'd worn to visit Angela in the hope of asking her for his first date.

People hurrying along Park Lane looked grey and preoccupied and that's how he felt. He checked Peter's written directions, turned into Oxford Street and walked along to the Corner House. Announcing itself in white paint and gold writing, it was a very fine building for his parents to see such a son. Why here? It was hardly to reward him? No. He understood. It was a big enough place, crowded enough for him not to be noticed; a place far enough away from Wandsworth to avoid anyone they knew; and it was a place that would emphasise his parents' dignity.

Inside, the choice of cafes and restaurants under the one roof was confusing. There were many people shopping at the counters, others ascending or descending the fine staircase. He wasn't sure which floor or doorway, but he had left enough time. Dad did expect punctuality.

The Mountview Café had many round tables with four chairs, padded for the small of the back and the seat. His parents were unmissable. They were the only people sitting stiffly at their white-clothed table without tea in front of them. As he sidled into the tea-room, so embarrassed and out of his depth, their static pose became even more rigid as though a joint paralysis had suddenly afflicted them. They had seen him, a young man who had once been their son.

Mother wore a neat hat that matched her green flecked jacket. Dad had removed his trilby. Otherwise, he was still the suited figure Bill had known as a child, who went away to work carrying his wig box.

Bill bent his upper half towards them. 'I'm here.' How stupid he sounded. He lowered himself into the third chair clasping his hands on his lap.

Mother looked at Bill warily. Did she think he'd jump up and thrash her? 'Are you well? You don't seem to have grown.'

Was that a compliment? She normally hated his size. 'Yes, thank you. I hope you're both well.'

Dad lifted his hand to summon the waitress, who came forward swiftly. Her formal cap, fitted black dress and frilly white apron made Bill feel oafish and clumsy. She glanced at him as if she knew he'd recently been eating from a tin dish in an Approved School.

Dad ordered tea and cakes as grimly as if the treat was prison refreshments.

Mother said, 'It's very nice here,' as the waitress departed with a swish of black skirt.

'It's been a while since we met,' Dad said. It was actually eight months. He didn't ask how Bill had settled. He'd be updated by Peter, of course, as often as he wanted, probably in the cloakroom at Chambers when no-one else was around to overhear the word *Bill*.

'You did receive the suitcase safely?'

'Yes. I have it. Thank you very much for packing it. Should I have brought it back?'

Dad waved a negative hand.

Mother said, 'We chose these tea-rooms. I enjoy the trio who play here.'

The waitress approached with her tray. No-one spoke during this arrival of tea paraphernalia. Bill had no words.

When the waitress left, Dad fingered his pipe, but placed it neatly in the glass ashtray. 'We must tell you about Kenneth's adaptations. He now has a bookstand for reading—'

The waitress came again and placed a cake-stand right in front of Bill. As though he could face eating cake! She whisked away to another table.

'—and the hospital have worked hard to get him a better prosthetic hand. He's still trying to use his left hand, but that isn't coming easily. Most fortunately, Dulwich College has been extremely sympathetic. When he cannot attend in person, tutors support Kenneth's studies.'

Mother cleared her throat, and fiddled with the tea things, arranging the cups, pouring milk and then stirring the tea in the teapot. 'Jill is doing quite well at boarding school. Sussex is far enough away for her to be protected from the fear of other girls knowing about you.' Her eyes raised to the highly decorated ceiling. 'The fees mean we have had to make many sacrifices.' She poured the tea into the cups, each three-quarters full, and passed them over.

Dad said, 'We do the best we can for Jill. She no longer has Dawn and Iris as playmates, of course. Their parents hardly nod to us should we cross paths.' He pushed the cake-stand forward. 'It can be difficult for her, occupying herself during the rather long holidays.'

'Perhaps I could help,' Bill said eagerly. 'I could take her out at the weekends.' Surely Jill would want to see him again?

Dad raised both eyebrows. 'Not appropriate. And Peter said you'd been asking about visiting your grandparents. We don't see how you can for quite a while.'

Mother took one dainty sip of her tea and placed her cup carefully onto its saucer. 'Best not to write, either. It was the most terrible, terrible shock for them.' Her eyes watered, an awful thing to see. 'Telling them what you'd done was the very worst thing I have been forced to do to my family.'

Dad took her elbow. Someone at the next table looked across. It must have looked as if Dad was preventing her from taking a cake.

She looked at Dad's hand, and then at the very white tablecloth. 'And now I'm so limited in the time I can give them.' She took another tiny sip of tea using her left hand and Dad released her other elbow.

'Is Colin—?' There wasn't any more Bill could say. His throat was too tight.

'What a blessing he's still there.' Dad waited for Mother to choose her cake and then he took the Eccles. He pushed the plate towards Bill.

Bill fiddled with his teacup, not taking either the slice of Madeira or the iced fancy.

'We've paid for them anyway,' said Mother, nodding at the cake-stand.

Was it best to waste the cake or ignore Mother's direction? He took the Madeira and crumbled a little edge into his mouth. He took a large gulp of tea to wash it down.

'None of your Brigville manners here, please,' said Dad, almost squirming.

'Sorry.' He concentrated on lifting the teacup to his mouth and replacing it carefully.

The three musicians took their places on a dais and played delicate music as they sipped their tea.

'Boccherini. How nice.' Mother nodded her head more or less in time. 'It makes a treat, a civilised tea like this, doesn't it?'

They enjoyed the rest of it without speaking.

As polite applause followed the music, Bill tried, 'I am assisting a photographer in Clapham, now.'

'Yes, we heard. That's good,' said Mother.

'Ensure you complete your apprenticeship with no blots on your service.' Dad raised the tip of his hand at the waitress, who hurried over with the bill.

Mother stood up, easing her jacket more securely onto her shoulders, sliding on her gloves.

Bill stood quickly and moved each of their chairs under the table, siting them as perfectly as the ones at the unoccupied tables.

Dad's coins chinked on the tiny silver tray in the waitress's hands. For the first time, she smiled before disappearing beyond the wooden screen. Dad reached down to his briefcase and brought out two books, *The Pilgrim's Progress* and *My Life in Jeopardy*. 'Improving texts, Bill. Something to read and think over until we see you next month.' He placed them into Bill's hands, where they weighed heavily.

'Thank you, Dad. Thank you for coming, Mother.' Should he shake hands?

But they had both said *Goodbye* while he was dithering, and turned away.

He watched his parents pass through the door and start down the staircase. The tea, the visit, was over.

He walked the first part of the journey back. It was still warm. He needed to stride down Park Lane to keep the greenness of Hyde Park in his mind before the bus took him the rest of the journey, past the dirty toothless mouths of buildings, back from being Wilson to being Durban.

Chapter Forty-one

The apprenticeship was moving into its second year. By now Mr Gibson was treating Bill almost like a partner. Bill dealt with all the work of the darkroom. He'd learned to produce proofs long ago and sets of immaculate prints. As for his own attempts, his portraits were often praised and Mr Gibson displayed the best ones in the window alongside his own.

He had become chatty in slack moments and even asked Bill's opinion on his choice of ties if he was going out for the evening. These ranged from dark green with spots to light blue with spots, whereas the ginger jacket remained the same, corduroy and slightly dusty.

Mr Gibson took his tea strong, with two sugars, though goodness knows where he managed to get his supply. One morning, with no customer due, he sipped his tea and looked philosophical. 'Bill, you're a good apprentice but more than that, you show real talent. You can take a good portrait; you can snap an interesting scene. Now you need to realise the significance photographs can have. It's not just a record of the moment, as people think of it. They come in to get a picture of their loved ones, but the result is also history.'

'I know. In a hundred years, married couples will look different. Perhaps they'll wear black.'

'More appropriate, perhaps.' Peter called Mr Gibson a cynic. 'You must make sure their grandchildren value the photograph you've taken. It's a responsibility.'

'I'll remember that. But I like photographing outside. This week I did someone disappearing under an arch, and rain falling on a pile of rubbish.'

'Yes, I've seen those in the darkroom. Promising. Now, I'm going to let you do some of the booked portraits, the females.'

Bill felt a blush, although Mr Gibson would never know about his early attempts using Angela. 'Thank you.' It was a compliment that he was being trusted.

'We have to progress, Bill. Photography is an Art. And photography is where artifice becomes reality. These film stars, they look unbelievably beautiful or handsome because of photography. Remember this. It's the lighting, the angle, the speed of your capture,' he leaned forward, wiping his mouth, and said almost in a whisper, 'And your understanding of what's going on behind their faces.'

Bill hadn't thought of that. It wasn't something included in his manual. Had there been something going on behind Angela's face, her meetings with Kenneth at the Evening Institute? What other portraits had he done that he could look at in this way? He had a sudden thought. 'I did take a photograph that almost isn't of a face, but it's special. I took it when I was little but it worked by accident. I hate it, but I'm proud of it. I'd almost forgotten, I don't know how. I always wanted to show it to a proper photographer.'

'Bring it in tomorrow, I'm fascinated.'

After tea, he went up to his bedroom and took out his album, still tied into its own box. He hadn't opened it since before the accident. The photos of his favourite people and places would make him too sad, and his well of sadness was already over-full. He wouldn't look at it now, but would save it, like a treat or reward, to relish after he'd paid his retribution, once Kenneth had decided what that was to be. He would just take the envelope from the box and leave the album unopened.

He undid the ties and put his hand under the album. The envelope wasn't there. His hand went to his stomach as he felt the familiar thud. He took the album out completely but there was no envelope, nor any loose photograph. The album had been left tied up on the bookcase beside his bed at home. At some point, one-handed, Kenneth must have taken the photograph; the second time he'd stolen a photograph from Bill. This time it wasn't because he meant to give it to another person. This time it really was destined for the rubbish bin. Kenneth would have taken it to destroy it.

He didn't need to check whether the album photos were safe. Kenneth would only be interested in the one of himself. He packed the album away. The missing photo was another loss; something of a past time he could never get back, and his own piece of art gone forever. He'd so looked forward to sharing that photo with a photographer who would appreciate it. It wasn't something he could ever recreate like a portrait of a film star.

When had Kenneth taken it? Immediately he got out of hospital, or only when he knew Dad was about to pack Bill's suitcase?

He couldn't even be angry, because this time Kenneth had some right to a picture of himself. If you were the subject of a photo, did you own it? Kenneth would think it fair. He had asked Bill not to photograph him, and it was taken at a time he was grieving.

He put the album away. He'd have to tell Mr Gibson that sadly he had lost the special photo. Mr Gibson would shrug and say he could take plenty more. But this was the one that began his career and told Kenneth's story. Even if he did meet Kenneth, the very last thing he could imagine of such an awful event would be asking for the photo back.

At work, photography was what he was supposed to be doing. At home, photography was an excuse for escape. He could put the camera around his neck and go out without it seeming odd, whatever time of the day or evening. He used the excuse to visit a café where other young people met, one of them who played a guitar. He used it for awkward times in the Durban home. Like when Angela visited. How embarrassing, or worse, was that!

'We've visited Angela many times as you know, but this is her first trip home for two years. You must take a low profile, Bill,' Peter warned.

'She's going to have so much to tell me,' Letty said hesitantly. 'It's just not the same on the telephone.'

He said quickly, 'I thought I'd take my camera somewhere this weekend. A bus journey, probably, to find different subjects. I'm practising scenes in different lights, you know.'

'Thank you, Bill, but be here when she arrives. Angela does accept that you live here.'

It was going to be another hurdle he had to climb.

On the Friday night, Angela arrived in a great flurry of chatter, Peter and Letty rushing to the door as the taxi drew up. He could see how much they had missed her all the time she had been away. They drew her indoors, one on either side of her, each of them asking and answering questions.

Even if nothing had happened in between, Bill would have been breathless to see Angela. He hadn't looked at another girl since bringing her pin-up poster. Because of her, he'd never had a girlfriend. Yet, it could never have been her, as he'd stupidly hoped that dreadful day. She had really encouraged him to fall in love with her, but of course she'd never have dated a boy three years younger. In a large sealed envelope, he had a pile of portraits he had taken of her just before the event, when he was practising portraits using her as a model. Truth – liking the excuse to get near her. He hadn't looked at these nor wanted to show them to Mr Gibson.

He watched her from where he waited at the open door of the lounge. She was wearing a blue coat. Her hair was shorter, neater, her legs shiny in nylons. She must hate him being here, a reminder of an awful experience and a scene she needed to blot out. She'd hate that she'd ever made a fuss of him.

He saw Peter take her coat. This was the right moment to show himself. There was no polite opening that he could sensibly use, such as *Nice to see you again.* She could hardly reply with the same.

'Hello, Angela.'

'Hello.' She hardly looked at him, as if he was a disreputable porter at a strange railway station.

Accepting her chilly greeting, he took her creamy white suitcase with its soft lid and carried it upstairs. He placed it in the pink bedroom, averting his eyes from the bed where she'd once paraded her favourite dresses for him.

'Thank you, Bill.' She put her hand on the case, as a signal that she was waiting for him to leave.

'I hope you've been enjoying your new position at work.'

'I have. Thank you.'

He stepped out of her room. She was politely distant and wary, like Mother was, as if there was some beast in him that might leap out. His mother, he understood. He'd confirmed the worst of her fears when she produced a boy child, but Angela, his long-time friend, the person who had wanted to hug him –her attitude to him now was hard to bear. He made for his bedroom, the muscles in his face taut.

Letty was on the landing. She took his arm and stepped inside his room with him, whispering, 'Remember, she was fond of both of you. And she was there where it happened so soon afterwards.'

He all but crumpled, remembering that scream.

'Try to understand. She knows you were quarrelling about her. She feels responsible.' Letty squeezed his arm sympathetically then slid back to Angela's room.

But it was the shashka he and Kenneth were quarrelling about, wasn't it, not Angela?

"She feels responsible." *Responsible*. That horrible word was weighing everyone down around him. It was as if he'd slashed at all their lives with the one stroke of the shashka. Its old story flashed into his mind, the Cossack soldier's dying words, '…mind its path, protect it well. It will inflict the most terrible wounds.' And it had, it had. He hadn't remembered those words at the time Kenneth snatched it, he hadn't heeded the warning. It had been there all along. He was the only one who was responsible. He slumped down on his bed, his head in his hands. And despite everything that he was responsible for, more loathsomely still, he was *glad* Angela was not going out with Kenneth.

He stayed in his bedroom as long as he could justify. He stood by the window to take deep breaths of the air beyond his window. He kept his eye on the church tower. It was more imposing, less cosy than the squat one on the village church he missed so much. How much more manageable things had been back in evacuation! What did it actually mean *evacuate*? He searched in his dictionary. Fancy never looking before! It meant *to remove to a safer place*. He was evacuated here, then.

He picked up his camera, a new roll of film, and trod downstairs. It was time to go out. He pushed his arms into his mac. You never knew when it was going to rain.

Chapter Forty-two

Months had gone by, marked by the Corner House teas. *Retribution* was always in his head, his whole being alert until the word left Dad's lips. The teas followed the same pattern: sitting near enough to the music for crucial words like *Approved School* to be masked; the neat waitress bringing a cake-stand bearing one iced cake with a cherry, one square sponge with a tiny blob of chocolate, one dry slice of sandy Madeira, one Eccles cake, and a pot of tea. Simmering in the teapot's steam each time was the question of when Bill would have to meet Kenneth.

Gradually, he dared ask about Kenneth in more than a general way. His parents told him that he hoped to study art history, that he spent a long time with his gramophone. He had managed to go back to choir and sang tenor.

Tenor! Before the accident, Bill had wanted to taunt Kenneth about still having a treble voice beyond the age of fourteen. His voice must have broken. Did it break at the moment of the accident? Was that Bill's fault too? But Kenneth would be eighteen next month.

Mother said, 'Kenneth's been given an upright piano. He practises the choral music, sounding out the notes with his left hand.'

Swallowing, Bill ventured, 'Is he getting used to the metal hand?'

Mother answered. 'Yes, but it often hurts where it joins the live flesh.' If Bill didn't shudder outwardly, his stomach did. Why did *live flesh* sound so awful?

Then Dad said the words, as if Bill's direct mention of the prosthetic had wreaked the evil magic. 'He'll probably choose to see you soon. Up to him of course, in his own time.'

Bill prayed for Kenneth's time to be long drawn out.

Art history didn't sound like a job. What work could someone as disabled as Kenneth do? Bill thought of his own work. He was so dependent upon his eye to the viewfinder, both hands to steady the sides of his camera. He couldn't imagine how he'd manage without one hand, let alone one eye. It was truly awful.

Little was spoken of, other than a request for Bill to outline his progress. He spoke of his study using the encyclopaedias, hoping this would please.

Dad nodded. *"The essence of knowledge is, having it, to apply it,"* Confucius.

He had tried to apply the knights' code, but he hadn't understood some of it, and Dad was not the person to ask.

Mother stood up, swinging a blue and grey scarf around her shoulders. Bill remembered it from long, long ago. He must have been only five years old, for the memory was how the scarf identified her from the other mothers waiting at the school gate, and by the time he was six he'd started walking home on his own. Dad should buy her a new scarf. Perhaps Bill could do so, or would she throw it away?

The piano trio were playing light popular music. *We'll meet again, don't know where, don't know when.*

'Herbert, are you ready?' she said.

Dad put both hands on the table, preparatory to standing. 'The thing is, we can't be doing this for ever.'

'No', said Bill, 'of course not.' He was too scared to ask whether Dad meant the Corner House teas or the caring of Kenneth. He watched his father stand, flex his shoulders, feel for his pipe. He never smoked at the table, Mother didn't like it.

'You'll recall there's the not so little matter of retribution.'

The word hit him, just as he had anticipated the trial of the tea had ended, and the thankful relaxation that always followed.

'Yes.' He hadn't really thought his pathetic sums of money went any way towards it.

'You realised when retribution was first mentioned, that it might well be appropriate later rather than sooner?' Dad must mean, *once you're earning more money.*

He nodded. The feeling of doom was more about having to see Kenneth and hear his choice of retribution than the loss of money.

...and I know we'll meet again, the music played on. Everyone knew the words to that Vera Lynn song. It was written for lovers parting, not for rivals renewing their conflict. Customers were humming along cosily as his parents sidled between tea tables to the exit, *some sunny day.*

'As long as you don't forget that.'

As if he could! He watched his parents walk down Oxford Street. They were going to choose some curtain material in John Lewis. The store was nearly rebuilt now after its bombing. Afterwards, they would go home. Would 'home' look much different these days? Had they got rid of the second bed, Bill's bed, in what was now Kenneth's bedroom? It must be difficult for Kenneth to climb to the top bunk, and now there would never be a time when Bill would occupy it.

Peter and Letty were always particularly warm when he got back after his monthly tea. He wiped his shoes and hung his mac beside theirs on the hallstand. Peter put his head round the dining room door. 'Glad you're back. We're eating early tonight. Go and tell Letty you're back.'

Letty was in the lounge, looking out of the French doors at the swathe of green lawn. 'Do you remember running up and down that with Angela when you were little?' She smiled.

'Rather! And your Anderson in the side garden. I remember lots of times being here. Often my parents didn't realise where I was.'

'Really? We were glad to have you visit. When Angela was a baby, I used to sit here with her and look out at the garden. I'd imagine her running around with a brother. I'd imagine a son playing cricket while she tended the flowers.' She laughed. 'Ridiculous fantasy. Angela never got into gardening and we never got our son. It wasn't to be.'

He didn't know what to say. Did she mean to underline that he had never been like a son? Or was it that he couldn't be like one now?

He asked if he should lay the table.

'No, it's done. Let's go in and eat. I'm going out to a musical concert with some friends and leaving you two men to enjoy *Bandwagon* without me.'

She had prepared a Macaroni Cheese, one of Bill's favourite meals.

'TTFN,' Peter quipped as she left. He was deliberately trying to sound jolly because of where Bill had been. He knew it was the tensest moment in Bill's month.

They cleared the table and did the dishes together. Bill felt a glow of closeness. Then he sensed Peter preparing to speak. He could tell something was coming.

When they'd finished tidying up, Peter purposefully moved to open the snug door. It had been kept closed all these months, even when Angela was home. If they went into it at all, Peter and Letty must have waited until Bill was well out of the way.

He turned quickly away but Peter kept hold of the door. 'Come along, we can't have part of the house taboo for ever.'

Bill moved his feet forward until he was standing at the entrance. A shudder went through him.

'Face it, Bill. The room is all right now. We'll go in.'
He took Bill's elbow, ushering him right inside.

The room was fully organized. Peter had finished the project. The military mementoes and photographs were arranged on the walls. The dreaded rug had been removed, ruined for sure, and now there was a neutral carpet almost reaching the sides of the small room. Slowly, he lifted his eyes until he took in the sight of the shashka fastened by clasps to the wall opposite the window.

Peter followed the direction of his eyes. 'Yes, I kept it. I did keep it. Whatever happened with it here, I can't part with it. It's just too important to me. And I contacted a history professor, a specialist in Russian literature. There is a book that is key to my shashka, apparently, but it's very difficult to get hold of in translation, and costs a great deal of money.'

Did Peter imagine Bill would still want to read about it? The opposite was true. He'd keep far away from the subject. That was safest. He concentrated his gaze on the clasps holding the shashka to the wall.

'Yes. I ordered these special wall clasps which are locked, so now no-one can just lift it down.'

'I wouldn't!' The thought of it was impossible. In a lower voice he said, 'I didn't.'

'We won't go into any of that, Bill. Leave the whole matter now. I just want you to get used to this part of the house again so that I can leave the door open as I want. I like to see my displays while I'm sitting in the lounge. I don't want the snug shut off. And you shouldn't shut off things. Everything is part of your life, part of you.'

'I wish it wasn't,' Bill said, cold to the root of his feet.

From then on, the door was left open. There were times when Bill saw Letty dusting in there and others when he saw Peter turning pages of a volume. Friends of Peter's now came and were taken to see his collection.

Bill didn't go in, but he could now manage to remain in the lounge with the snug door open.

He had just passed it without looking, when Peter took him aside and gave him a paper bag from Boots. 'Shaving kit. You need to start shaving. A few tips, let's go upstairs and I'll show you.'

Bill put a hand to his jaw. He had felt the down getting wirier but he still thought of himself as a child, and children don't shave.

Peter demonstrated the best technique to him in the bathroom. 'There you go! Now you'll have to do that regularly, and soon every day – the curse of the man,' Peter laughed.

Afterwards, feeling his smooth, though tingling upper lip and chin, Bill looked in the mirror to see the truth. The thing was, he hadn't really been looking in the mirror, hadn't done so for a long, long time. Had the last time been the day he smartened himself up to give Angela her pin-up picture?

THE day. That day. It had stopped everything. It had stopped him looking in the mirror, it had stopped him finishing school, being Head Boy, Captain of the football team, as well as going round to help Nanny, helping to bring Ted back to his old self. How had they all been managing? He could have been there once a week, twice a week all this time if only…

And now he shaved and was a man.

He strode from his bedroom. It should be possible to make a few of his own decisions. He was a working man, being paid wages, paying his way.

He found Peter and Letty in the kitchen. 'Is it all right if I visit my grandparents on Sunday?' he said.

Peter and Letty exchanged glances. 'They haven't said not to, have they?'

'They haven't said anything. I haven't seen them since…'

312

'No. Well, it's not for us to say. Phone your parents if you think you should check.'

But he didn't think he would. He never telephoned his parents. His father had telephoned him twice, otherwise, messages came via Peter. That was safest. Mother and Dad had said it was better not to visit Nanny and Grandad for a while. A while had passed.

On Sunday he threw on a coat and took the bus to Wandsworth. He walked up the hill to the place he'd so loved all those Sundays of his childhood, before evacuation. He smiled, remembering Ted upside down, his trousers flapping. Now it was a new Sunday. Surely, they would be pleased to see him now he was on an upward path?

Ted opened the door. He wasn't as closely shaven as Bill, the stubble adding to the grey bony look of his face. 'Yes?'

'Ted. Uncle Ted, it's me.'

'Bill?' There was a pause as if Ted was remembering what to do. Then he clapped both hands on the tops of Bill's arms. The palms, the fingers felt light, hardly making a dent. 'Didn't recognise you at first. You're out, prisoner of war! They let you out. Long time.' He took Bill's elbow with a lean white hand and came out of the front door. He walked Bill round the side of the house. 'Where have you been?'

It wasn't clear what Ted knew, what he understood but it was clear there weren't going to be any handstands. He looked at Ted, wondering where to begin.

Ted put a hand to his hair. 'Oh yes, Sis did say you'd got out of the Approved School. But you've been sent somewhere else...'

'Only to a friend's house, Dad's friend. I'm not far away. Fulham. If Colin's not here anymore, I could come over and lend a hand.'

'Lend a hand, that's what Sis does every Saturday, when Bert takes Kenneth out.'

Dad hardly ever took Bill out. Why did he take Kenneth?

'And Colin is still here. He helps. He got me some work at the refrigerator factory in Streatham. Only a few hours a week, but still.'

Ted was looking better. Lean and still a little odd, but better. Did Bill look worse? Ted was still holding his arm. 'You've had your punishment. You had a sword fight, slash, slash, someone gets hurt.' He picked up the garden fork and waved it. 'We're taught to fight, then when we do, we get punished. I know that, Bill.'

He took the fork away from Ted and leant it against the fence. 'I was lucky, Ted. War's ended. I'm nearly seventeen now and I've had none of what you suffered.'

'A year's time or so, you'll have National Service.' He came forward to Bill and grasped his arm tightly. 'I don't want you to go to war.'

'No, all right.' He'd better not argue, but people did have to go to war to defend their country. Several of the lads at football were already on National Service. Even Dad had served in the war. 'Where's Nanny?'

'Kitchen.' Ted looked at his hands, brushed them together.

They went to the back door. Bill hesitated. He wasn't expected. Coming in this way might startle Nanny. He didn't want to alarm her. 'Wait, Ted.'

Ted called out, 'Mother! Bill's come over.'

Nanny came to the back door, but slowly.

She would have known all along, and so would Grandad, that the damage to Kenneth was an accident, a total accident.

She set eyes on him, watery eyes. There was a long pause.

'Bill,' she breathed heavily. 'Bill! We didn't know you were coming.' She breathed again. 'I'm glad to see you're all right. Quite a man, now. Let's go and sit down with Grandad. Ted, you go and dig that trench for the potatoes, there's a good lad.'

Ted had been relegated to a younger child's role. He wasn't normal, he needed looking after, telling what to do. He looked at Nanny vaguely, then returned to the garden.

Nanny took Bill's arm. 'It was a terrible thing, what you did.'

He started to speak.

She paused, rubbed her ear. 'What's that? I can't hear well.' She led him into the sitting room.

Grandad was sitting in his chair, just like last time, only lower, slumped, as though he'd been sitting all these months waiting for Bill. He looked up, blearily. 'Colin – bring me…' He stopped.

Nanny said, 'It's Bill. Bill, come to see us.' She brought him forward, pointed to a low chair padded with the cushions she had embroidered while pregnant with Mother in 1907.

Grandad watched Bill sit on the low chair with his large knees poking upwards. 'Well, well, here you are, Bill. We knew you would come, eventually, whatever they said. So you've come to explain the whole dreadful thing to your old folks?'

'It was an accident, Grandad. I didn't mean to hurt him at all. He was going to pick it up. I went to stop him, grab it.' The act was so far behind him. He could put an end to it now, surely. 'That's how it happened.'

Grandad looked unimpressed. 'Some accidents are actions in the mind of the aggressor first.'

Bill's mouth closed. Was Grandad going to quote things? Had he caught the habit off Dad? But then he realised these were Grandad's own words, words he really meant.

Nanny fed in, 'The trouble is, Bill, you were always jealous of your cousin. I know he was petted, with his looks and sweet ways. But you had your health, you could always do things.'

'Jealousy's a dreadful thing, leads to worse,' said Grandad.

Jealous? Bill wrestled with the cushions beside him. *He*, jealous? It was Kenneth always trying to get his stuff, his friends, his family, everyone and everything in his life. It was Kenneth who had his home now. He turned his face to Nanny, deliberately showing his confusion.

'Yes, you were jealous, you know, Bill. Your mother explained the situation ages ago. He had the pretty manners and got the praise, so you were always complaining that Kenneth had hurt you, taken something of yours. You found it difficult to share, even though you had far more than he did. You didn't like him moving in despite he'd had the great sadness of losing his father in that dreadful way. And then he got keen on the same girl as you, and that did it. That's what we heard. We read it in the paper.'

Bill pushed at his head with the heel of his hand. 'I'm trying to help make things better for Kenneth. I've been working, since I finished serving my time.'

There was a pause, Nanny looking down at her hands, Grandad nodding.

'I'm working at a photographic studio.'

Nanny said, 'It's only right that you do what you can for Kenneth.'

'Yes. And I thought I'd come over to see you, to see if I can help. Like I used to.'

Grandad sounded gruff, proud. 'We manage all right. Colin helps us in the evenings, keeps an eye on Ted and takes him around a bit. Your mother comes most

Saturdays. She shows Ted what has to be done during the week. He can do things not too badly.'

'But I could do more, queue for your rations, cheer Ted up. I could visit you, ask your advice.' He paused, looking at them both, waiting. Nanny was silent.

Grandad stroked his chin. 'No. I'm a prisoner in this chair just as much as you were in your prison school. I haven't anything left these days, no energy, no talk, no advice, not on this scale.'

Nanny touched Bill's arm. 'We're old folk now, too old. We've had our time. It's nice you came to see us, but it's best you remember us how we were. And we'll always remember you how you were, like we do with Ted.' She stood up, the action and her words robbing her of her breath.

'That's for sure.' Grandad nodded slowly. 'We'll remember all the good things. All those Sundays. And if we've guided you at all in the past, you can remember that.' He leant forward as best he could on his wasted thighs. 'Off you go, Bill.'

Go! 'But, I just wanted to—'

'Try and lead a good life now.'

'I will, I am. I'm doing well. I'm going to be a photographer,' Bill's words spilled out.

'Yes, your mother did say. That's good. We'll be proud if you do well.' He sat back, as if his work on Bill's behalf was done.

Nanny asked, 'Would you like a drink before you go, Bill?'

He shook his head; he could hardly swallow as it was. 'No thank you,' he muttered.

She moved to the door.

'G'bye, Grandad,' he bent forward, low, hoping for a handshake or something. 'I can— I could come again, when you like.'

Grandad put a brown speckled hand on Bill's. 'Leave it, Bill. Let it be. Things are best as they are. You've shown you care, that's all that matters now.'

Nanny was still at the door, waiting. It was as if she couldn't bear for him to be there any longer. Bill gave her a hug, but she had no substance. He could feel bones where the cuddles used to be. He moved back, scared of crushing her.

They walked down the hall. He looked back to the garden door expectantly. One of the coloured panes in it was cracked.

'No good calling to Ted,' she said. 'He'll have forgotten you're here already. I've probably got to go and remind him what he was doing.'

'But I could...'

'He works a few hours a week now, under supervision. It's doing him good. And he amuses himself, collecting postcards, rearranging them. He listens to the wireless programmes, and all the repeats. He can do things for us, so don't you worry.'

Bill stepped across the threshold. Was it really for the last time?

Nanny blew him a kiss. 'You were a lovely little boy, whatever's happened since.' And then she closed the door.

Chapter Forty-three

Bill stood at Nanny's gate for some moments. Had Mother known it would be like this and tried to protect him from the hurt? She had said it would be better not to visit. Now he had seen that for himself.

He walked down the sideway to the patch where he'd worked on the carrots, and then returned to the road where Ted had shuffled home from Dunkirk looking like a scarecrow. The war had done that, that's what wars did and why Ted and Dad both thought you shouldn't fight. But Grandad, Mr Durban, Churchill and everyone in the posters said you should fight to save what you loved.

What he'd done to Kenneth was after the war and wasn't to save anything except something he'd wanted. The shashka didn't need protecting. If he'd left it alone, Kenneth would have put it down, certainly hung it up again before Peter came home. And now Kenneth had lost what mattered most to him, his looks and being able to paint things and even how he saw things. No wonder Bill had lost his family. It was only fair. His eyes filled as he held the house in his gaze. Every part of it reminded him of the warmth and fun and love he'd had when he was little. He couldn't believe Nanny and Grandad weren't there for him now.

He walked to Wandsworth High Street for the first time since his crime. He looked in the shop windows, the same shops that he'd queued outside with Mother, the butchers where he'd picked up Nanny's meat ration. He walked past the common, the defunct shelter, the roads where direct hits had occurred, a row of prefabs where children played in their small patch of grass behind a picket fence. A woman, their mother, stood, her hands akimbo, her mouth moving. She was talking to a passer-by in a hat with a feather. 'And we've got a fridge,' she said, 'so some good came out of it.'

'A refrigerator! Well I never!' said the passer-by and the feather in her hat nodded.

A fridge, like the Americans. That's what he'd like to buy for Nanny, but she wouldn't want one. She'd say she was happy to have that wooden safe with the wire door. Joan Youldon would be over the moon to have one, and the electricity to run it. One day he'd do that, when he earned enough money.

But it was Kenneth he should be buying things for. Retribution. He should provide something that meant Kenneth could work, and go properly into the world Bill had ended for him. But what?

He walked on and on, past the common until he reached the slides and roundabouts that he'd played on while Dad sat and smoked his pipe the week Jill was born. Mr Durban had given him pipe cleaners, and Dad had shown him how to make little men with them. It was the only time he remembered Dad playing with him, those few minutes.

It was as if his life was unravelling like those old jumpers that had to be re-knitted into socks for soldiers. He remembered Mrs Pawsey's attempts and the wrinkly wool, the messy balls. Unravelled. That was just how he felt.

A man was coming towards the swings, so he walked slowly away, but the man followed, picked up speed and slapped him on the back. 'It's Bill, isn't it?'

'Colin!'

'Why haven't you been over?'

'I just have. Mother warned me not to. They don't want me to come. They've said it's better not to. I could help, but—'

'That's tough. Still, it's been a shock for them. The old folk were kids in Queen Victoria's time, things were

320

different then. People went wrong, and that was that. But Ted will still want to see you.'

'Yes, he was all right to me. It's good about him having that work at your firm.'

'It's done him good. Look, I can bring him over to the place you're staying.'

'Fulham, not far. That will be super, if you can.' Bill felt his whole body lift with hope. At least he'd have Ted. He paused. 'You should know, I'm called Bill Durban, these days. Dad decided.'

Colin raised his eyebrows. 'I see. That's quite a thing. Listen, let's go and have a bite somewhere. Got time?' He walked back towards Wandsworth High Street, and although he needed to go in the opposite direction, Bill wasn't going to pass up the chance to sit and chat with a friend who was helping his family.

Colin led him into the small cafe where they sold pies and mugs of tea. He bought one of each for them both and put them on a table. 'Here, tuck into this.' After the first few mouthfuls he said, 'I know you've had to be banged up, but I never believed you had it in you to be vicious. I told your grandparents that.'

'Thanks.'

'Listen! This'll cheer you up. Remember you asked me if I heard more about Ted's injury I was to let you know on the QT? Well, while I've been living there, Ted's come out with the odd mention of action in Italy. After all, I served there too, and sometimes I chat to the old man about it. He takes a keen interest in operations, anything about the war, see.'

Bill leant forward, his knife and fork crossed over the pie. 'What was it?'

'The reason Ted flipped his lid? His platoon had it particularly rough, the position they were trapped in. The enemy was attacking from the hill above them, and each dawn foray ended with more men lost. Ted only had one mate left out of the conscripts, the others were regulars. It had been pouring with rain for days so they were struggling along in thick mud. They were covered in it and moving around was a slow hell. Supplies had been held up as well as letters from home, so spirits were about as low as they could get. The next time they were under fire, Ted saw his mate fall. The mud stopped him getting a hold to drag him to safety, so he lay on top of him to protect him. That's when he got the bullet in his backside. It wasn't from trying to escape.'

Bill's heart seemed to swell under his chest. 'So Ted was a hero.'

'Sort of. Only when the firing stopped, he found his mate was dead, and that's what did his head in.'

They finished their pies while Bill took this all in. What Ted had suffered was awful, yet Bill felt a glow. Ted had acted bravely; he had put his friend first. 'My father believes Ted never recovered from the three days in the sea at Dunkirk, waiting for rescue. The troops were under fire while they waited.'

'I wasn't in that show. I've always counted myself lucky. Poor old Ted. But he's better, he's definitely better. He manages the part-time work, and there's some guy linked to the Resettlement Office that's started seeing him. A sort of doctor, I think, but they just talk.'

'I'm glad if there's any help for him.' Now he could talk freely to Peter about soldiers losing their nerve, for Ted had tried to protect his friend. His last friend. 'I'm glad Ted's got you, Colin.'

'Ah, and there's more news. I have a young lady, these days. We've been going steady this last year. The plan is we'll get married and your grandad has said we can live there. The stairs are too much for both of them, so they're going to move out of their bedroom and let us have it. We'll all eat in the kitchen and the old folks will use the dining room as their bedroom.'

Bill couldn't find an answer. It seemed very shocking that the house would be so turned around.

Then Colin said, 'Peggy, my wife-to-be, has worked up at the hospital assisting the nurses so she's picked up a lot. She's going to look after them both, see. Your nan won't have to worry about housework or cooking. The old folks will have all that done for them.'

'Really! How super. Mother will be glad.' The news helped lift away the heavy sadness of parting with Nanny and Grandad. He wrote his address and telephone number down for Colin on a back page of his diary, and set off for Fulham. 'Don't forget about bringing Ted over, will you?'

Peter was in the hall when he got in, folding piles of newspaper ready to tear into strips for the boiler. 'They say we're in for another vicious winter. That's nice to look forward to, isn't it!' He looked up at Bill. 'Not a good idea, to visit then?'

'No, not really. I can't go again.' He firmed his jaw. 'But there are some good things.' He told Peter about Colin and his wife-to-be. 'It will be so much better if Nanny doesn't have to worry about housework and cooking. Colin says he'll bring Ted over to Fulham to see me. Can they come here; would you mind?'

Peter was glad for him and so there was something new to look forward to. No-one had visited him here so far. He went up to his bedroom and sat on his bed. From there he could see the tree next door, virtually leafless. It had seemed chilly lately, but perhaps worse was in store.

He opened his chest of drawers. There was one knitted V-neck, a relic of Aunty's handiwork, now too small for him. One jumper had been school uniform in those days when he'd been a prefect. He'd had a thicker one at Brigville but it had gone for rags, worn-out and outgrown. There was only one other jumper, rather a thin one. He wouldn't have enough to keep him warm this winter.

His bottle of shillings was half full. He always put in a shilling whenever he still had one left at the end of a week. Upending it, Bill found the contents came to twenty-seven shillings. He put thirteen on one side and fourteen on the other. He wasn't particularly superstitious but he took the fourteen, not the thirteen, downstairs to Peter.

'Peter. I've been saving. This is for Kenneth, to help with his singing lessons. Can you pass this onto Dad, please?'

'That's the spirit, Bill. I'll do that.'

Bill would need the thirteen shillings for a warm jumper before the month was out and warmer trousers if it was going to get much colder. It was already a monthly problem getting his one pair of good trousers back from the cleaners in time for work on Monday.

Peter said, 'On a cheerful note, Bill, I saw Gibson at the club. He said that you're an asset. Business has looked up since you got your hand in. He's taken on a lot more bookings.'

It was true. Mr Gibson had also encouraged him to experiment and let him borrow equipment. The studio had some American magazines lying around and they were good for sparking new ideas.

As far as his career was concerned, things had got to the point where he'd stopped being frightened of the future, except for the one threat of doom. Retribution.

Chapter Forty-four

When he heard that Angela was to spend Christmas and New Year with the Durbans, Bill wondered how he could possibly manage the awkwardness of the situation. Because he'd taken no holiday from work so far, Mr Gibson had given him from Christmas Eve until January 2nd off, so it would be difficult to escape the house. Luckily, Alan rescued him. On one of their many get-togethers after work, he invited Bill to stay for the entire holiday. Bill clapped him on the shoulder. 'You're such a topping friend. Thank you!'

Christmas was a good week. The Routledge parents were their usual kind and interested selves, as though Bill had never been a criminal. Somehow Major Routledge had found a ham, and there were vegetables from Alan's patch as well as trifle, and a cake and some dates that Mrs Routledge had been given at work. They played different board games during the week, and when the rain stopped, he and Alan worked on the garden borders, or went down to Thornton Heath for a kick-around with his friends.

The Routledges all wanted to see his photographs, his original album and all the loose ones, loads of them, that he'd taken since joining Gibson's studio. It was so good having people interested in his efforts.

The three of them had bought him a Christmas present: a large portfolio he could never have afforded himself, with padded covers and useful slits for the photograph corners.

Mrs Routledge painted a heading on the first page with white poster paint, 'New Year 1949', and suggested he put in photographs taken of them that day using the flash equipment Mr Gibson had lent him. His Christmas present to Bill had been four bulbs for the flash gun that attached to the camera, and it was exciting to try it out.

Although Bill timed each take carefully, Mrs Routledge couldn't help flinching when the flash went off, so he knew there'd likely be only one of the four that was any good. He threw the used bulbs away, wondering when he'd be able to afford some more. There were so many more possibilities with a flash gun, like night-time studies. He was going to try that next.

During the month of January, he compiled his best photographs and put them in his new portfolio. He ordered the pages carefully, presenting a full range of studies. He checked out whether Peter and Letty liked each one before including it. 'You can't trust your own judgment.'

By February, the album was full and organised, and he felt ready to show it to Mr Gibson. He took it to work in the large portfolio messenger bag that Peter and Letty had given him. It was second hand, of course, but was a super useful thing to have.

As he hurried towards the studio he could see that Mr Gibson was waiting at the entrance grasping a white envelope. Could it hold something about his past? 'Is something wrong, Mr Gibson?'

'No, something's right, very right.' He gave Bill an embarrassed hug. 'Your pic of brewery horses in the snow won the *Photographic Monthly* winter competition.'

Bill's breath left him, 'No!' He shook his coat off quickly and took the envelope.

'It's in the name of the studio of course, but I'll make sure you get full credit.'

He took the letter. He hadn't dare to hope that his photo would even be placed. He had actually won?

'I've already rung the local rag.'

Bill couldn't speak. The last time he'd been in the paper it had been for something truly awful. But that was in a different name.

Mr Gibson bounced on his feet as if he was about to start dancing. 'You've put my little studio on the map. I'll have the trophy to display in the window, thanks to you. But the fifty-pound prize, that's solely yours. Only fair.'

'Gosh!' That was an immense amount, half the fare to America.

'You're gobsmacked, aren't you? As for me, my studio will be listed in *Photographic Monthly* forever.'

He noticed the large album under Bill's arm. 'What's this, now?'

'I've put a portfolio together, as you suggested.'

Mr Gibson sat down. 'Go and make some tea while I look through it.'

When Bill brought back the tea, Mr Gibson closed the album and said, 'These are good. Some, very good. You're getting to the point where I've no more to teach you. When your apprenticeship ends, you don't have to go to a bigger studio to work. I'll make a job for you here. We'll take on corporate work, if you want to stay.'

'Definitely!' Bill couldn't imagine leaving. Where would he go?

'I can't increase your wage by much now, but I'll help you sell your work to magazines. That'll bump your income up. You could even think about having your own studio when you're twenty-one.'

'Really!'

'Yes, when it comes to it. Get your National Service over, save as much as you can, then set up on your own, as long as it's not in Clapham. I don't want you as competition! I already have *Jerome, branches everywhere!* to contend with.'

He laughed, and Bill laughed too, a well of excitement surging somewhere in his middle. His own studio! But it certainly wouldn't be in Clapham, not even in South London.

'You should make a plan. It's something to discuss with Peter. First of all, upgrade your equipment. I can help you with that. Then price out for a studio, materials, processing and charges for customers. Best to have a future ready, as soon as you get back from wherever you're sent to serve.'

He went home, not hearing or seeing anything around him, and reported back to Letty and Peter. Their delight at his win was almost as warming as his own. 'I don't know whether I can be a businessman, but it would be my dream to have my own studio.'

Peter grabbed a lined notebook and a pencil. 'Magnificent. You've stuck at your study and now it's paid off. Let's work out some figures. Stay with Gibson till you're eighteen. You could defer your National Service if you're on a course of study.'

'But I'm not, and I don't even have School Certificate.'

Peter sighed.

Letty said, 'Or you can claim a Conscientious Objection. Your father's a pacifist.'

'No. I shall serve. I want to do my bit.'

'Good man. Do your service, then. Get a good record, and after it's over, you can make your move.'

Bill clasped his hands tightly on his lap. It would mean a move in all senses. Something else to face; excitement and sadness mixed.

Peter lit a cigarette and blew the smoke towards the window. 'The photographic prize plus Mr Gibson's suggestion; very good news to give your parents tomorrow.'

'Yes,' Bill nodded. The following day was his monthly Corner House tea, and at last Dad and Mother had

328

something that might make them proud of him. What would they say at the idea of his having his own studio?

His heart thumped a touch on the way. He was a little late as he passed the Brasserie and he leapt up the staircase, two at a time, to the usual tearoom. He sidled past the musicians who were just moving towards their dais, and looked for his parents' familiar backs. He spotted them. But there were three backs. There was no mistaking the curls. The back of the head was unchanged.

It had to happen, he'd known that, but they hadn't warned him. They should have. It wasn't fair. He paused and took a breath before stepping between the tables to show himself, and to see Kenneth face-on for the first time since the shashka had damaged it.

He managed a careful *Hello*, directing his gaze to the middle of the table.

'Bill.' His father spoke, but was too busy kneading his knuckles to look up.

'Kenneth thought he'd join us today,' Mother said, waving away the waitress for the moment.

The slight figure in the Dulwich College blazer leaned forward. His intent stare from his one eye made Bill's knees weaken. A satin eye patch covered the right eye. The reality of a familiar but damaged Kenneth was worse than his imaginings. The challenge in the stare was, this time, fully justified.

He sat down with a thump. Mother started, and he muttered, 'Sorry.'

It felt a lifetime since he'd seen Kenneth properly. The last time he'd been a hump in a hospital bed. He took in the eye patch, the wormof a red scar beneath it spoiling the peach-like face. He must keep the shock from his expression. He tightened his face muscles. Automatically he held out his hand.

With a wry smile, Kenneth held out his left hand and the two hands met over one side of the white tablecloth. It was like holding hands as a child instead of the formal gesture he'd intended. Instantly he felt a deep blush cover his face.

'I find people prefer the wrong hand to a metal one,' Kenneth said ironically, flicking back his right sleeve to show the ugly thing. Technicians must have made some attempt to humanize it, but it was still crude: a parody of Kenneth's sensitive white hand with its long fingers.

What could he say? It wasn't as if he'd never rehearsed his words. He'd dark-dreamed them often enough. But now no words would come.

Kenneth had less difficulty. 'Well, one of us hasn't changed much in the last three eventful years. You're still built like a football player. I suppose you still do play?'

Bill tried to nod calmly despite inwardly cringing.

Dad raised one hand, twitching his fingers to alert the waitress.

Mother cleared her throat and said in her highest voice, 'The singing lessons have gone really well, Bill. Kenneth's in great demand for solos as well as for his contribution to local choirs.'

'I just need transporting,' said Kenneth with a lift of his left eyebrow. Did the right one still work or was that damaged too? 'My health is still a little frail for public transport.'

'I hope to get a car soon,' said Dad. 'That will be a great help, as other choir members can't collect him every time. But it's a bit beyond me at present.'

Bill nodded and concentrated on the rise and fall of his stomach. He'd never been to sea, but it felt as though he was rocking to-and-fro on a see-sawing deck.

The waitress came for the order. They'd always had the same but this time Dad turned to Kenneth first and asked if he wanted anything special.

Kenneth turned his good eye upon him and considered. 'An egg sandwich would be so nice, Dad.'

The waitress was an older woman. She bent towards Kenneth solicitously. 'The sandwiches are meant to be the set variety, but I'll make sure there's an extra egg one for you, sir.'

Kenneth treated her to his dimples. He still had both of those.

There was a distant rustle as the trio took their places. Bill's applause was much more enthusiastic than before. He couldn't wait for the music to start. It would prevent the need for conversation. The violinist tuned up and a medley of romantic music began.

'Schubertiana,' said Kenneth.

'Delightful,' said Mother.

Dad was looking tense, or was it anxious? He couldn't be more so than Bill. What statement or demand would come at the end of the tea and cakes, or was this occasion merely that Kenneth felt ready to reacquaint himself with his attacker?

The waitress came with the tea, placing the pot by Mother and smiling at Kenneth who was humming along with Schubert's *Trout*. She returned with the food.

For once, the cake-stand would not have one of its four cakes left at the end, always the dry sandy Madeira. Bill kept his eyes on the safe yellow rectangle. It would be left to him to eat it. He waited to be proved right.

They began with the sandwiches. Bill handed them around, deliberately averting his eyes when Kenneth took his with a metallic click against the plate.

Mother, nibbling at an eggy triangle, said, 'Won't it be absolutely magnificent when there is butter again? War's well over but things seem to have got harder and harder.'

At that point Kenneth's metal hand clonked accidentally on the plate and his serviette fell to the floor. Before Bill had time to react, Dad had leapt up and retrieved it.

Instantly, Bill saw how things must be and understood the grey in his father's face.

Dad placed the serviette close to Kenneth's left hand. Then he leant towards Bill. 'For his new career, Kenneth is to be an art historian.'

Kenneth smile conveyed pain bravely borne, rather than pleasure. 'Prevented from creating Art myself, I am to analyse and appreciate the Art of others, masters of past work.'

Bill put his sandwich down. It was the meat paste one. How sensible a solution, for Kenneth to have a place in the artistic world without need to wield a brush; but how stinging a transcription of his situation.

Mother said, 'If his Higher School Certificate results are to expectation, he will undertake a BA course at the Courtauld Institute.'

There was a pause. Bill had never heard of it. As if in celebration, the trio began playing a march. Kenneth probably knew its name.

Dad continued the train of thought. 'A most prestigious institution. Anthony Blunt heads it, leaving his questionable politics behind, I trust. A great honour if Kenneth gains a place there.'

'It's quite near here, in fact,' Mother added. 'Portman Square. So convenient for Selfridges.'

'That's – super. Impressive,' said Bill, bemused. He had no idea why art historians or Kenneth needed Selfridges nearby.

Kenneth moistened his lips. 'Mama is delighted to hear this, of course. But the exams are yet to be faced. One mustn't count one's chickens.' He looked modestly at his second egg sandwich.

'If all goes well, he'll start in October. But he still needs physical support at home.' Mother added, 'When your father's away, it falls to me.' Her expression was pained.

In the following pause, Kenneth began to reach for the cake-stand and Dad quickly proffered it. After a mouthful of the lemon fancy, Kenneth explained. 'At the Courtauld, the note-taking during lectures will be beyond me. My left hand is very clumsy and my right,' he gave a tinkling laugh, 'will need a wealth of practice.'

What did that imply? Bill waited.

'For his course, he will need an amanuensis,' said Dad.

'Amanuensis? Is that something you buy?' Bill prepared himself for the price.

Kenneth smiled at Mother, the corners of his mouth turning up while his upper lip moved down in a way Bill remembered so well.

'It's a person, Bill, someone who takes notes from what you say,' Mother said. 'At school, the boys have taken it in turns to do this for Kenneth.'

Bill bit the inside of his cheek. If they were saying he had to take the notes, how could he go to work?

Dad corrected his guess. 'Kenneth will have to interview candidates for the amanuensis, a paid position.'

There was his fifty-pound prize. That should cover it. It would be the retribution Dad had suggested, something to really help Kenneth back into the world he wanted. He felt his stomach muscles soften. What a relief it would be to have the retribution sorted.

Kenneth was leaning forward. 'But enough about me. Let's hear what you're up to, our strong member of the family.'

Everything Kenneth said now would be laced with sarcasm or making a weighted point. How was it best to respond? It was like being a fencer with no lance.

'Yes, Bill, how is your progress at the photographic studio?' said Dad, the pinch of his nose suggesting a touch of interest.

The pianist was now taking the forefront of the performance, his arpeggios rippling away while the violinist and 'cellist merely gave the odd stroke to their strings, or so it looked to Bill.

He toyed with his pastry fork, its handle greasy with sweat. Mother had foisted an egg sandwich on him, sliding it onto his plate while the three of them continued with cake. He forked a piece of egg white, hoping it was soft enough to slide down his tense throat.

Kenneth's left hand was imitating the delicate tinkling of the solo piano part.

Bill had hurried here eager to tell of his win and the plan he'd worked out with Peter. But now, in Kenneth's presence, these achievements would feel like an insult.

Dad persisted. 'You must be progressing by now? Does the photographer let you use the equipment yourself?'

That stung. 'Yes! All the time! Mr Gibson, the boss, lets me take some of the portraits. He's put some in the window. Also, I won a competition with a photograph I took in my spare time. It will be on the front of *Photographers Monthly*.'

'A journal, is that?' Dad indicated that most people would never have heard of it.

'Front page?' said Kenneth.

'With your name beneath it?' said Dad.

Bill looked down. 'Inside the journal.'

Applause broke out in the tea-room. The trio had finished the selection. Kenneth fell quiet, unable to clap.

Mother's token tapping of her fingertips lasted only seconds. Then she joined Dad in asking more questions about Bill's work.

He answered, relieved to be on safer ground, and ended, 'Mr Gibson thinks I'll be good enough to set up my own studio before I'm twenty-one. After National Service, I plan to move on, live independently.'

'Live independently,' Kenneth repeated in a dreamy voice. 'How enviable.'

'Your own studio?' Dad queried. 'That sounds risky. But you'll probably think better of it by the time you've finished National Service.'

'Better to be employed by a known establishment,' said Mother.

Bill looked at them for signs of some satisfaction. Was *photographer* an acceptable occupation, one they could admit their son was following?

'I knew Peter would provide a sound guide and influence on you,' Dad summed up.

Mother's interest had waned. 'You haven't had your Madeira, Bill.'

'I thought Kenneth would like it,' he fenced.

Kenneth shook his head and wrinkled his nose.

The trio began 'The Skaters' Waltz', a piece he'd heard on the Routledge's gramophone.

'How I used to adore waltzing,' said Mother. 'I suppose those days will never come back for me.'

'I'm hardly in a position to take you, am I?' said Dad.

'If only I could,' said Kenneth regretfully.

Bill looked at the crumbs on his plate. It couldn't be long before Dad brought an end to this ordeal. Nothing definite had been said about what he was supposed to do or offer. There hadn't even been a quotation, only the talk of an amanuensis. Was that to be it, the retribution, or not?

Dad stood. 'I'll pay the bill. One day it may be you doing this, Bill, taking us to tea.'

Bill reached for his wallet that he knew held only two shillings. 'I can contribute.'

Dad waved a hand. 'Another time, perhaps.'

Mother moved her chair wide from the table, a too visible statement that otherwise Kenneth might bump into it as he moved from the table.

'Well, then,' said Dad. He rubbed his hands together as if ridding them of sand from the Madeira which finally

335

he had been the one to eat, muttering, 'Waste not, want not.' *Ridding* was clearly in his mind for he went on, 'Now that Kenneth has met with you, I think this marks the last of our teas here. Kenneth can think about things before a new meeting.' Dad looked at Kenneth. 'Just the two of you, if he feels that's better.'

Kenneth inclined his head. He still hadn't said anything about retribution.

Dad picked up his rolled umbrella. 'You could come to the house, perhaps. What do you say to that, Kenneth? Just for a cup of tea, a conversation—'

Kenneth said, 'If Bill's not averse.'

Bill felt totally averse to it. Dad saying '*the house*' instead of '*home*' didn't help. He gave a nod, more in recognition of Kenneth's allowing it than in agreement with the idea, one he hoped would just melt away.

Dad took Mother's elbow. 'We'll let you know, Bill. *Tempus fugit.* We must be off. I have to pack my files. Sessions in Winchester begin Monday.'

Bill read Mother's face as '*And I'm left to cope alone*'. He was so, so lucky that Peter had taken him in and he hadn't had to endure these things daily, not that he'd have been allowed home.

'I suppose that photography could be considered an art form,' conceded Kenneth as if his mind had remained in an earlier conversation. 'And one that pays, it seems.'

Bill made a minute raise of his shoulders, the nearest he could get to a non-committal acknowledgement. 'Goodbye,' he said, nodding to each of them. He tried not to show his great eagerness to escape but his feet betrayed him. 'Thank you for the tea, Dad. It's wonderful about your art history, Kenneth.'

He could have sworn that Kenneth made a regretful glance at the metal appendage where his drawing hand had been. Certainly the fingers twitched upwards in a gesture of some kind.

'March of the Toreador' accompanied Bill's eager strides to the staircase. He could still hear the strains as he negotiated the press of bodies around the food hall and squeezed thankfully to the exit.

Chapter Forty-five

He'd been dreading the moment of facing Kenneth ever since Brigville. Now, even months after the final awful Corner House tea, he didn't feel he'd recovered from it. Since then, he'd concentrated on his work, and felt heartfelt gratitude each week that went by, that he wasn't having to endure another meeting.

He'd posted fifty pounds as soon as he'd received his prize, addressing the envelope to Dad to ensure that he would know Bill was paying for an amanuensis. As he watched the letter drop through the open mouth of the letterbox, he prayed that this would be accepted as retribution.

He had a plain postcard from Kenneth stating, 'Received £50, thank you.' He heard nothing more, and Dad had said nothing to Peter.

Then Mother telephoned. A telephone call from 'home' was a rare and tense event. Would it be a crisis, a demand or a belated acknowledgement of the money he'd sent as appropriate for Kenneth's retribution – what Alan called his Sword of Damocles?

'How are you, Bill?' she didn't wait for an answer. 'Kenneth feels ready to have you visit here, at the house.' The tone suggested that gratitude would be the appropriate response.

'Thank you.' How could he delay it? 'Would it be more convenient for you if I wait until Dad is back from Sessions?'

'Not necessarily.'

The years of separation from Mother were not long enough to miss the hidden command. She needed him to come now, for some reason. His instinct told him he should go immediately, his stomach felt differently. At that last Corner House meeting, Dad had said 'just for a cup of tea'. He would act on that.

'Shall I call by for a cup of tea after work on Friday, then, my half day?' Going soon would avoid agonizing about it for days and nights.

'Thursday would be better. I have friends on Friday.' Of course, Mother wouldn't want Bill seen, not in daylight especially.

'I'll come after work, then. It will be just before seven by the time I get there.'

'That's quite suitable for us. Until Thursday, then.'

He held onto the receiver after he'd rung off, as if that would delay his visit. It was going to be dreadful to see his old home. It was not far off three years since he'd set eyes on it. He visualised the door opening onto it all. What was familiar would underline his loss, and what was changed would underline his distance from his family. But he had to go.

He'd come home that Saturday of the last meeting muttering, 'Kenneth was there,' and Peter and Letty looked sympathetic. Bill never knew if they had additional information. Now he went into the lounge to tell them what he had to do after work on Thursday.

The day came, and heavy rain with it. Peter walked to the bus stop with him, holding his large umbrella over them both. They both travelled in the same direction to work but on different buses.

The puddles splashed around their feet as they marched to the bus stop.

'You're a good soul, really, Bill. Believe that. Just have a cup of tea with your mother and Kenneth. It breaks the ice, you know. You needn't make more of it than that.'

Bill shook his lowered head. Peter was clearly warning him that the invitation was not Mother's prelude to having him back home. 'I wouldn't. But they have plans for me. I'm sure.'

Peter didn't seem to take that in. He pressed his hand on Bill's shoulder. 'Remember, although there are all these difficulties you have to face, you have a lot of very good things ahead.'

Bill's bus came first, splattering them both with muddy water. 'Thanks, Peter.'

'Good luck. Stay positive.'

Once at the studio, Bill made an excuse to work in the darkroom all day. It avoided his tension showing itself to Mr Gibson, who remained completely unaware of Bill's life, an ignorance that was most comfortable for them both.

When Bill emerged into the light of the street he felt like an unearthed mole. He was greeted by relentless rain. He started for the bus, but, suddenly disorientated, had to stop and think how to get to his old home.

The rain had not lessened when he left the bus in Wandsworth. He didn't now have the protection of Peter's large umbrella. He would have to rely on a handkerchief to dry off his face and hair when he arrived.

He approached his old road viewing it like the visitor he now was. Forty-three, Primley Road was still one of its kind. No colour on the gate or paintwork marked it out as different from the rest of the street, or as the kind of house where a couple might have a criminal son. He kept his head down and his coat collar up just in case neighbours might see him in the dusk, and hurried towards the gate. His shoes were suffering from the rain and the state of the pavements, ensuring a lessening of his welcome.

When he reached the front path, he tried to dab himself dry with his handkerchief and the precious piece of napkin fell out into a puddle. It felt like a bad omen. He picked the sodden fragment up and put it in his left pocket as he moved to the porch.

There'd been such a hurricane of events since he'd opened this front door with his own key. He certainly didn't have one now. Ding-dong, the bell chimed with ironic cheer. Mother answered and almost pulled him inside.

'Did anyone see you?'

'I don't think so.'

She took his raincoat and hung it on the peg next to Dad's trilby.

'You're soaked.'

'Yes, I'm sorry.'

'Best to leave your shoes here, then.'

She went to the cloakroom and brought out the hand towel.

'Thank you,' he said, drying his face and hair. But the damp from the napkin seeped its reminder in whatever position he stood.

Mother said, 'I'll put that towel in the laundry in a moment.' She looked him up and down, appraisingly. 'Of course, you're hardly a youth anymore, at least no-one would think of you as one.'

Of course, she was comparing him to his pre-criminal appearance using what might be the neighbours' eyes. 'You look like a working man now.'

'Well I am.'

'Yes. I'm sure you're very competent at what you do.'

'Would you like to see some of my latest work some time?' As soon as the words had left his mouth he knew they were ill-judged.

Mother's eyes closed briefly. 'Some time, yes of course. Kenneth's in the garden room.' She took the towel from him and went towards the kitchen.

Bill couldn't help looking around, breathing in the crushingly familiar smell of lavender polish. The stairs had a new carpet. It would be crass to comment upon it.

Mother had gestured towards the garden room door, so he moved towards it.

Inside the open door, he saw the bookcase that had once held a few *Readers' Digest* abridged novels, his annuals, an atlas and the set of Home Encyclopaedias, now displayed a hard-backed series, *Gems from the Art World*. These provided a safe enough place for his eyes to focus on as the next stage of his drama unfolded.

Kenneth turned from his contemplation of the garden at night. The sight reminded Bill of a scene in a Noel Coward play. Peter had taken him to see it not long ago. Would Kenneth break into song?

'Bill. Welcome. Is Marcia making tea?' Kenneth asked, musically enough.

Marcia now. Bill supposed that figured; *Aunty* didn't sound sophisticated. 'I didn't ask her. How are you, Kenneth?'

'As well as can be expected. I struggle on.' With his good hand, he smoothed down his finely knitted jumper patterned in small jewels of colour, perhaps the first jumper he'd owned that wasn't hand-knitted by his mother. 'How does it feel to be here again?'

'As difficult as can be expected.' He jolly well wasn't going to pretend, and there were limits to what he would tolerate. Peter had said to draw a line under it somewhere.

'Will you want to look around?'

'Not really.'

'Ah.'

There was a pause.

Bill looked around the room while he could. It was more or less unchanged. 'How is the amanuensis?' He needed a clue to see if his fifty pounds had been an acceptable gesture of retribution.

'Still interviewing. I've given one or two a trial. There's time before my course begins.'

Bill's heart sank. The gesture clearly hadn't been large enough. The sword of Damocles was still raised at the ready.

'Shall we go into the front room? That's where we usually take tea.' Kenneth was beginning to sound like an old married man.

It was a long way past tea-time. It was also a long time since Bill had had anything to eat. It was unlikely he would be offered actual food here, and he might not feel like eating when this ordeal was over.

'Come.' Kenneth led on, his remaining eye showing the way. He'd adopted a tilt of the head as a way of operating one-eyed. Bill followed, the guest. The hero opened the front room door.

Kenneth obviously wanted Bill to see that Aunty's furniture had all gone. The pouffe and the chairs with their lacy arm covers were back just as they'd been before the war. With a jolt he remembered sitting in here the very first time he'd met Kenneth, the little boy with knife pleats on his shorts, pushed forward by terrifying Uncle Frank.

Kenneth sat in one chair and waited for Bill to take the other. Bill took his time, looking around before sitting down. The left side of his trousers was uncomfortably damp, and he shifted position. 'You must miss your mother, all her things.'

'One grows up. I could have gone to America, I could go now, any time, but I shan't.'

'That seems hard.'

'A lot of things are hard.' He waved the good hand. 'She telephones once a fortnight. They can afford it.'

A gust of wind, followed by an increased downpour against the window, filled the silence.

How long could Mother possibly be bringing the tea, or was this interim deliberate?

'I miss Aunty,' he said voicing his thoughts unwittingly, then fabricated a cough to cover them.

'I doubt if the feeling's mutual. The youth who ruined her lovely boy!'

He swallowed his misery at the thought of Aunty's loathing. 'I'm really sorry she's gone.'

'I let her go; partly from kindness. She couldn't bear to see my injuries, to see me face hospital or the aftermath of surgery. I thought I'd save her from witnessing it, over and over again. Anyway, you know very well that I didn't want to go to *A*-merica with *Duh*-waine.' His sarcasm died suddenly. He leant forward. 'My mother has been taken as well as my eye and my hand. You had a hand in the Dwaine part, too, didn't you?'

Bill's breathing was hurting his chest like a runner who shouldn't tackle hills. If he had anything to say he hadn't breath to say it. Thankfully, he heard footsteps.

Mother tripped in with the tea. 'Not too early for you, Kenneth?'

'Perfect, Marcia. Grateful as always. I shall have to find some little thank-you, later.'

What might that involve? Bill kept his eyes on the tray of tea. Mother tweaked the tea cosy, ready to pour. Bill remembered Aunty knitting it for Mother's Christmas present during evacuation. She'd used the red and cream wool from a child's jumper that Kenneth had unravelled. He was good at that.

Mother began a litany of Kenneth's events. He imagined her speaking to her Ladies' Circle in a similar way. 'Kenneth will be on his way to read History of Art at the Courtauld in September. He's been a soloist at Wandsworth's Choral Society on many occasions, and now he's been chosen to join the tenors for Bach's B minor Mass to be performed by the Southern England Philharmonic at Christmas. Such an honour!' Kenneth held up his good hand.

'Enough about me, Marcia. Bill won't have a clue about oratorio, collections or artistic movements. Mustn't bore the poor chap.' He turned to Bill, politely. 'Do you still play football, then?'

Bill nodded.

Mother shuddered. 'In rainy weather, all that mud. Your kit must be horrendous to wash.'

He nodded again, guilty as charged. She'd be so relieved it wasn't in her wash-load. 'I play Saturdays, left wing usually. We train Wednesday evenings.'

'How vigorous,' Kenneth said. He paused. 'I still go to watch my cricket team, in the summer.'

His voice trailed off, weary after emphasizing the *watch*. Mother's cup clinked gently on its saucer.

A horse and cart clattered past, *Any old rags 'n' bones, rags 'n' bones*. It was surely the same man who'd always come past at home times? The man had been old even then.

'Really!' exclaimed Mother. 'In the evening! And I wish he'd confine his calls to the main road.'

What should be said next? What was coming, if anything was coming? How long was long enough? When could he politely leave? He drank the rest of his tea.

'How are your prospects now?' said Mother.

'Good, Mother.' He started to tell her about the pictures that magazines had bought, the competition wins; his further plans. After the halting exchanges this topic was a relief, and his enthusiasm filtered through his reserve.

'I'm glad,' said Mother, 'that you're making good. Your father will be really pleased. Competiton wins: your name will be under your photographs, of course.' She paused, and as if he didn't know exactly her train of thought, 'Perhaps you should return to your own name in the future. William Wilson, the photographer.'

He didn't answer. Kenneth's legs stretched into the middle of the room, and he crossed one foot over the other. His smug expression emphasized the Wilson in him. Bill remembered his own dismay when he first met Kenneth, discovering that he wasn't the only Wilson in the world.

Mother repeated, 'William Wilson?'

'Is that what Dad thinks my name should be?'

'He does. Now.'

He allowed a pause. 'It's best I keep to *Bill Durban.*' That was the man he'd become.

Mother's eyes widened. He sensed outrage. 'I shall have to tell your father that.'

In the silence, he imagined Mother waiting for him to change his mind. He kept still.

Kenneth gave a small cough. 'So you're doing well as a photographer. Moving towards that *independence*,' he said thoughtfully.

'Yes.'

Mother started gathering the cups.

It was an appropriate time to leave. How wonderful! There wasn't to be a new demand. Bill rose. 'Thank you for tea, Mother.'

'Was there anything you'd like to collect, while you're here?'

This was her way of saying this would be the only opportunity. There were things, and he hadn't known how to ask. There was his bravery medal hidden behind Kenneth's picture. There were his letters hidden in Dad's study. Should he admit to that, or chance losing them forever?

'There is something I left in the bedroom,' he started carefully.

Kenneth smirked. 'Wouldn't I have noticed it? I passed over your bits when Dad packed your suitcase at the end of your sentence.'

Oh, what did it matter now if he revealed the hiding place? He wasn't ever going to need it again, after all. 'I hid something important.'

Kenneth's one eye gleamed. 'Ah. Tell me where, I'll get it.'

Bill didn't want to go up himself and see the room changed into Kenneth's enclave. In any case, Kenneth would follow him and see the hiding place, so he stayed where he was. 'Thank you, Kenneth. If you could bring your picture down, the one Aunty framed for you, I'll show you.'

Kenneth disappeared upstairs. Bill turned quickly to Mother. 'There's something I put in Dad's study, please.'

She raised her eyebrows. 'You had no right. Get it quickly then.'

The study was unchanged, as he'd predicted, but now he was tall enough to reach up to the legal annals. With a shudder he remembered the last time he'd done this – to collect the fatal pin-up poster for Angela, that dreadful day. He removed his precious shashka story and the letters and slid them into his pocket quickly. He could hear Kenneth coming downstairs. He moved into the hall before Kenneth reached the bottom stair, the bravery medal in his good hand. He dangled it from its ribbon. 'A treasure behind my picture! A touch of embarrassment, now, I suppose? But I admire your choice of hiding place.'

He didn't answer but stood at the bottom of the stairs, which prevented Kenneth coming further.

Bill was angry now. Kenneth had asked for this. He took his medal from Kenneth and put it in his top pocket. 'There was one other thing.'

Mother was behind him and he turned, not wanting her to miss his words. 'An important photograph is missing from my album.'

'But your father packed your album when you first moved into Peter's.'

He turned back to face Kenneth. 'Yes. But the envelope with this particular photograph was no longer *under* the album, *inside* its box, which was still tightly tied.' He let his words fall out singly to ensure their import wasn't lost on Mother.

She said defensively, 'You must have so many photographs, Bill. The loss of one can't matter. Don't be self-important.'

'Was it a photograph of me?' said Kenneth, airily.

He resisted making the retort *You know it was.* His old home mustn't hold anger and bitterness as its last memory of him. He said in his most generous tone, 'Yes, it was, Kenneth.'

'Then we must aim to replace it.'

'There, you see,' Mother said with a triumphant flick of her shining hair, 'Kenneth is putting things to right.'

He took a step back and Kenneth descended the rest of the stairs.

Hadn't Kenneth destroyed it after all? Did he mean to post it back to him? Bill had a surge of hope. It was one of his earliest photos, his first really good one, his own piece of art, even if it was from a sad and awkward time. It would interest Mr Gibson. 'Thank you, it would be really good to have it back.'

'Replaced,' said Kenneth. 'I shall have to let you know how. After all, we still have the ultimate to discuss.'

The sword of Damocles. How could he have imagined that it would not descend?'

Mother was moving down the hall with small steps and the two of them followed her, as if threaded together.

As a last thrust towards ownership Bill said, 'When will Dad be back? It's some time since I've seen him.' Now Mother would have to invite again, surely?

'He's back on Sunday to a really busy time. He says the court list is over-full with crimes committed by youths who've lacked discipline during the war years.'

His cheeks flamed. Mother would never forgive him, and now it was clear that Dad did not want to see him in this house. They were both conveying that this was no longer 'home'.

Kenneth raised his right hand, as if displaying the prosthesis for the first time. 'A thought, Bill. Mama has been asking for a recent photograph. I also want one for the alumni book at Dulwich College, to leave my mark, you might say. And now I need one to replace the one you lost.' He smiled sarcastically. 'So please arrange a sitting at Gibson's. Who better to take my portrait than my prize-winning photographer cousin?'

Bill tensed. He couldn't refuse. It would be turning away Mr Gibson's business. Mr Gibson might get other Dulwich College school leavers coming, a profitable avenue. He nodded at Kenneth, unable to find the words.

'I am preoccupied now with preparations for my History of Art course. It may not be for a month or two, but I shall telephone Gibsons for an appointment. Ask him to get hold of a decent chair, will you? And a suitable backdrop. I want to set the right scene.'

Now was certainly the time to go. Mother and Kenneth both stood by the front door with him. It was totally dark outside.

'Your trousers seem wet,' said Kenneth indicating the growing patch on his thigh.

'My handkerchief fell onto the path.'

'How unfortunate. You must have been uncomfortable all through this visit.'

He wouldn't answer that.

Mother handed him his raincoat. 'Your father will be in touch.'

The words hung heavily, as the front door opened onto a heavy drizzle of rain.

Kenneth peered out at it. 'Nasty. Shame you haven't an umbrella to keep the worst off.'

Bill lifted his collar and hunched his shoulders in preparation.

'You'll just have to walk briskly,' Mother added, as she closed the door.

Chapter Forty-six

Kenneth certainly took his time before telephoning the Gibson studio; two months in fact, but then requested the entire morning for his sitting. Mr Gibson borrowed two chairs from the neighbouring second-hand shop that stretched to the occasional antique. 'I trust one of these will suit,' he said, dragging a Windsor and a green velvet regency affair behind him.

Kenneth also requested a gramophone. 'I can only relax with music in the background, because of my condition. And make sure it's a fine model, to look right beside my chair. *His Master's Voice* would be good.'

'Fussy bugger, your cousin,' Mr Gibson said, after the phone call, 'if you don't mind my saying.'

'I don't.'

'Why don't you send him elsewhere to be photographed, save yourself the aggro?'

'This is something I have to do. It's—' How could he explain? Mr Gibson knew nothing about the accident. 'There may be quite a number of proofs, and several prints, some framed. I want to meet all the cost.'

'Are you sure?' Mr Gibson's eyebrows shot up, but he was not one to probe. 'Do you want me to stay when he comes, the Lord Muck?'

'Thanks, no. Best not. He has a metal hand; he might feel awkward about posing in front of anyone else.'

Mr Gibson immediately became understanding and on the day, made himself scarce, probably glad to have an entire morning free.

Bill prepared the scene: the books, the vase of dried flowers, the chairs, the gramophone standing on a rotating bookcase. He owed the second-hand shopkeeper a few favours now.

Mr Gibson owned three different backdrop screens: the romantic landscape, the library, the misty sea-scape. Otherwise he used a plain white, or the outside of the studio between surges of traffic. Kenneth was bound to choose the library backdrop.

Everything was ready. Bill waited by the door like an expectant shopkeeper. Would meeting the expense of these photographs satisfy Kenneth's need for retribution? After such a prolonged period of dread, it would be such a relief to go for National Service with none of that in his emotional kitbag. Whether his photographs could satisfy Kenneth, the ultimate in difficult customers, was anyone's guess.

He'd phoned Alan about it who'd advised: 'Prepare for the worst, be glad of anything less.'

The studio clock told him Kenneth was due. He watched a large cloud lower itself on the top of the buildings opposite and imagined Kenneth on a throne in its midst. But at that moment, a car drew up outside and an older lady in a neat suit and a fox fur opened her door, and tripped round to the passenger door where Kenneth was stepping out.

'Thank you so much for the lift, Violet,' he said, dipping his head to indicate appreciation. 'I'll see you at choir.'

Bill felt he was nurturing a star rather than a cousin. Kenneth's black velvet jacket, the matching eye patch, a cream silky shirt and a purple cravat suggested stardom. Was Kenneth really intending to turn up for his lectures in this garb? What could Bill say, apart from, 'Everything's ready, Kenneth. Come in.'

Kenneth had brought his own record to enhance the sitting. 'Some Gilbert and Sullivan will lighten the mood, I think. I assume you'll take a number of *shots*, is it called?'

'Not really.'

'A number of proofs from which I can choose, then. Choice is everything, don't you think?'

Bill showed him the three background screens, and Kenneth opted for the library one, as expected.

Bill displayed the chairs: the ordinary studio one, pillowed to support babies; the Windsor chair, the low velvet armchair, the high-back leather armchair, green and shiny.

'Take that velvet one away. Why would I want to sit so low? It has to be this one,' Kenneth grasped hold of the leather wing of the high-backed chair. 'I just love it.'

Bill moved the Windsor chair nearer him. 'Try this first. It's plain and won't argue with your clothing.'

'Hate the wooden arms.' Kenneth sighed and slid into it, placing his prosthetic hand heavily, so that it clanged a protest. He watched Bill move to the camera and disappear under the hood.

Bill didn't need to do so, but it avoided the awful situation for a few moments. How was he going to manage this: treat Kenneth like a film star or a cosseted patient, or ignore the affectations and risk some come-back? Goodness knows, he'd suffered enough from those in the past.

His deliberations were interrupted by the sound of Kenneth opening the lid of the gramophone, placing his record on the turntable. He wound the handle many times. There was a light click as the arm was lifted and placed down upon the record. *A wandering minstrel, I...*

His nerves raw, Bill heard it first as *A Wandering Minstrel Eye* and had to listen for several repetitions before he understood the words. He emerged from under the cloth. 'Are you ready, Kenneth? How would you like to sit?'

Kenneth was humming along with the melody. He placed his velvet covered arms on the wooden ones of the Windsor chair and closed his eyes briefly. 'You can try me on this, but I think we'll need to transfer to the wing chair.'

Bill arranged the lighting, highlighting Kenneth's good hand, its fingers extended delicately. He returned to his hood and took two pictures.

Kenneth stood and stretched, his good eye focussed on the green leather chair. It wouldn't set him off so well, but it pleased Kenneth.

Bill swapped the chairs' positions and motioned to Kenneth to sit down. He looked as if he might break into song. Did he want a photograph of himself singing? Anything was possible.

Our wonderful tenor, Bill imagined the mainstay of the choir saying, as she came to collect Kenneth every Tuesday and Thursday evening.

'A thing of shreds and patches...' Kenneth's tenor joined with the one on his record.

'Do you want the same pose or shall I take you from one side? If so, which side?'

Kenneth stopped singing. 'Now which side would that be? Can you possibly work that out, Bill?' He sat down in the green leather chair, sliding his legs to one side and then the other, his head inclined to match. 'Try this pose, will you?' He angled himself to one side, his legs partly stretched out.

Bill took the picture, but said, 'You hardly look relaxed.'

'...A dreamy lullaby, da, da-di, di-da-diddy da,' Kenneth continued. Was that intended to taunt?

'Just move around as you would at home. I'll take several and we'll see which ones work best. How about one standing, perhaps holding the back of the chair?'

'Ah yes, good idea. Follow my movements, then.' Kenneth stood, turned a touch to the left, posed to right, sat, rested back, and leant on his knees.

Bill adjusted the lights, then took photographs of all. 'That should do it, Kenneth.'

Kenneth stood up again, staring down imperiously at Bill, hunched near the camera's hood. He assumed Bill had finished but another press of the button, Bill's hand tucked behind him, captured the moment. *Me boss, you worker,* that was Kenneth's expression and Bill knew it was in his mind.

Kenneth hummed on, '*Da-diddy, da-diddy da.* I'll enjoy *The Mikado* while you work away. Just carry on if you need to take your frames to the darkroom.'

Some instinct stopped Bill from leaving Kenneth in the studio with all the expensive equipment while he went down to the darkroom. He would delay that until Kenneth had gone. He bustled about, tidying things a little, waiting.

When the record came to an end, Kenneth stood and lifted the gramophone's arm to put it gently on its rest. He removed the needle. 'Past its best. Throw this away, will you?'

Bill took it over to the waste bin. It wasn't all he'd love to throw away. He had finished all the fiddling about he could reasonably make. He felt anxious, queasy. More than the awfulness of having Kenneth as a sitter, he needed Kenneth to just go. It was dreadfully uncomfortable having him in this territory, territory that wasn't even his.

Suddenly he located the discomfort. The last time he'd been left in charge of a premises with Kenneth present, it had been the *event* itself. He stepped forward. 'I shall do my very best with these photographs. Obviously I want Aunty to have one that she'll really treasure, and I want you to be satisfied too.'

'And I want you to have a replacement for the one you lost,' Kenneth said with an irony he meant Bill to absorb.

'Can I just check, Kenneth. Do you have any objection to possible public display of your photograph?' Mr Gibson might choose to display one, and he had the say about what went into the windows.

'Will it say who I am, that I'm studying at the Courtauld?'

'It certainly can.'

Kenneth nodded, his tongue exploring the side of his mouth and then his lower lip, apparently with great satisfaction. 'I'm meeting Marcia at Arding and Hobbs now. The proofs?'

'They'll all be posted to you for your consideration.'

'No hurry whatsoever. Quality before speed, wouldn't you say?' That was a barbed comment about Bill's swift movements between camera, table, desk and chair, agitated about getting Kenneth to go.

As if to underline the point, Kenneth strolled slowly towards the door, flexing his neck and shoulders.

Bill screwed his fingers into fists. He must make an arrangement for finalising this matter, once and for all. 'I'll meet you at Fullers for tea when the prints are ready.'

'The ultimate discussion over tea. Yes, very civilised. Don't worry about calling a taxi, I'll walk.'

Chapter Forty-seven

'Absolutely smashing!' He came off the phone to Alan, grinning. 'Alan's father has pulled strings so that Alan and I can do our National Service together.'

'That is a bonus,' Letty said, as she handed him a pile of ironed clothes. 'He's got his Higher School Cert, then?'

'Yes, but hasn't decided what to do until after National Service.' It was the one matter that made Bill feel he was ahead of Alan.

This good news was one of the plus things of Bill's plus and minus month. Since he'd received his call-up papers, he'd been busy trying to leave everything in good order. There were a lot of things to settle.

Mr Gibson had given him photographic equipment small enough and suitable to take in his kit. 'Insure it! And I'll look after all the rest of your gear until you get back and set up your studio. Maybe the army will make use of your talent and you'll take military photos one day.' He gave Bill a week's paid holiday. 'You've earned it. I'll do anything that's unfinished.'

Bill gladly left him with the task of preparing Kenneth's proofs. He'd not had the stomach for looking at the negatives and had the excuse that Kenneth wasn't in a hurry while he was so engaged on the beginning of his Art History course.

'The awkward cousin! I'd better promise to send off the proofs as a priority,' Mr Gibson grinned.

It was a terrible wrench for Bill to move out of his room at the Durbans' and know that he wouldn't be back, not to live, but it was the right time. Angela was moving back home. She and her fiancé, Vincent, planned to marry in the spring. Finding somewhere to live would be difficult for them; meantime they could live with her parents. Bill would be over twenty when he came back, nearly an adult. Anyone would expect him to find his own accommodation then.

Peter and Letty went over the figures again for setting up his own studio. Peter had seen a likely premises in Stockwell. Bill didn't say that South London was not where he'd settle, for he knew they'd assume he would want to be near them.

When he changed his name by deed poll, it was like a christening. Letty and Peter said that he was like a son in their eyes and they'd celebrated with dinner at a venue only known to the barristers Peter worked with. 'This has caused a certain chilly atmosphere between your father and myself, but he accepts that originally it was his own wish for you to lose *Wilson* so can't object if you decide to stay *Durban* now.'

Bill was happy to be a Durban, especially as the name would otherwise have been lost when Angela married. He imagined her having a son, and the item he would inherit, and how the Durbans would protect him from it until he was adult, warning him of its heritage, using the dreadful story of Bill and Kenneth.

Now it was a relief that he wouldn't ever own the shashka himself. He didn't need its imaginary power. What Peter Durban had given him was infinitely more valuable.

There was one thing he could do related to the shashka, that would be appropriate and also of real benefit to the shashka heritage. It was very expensive, as Peter had predicted, but Bill had managed to track down the copy of the ancient book the professor of Russian history had told Peter about.

In the Charing Cross Road shop, the bookseller brought the dark covered volume out. Bill no longer wanted to know its contents, only that it was the story

Peter needed. He put his own book on the counter, the Dutch history. The book-seller examined it closely.

It gave Bill a strange thrill to discover that when Kenneth had opted to have the German grammar, he'd left Bill with the treasure. The thrill was increased by the thought that Dad had given his own son the prize, even if he hadn't intended to. Now that prize was being used to achieve something otherwise unattainable. The book-keeper was happy to make an exchange for the price of five pounds to Bill.

Bill left the shop with a glow. He wrapped his treasure up carefully, adding only a small card to tuck inside the front cover. 'Thank you both for ALL you've done for me.' He would leave it for Peter to find in the snug, once Bill had moved into the barracks.

Colin brought Ted to see him before that. They sat on the Durbans' sofa, drinking tea.

Colin jerked his head towards Ted, whose face was nearly as long as it had been after Dunkirk. 'He doesn't want you to do your National Service, Bill.'

'You know what I said, Bill. You could go for deferment. Don't let them take you to war. You might have to fight in Korea.'

Bill put his arm on Ted's shoulder. 'I don't like war either, but I want to serve my country. I haven't any qualifications, but I'll have a record of service and I'll make sure it's a creditable one. You understand, Colin, don't you?'

'Yep. But I'm not your uncle.'

Ted was pulling Bill's sleeve. 'Listen to me. Don't go.'

'Ted! Think how your job has helped put you back to rights? Well, doing National Service will achieve that for me. I'll feel I've made myself acceptable.'

A few days later, he made his goodbyes to his parents. 'Are you sure about this?' said Dad. *This*, as Bill knew, referred to everything from doing his military service, through photography as an occupation, to changing his name.

Mother said, 'You'll be a man when you get back. National Service is supposed to be very character-building.' She made a move towards him that he momentarily thought was going to be a kiss, but she just corrected his cuff that had turned itself back a little. It was her moment of warmth; the amount she could spare. 'Look after yourself,' she said. Hadn't she conveyed that instruction, years ago?

He'd first looked after himself on a journey to the country where he'd found people who'd made him feel like a prince. And that's where he went next, half-expecting it all to be a myth in his mind, but it wasn't.

It was totally dark when he passed the chicken hutch and tapped on the door he'd last seen as a twelve-year-old, heart-broken to be leaving. He had something to return, the remains of a napkin, the missing one of its set. He had a lot of missing gaps to talk about, and now he could be totally frank.

It didn't take a day to confirm that, whatever he'd done and might do, Bill had his secure place in the Pawseys' hearts.

Mr Pawsey waved his glasses. 'You'd better not leave it longer before popping down to the Youldons, Bill. They'll all be waiting for you. And come straight back afterwards. The missus has made up your bed ready.'

His heart jolted as he got to the dim lane of little cottages and saw the door where Mrs Youldon had taken him in when no other housewife would. He peered down the side of the cottage. Only a sliver of moon helped him pick out the fence, the outline of the privy, the trees behind the cottages, the view he'd had that very first night away from home, a lonely, scared child, sharing the space with Alan, another evacuee feeling the same way. Bill couldn't get back to that innocence, a time when he'd never done anything worse than make a noise in his mother's back yard, but he'd made changes and returned here. He knocked.

Tim opened the door with one brawny arm. His face went first blank then it flushed with delight. He said nothing, but turned to his mother and sister, opening the door wider. The two women looked up and behind them Bill saw the photograph, one of his first efforts, the children as they had been then, Sally giggling and hanging on to Tim.

Joan Youldon came forward. 'Bill? *Bill*!'

Sally, now the same size as her mother, stayed sitting, wisps of hair hiding her eyes but not her joy. 'Hello, Bill,' she said quietly, her mouth quirking upwards at the sides.

He moved behind her and placed his hands upon her shoulders, feeling the slight bones under his fingers. The sensation reminded him of how he'd once held her tiny figure up from the icy water.

'How are you all? How have you been?'

'I can't believe you're here, Bill.' Joan Youldon held both hands to her neck, gaping. 'You're so – fine.'

'No!' He gave a gusty laugh. 'Hardly! I said I'd come. You don't know how long I've been longing to. Years!'

'Mum never believed you'd manage to,' Sally said, as though they'd discussed it many times, 'but I did.'

Four days with the Pawseys and the Youldons, confirmed his plan to set up his studio in the county town there. 'Two years,' he said to them all, 'and I'll be back, this time for good.'

Tim would be taking his turn at National Service in a few years' time. Bill would be needed.

'We will be waiting for you,' Mrs Youldon said. 'Really.'

Then Sally: whatever women he met in the future, none would have the look in Sally's eyes as she said Goodbye. This village was where his future belonged. He let them know.

That evening, he let the Pawseys know. Their faces showed the joy that he'd hold onto if National Service got grim. 'God willing, we'll still be here when you get back, Bill. And you spend your leave here, mind.'

Otherwise, it would only be Alan he'd tell his plans to, until well after National Service.

He left Kenneth until last. After all, there was no question that he and Kenneth had the most to settle.

He checked the finished photographs at the studio briefly. All the proofs had been satisfactory. Kenneth wanted prints of all of them. Mr Gibson had enlarged and framed three. One was for Aunty. It would prepare her for the reality of Kenneth as he was now, before she came over in May for the Festival of Britain. Afterwards, would Kenneth go back with her and sample the much more comfortable life that Dwaine could provide? For his first love, Art, he'd surely prefer to remain, at least until the end of his studies at the Courtauld. But as he'd said, having a choice was good.

A bright green scarf and the velvet eye patch identified Kenneth in the crowd as Bill approached Fuller's restaurant to meet him. The Corner House teas had established the idea that a dainty tea-table in a neutral environment was the most fitting place to settle heavy matters. In such a place, raised voices, conflict, aggression would be unimaginable.

He ushered Kenneth to the rear-most table where they would benefit from more privacy. Until the waitress took their order, they discussed the course at the Courtauld and Kenneth's arrangements for study, including the amanuensis Bill had financed.

'I've settled for a very nice girl. Attentive, and not too much to say. She'll suit my needs well. I use my left hand between times, but the writing's so poor that I'm getting her to take the pages home to rewrite. She doesn't seem to mind the extra chore. She has a good craven attitude.'

Bill said nothing. He didn't envy the girl.

The waitress brought the tea, and the coffee walnut cake that Kenneth had admired.

Bill said, 'I'm glad you approve of all the proofs, Kenneth. The prints will arrive tomorrow, including the framed ones, so I hope you'll be at home to receive them—'

Kenneth nodded, looking pleased.

'—because I'm due to start my training, as you know.'

'National Service. I haven't been called up, of course.' His prosthetic hand lifted slightly. 'What a shame I can't serve.' He dropped his sarcastic tone. 'Perhaps I should be grateful that you've saved me from the experience. Square-bashing, wielding an instrument – it's hardly me, is it?'

Bill looked at his hands. 'I hope I'll be wielding a camera. However.' He must get things entirely settled. 'The whole set of proofs and prints, I hope they're a suitable gesture towards – everything.'

Kenneth took another slice of cake. 'My compensation? I had intended something more retributive, but now you're off to National Service, perhaps to be killed or maimed in war, perhaps I should be satisfied.'

'Killed or maimed? Is that what you hope for?'

Kenneth closed his eyes briefly. 'You could have deferred, even claimed to be a conscientious objector. I would.'

'No, I won't. I will be serving for both of us, Kenneth. That seems only fair.'

'You'll take that risk?'

363

Bill felt stronger, the heavy dread of retribution dissipating like used tea-leaves. 'I'm sure we'll both have a good future.'

'As we both have a past,' Kenneth took the napkin and wiped the coffee cream from the white fingers of his left hand, 'if not a good one.'

Was Kenneth referring to his own mean acts? Bill stood up. He'd had enough. He moved away from the tea table and in order to shake Kenneth's good hand, held out his left hand

Kenneth looked at it, and then shook it, a firm shake. His face lost its sardonic expression. 'Come back safe. Whatever else, you're the closest I have to a brother.' He flicked his green scarf over the shoulder of his velvet jacket and left, the eyes of every customer following him to the door.

Bill was so stunned by Kenneth's words that the waitress had to ask him twice to pay the bill before he heard her. If he never saw Kenneth again, he could never lose the memory of his dramatic presence.

Some instinct made him hurry back to Gibson's studio to ensure the prints had been packaged and sent.

Mr Gibson had not yet gone home for the night. 'Bill! A most propitious swansong! I've sent off the prints, all very good. But *this* photograph is unlikely to be surpassed by anything in your future portfolio.' He brought out the picture Bill had taken when Kenneth had assumed the sitting was finished.

The nonchalant stance defied the black patch as signifying anything other than a fashion statement. Everything in the picture screamed a drama: the imperious expression, the quizzical remaining eye under a raised eyebrow, the black velvet jacket and bright cravat, the delicate artist's hand outstretched on the back of the green leather chair, the prosthetic one hanging limply in front.

364

'This will be on the front cover of *Hidden Power* in November.'

'*Hidden Power*?'

'Yes, it's the new, most prestigious London magazine for the Art world.' He held out a copy. 'This is August's issue. Any photographer would give his right hand to get a pic in this mag.'

A shudder went through Bill.

Mr Gibson raced on enthusiastically, oblivious to his gaffe. 'I knew it was a winner as soon as I saw the negative. I nearly rang Peter's, but remembered you'd already moved out. What a stunner!' He waved the photo in front of Bill's face.

Bill flinched.

'Super work! One look and the reader's full of questions. I sent it off directly it was printed and they snapped it up. Quite a stunt to hit the front page, just as you're off to National Service!' He struck the journal's front. 'Just imagine your stunner right here!'

Bill took the current issue of *Hidden Power* and turned its shiny pages.

'Now you have to pen a paragraph about the sitter.'

'Paragraph?'

'To write the background to the picture.'

The journal slipped from Bill's fingers and he bent to pick it up. 'I'm not a writer.'

'He's your cousin, eh? There'll be so much you can write. His whole stance shouts for explanations. I tell you, when you're famous, it will always be this photograph that everyone remembers.'

Bill sat down heavily.

Wherever he went, Kenneth, and the question of his injuries, would always be with him. Kenneth had manoeuvred his lasting retribution.

TO THE READER

This ends the trilogy, A RELATIVE INVASION

Thank you for reading about Bill and his world. Writers are always grateful for reviews. Please consider writing one, however brief, on Amazon and/or Goodreads.

If you'd like to try my other books, you can see them here:
http://www.amazon.co.uk/RosalindMinett/e/B00J5LZXLG   or order the paperbacks from Foyles and other bookshops

Me-Time Tales: tea breaks for mature women and curious men. *Ironic short stories with a dark edge. All kinds of women unlocked.* www.amazon.com/dp/B01DGLI484

Curious Men: (forthcoming, 2017) *These idiosyncratic males need their own short stories away from women.*

Crime Shorts, an e-book series:

No. 1. A Boy with Potential. *A choirboy's sinister discovery.*
No.2   Homed. *Who is guilty, the child or the adult?*
No. 3   Not Her Fault. *Why does the murder of a young boy obsess a grown woman?*

I blog about writing at www.characterfulwriter.com

Lightning Source UK Ltd.
Milton Keynes UK
UKOW03f1903050517
300607UK00002B/172/P